RISE OF THE AUTOMATED EMPIRE: FINAL ASSEMBLY
BOOK ONE OF RISE OF THE AUTOMATED EMPIRE

Dennis M. Myers

Theogony Books
Coinjock, NC

Copyright © 2023 by Dennis M. Myers.

All rights reserved. No part of this publication may be reproduced, distributed or transmitted in any form or by any means, including photocopying, recording, or other electronic or mechanical methods, without the prior written permission of the publisher, except in the case of brief quotations embodied in critical reviews and certain other noncommercial uses permitted by copyright law. For permission requests, write to the publisher, addressed "Attention: Permissions Coordinator," at the address below.

Chris Kennedy/Theogony Books
1097 Waterlily Rd.
Coinjock, NC 27923
https://chriskennedypublishing.com/

Publisher's Note: This is a work of fiction. Names, characters, places, and incidents are a product of the author's imagination. Locales and public names are sometimes used for atmospheric purposes. Any resemblance to actual people, living or dead, or to businesses, companies, events, institutions, or locales is completely coincidental.

Cover Design by J Caleb Design.

Ordering Information:
Quantity sales. Special discounts are available on quantity purchases by corporations, associations, and others. For details, contact the "Special Sales Department" at the address above.

Rise of the Automated Empire: Final Assembly/Dennis M. Myers -- 1st ed.
ISBN: 978-1648558986

*In memory of my grandmother,
Della Sheffield Baker*

*When I was in sixth grade, she handed me a paperback copy of
The Star Beast by Robert A. Heinlein.
That changed my world forever.
Several of the older books on my shelves were either given to me by,
or inherited from my grandmother.
I credit her for sparking a love of reading and of science fiction.
She's the one who took my little brothers and me to see that famous movie in
1977.
I had no idea what it was when the crawl started.
Thank You, Grandma!*

The Aviary

Monday, September 20, 3288, 13:45

Dawn Sheffield slid gracefully into line behind a mother and son as they headed to the shuttle boarding gate. The waiting area was well lit from overhead. The concrete floor, still damp from a recent removal of lunar dust, reflected the lights.

The boy fidgeted, hopping back and forth in front of his mother. He stopped for a moment, then jumped high over his mother's head.

She grabbed one ankle and pulled him back down, then pushed him into place by his shoulders. "Jordan, I told you before. No more jumping."

She released her grip. He jumped again and sent himself into an uncontrolled backward tumble. His feet flew out of his mother's reach.

Dawn put her hands up and caught him to avoid being landed on. He scrambled down and wiggled free.

"I'm so sorry," the mother said. "Jordan, apologize."

The boy crossed his arms. "It was an accident."

"Apologize. Now."

Dawn stood quietly, locking eyes with Jordan.

He stood for a moment, his steely blue eyes defiant, and he looked down at his feet. "Sorry."

"Apology accepted." Dawn smiled at the mother and pointed in the direction of the shuttle. "The line's moving."

The woman turned, took her son by the hand, and followed the other passengers through the airlock into the shuttle.

Dawn looked down the length of the cabin. She spotted her meki, a familiar glowing spool of blue thread with a silver needle, floating above a seat halfway back on the left. When she looked directly at the meki, her seat glowed. The floating image faded when she sat down. Looking about the cabin, she watched as the other passengers found their seats by following the mekis only they could see.

Jordan and his mother sat in front of her. Dawn twitched her eye, and names appeared above their heads. CHERYL AND JORDAN AUDREY OF GRISSOM PARK. Being from Moretus Plains, Dawn was familiar with the place. The two large communities had been built near each other on the floor of Moretus Crater. Over the centuries, they'd grown together, yet maintained their different styles. Grissom Park was dominated by a dome over a smaller crater in which a large, open park had been built. Low, sprawling structures spread in a circle around it. Moretus Plains used towering apartment blocks with public establishments gathered at the lower levels. Where the two communities met had been handled organically, so while they flowed together, it was easy to tell them apart—a detail only visible from the outside.

Jordan yelled at his mother, loudly proclaiming that she stank, and he didn't love her anymore. He stomped his feet so hard he came up out of his seat. Cheryl grabbed his arm and pulled him back down. She twisted over him to latch his seatbelt. The boy pulled against the restraints and started yelling again. With an air of finality, Cheryl waved her hand and poked her finger at controls only she could see.

Jordan went still. "Hey. Turn it back on."

Cheryl shook her head. "Sit quietly for a while, and I'll consider it."

"Mom, don't be like that. My friends were watching. Let me back on. I'll be quiet, I promise."

"It's too late, Jordan. You had your chance. While you were busy entertaining your friends, you were mean to me and making me angry. Is that the kind of person you want to be?"

Jordan crossed his arms and sank into his seat.

"Now you can sit and think. When we get to Zeeman, if you're calm and polite, I might let you back online. Maybe."

Jordan's face turned red. He was about to start yelling, but something in his mother's eyes made him stop. He took a deep breath and sat back in the acceleration couch.

Dawn brought up her display and selected the news stream. She chose the latest trending story by Tony Renard. She watched as he connected a few minor coincidences and claimed there was a serial killer on Luna. The idea unsettled her. After the video, she took a moment to check in on her family. Uncle Keegan was with Etto at the restaurant. Her sister Fawn was attending a sporting event with Buck. She even checked on Adi and Evren, her sister's friends. They were at the same event as Fawn and Buck. Dawn relaxed a little. Tony was probably just out for more ratings.

Dawn was looking forward to her week-long vacation at the aviary in Zeeman. She wanted to put wings on her arms and take to the skies again. It felt good to worry a little less about her sister. Ever since her sister had come of age, Dawn had felt less pressure to stay close.

The shuttle doors closed, and a slight change in pressure meant they were close to departure. Dawn pulled up images of the electromagnetic rails they'd be using to launch into a ballistic trajectory over the South Pole. She'd ridden shuttles like this a few times in her life, but the thought of freefall still twisted her stomach.

Soon, reminder lights appeared, along with a soothing voice over the intercom. "Please ensure you are sitting comfortably all the way back in your seats, and you are strapped in. During acceleration, you will experience nearly six times lunar gravity, and you will feel like you are lying on your back. This will be abruptly replaced by weightlessness. We ask that you remain in your seats for the duration of the flight. Once we have risen to a suitable altitude, the capsule will rotate, and you will be able to see the lunar landscape above you through the transparent canopy. All passengers have been secured. We thank you for your cooperation. We will be launching shortly."

An array of a dozen indicators appeared in front of her. Dawn watched as they turned green in small clumps. Once everything was completed, the lights were replaced by a countdown from five.

The launch pushed Dawn deep into her seat. Her thin frame had a decent build for someone born and raised on Luna, but it was no match for the thrust launching the shuttle out of the crater. Weightlessness, as if they'd stepped off a cliff and were endlessly falling, came as abruptly as advertised. She could see the Earth to her right, low in the black sky, and realized the thrust she'd felt would be normal gravity down there.

The shuttle rotated until the Moon appeared above them. The landscape receded rapidly as they rushed by. In the darkness of the night, every shade of gray came into view. The starkness of the surface was broken by scattered settlements, splashes of color and light.

Dawn noticed the small indicator that told her the view had switched to simulated. Jordan let out a yelp.

"I can't see anything," he said. "The sunscreen came up, and now it's all blank."

"Well," Cheryl said, "the view is still nice for the rest of us."

"Mom, stop. Let me back online. Please?"

"I took it away because you were being hurtful. Why should I give it back to you? I could keep you offline until you get back to school."

Jordan paused for a moment. "Okay. I get it. I'm sorry. I was too excited, and I wasn't listening. I'm listening now. I promise I'll try to be better next time."

Cheryl sighed and ruffled his hair. "That's all I ask, Jordan. Try to be your best." She waved her hand to restore Jordan's connectivity.

He sat back and looked out at the restored view of the passing landscape. He raised his hand and pointed. "There's Ashbrook Observatory. That's what I wanted to see. It's the highest structure on Luna."

Dawn followed where he pointed and recognized the iconic structure, as well as the city below. Meshabu was one of the oldest cities on Luna. A few of the original structures had been preserved in a museum deep inside the complex. Her parents had taken her there when she and her sister were children. Before her parents had passed away. Dawn took a deep breath and exhaled. She cleared her mind and took in the scenery.

Soon the capsule rotated again, putting the surface under them once more.

"Please ensure you remain seated for the next few minutes. We will be turning the shuttle so that we are traveling backward and entering the magnetic net shortly after that. As the shuttle slows, there will be some rocking sensations, followed by a sudden resumption of gravity. Again, as with takeoff, you will feel nearly six times your normal weight for a few moments. Please don't try to move during this time. Once we have slowed down, the ride will be gentle and smooth to our destination at Zeeman Plaza. There may be a bit of a rumble as the craft is cleaned. Removing dust upon arrival is standard procedure. We appreciate your patience."

The landing came as described, eliciting a shout of joy from the boy. The shuttle came to a stop, and the pressure changed slightly, indicating the hatch was opening. Soon they stepped out onto a wide platform. The damp shuttle sparkled in the lights. Dawn smiled at Jordan as he and his mother headed to the southern end of the plaza. She swiped her display and selected her destination. A glowing blue line led her north to the aviary apartment complex.

* * *

Dawn slid along the large corridor, tiny air jets in the floor whisking her along. She leaned forward ever so slightly and gained speed, passing several fellow visitors along the way. The gentle rightward curve put the farthest end out of sight, but not without giving Dawn a sense of ancient grandeur. Ornate hanging light fixtures far overhead illuminated the structural arches that gracefully lined the walls. From here, it was hard for her to imagine how high up the crater wall she was. Her glowing blue line cut through the space, leading to the room she'd reserved.

Every dozen meters on the right side of the corridor was the entrance to another suite. Each entry displayed artwork selected or created by the occupants. Some were animated; others were still. Many were displayed in three dimensions, showing a false depth set into the panel.

She leaned back and slowed as she passed an entrance displaying an artist's rendition of a waterfall. The motion of the water, coupled with the flight of an occasional bird, made her smile.

Her glowing line ended at a familiar drawing of a tall, pink flamingo wearing a miniature bowler hat standing in shallow water. As she approached, the bird grinned with comically large human teeth. The panel slid aside, knocking the animated bird off balance. Dawn entered her temporary apartment and looked around. "This will do nicely. Service, does the balcony open directly to the aviary? Will I be able to fly from there?"

The Southern Lunar Communications Service answered in a pleasant male voice, "Affirmative. This apartment was designed to be suitable for flyers of intermediate to senior skill levels."

"Wonderful. Is my workshop set up and ready?"

"Affirmative. The Zeeman Transport Service has already delivered your selected materials. The additional equipment you requested has been installed."

"And my wings?" Dawn asked. "Where are they?"

"They are in the Welcome Center. You have been requested to complete three hours of refresher training before being approved for flight."

"That's disappointing. How do I avoid the three hours? Is there a shortcut?"

"The exact duration of your training depends on your instructor," Service said. "In general terms, they are far more concerned with your knowledge of safety procedures than your skill at flying."

"Do I need to be there at any particular time?"

"Training sessions begin every hour on the hour."

The transparent panel slid aside silently as Dawn stepped out onto the balcony. She admired the wide-open view as a gentle breeze caressed her face. Much of the soaring structure overhead was transparent. The black, star-filled sky shone through between tremendous illumination panels. The dome's edges had been built into the rim of a small crater. Twenty kilometers above the crater floor, in the center of the dome, was a cluster of open structures. Dawn twitched her eye to activate her data feed. The hanging structures were joined by the label THE RAFTERS. A series of wide terraces followed the gentle slope down from the rim, bursting with trees and dense foliage. Various labels hung over them, such as BIRDSONG FOREST to her left, and THE HIVE beyond that. The right was dominated by ELYSIA, THE DARK FOREST, and GREEN MEADOWS in the distance.

The protective dome held the atmosphere in, while filtering out harmful radiation when the sun was up. Immense lights provided false daylight for times like today, when the sun was down. She could see the entire distance to a forest of tall trees at the far side. Floating above, embedded in the scattered clouds, were the words THE GREAT FOREST.

Elysia, the closest on her right, was where people pretended to be Angels. Pale, heavenly structures were built on a wide terrace. Angelic flyers dotted the white landscape. Beyond that was a grove of giant, multi-colored mushrooms labeled FLUTTERWING FIELDS, among which fluttered butterfly-winged people. The mushrooms reminded her that her favorite pair of mycelium leather boots were getting old. On impulse, she swiped her display and requested a new pair be grown for her. She thought about the wide variety of materials she used to create clothing that were grown from mushrooms. That type of mushroom, and even the majestic, towering mushrooms in the distance, were very different from the little ones her uncle served in his diner.

In the center of the dome, dozens of flyers circled a warm updraft that bellowed from a large, hexagonal grate in the crater floor. The rising air allowed them to reach great heights, including The Rafters.

They were like specks of dust slowly swirling in a breeze. Dawn waved her hand over the labels, dismissing them. The people behind this entertainment center used augmented reality sparingly. Place names and flight warnings were about it.

Dawn looked down, and her chest momentarily tightened. She hadn't realized her room would be this far above the crater floor. Her lips curled into a smile. It was exhilarating. At almost five kilometers directly above the near end of the children's playground, the view was immense. She thought she could hear the sound of children's laughter floating on the flower-scented wind.

Dawn stepped over to the adjacent sliding panel and entered her bedroom. It smelled of fresh linen and flowers. Crossing the room took her to a short hallway. To the left was the main room and kitchen, and ahead was the fresher. On her right was her temporary workshop. She stepped inside and looked around. The cloth she'd selected was arrayed on a large table to one side, and in the center of the room stood a small, full-body mannequin that appeared to represent a young girl.

Dawn frowned. "That doesn't look much like her, Service."

"You did not specify an exact replication of Carlene Sullana's face," Service said. "You only specified accurate body measurements and flex points for the express purpose of creating a dress."

Dawn shook her head. "I know. I remember. But that looks too much like she did when she was a teenager. She's a tiny woman, but she's in her thirties. I need to be thinking grown woman, not little girl. See what you can do, will you? I'm going to use the fresher, then go get my wings."

* * *

When Dawn reached the Welcome Center, she found herself in a large group of people of various ages. They were ushered into a circular hall with several rows of seating around the perimeter. In the center of the room was a small platform.

A young man stood on the dais, directing people to their seats. His meki was a glowing blue orb that floated directly above his head. It indicated that he wasn't actually present, but rather a shared bit of augmented reality. Dawn wondered for a moment if he was a real person or a software simulation.

"Once people are all seated," he said, "we can get started. More seats right over here. Plenty of room for everyone." The crowd milled about, leisurely finding seats.

Dawn found herself seated between a woman about her own age and an older man. The man waved his hands through the air, swiping and flicking controls visible only to himself, while the woman smiled at Dawn. Her golden eyes sparkled as she introduced herself. "Hi. I'm Sheena. This your first time?"

"Nope. Third. I think it's my new favorite place on Luna."

"This is my second," Sheena said. "Which I know is strange, because I live just on the other side of Zeeman, up on the ridge. How long are you here for?"

"Five days. I set up a workshop, so I might stay longer if I feel like it."

"Workshop? What do you do?"

"I create outfits for people," Dawn said. "Mostly fancy dresses these days, but I take almost any request. You got a thing?"

"Yeah, actually. I do a lot of acting. Mostly old classics, from the 23rd century on up to the turn of the millennium."

"I saw something recently. It was a story about the first manned mission to Proximus. But wait, that's older, isn't it…?"

"Yeah, like that," Sheena said. "Not quite so old. But my friend Donny played Commander Groseclose in that one."

"I remember him. He was good."

"Anyway, where you from?"

"Moretus Plains," Dawn said, "right next to Grissom Park. You know it?"

Sheena furrowed her brow. "I think so. Big, interactive theme park, right? Lots of custom augmentation?"

"That's the place. I take it you've never been?"

"Not my kind of fun. I prefer real things, like strapping fake wings to my arms and pretending I'm an Earth bird on the Moon." She giggled.

Dawn laughed. "I like bird wings, too. I tried butterfly wings my first time, but they don't really let you soar, swoop, and dive."

The young man on the dais spoke much louder. "Your attention, please. This first hour is a basic safety tutorial. For newcomers, this is the first of several hours of instruction. For those of you in review, it's simply a basic reminder before you go on to your practical groups." With a wave of his hand, he and his meki quickly faded out, and the room darkened. A lifelike animated display showing the basic concepts of flight safety took his place for the next hour. The frequent use of humor kept everyone's attention.

After the review, Dawn found herself in the same group as Sheena. They took extra care adjusting the wings to their arms and shoulders. Dawn's were patterned in the colors of a bluebird. Sheena's were also mainly blue but had a splash of red where they joined together, and again in the tail feathers.

"What kind of bird is that?" Dawn asked.

"It's called a macaw. A kind of parrot, I think. Yours is a bluebird, right?"

Dawn lifted one wing and spread the feathers. "I love the blues. I know I should've paid more attention to flight characteristics, but I really loved the colors." She took a moment to tie her thick brown hair into a short ponytail. Sheena's curly hair was tightly braided in the back, perfect for flying.

When everyone was reacquainted with their personal wings and how to operate them, the group migrated outside onto the aviary floor to an awaiting open-air tram. The tram whisked them through the first-timer training zone to an area called the Newbie Nets.

The young man popped back in with a little flash and raised his hand. His voice was still amplified. "Everyone, filter your communication and display to Raha Two. Ignore everything else. No distractions, please. Raha Two will allow me to send you instructions, in addition to being your flight display. Remember your display colors. Blue means expert. None of you here qualify for that. Green means intermediate. That's all of you. Yellow means junior, like the folks we passed in the first-timers' zone. Yellow means watch out, be careful. Orange is used to denote someone having difficulties, and red means they need help right now. Broken wing. Dead electronics. Anything that puts their life in danger, or yours. Now, everyone go ahead and take off; stay above the nets. Watch your neighbors' flight paths. After a while, I'll visit you. Once you perform the actions requested, I'll release you. Then you can make your way south to the updraft and go anywhere you like. Any questions? No? Good. Get up there."

Dawn and Sheena raced each other into the wind. Taking off quickly, they steered themselves out over the gigantic nets. Dawn stretched her wings and tested their limits.

Sheena signaled that she was getting her instructions, so Dawn glided back toward the tourist complex, staying above the safety nets. Not long after, the young man and his meki appeared to her left, floating through the air on a pillow. Dawn realized his glowing orb meki was an egg. He gave her a series of simple requests. Glide left, climb quickly, dive—basic moves she was already confident in. Eventually he smiled and saluted, aiming her south into the updraft. His image faded out. She circled the rising plumb of warm air. She took large, easy circles as she gained altitude. In a few moments, she was near the top.

There were dozens of perches and a line of little shops up in The Rafters. She looked for Sheena and found her perched near a little snack shop. Dawn joined her, but almost missed the landing.

"Whoa," Sheena said. "Slow down there, whiplash. You'll make me spill my iced blueberry latte." She grinned. Her wingtips were folded back so she could use her hands. She balanced on a perch designed to accommodate flyers with nearly any type of wing.

Dawn inadvertently looked down and felt the stirring of vertigo. "Damn. Long way down."

"Yeah, but even if you had no wings, you'd never hit bottom. Too many rescue drones hidden everywhere." Sheena nodded in the direction of the closest drone docking port. "Those things move fast in every direction. Break your fall, not your neck. At least, that's what they promise. I wouldn't want to test it, though."

"I know. It's still a long way down." She smiled at Sheena. "I wasn't sure if you'd be waiting for me."

"Maybe. Or maybe I just wanted to get high and drink coffee. Wait, not what I meant. Want some coffee?"

"No, thanks. I'm ready to fly."

"Where are you headed?" Sheena asked.

"Last time I was here, I spent a lot of time over in Birdsong Forest. I want to try somewhere new this time."

"There's a place just south of there called Evilwood. I haven't been there yet. Restricted, adults only. Saw it last time I was here, next to the Demon Enclosure." She pointed generally out and down. "Just there, south of Birdsong."

Dawn swiped her display, using her directory to call up details about Evilwood. Some sort of interactive spooky zone, like a haunted forest, only with giant bugs and slimy, creepy things with too many legs. She laughed. "Oh, yuck! It looks nasty!" Dawn looked out and down again. She pointed. "I see it, southeast of us. Other side of the obstacle course."

"Yup. Creepy, nasty place." Sheena slowly sipped her drink with a smile.

"Horrible smelling too, I'll bet." Dawn climbed off her perch and stretched. "Race you!" She dropped off and spread her wings, falling into an easy dive in the direction of Evilwood. The light gravity made her actions slow and graceful.

Sheena took one last hurried gulp of her coffee, tossed the container into the closest recycler, and headed after Dawn at a much more aggressive angle.

They spent much of the afternoon exploring the tangled haunted forest of Evilwood. Random animated character interactions made the experience slightly spooky and highly comedic. The thick canopy overhead gave the forest a dark, foreboding feeling. Mist clung to the ground in patches. With all the other people exploring, there was simply too much laughter for the place to ever be too frightening.

Later, they participated in an interactive drama, where a fairy army was invading to battle an insect horde. Many of the fairies had long, pointed ears as a body modification.

The ending of the battle was delightfully unexpected, as the fairy princess ended up kissing the insect chief. They then proclaimed their love and sang a duet. Everyone laughed and cheered.

After the make-believe war was all settled, everyone was invited to a Fairyland Feast in the nearby Great Forest. Dawn and Sheena found themselves swept along with the crowd, enjoying it all as they made the short flight.

Tucked away in a corner of the Great Forest, Fairyland turned out to be an adventure all its own. Tall trees had ornate living spaces carved into them in an archaic fairy style. Down in the clearing where the feast was held, there was a stage and a dozen large tables with long benches. A five-piece band of fairies started playing, only to be invaded by insects early on. The resulting band had a dozen characters and played brilliantly entertaining music. Everything was made to look as if it were carved from wood or chiseled from stone.

The two of them ended up seated at a table surrounded by a mix of fairies, birds, and even an angel, who introduced himself as Elam. His wings came from his back, attached at the shoulders. His brilliant white feathers smelled noticeably of fresh-baked cookies.

Sheena chuckled. "Do all angels smell like cookies?"

Elam laughed. "Only the real ones."

Dawn shook her head with a half-smile. A small, glowing pink heart appeared in front of her. It was her sister's meki. She tapped it to accept the call. "Hi, Fawn."

Her sister's face floated in the air, smiling. Long, pointed ears flicked forward. A wild auburn cloud of hair floated about her head. "How's the flying?"

"It's fun, but it's only been a day. You can't possibly miss me already."

"Who says I can't?" She stuck out her tongue.

Sheena noticed Dawn was on a call and politely turned to engage in small talk with others at the table.

Dawn put her hand over her heart. "I love you, little sister. Now go pay attention to Buck. I'm having a great time, and I'll tell you all about it next week, I promise."

"Buck is working on a new candle. He's trying to concentrate, so I'm leaving him be. What are you doing now? Do I hear music?"

"Yes, there's music, and people are dancing. I was sitting here talking to a friend I met today."

Fawn gasped. "A new friend? You?" She crossed her arms. "Prove it!"

Dawn shook her head. "Brat." She turned to Sheena. "My sister wants to say hi."

"Sure," Sheena said. "Share me in."

Dawn shared her display. "Sheena, this is my sister, Fawn."

"Hello, Fawn. Nice ears. Deer?"

Fawn grinned and twitched her ears. "Yup."

"I thought they might be. They match the name. Did you do your eyes, too? They're like big chocolate marbles!"

"Nope, those are natural. Dawn, give her the full picture."

Dawn adjusted her display to show a miniature Fawn standing on the tabletop, clomping both her hooves and wiggling her auburn tail.

"Impressive. That's a good look for you."

"Thanks. I have a matching boyfriend, too. Buck."

Sheena laughed. "A matched set."

The music grew louder, and the lights dimmed throughout the dome. Dawn checked the time. It was right at 18:00, the beginning of the two-hour twilight between the day and night cycles in the aviary. Several people were setting serving platters on the buffet table.

"Okay," Dawn said, "they're serving dinner now. Give my love to Buck. I'll talk to you later."

"Bye! Sheena, nice meeting you."

Sheena waved. "Take care."

Fawn faded as her meki bounced away.

Dawn shrugged. "She's a little overly dependent on me. Not so good with separation."

"No worries," Sheena said. "She loves her sister. That's all that matters. Let's go get some food."

After dinner, they were invited on a tour of the village. Elam the angel followed along with them. After the tour, they sat back at one of the long tables. The band was playing a mix of old and new music.

"Dawn and Fawn?" Sheena tilted her head and smiled. "Were your parents into rhymes?"

Dawn shook her head. "She was Debbie until she got the body mod. She changed her name. Buck didn't change his officially, but he uses it everywhere now."

"Where did she get the idea? I don't think I've ever seen a mod like that before."

"It's based on an old image she found. A hand drawing of a nude girl with hooves for feet, a tail, long, flowing head of reddish-brown hair, and long, pointy ears. There's also a tuft of hair at the bottom of each shin."

"Do you make her outfits?" Sheena asked.

"Some. She wears a lot of skimpy outfits and isn't afraid to go into 'full art' mode when the thought crosses her mind." Dawn chuckled. "I thought for a while she'd end up being a nudist. Some of her own outfits have flair, but way too much glitter for my taste." She shook her head and smiled. "Then there are times when she hits all the right notes and puts together something truly impressive."

Sheena laughed.

Dawn's shoulder felt stiff. She stretched it. "I think it's about time for me to get back to a warm bed. My arms are getting sore. Not used to so much work."

"Be sure to stretch before you go to bed," Sheena said. "Stretch again when you get up in the morning. It'll help."

"Got plans tomorrow?"

"Not yet. Want to meet up for breakfast somewhere?"

Dawn considered it. "Sure. My place is over near the Angels. I think I remember seeing something about a bakery there that makes some really good morning food."

Elam leaned in. "That would be Irma's Cottage in Elysia, only it's more like a cafeteria now. She still makes everything herself, but she's got quite a crowd. A good time is right after daybreak, 6:30 or so."

Sheena groaned. "Just a bit earlier than I had planned. What's the crowd like at 7:30?"

"It's crowded," Elam said, "but the line is really never all that long. I think it'll be worth your wait."

"7:30 is more my style," Sheena said.

Dawn reached out and touched Sheena's hand. "See you there around 7:30."

They flew most of the way across the dome together and parted ways as they neared the tourist end. Sheena's balcony was down closer to the first-timers' area. Elam circled for a moment, as if hoping for an invitation. He drifted over toward Elysia, gliding past Dawn and waving.

Dawn landed with a light *thump* on her balcony. The panels opened for her as she walked in, unstrapping her wings. After freshening up a bit, she went into her workshop, where a full-sized exact replica of Carlene Sullana, fully colored and highly detailed, was standing there to greet her. Dawn giggled. "That's *not* a little girl." She shook her head and went to the living area. She called up an unfamiliar list of old shows. "Service, where's my entertainment list?"

"Your personalized list is in the database of the Moretus Central Entertainment Service. It has not been transferred to the Zeeman Entertainment Service."

"Please copy it here. I want to pick up where I left off."

"Acknowledged." A few moments later, she was watching the next installment of a familiar show.

* * * * *

Coffee

Tuesday, September 21, 3288, 6:00

He awoke in a foul mood. Nothing different from the day before. He stretched and rolled over. Tossed the covers and groaned. The walls of the room were bare. He pushed himself out of bed with one arm and bounced into the fresher with minimal effort. A warm shower followed by warm, dry air was bland and pointless to him. His reflection was the face of a stranger. The nose still looked oddly straight. It would take getting used to, but it looked much better than the previous version. He skipped shaving and wandered into the kitchen. "Coffee."

The order had been set to produce one hot four hundred milliliter mug of coffee with thirty milliliters of cold creamer and five grams of granulated sweetener. It never varied. There was no need to change it.

He inhaled deeply, smelling the rich aroma. A cautious sip let the warmth flow down his throat. It was the perfect taste in the morning. Some days, it was his only pleasure.

Barely moving his legs, he trundled into the living area.

His walls were all opaque, blank. An empty canvas, except for one shelving unit, upon which were nearly a hundred small statues in various sizes, styles, and colors, mostly women with a smattering of men. All were in various poses of bondage and distress. Many looked horrified, broken. Some were missing limbs. He glanced at them, then sat in his chair.

"News." His display wall showed a large grid of thumbnail news feeds. He selected one near the top, expanding it to play. He repeated this over and over, watching a variety of different feeds and sipping his coffee. This went on all morning, every morning. It was always the same.

One particular story made him laugh. Some fool named Tony was doing investigative reporting about missing young women from Schrodinger.

"Could there be a serial murderer on the Moon?" Tony asked. "It's happened before. It could be happening now. He could be watching this show. I hope I don't piss him off."

"You can't piss me off, Tony. You can't begin to guess where those projects ended up. Have fun chasing shadows." He went back to casually browsing the news feeds. Another one caught his attention. He paused and furled his brow. "Vondur, repeat that." It was a story about two groups of teens that had been playing outside their communities in Minkowski Crater. When one group saw the other, they threw rocks. The resulting fight had cracked one boy's helmet.

That was different. It had real promise. He felt a sense of anticipation as he watched all day. Parents shouted at each other as he waited for an escalation of the conflict. Things settled down that night, and people went back home. News feeds began dropping the story, moving on to other topics of little or no interest. He reviewed the incident in his mind. Could this be the opportunity he'd been waiting for?

"Vondur, have there been any developments in my current project?"

"Negative. Nominal indications, minimal output."

"Increase supplementation and maintain stability. I'll pick it up tomorrow."

"Acknowledged."

"Now, give me everything there is to know about those two communities in Minkowski, with particular attention to their structures."

"Acknowledged."

"My orders were to stay low until I was activated. Stay low, they said. Ten fucking years I've stayed low, Vondur. Ten. Do you think it's time to make some noise?"

"Unable to answer. This service does not have opinions."

He scoured the information that had appeared on his display. He pointed to one of the structures. "Show me the plans for that one."

* * * * *

Ganymede

Tuesday, September 21, 3288, 6:57

The ship's control room was brightly illuminated by flat screen displays at various stations. Tong Sianothai, captain of the *Pang Yu*, perched in the center behind a series of rails. This was the Conn. Forward of that was the navigation console, and on the starboard side, the weapons stations. The inner hull was a tight pattern of colored pipes and conduits.

"All hands," Tong said, "station the maneuvering watch." He swiped his display, and a loud, bonging alarm sounded. It rang several times.

"Got it, Cap," said Kip, the ship's engineer. "We're all up. You can kill the alarm." She floated into the control room from the forward passageway, guiding herself along mounted handrails. Her straight black hair was braided and pinned back. She gave Tong a sidelong glance with her deep brown eyes. She winked and grinned at him.

Tong silenced the alarm and winked back. "You never let me have any fun, Kip."

"I'll take you to Bujo's when we get back and show you what real fun is."

"I'll pass. I'm not into pain."

"Aw, come on, Cap." Jake floated into the control room from aft. "A little pain never hurt anyone."

Kip laughed. "Jake will join me, won't you?"

"Bujo's? Sure, I'm in again. You took me last time, remember?"

"Oh, yeah, maybe." Kip grinned and rubbed her forehead. "It's a little foggy, kid."

"We're stationing the maneuvering watch, Lieutenant Kiputh," Tong said. "That means you're in Engineering, right?"

"Yes, sir. Moving along, sir. Right away, sir." Kip angled her body in the direction of the aft passageway and pushed off with her feet, deftly using grab holds to guide her.

Vin floated past Kip in the opposite direction, greeting her politely. He handed her one of the five coffee bags he was carrying. "Light and sweet."

"Yup. Thanks, Vinny." She caught the warm bag with practiced ease and continued floating smoothly aft.

As he entered Control, Vin passed a bag to Tong and to Jake. "Where's the ensign? Did I miss her?"

"Nope. I'm here." Brenna floated into Control, her hair slightly unkempt and dark circles under her eyes.

"Are you qualified yet?" Vin asked.

"No, sir. Not yet," said Brenna, the newest member of the crew.

"Then why should I be bringing you coffee, non-qual?"

She half-smiled. "Because you're such a wonderful, caring individual, thoughtful of your shipmates, sir?"

Jake shook his head. "That's laying it on a bit thick, don't you think?"

Vin snapped his fingers at Jake. "Hey, you shut up, kid. This is about the only joy I get. Yes, Ensign. I'm such a good person, I grant you the bean of the gods." He shoved a warm coffee bag in her direction. "Now get back aft and study hard. Get qualified soon. We have a week in jump, and you need to be able to stand watch to make sure your boss gets some sleep."

"Yes, sir, thank you, sir." She caught the coffee bag, then headed back aft with far less grace than her superior officer had a few moments earlier.

"If she doesn't finish her quals on the first watch, I'll go give Kip a break," Tong said.

"Oh, I'm sure she's about ready," Vin said. "I checked before I came up. She's only got one system test left, then she takes the full review. I think she'll get it first watch. Just don't tell her I said so." He settled into the navigation station, poking and swiping at his display consoles.

Jake settled into a cluster of sensor displays, swiping at them as well, checking his system's status and running tests.

Tong looked at his indicators and frowned. He poked his display and selected the ship wide communications circuit. "Engineering, Conn, report your status."

"Engineering, aye," Kip said. "Passing through Machinery Two, Cap. Give me a minute."

"Conn, aye," Tong said.

A few moments later, Kip said, "Conn, Engineering, Engineering watch set."

"Conn, aye," Tong said.

"Conn, Nav. Nav watch set," Vin said.

"Conn, aye," Tong said.

"Conn, Ops, Ops watch set," Jake said.

"Conn, aye," Tong said. "All hands, prepare for jump. Engineering, Conn. Report pre-jump status."

"Report pre-jump status, Engineering aye. Stored power at 100 percent. Heat sink is at 175 Kelvin. Reactor at 100 percent. I have a green board."

"You have a green board, Conn aye. Navigator, verify your coordinates."

"Verify coordinates, Nav aye. Sir, my coordinates are verified. I have a blue board."

"Verified with a blue board, Conn aye. Ops, Conn, report all contacts within one hundred kilometers."

"Report all contacts within one hundred kilometers, Ops aye. Conn, Ops, we have one contact, designated L-14. Contact is at 99.4 kilometers and opening. No other contacts within range. We are clear to jump."

"Clear to jump, Conn aye." Tong watched as the one remaining contact passed the hundred-kilometer mark. "Engineering, Conn, commence the jump."

All five braced themselves as the jump engine, being fed massive amounts of power, routed energy through a grid embedded in the outer hull. Slowly the grid began to glow dark blue, then brilliant blue, and finally pure white as it twisted spacetime slightly and pushed the ship into a different dimension. Seen from a distance, the brilliant white light appeared to simply shrink and fade rapidly away, leaving nothing behind.

"Conn, Ops, jumpspace detected," Jake said. "Jump transition complete."

"Jump transition complete, Conn aye. All hands, the jump timer has been started. Secure from the maneuvering watch, set the jumpspace watch, sections one and port. Or should I say, *re*-port back there. Not to put any pressure on you, Ensign Dotseth, but you have six hours to get qualified." He turned off his broadcast. "Who has first watch? I forgot to look."

"I do, Cap," Jake said. "You're on second. Vin gets third."

"Perfect. Come on over. Lieutenant Tory, the *Pang Yu* is in the first hour of a long jump. Expected exit at hour one six seven. I haven't checked, but the power storage banks are empty from the jump. Heat sink is at 175. Lieutenant Kiputh is on watch aft. We have two broken Assegai missiles forward. All forward batteries are empty. In the missile compartment, magazine four is jammed. Missile battery four only has 108 loaded because of it. Since that affects our entire loadout of Cutlass missiles, battery four is offline. Batteries one through three, our lovely Barong missiles, are fully operational and loaded with 160 each. Their magazines are at 790 each. Potable water tanks are full; ballast tanks are in trim. Oxygen at 20.14 percent."

"Aye. I relieve you, sir."

"I stand relieved," Tong said. "Ship, Lieutenant Tory has the Conn."

"Acknowledged," the ship said.

"Did we ever figure out why the Cutlass magazine jammed?" Jake asked.

"Why?" Tong asked. "Because some jackass corporate type cut corners to pad their fat ass, that's why."

"I see, sir. Thank you, sir."

"Drop it, Jake. I'm not mad at you. It's frustrating that we have to upgrade our missile systems so damned often because the corporate types want to make more money from it. The Assegai missile worked fine and was a lot smaller than the Cutlass, or even the Barong. We're a perfect example of corporate greed. Three separate and incompatible missile systems for essentially the same class weapon." He took a deep breath. "I'm going to go rest for a while before my watch. Stay awake and keep an eye on the oxygen. It's not out of spec, but it's a touch low."

"Aye, sir. I'm on it."

Tong headed aft to the compartment known as Ops Two, where he caught up with Vin in the ship's galley.

Vin was preparing himself a meal in the tiny space full of stainless-steel appliances. "Want something to eat, Cap?"

"Yeah, I'll get it when you're done. Feel like watching something? I'm not going to start the drills until tomorrow."

"I was thinking of watching *Conquest of the Waters of Europa*. Interested?"

"I don't know," Tong said. "I've seen enough explosions for a lifetime. I wouldn't mind seeing *Escape* again, though. It's my favorite of the series so far."

"That one always makes me cry."

"Oh, yeah, when what's-her-face dies. Yeah, that's a great moment."

"How about a comedy instead?" Vin asked. "I think I'd rather laugh."

"Comedy is good. Got anything in mind?"

"There's a new series out of Aretha's Halo I've been meaning to watch."

"*The Real Woman?*" Tong asked.

"Yeah. You've heard of it?"

"Yup. Watched it all last refit. Sorry."

"Don't want to watch it again?" Vin asked.

"Let me say this, it's a great show, but a lot of it's because of how twisted it gets. Once you know the twists—" Tong shrugged "—well, it's more of a watch it one time and hope for more shows."

They floated into the crew's lounge, a semicircular nook with padding arranged so crew members could space themselves out and still have a good viewing angle for their shared entertainment.

"There's a new one from Media Ultima," Tong said. "It's set on Mars. Called *Uncle Martin's Broadcast*."

Vin swiped his display. "Oh, hey. Six stars. All right. Let's watch that one."

Tong swiped his display and queued up the first of many episodes. Their only interruption was when Ensign Brenna Dotseth passed her final watch qualifications.

* * * * *

Elysia

Tuesday, September 21, 3288, 7:24

Dawn arrived at Irma's early the next morning. The building was an enormous, yet rustic cabin. The beams had been crafted to look like real wood. An oversized balcony in front allowed flyers easy access inside, while large, open decks on each side wrapped around to the back. There was a line, but it didn't look too intimidating. She could smell the intoxicating aroma of fresh bread and sweets. She'd been waiting in line a few minutes when Sheena landed beside her with a clumsy flourish of her wings.

"Whoops!" Sheena said.

"Careful there," Dawn said. "Here, I saved your place."

There was a grumble from someone behind them. Sheena touched Dawn's arm, turned, and smiled. "Sorry!"

They each picked out delicious-looking pastries stuffed with various proteins and settled down at a table for two on the expansive deck outside.

Dawn activated her display and looked at the map of the aviary. "Where should we go today? Any ideas?"

"I really enjoyed the fairies," Sheena said, "and I want to spend more time there, but I think today it might be more fun to explore someplace new. Where have you never been?"

"Let's see. That was my first time to Evilwood and Fairyland. I'd never been in the Great Forest before, and there's the Demon

Enclosure, and the Hive." Dawn lowered her voice. "Behind those is the Fantasy Land Adult Playground." Dawn glanced at Sheena. "Way at the back of the Great Forest is Squirrel Town, and the Acrobats, of course. I've been to Green Meadows and near Clifftop. Here's something called the Dark Forest. It's next to the Night Flyer caverns. Never been there. What about you?"

Sheena looked at her display as well. She swiped her display to share it with Dawn. "Okay, so I've marked the areas I've been to with red. Green is where I haven't been."

Dawn waved her hand to accept Sheena's map and copied it onto hers. Dawn looked it over. "Wait, you've been to the Demon Enclosure and the Adult Playground? Oh, do tell! What was that like?"

Sheena grinned. "It was okay. The playground, that is. The Demons were just a bunch of guys in bat wings with certain... *enhanced appendages*, shall we say. The playground is naked flying and hookups. I tried it. The naked, not the hookups. Not really all that exciting." She laughed.

Dawn laughed, too. "Right, that's off the list. That kind of leaves the Great Forest, which we both loved and want to explore more of, and Squirrel Town on the other side of that. Neither of us have been in the Dark Forest or the Night Flyer Caverns, but that sounds like a nighttime adventure. And it looks like this is the first time for both of us here in Elysia."

"Want to just explore around here for a while?" Sheena asked. "That castle over there looks amazing."

"Sounds like a plan. That reminds me, do you see Elam anywhere?"

Sheena gave a lopsided grin. "More like the cookie fairy, wasn't he? I can't get over how much he smelled like cookies."

"He sure seemed like he was interested in you," Dawn said. "I'm surprised he isn't here now."

Sheena shook her head with a smirk. "I think he's smarter than that."

After eating, they took to the sky again, flying over an area mostly inhabited by people wearing angel wings. The ground was white and covered in mist.

"What's all the fog about?" Dawn asked.

"This is supposed to be Paradise or Heaven, like the afterlife, so that's not fog, it's clouds."

"So it's clouds, which is condensed water vapor, but at ground level, as opposed to fog, which is ground-level condensed water vapor." Dawn chuckled. "I see. Makes all the sense in the world."

"It's all imaginary, anyway; just go with it."

They spent the rest of the morning swooping over the white landscape, perching on castle walls, and exploring a grove of apple trees. They swooped close to the clouds and looped back to see the mist swirling, once revealing a couple of children who'd apparently been hiding from their friends.

Closer to midday, as they explored the castle grounds, they came to an opening that led to a hidden courtyard. Several young girls played on the grounds, each wearing matching angelic outfits with light, feathery wings.

Dawn took note of the style of their outfits and tilted her head.

"See something interesting?" Sheena asked.

"Actually, yes. See how the bottom of their outfits look like a thin, almost ethereal skirt? Look what happens when they jump." Dawn pointed. One of the girls jumped, and what at first appeared to be a single delicate layer of cloth grew extra layers of modesty as it tossed about. "See. It's so thin and light but look at all the extra layers that just appeared. I love that design!"

Sheena giggled. "I forgot. You make dresses."

Dawn swiped her personal display, making notes and capturing images. "Yes, mostly dresses, but I don't limit myself. That's what I love to do most. I'll look it up tonight."

"Hey, Dawn, you hungry yet?"

"A bit. Could use a shower, too. My place?" Dawn pointed up to the general area where she was staying.

"Sure," Sheena said.

Dawn swiped a copy of her location meki to Sheena so they could both see where to land. Dawn swooped up and over her railing. She touched down lightly and strode into her living space. Sheena followed with more of a thud and stumble approach.

Dawn ducked quickly into her fresher. "Be right back." Several minutes later, as she was done freshening up, she heard Sheena shriek and giggle. Dawn left the fresher, only to find Sheena still giggling right outside.

Sheena pointed a shaking finger at Dawn's workshop. "There's a naked girl in your workshop!"

"Yes, dear. It's called a mannequin. I use them to make dresses."

"But it's a naked little woman!"

Sheepishly, Dawn shrugged. "It did turn out a little more detailed than I usually go. The original looked like a little girl, so I asked Service to make it more specific to the person I'm making the dress for." She shrugged. "She's the one I want to try that trick with the gossamer skirt on. She's small, so I think the effect will look nice, and I'll do the top with a deep neck to show off her cleavage. If I do it right, it'll look like it's constantly just about to fall off her, but won't even show a tease."

"Can you make it adjustable?" Sheena asked. "What if she *wants* to tease?"

"Oh, sure. That's a slider in the app. I like to give people options, but I always think about my default settings first."

Sheena hopped toward the kitchen. "What's for lunch?"

They shared a quick salad and settled on the Great Forest for their next stop.

Dawn looked through the local event schedule on her display. She swiped her display to share the event with Sheena. "There's an acrobat show in half an hour. If we hurry, we can still fly and make it!" She bounded to the balcony, spread her arms, and let her wings strap themselves into place.

Sheena followed, her wings strapping on a little slower, then dove off the balcony, gathering speed to catch up.

Dawn was soaring from her balcony jump, straining hard, stroking the air with her wings to gain altitude. If she climbed high enough on her own, she could go straight through the center of the updraft, catching a lift, and then on to the Great Forest, saving some time. She looked back at Sheena, who was struggling a little to catch up. Once she felt the updraft, Dawn spread her wings wide to catch the gentle breeze. She glanced back under her wing to search for Sheena.

Her display flashed red. Impending collision. Too late. A body slammed into her like a ton of dead weight. She felt a deep rip inside her back. In a tumble of confusion, pain, and entanglement, the person she'd collided with grasped her legs. Her nanomedics rushed into action. Her spine faded into a dull ache. She quickly assessed the situation.

They were falling, fast. The man clutching her legs had no wings, and she couldn't move her legs. Her wings weren't catching enough air. She quickly adjusted her wings and spread them wide to catch as much air as she could. "Hang on and don't let go." His answer was muffled, but he was still there.

As their fall slowed, Dawn was facing north. Despite the nano-medics, her discomfort grew. She could feel her back stretch in ways it shouldn't. The Newbie Nets came into view. Hoping to make it, she aimed and thrust her wings with as much power as her arms could deliver.

Within seconds, she saw they were going to miss the nets. A large, padded rescue drone arrived in time to help lift her passenger, and they barely made the nearest net in a painful tumble.

Dawn went face first on the net. She could see people below her looking up and pointing as she lost consciousness.

* * * * *

Projects

Wednesday, September 22, 3288, 6:00

He awoke in a foul mood. His dreams had been vivid, violent. He thought about the previous day's conflict. Kids starting a fight. Such an easy target. It was time to act.

He got out of bed and headed to the fresher, then he wandered into his kitchen. "Coffee." He inhaled deeply, smelling the deep aroma of the coffee. He repeated his routine and trundled into the living area. "News. Search for Minkowski." Nothing. It was all calm. A flash from his dream made his heart race. "Time to get started."

With a poke at the news story and a few well-placed swipes, he called up his map of the crater. The two communities were in close proximity.

"Vondur, new project. I need you to acquire explosives and a bot in Minkowski to work outside. Enough to crack the dome right about—" he pointed into the display "—here. Make sure you use that special protocol of yours. No traces."

"Acknowledged," Vondur said. "Beginning search."

He sat back and relaxed for a moment. This unusual service had an amusing array of talents. A very lucky find. Or had it been a gift? A tool for his mission? It was a memory he knew he had, but it wouldn't come to mind. There were a lot of those. He shook his head. Enough of that. He had work to do. "Vondur, how long until the fireworks?"

"The required equipment has been located and secured. Transit will take several hours. Query, do you wish the delivery bot destroyed in the explosion?"

"Negative. Run that sucker out and hide it in a hole. I want it to look like an attack from the other group."

"Acknowledged. An exit path is being calculated."

"Let me know when it's ready," he said, "and make sure you have a camera set up so I can have a good view."

He got up and stretched, then he headed into his workshop, where his other project hung by her hands from the ceiling. A squat bot sat next to the young woman. Her eyes filled with fear as she saw him approach. Her mouth was taped closed.

"Ah, you're awake. Good. By now, you've figured out that I've taken you offline. I'll bet you're wondering how I did it, or you're wondering why. No matter. I'll explain everything. Slowly. The first thing you should know is, I've disabled your medtech as well." He walked over to a table where an assortment of tools, many with sharp edges, were laid out and contemplated his choices. "No pain relief for you today." He waved the door closed.

* * * * *

Discovery

Wednesday, September 22, 3288, 6:25

Elliot Humboldt spent time every morning looking in the mirror, grooming his gray hair, washing his face, and making sure he presented an image to the public that was immaculate. A personal grooming bot trimmed his hair impeccably. The resulting excess floated like dust in the air until it was promptly vacuumed up by the automated cleaning bot below. Elliot watched them work, imagining himself a bastion of integrity. At least, that was the appearance he wanted to give.

He paused to look at a recently arrived image of Lauren and their daughters. From time to time, his wife updated the display with images to encourage him to stay focused on his task. With his wife and daughters living back on Mars, he was free to focus on gaining more power.

He noticed that Danielle was in her track outfit. He felt a surge of pride. She'd probably make the finals again this year. Competing in the Olympics was her greatest achievement. Doing it again would add to the greatness. When his attention returned to the image, he realized there was a fourth person. Peeking out from behind a set of flowing drapes was Leslie's daughter, Ella. One of his grandchildren. His heart swelled with pride. "You are the reason I am here, little one."

As director of Offworld Trade for Yolo Consumer Goods, he was the second most powerful director of the second most powerful corporation in the Corporate Federation. Yet even in that rarified air, he was unsatisfied. "Too many seconds," he said to himself. "I keep settling when I should be pushing harder."

After dressing in professional attire, he walked out onto the balcony. His view over the interior of the orbital station didn't impress him as much as it might others. Over a dozen stories below, he could see too much green grass, too many colorful flowers. He missed the red soil and pale blue-gray skies of his native Mars. The color had matched his eyes. Green didn't fit into his world view. Kigyo Station was built by Earthers. On the rare occasion he looked outside, there in the field of stars was the dying Earth. His only joy here had been finding that, at this particular level, he experienced Mars-normal gravity.

He sat at a small wooden table and waved at his personal display. He quickly selected items from a breakfast menu, then went on to review his other activities. His current goal was the elimination of Yolo's senior director, Wayne Preville. Preville was the only person above him at Yolo. If it were engineered correctly, Wayne's fall would lead to his own rise in stature. No one else was as well positioned as Elliot was. As he scanned each line, he noticed a golden indicator next to one of those research projects.

"Bil, I see an indication you managed to open the subject's personal files from university. What did you find?"

The Backoffice Interplanetary Logistics Service answered in a soothing female voice. "The subject kept a video log of sexual encounters while at Viking University in New Zubrin. Several of the encounters include unusual conduct. Further review is required."

"What do you mean, unusual? Show me one."

The images appeared before him. In the slowly unfolding recording, the young couple was holding hands, talking, and occasionally kissing. A window behind them allowed the afternoon sunlight to stream into the room. The red-headed young man attempted an advance and was rebuffed. After the second time being turned away, he excused himself and said he'd be right back. However, in the few minutes he was gone, the young woman abruptly passed out. When he returned, he swiftly went to work, removing her clothing and gratifying himself.

"Enough." Elliot waved the display away. "This pattern repeats?"

"Affirmative."

"Where did he go when he left the view?"

"Unknown," Bil said. "No recordings exist beyond this portion of each encounter."

"Do you have the identities of these women?"

"Affirmative."

"Let me see." He scanned the list, then caught himself in surprise. "No. No, this is too good." He sat back and contemplated his next move. "This will do nicely. Oh, you silly man. I'll bet you never expected she'd end up so very close to you. Keep digging, Bil. I want to know more about what Preville was up to. I need to know how he did it."

"Acknowledged."

Elliot sat back and closed his eyes. He imagined himself celebrating his triumph. "Bil, I want to celebrate. Something special. What was that whiskey we used to drink, back in the '70s?"

"There are twenty-eight different brands of whiskey in your history between 3269 and 3280. Please be more specific."

"I remember that it was from Scotland. A rare label, because the distillery had been destroyed in the war. August Monarch opened a bottle for his fiftieth birthday, if I recall."

"During that time frame," Bil said, "Executive Director Monarch drank Dogson Black Label Scotch almost exclusively."

"Oh? Why did he stop?"

"As of 3281, there was one surviving, unopened bottle. It is currently owned by Malcolm DeRyke, senior director of the Earth Grid Corporation."

Elliot frowned. "That would be the brand. Is it on station?"

"Unable to confirm."

"Dig into it. Find out the exact location of that bottle."

"Acknowledged," Bil said.

"Also, do some detailed research on Malcolm DeRyke, include the whole top leadership of EGC. Let's see if we can find some leverage. I want that bottle."

"Acknowledged."

* * * * *

The Meme

Wednesday, September 22, 3288, 14:40

Dawn awoke in a light blue room that smelled faintly of antiseptic. The taste in her mouth was horrendous. She blinked hard to clear her eyes in the dim light.

"I see your eyes opening," Sheena said. "Are you here now?"

Dawn took a deep breath. She smiled weakly at Sheena. "Are we going to miss the show?"

Sheena laughed. "That show was yesterday, but they say you're almost ready to leave, so we might make today's show. Maybe we'll take a tram this time, okay?" Curly brown hair rippled gently around her shoulders as she dabbed tears from her eyes.

"I've been out a whole day? How bad was it?" Dawn smacked her lips. "Need to rinse my mouth."

"Broken back, torn ligaments, fractured hip. Enough that they kept you under until now. Check your display." Sheena found a little bulb of mouth rinse and handed it to Dawn.

Dawn took the bulb and popped it into her mouth. She waved her hand in the air and activated her personal display. She checked her body. The damage had been repaired. New tissue was in place and all hooked up. Sheena was right, she was almost ready to go. She checked the history and gasped, choking on the forgotten mouth rinse.

Sheena held a waste container to Dawn's face, letting her spit the rinse out. "I know, right? That guy really messed you up. He got off with a broken ankle and banishment. He can't fly here anymore. Check for yourself. You were probably asked about it."

"Who was he? How did it happen?" Dawn found she'd been asked for input on the banishment. The system default was permanent, but she could opt to have it lowered.

"He's a drop junkie. There were five of them. They all dropped from the rafters with one wing each at the same time, right down the middle of the updraft. Most of the time, they just spiral down really fast to a hard landing. This time, you ended up right under him. His wing was ripped off during the impact. But it gets worse. He's not just any drop junkie. He's Archer Maliwan, one of the most popular sports feeds. He's got a huge following. Lots of onlookers were streaming the fall. And then..." She shrugged.

"What? My broken back is famous now. What of it?"

"You know," Sheena said, "you're really beautiful, right?" Sheena blushed. "And then he's got this back full of really nice muscles, and you're falling with wings fully stretched out, and the look on your face... and where his face was..."

Dawn frowned. "His face?" She tried to remember. Then she pulled up her display and looked herself up. The image really was quite remarkable. "Oh, good grief, that's enhanced!"

"Yup. One of his followers took a snap, spruced it up, and there you are, an erotic meme going viral."

Dawn laughed. "The extra color in the wings is beautiful, but the expression on my face was *pain*, not joy." She looked thoughtful for a moment. "I like the little flourishes they added to my outfit. Nice touch. But my eyes aren't green. Not always, anyway."

She swiped into a biography of the man who'd hit her. Archer Maliwan was a little older than she was. "His history shows him jumping from heights and climbing things. Here's a bit with him in a hopper. Ah, he used to play with the Mustangs." She shared her display with Sheena. "Now he does speed challenges. He generally seems to enjoy pushing the limits. There's a few posts about safety here, too." She read for a few moments. "Looks like he jumps here twice a year. Still, accidents do happen. I think I'm going to let him off with a year. I mean, it was stupid, and painful as anything, but permanent still seems like a steep price."

Sheena chuckled. "Softie. But yeah, you're probably right. System defaults can be a little steep. I think they were set before nanomedics were a thing, and no one's suggested we call an assembly to fix it." She shrugged. "I promised Fawn I'd have you call her as soon as you woke up."

Dawn sighed. "Was she a bother?"

"Frightened silly. I had to tell her friends to stop her from jumping a shuttle. She's fine, though. We had a good talk."

"Oh?"

Sheena swiped her hand and poked the air.

Fawn appeared at the end of Dawn's bed, looking worried. Her glowing pink heart meki floated above her head. "Hey, you, what's going on? Are you okay? That was a big hit you took!"

"Yes, it was," Dawn said. "Broken back and everything. Nothing permanent. I'm fine now."

"Sure am glad. But hey, did you see the meme? It's absolutely stunning!"

"I saw it. It wasn't nearly as fun as it looks. That's pain, not joy."

"Yeah, I got that." Fawn giggled. "Next time, try the fun way."

"In your dreams. Poke Buck for me and give Adi a hug. I'll see you in a couple more days. Oh, and don't forget to go visit Uncle Keegan and Etto."

"Yup, yup. Hugs." Fawn faded as her meki bounced away.

A nurse entered the room. "Good to see you awake. How do you feel? Are you ready to test out the repairs? Can you step out of bed, please?"

"I feel fine. Minty fresh." Dawn grinned as she hopped off the bed.

It only took a few minutes for Dawn and the nurse to verify that she was fully repaired and there was no lasting damage. Shortly, Sheena and Dawn were back in the open air, stepping out on a wide balcony ten meters from the crater floor.

"You know, it's been a long time since I made a new friend like this. When I was younger, I used to go out all the time, meet new people, try new things." Dawn sighed. "I guess I pulled back on that part of my life when our folks died. I felt like I had to do right by my sister, whatever she wants to be called."

"She told me how you lost your parents." Sheena shook her head. "Such a shame. How does bombing the remains of a failed Mars colony and killing innocent tourists help anyone's cause? It seems so pointless. Sorry."

"It's okay. They took a romantic holiday to New Zubrin, and some anti-corporate terrorists were having a bad day." Dawn shook her head.

"Should I be flattered," Sheena asked, "or was I just the first opportunity you had to make a new friend?" She smiled. Entrancing sparkles reflected in her golden eyes.

Dawn felt her face flush and laughed nervously, then stopped and frowned. "Oh, that's right! I've lost a day. Today is Wednesday. I wanted to make that dress last night and send it off so Jon would have it today. He wants to give it to his wife, Carlene. Her birthday is tomorrow. I really want to get it done."

"No worries." Sheena waved her hand. "You go make your dress. I'll find something to keep me occupied."

"Sure thing. Here." Dawn pulled up her display and sent Sheena a little dress status display. It currently showed the mannequin.

"Oh, thanks. A tiny naked woman!" Sheena giggled.

Dawn smirked and dashed to the lift, headed back to her workshop. On her way up, she sent a message to Sheena. TRY ME FOR BREAKFAST AGAIN IF YOU LIKE.

* * * * *

A Cloud of Dust

Friday, September 24, 3288, 0:15

He stepped out of his workshop, unsatisfied, his apron soaked in blood and tears. He shook his head to clear his thoughts.

"Project update," Vondur said. "Everything has been made ready. The camera is now active. Your command is required for detonation."

He sighed. "Let me clean up first. Oh, and make sure the project in my workshop stays fresh. I'm not done yet."

After a quick trip to the fresher, he was clean and dry again. He sat in his chair and activated the large wall display. "Show me."

The display resolved into a view outside a structure, near where the central dome met metal. The landscape was bleak and gray, the pitch-black sky filled with brilliant stars above.

"Blow it."

A quick flash of light and a cloud of dust. The dust settled slowly in the lunar gravity.

"That's it? That's all there was?"

"Affirmative. The dome has been compromised. Emergency services are responding."

He nodded slowly. "Might be enough. Search the feeds again. Keep looking until something comes up. While you're at it, get more explosives. A lot more. And eyes. I want to see what's going on inside. Make sure you're not detected."

"Please specify the quantity of explosives requested."

"What are my options?"

"The only source of materials able to be rapidly assembled into explosive devices with a low probability of detection are located in the Manywydhan Multi-Materials Automated Mining Complex, west of Minkowski Crater. The security system is outdated. Detection can be avoided. Current inventory shows that an additional fourteen devices can be created with the same explosive impact as the previous example."

"Excellent. Do it."

"Acknowledged."

It felt good to have something new to do. This could be quite an exciting project if he worked it right. A push in the right direction, a shove in the other. *They'll be fighting in no time.*

* * * * *

Moretus Plains

Saturday, September 25, 3288, 11:20

Her time in Zeeman had come to an end, and Dawn took a local slide tube to Heinlein Loop Station, a few kilometers from the aviary. The tube was an enclosed beltway that whisked people rapidly from place to place while they stood or walked. She'd taken a shuttle the week before and decided to ride the loop home in the hopes of having a more scenic view of the lunar landscape. The cylindrical loop cars, smaller than shuttles, were designed to travel through a system of transparent tubes that stayed close to the surface or dug under it where needed. They were equipped with large transparent canopies, making sightseeing easy. She joined a line of passengers as they entered the airtight cylinder. She followed her meki to her seat, as always, then waited patiently as the craft was sealed. After a few minutes, they were moved into the airlock. Lights inside held the darkness at bay.

Once the air had been pumped from the chamber, a warning light and a gentle chime told people to brace themselves. Moments later, Dawn was gently pushed back into her well-cushioned seat. The craft accelerated with a smooth, silent burst of electromagnetic power.

They emerged from darkness. The transparent panels allowed them to see the brilliant stars against the black skies and the silvery landscape speeding past. Dawn could see a wide variety of structures scattered about the bottom of the crater as they began to curve and climb to the rim. Her display showed names for significant landmarks.

Once the craft reached five hundred kilometers per hour, there were no more accelerations or decelerations. Curves were kept as gentle as possible, as were the inevitable climbs and falls. Dawn placed herself offline, sending any non-emergency communications into her queue, as she often did. She reclined and let herself drift as she watched the landscape pass by.

The view over Drygalski Crater was magnificent. On the opposite side of the craft were the southern range mountains. Lights dotted the entire landscape, revealing human settlements everywhere, with the dense cluster outlining Meshabu shining the brightest.

As they neared Moretus Crater, they crossed into daylight. The transparent panels became slightly opaque to protect the inhabitants from too much solar radiation.

An indicator flashed in front of her eyes, a warning that they were experiencing a quake. That didn't bother Dawn. Quakes were a common occurrence on Luna when the sunlight came or went. This one was short. It only lasted five minutes.

A few minutes after the quake, they decelerated. Another trip through the airlock, and the passengers were free to leave. Dawn stepped out into the Moretus Peak loop station. It was built into the top of the central peak of the crater, and loops from every direction converged here. There were transparent drop tubes leading in all directions that used gravity and air to allow people to fall and glide to a lower destination. Dawn took the drop tube labeled MORETUS PLAINS. She found the drop and glide enjoyable. It reminded her of flying. After easily stepping from the end, she headed for a longer slide tube to her block. She leaned in the direction the sliding belt was going, then jumped in.

It had taken her weeks of practice when she was a child to get the hang of mounting the slide tubes, but once mastered, it had become a primary escape route for her adventures. Thinking of that time of her life made her think about her parents. She still felt the hole in her chest they'd left. It had been such a sudden and pointless tragedy.

Once at her destination, she slid off the end with practiced grace and walked along the wide passageway. Neighbors greeted her with nods and smiles. Some of them Dawn knew by name. Others had names conveniently floating above their heads.

She came to an intersection where two wide passages converged into a tall open square. A large apple tree stood in the center, surrounded by a small green garden. Children were playing in the grass. Deeply rooted, the tree's towering branches offered fruit to those willing to jump high enough. Larger children were taking turns picking apples and passing them to the smaller ones. Several birds had made nests in the upper branches, well out of reach. They wheeled about freely in the open air above the leaves.

At one corner of the square was Keegan's, one of Dawn's favorite places to eat. The large red and white sign lit the entire corner. She bounded through the tall stainless steel and glass front door and was greeted with a boisterous welcome by the chef himself.

"Dawn! Good to see you! Where have you been all week? No lunches, no visits, no hugs. Oh, dear, I'm feeling faint just remembering the torture!" He pretended to brace himself against the chrome countertop. There was an ever-present hint of mischief in his deep brown eyes.

"Uncle Keegan, you big lug. I went flying, remember? I told you before I left." She took one of the red padded stools at the counter facing the large man.

"You did no such thing. You neglected me. What'll you have?"

"I did tell you, and you could look me up online anytime. Salad to go, please. Make it a Bakersfield Apple. Hello, Uncle Etto." She waved at the bartender, who'd poked his head around the corner. He waved back with a warm smile.

"Online? That's silly. Why would I go online to find you when you and your sister are always here? They came in, your sister and Buck, with those two friends of theirs. But no Dawn." He'd assembled most of the salad as he spoke. With a flourish and a grin, he diced an apple and scattered it on top with a light dusting of spice. "Lid?"

"Yes, please."

He handed her the container filled with fresh salad. "Good to see you back. Hope you had fun. Oh, and loved the meme. Spectacular!" He nodded with a grin, one eyebrow raised.

Dawn groaned. "Thanks. See you soon, promise."

She headed for the nearby lift and stepped in. The transparent enclosure allowed her to see the entire central square before entering an opaque tube as she passed through several levels.

She stepped off at her floor and slid along the familiar corridor. She saw her large friendly pink bird near the end. The flamingo tipped his bowler hat, and her door slid open. This time the motion made him stumble and drop his hat. That caused him to scramble for it in a crazy attempt to keep it out of the animated water.

Dawn's rooms weren't large, but they were comfortable. The entrance opened to the entertainment room, containing seating for friends to gather with a low table in the center. Buck had given Dawn several handcrafted candles. Her favorite decorated the center of the table. A faint but detailed scrollwork pattern added detail to the walls. To the left of the entrance was a small kitchen area. The far wall was transparent, showing a view out over the city. Near the edges of the window, a delicate etching framed the view. It glowed in the sunlight. In the pitch black sky, the sun peeked over the rim of the crater, its brilliance dampened to a safe level by optical filters. Gazing at the slim crescent Earth reminded her why she loved the view, although she preferred it when the sun was down.

Further to the left, a hallway led to her fresher, sleeping chamber, and work space. It was much larger than her workshop had been in the aviary. Huge bundles of cloth in a variety of textures, colors, and patterns were stacked neatly on deep shelves. Long racks of clothes filled the walls. A large workbench in the center gave her space to do her work.

"Service, any messages in my queue?" she asked.

Four mekis appeared in the air in front of her. Two were her sister's familiar pink heart, one was a brass coin she recognized, and the last was a glowing green jewel. "Four new messages from three individuals. Would you like a summary?"

"No, thanks. Play them in order."

"From Jon Merrill."

A deep male voice came from the transparent wall as an inset blinked into existence showing his head and shoulders. "I wanted to let you know that Carlene loved her new dress. It really was the perfect gift. Again, my deepest gratitude, Dawn. I'll be sure to recommend you to all my friends."

"Would you like to respond?"

"Send a modest nod. Save it to my happy list. Next message."

"From Sheena Raku."

Sheena's head and shoulders appeared. The glowing green jewel floated above her head. "This went to your queue, so I'm assuming you'll see it when you get home. Hope you had a great trip. I just wanted to say that I enjoyed your company this week. Call me sometime."

"Would you like to respond?" Service asked.

"Send a smile. Mark it for follow up tomorrow. Next message."

"From your sister, Fawn, first of two messages."

Her little sister's voice and image replaced Sheena's on the screen. "Dawn! You've got to come see it! We're all headed down to the festival tonight. It'll be amazing. Please join us!"

Her sister had always been impetuous. That was one of the many reasons Dawn preferred to remain offline. Constant communication sometimes disrupted her thought processes.

"Would you like the second message?" Service asked.

"Sure." She sat and opened her salad container.

"Dammit. I hate when you switch off. I want to show you something really great. I'll be sure to record it. Let me know when you get back! Please! Love you!"

"Service, what time do Fawn and Buck expect to be at the park?" She poked at her salad with the fork her uncle had provided.

"Approximately 16:30."

"Tell her I'll meet them there."

"Acknowledged," Service said.

She sat and ate the salad, then decided to take a short nap. "Service, wake me at fifteen, please."

"Acknowledged."

She wandered into her bedroom, tossing off her outfit. She stretched out on the bed and relaxed, letting her eyes wander over the bland ceiling.

A glowing white butterfly fluttered into Dawn's field of view. She recognized the meki at once, although it had been a long time. She sat up, turned, and dropped her legs over the side of the bed. With a hesitant finger, she touched the meki. "Hi, Carlene."

"Hi, Dawn. I wanted to tell you how much I appreciate the dress. It's beautiful."

"It was all Jon's doing. You know that."

"I know he asked for it," Carlene said, "but I would have thought you'd say no, given our history."

"Why would I say no to you?"

"You blamed me for the death of your parents. It might have been a long time ago, but I do remember that."

"Blame you?" Dawn shook her head. "No, no. Not at all. I don't blame you."

"I remember you being very clear about that. You said it was because of me that your parents died. Loudly, too, I might add."

Dawn's heart caught in her throat. "I see. And you took it to mean that I thought it was your fault." She sighed. "I was young and inarticulate. I blamed *myself* for choosing to stay near you instead of going to Mars with my parents."

"Then you and Fawn would both be dead, too. You know that, right?"

Tears grew in Dawn's eyes. She looked away. "They were going to take us to the World of Barsoom, that big amusement park in Dogana. Because we weren't with them, they went to the old ruins instead. They wouldn't have been there if we'd gone, and they wouldn't have died."

"There's no way you could've known that, Dawn. It's not your fault."

Dawn shook her head. "I know it in my head, but that inner teenager of mine still believes it in my heart. But please, I never meant to blame you. I didn't mean to push you away."

"We were young. It was hard. I know that now. I'm sorry I couldn't figure it out back then."

Dawn attempted a half-smile. "Yeah, but then you wouldn't have met Jon."

Carlene wiped tears from her eyes. "I know. I got lucky that way. How about you?"

Dawn shook her head. "Not really. Not looking."

"Oh, good lord, Dawn. Haven't you even had a date since then?"

Dawn blushed deeply. "Well, kind of. Maybe recently. I don't know."

"Give it a chance, Dawn. You deserve to be happy. You're a wonderful, loving, caring soul. Others see that in you, too. Just don't chase them away."

"Thanks. Look, I need to get going. Let's keep in touch, okay?"

Carlene smiled. "Definitely. Talk to you soon."

Dawn swiped her display, and the image cut off. She collapsed back onto her bed and buried her face in the pillows.

* * *

Dawn reached the wide entrance to the park just after 16:30. A few meters to the left was the large rock structure that supported Virgil Falls. The path split into two directions through the trees. Fawn's pink heart meki greeted her and flew down the path that led to the creek, leaving a trail of glowing pink glitter. Dawn followed the glitter. As the sound of the waterfall faded behind her, she came to a clearing near the shore of the creek. Fawn jumped up from the tall grass and somersaulted before landing and bouncing over to hug her sister. Adi, Evren, and of course, Buck, all sat up.

Adi wore a white blouse with an old-fashioned vest and skirt. The orange and purple fabrics complimented her green hair. A hint of cinnamon sparkles decorated her tan cheeks. Evren's outfit was fit for a medieval prince. His large frame emphasized Adi's diminutive stature.

Dawn looked them over. "You two look nice."

Fawn grinned and bounced back to Buck.

"Thanks," Adi said. "You didn't feel like decorating?"

Dawn shook her head. "I only wanted to come down and hug my sister. I didn't even check the theme."

Fawn laughed. "Medieval fantasy. Buck and I fit right in."

Adi twirled, showing off her dress. "We thought going as royalty would be fun."

"Don't look at me," Evren said, "I just do what she tells me. Buck's lucky, he doesn't need a costume."

Buck pulled at the straps of his leather overalls. "What do you call this? This is perfect for a medieval setting. Comfortable, and they look good with the body mods, right?"

"Of course, they do," Fawn said. She leaned in and kissed him. His light skin flushed red.

Dawn turned to Adi. "Your dress is beautiful, Adi. Good lines, perfect colors, and I love the lace. Oh, and is that a little bit of glitter in that lace?" Dawn tilted her head at Fawn. "You did this?"

Fawn grinned and nodded.

"Your restraint on the glitter is improving. I like what you've done."

"I do, too," Adi said. "It's the prettiest princess dress I've ever had."

Evren laughed. "Now you sound like you're twelve."

Adi crossed her arms. "Take it back."

"Or what?"

"Or I'll toss you into Ivan Creek."

"Fine," Evren said. "You don't sound like you're twelve."

Adi grinned.

Evren grinned. "Ten at most."

While Adi and Evren wrestled each other, Fawn leaned over to Dawn and said, "I did his outfit, too."

"It's nice, but maybe a little too form fitting in the backside."

Fawn shrugged. "That was a special request from Adi."

"What," Buck said, "so she could see his backside all day long?"

Dawn laughed.

"Yes, silly," Fawn said.

Buck turned around and flicked his tail at Fawn. His trousers were nowhere near as form fitting as Evren's.

Fawn laughed. "You don't need to show off, Buck. I like it like that."

In the distance, a shriek and a splash told them they'd reached the creek.

"Let's go see who's wet," Dawn said.

Fawn giggled. "I'm betting Adi won." She bounced in the direction of the creek.

Dawn and Buck followed. When the creek came into sight, Dawn laughed. Both Adi and Evren were drenched from head to toe.

"I won," Adi said.

"Did not," Evren said.

"You got wet first." Adi pushed him back into the water and climbed up to where the others were standing.

"You got more wet than I did." Evren climbed out of the water.

"Damn. Do you know how see-through that shirt is now?" Adi looked down and laughed, pulling the blouse away from where it clung to her body. "It'll dry."

Fawn pointed to the path they'd come from. "Let's follow the path back around to the pavilion. By the time we get there, these two should be a bit dryer. I want to see who else is here."

Not long after, they approached the pavilion and encountered a group of children playing a game. Their hands were moving, tossing an invisible object.

"What are they doing?" asked Dawn.

"It's nothing until you turn your eyes on, dinklehead," Fawn said.

Dawn smirked and swiped at her display. She selected the augmented reality feed from the park. Her view transformed. All hints of the dome evaporated under sunny blue skies. A winged horse was flying in the distance overhead. The children tossed and chased a spinning golden orb that changed direction at random intervals. It left a trail of tiny bubbles as it went. Dawn thought it was rather nice. In the far distance, well outside the real dome, she could see two giants playing catch with a boulder. Their mekis resembled lit torches. Several other virtual fantasy creatures dotted the landscape, as well as people enjoying the park.

Out of nowhere, Fawn exclaimed, "That's horrible! Someone should stop those people. They must be crazy." She waved her hand in mid-air, dismissing a display only she could see.

"What is it?" asked Dawn.

"News feed, Dawn. Check your news feed. It's fighting. We have people fighting each other on Luna. It started while you were gone." She swiped her display and shared the story.

Dawn caught the news item Fawn had tossed. Ever since their parents had been killed, Dawn had found conflict like this unsettling. Having the fighting so close to home made it all the worse. She played the story and searched for more information.

While she'd been offline, gliding through the skies of Heinlein Aviary with Sheena, two small groups of youths playing out in the space between the refugee communities in Minkowski Crater had been fighting. One group had started throwing rocks at the other, who'd then retaliated. In the end, one boy's visor cracked, and the alarms went off. Everyone was whisked back to their respective communities. No one was hurt, of course, but that spark had set off a firestorm of social media overreaction. Parents in both Ablom and Takiyama had exchanged heated words at first.

Usually, those sorts of things settled back down. This time, someone from Ablom had apparently set off a small explosive near Takiyama's central dome. The resulting crack took hours to fix and frightened the residents. People were now protesting and chanting angrily for payback.

A pair of squirrels chasing past broke her concentration. They had tiny little acorn mekis, meant to remind people that they weren't real. The capes and flamboyant hats should've been enough of a giveaway. She laughed as they pulled out miniature swords and started a swashbuckling animated fight. Evren and Buck decided to chase them, laughing and running through a stand of trees. The squirrels forgot their previous battle and took turns hitting the men on the head with acorns tossed from high above. Dawn shook her head when she realized the animated characters were grabbing each other's meki to throw, only to have it light back up after the toss.

They spent the next hour strolling through the park. Dawn kept glancing at the news feeds. Even though the situation hadn't changed, her apprehension grew.

There were various staged entertainments scattered throughout the park. Later, while the others were participating in a couples dance at the pavilion, Dawn decided to look for some background information on the refugee communities. She found a segment recorded by Tony Renard the day before.

"Hello again," Tony said. "Welcome to the Tony Renard Show. I'm Tony Renard. Tonight we have an exciting story for you. Of course, by exciting, I mean a little scary, and with plenty of stupid people. What's worse than a bunch of scary, stupid people? Two groups of scary, stupid people trying to blow up each other's domes."

Tony spun into a new camera shot. "Look," Tony said, "in case you grew up on Earth or something, let's be clear. A lot of times, an entire community is referred to as a dome, and sometimes that can be confusing when we talk about a dome on top of a community. Case in point, the community in Minkowski called Takiyama. It's an older community, so it has a pretty good-sized complex above and below ground. Like a lot of us, they have a real dome over their central park. So, when we say someone cracked their dome, we don't mean their community, we mean the big, round thing with a park underneath. It's almost always the largest open space in a city. All air, no bulkheads. And yeah, some ignorant lowlife set off a bomb. Cracked it. Most people are blaming Ablom, you know, because of that whole rock-throwing thing.

"So, who are these people, and what makes them so different from your average Loonie? Well, as far as the populations go, they're relative newcomers. See, back in 3202, when Yellowstone blew, a lot of folks lost their homes back on Earth. Survivors didn't have anywhere to go. As the years went by, and things didn't get any better, they asked for help. In 3206, our grandparents rose to the occasion. They called forth the Ninth Lunar Assembly, who decided to let some folks from near the devastation come here to live. Seemed like a nice thing to do, I suppose, and it was pretty easy, too, because Earth still had all those elevators. So these folks came here, and they named their new community The Ablom Refuge. You've heard of them, right? And everyone lived happily ever after."

He spun to a new camera angle. "Or did they?" He shook his head. "Nah, 'cause Kagoshima went in 3207, less than a year later. So, history repeats itself. In early 3208, the Tenth Lunar Assembly decided to do exactly the same thing for a bunch of folks barely surviving in southern Japan. You guessed it, that's how Takiyama got its name. And guess what, they put this new group right next door to Ablom. I mean, what harm could there be in that, right? Yeah, see, the first group, they were all Mormon Catholics. Now guess what the new guys were? Go on, guess... Nope. You're wrong. They were Southern Orthodox Neoshinto, which probably doesn't mean anything to you, but let that sink in a minute. They took two groups of people from Earth... Earth... both very religious types, from completely different parts of Earth... and made them neighbors on the Moon.

"So fast forward to last week. Are they friends? Oh, hell no. They hate each other so much that when their kids met out in the harsh vacuum, they threw rocks at each other just for fun. I guess they think it means hello. Then the group they said hello to said hello right back.

You guessed it, more rocks. One cracked visor later, everyone's rushed back inside, and parents are a little bit cranky. Can't imagine why. They were only saying hello, right? So then someone set off a bomb. A bomb. On the Moon. Who the hell thinks to do that? Well, that's the story I know. I'm Tony Renard, and I think we need to do better."

A news update flashed in. Takiyama had officially closed the slide tube between themselves and Ablom. They'd stationed several guards and shut down the blowers. They were only allowing their own people to enter their community and turning back everyone else. The resulting online debate was getting more difficult to follow, but a consensus was growing that something should be done.

Dawn hadn't noticed that the dance had ended, and the two couples had returned.

Adi touched Dawn's shoulder. "What are you looking at, Dawn?"

"I was wondering what all the fuss was about." She dismissed her display. "It looks to me like this could get out of hand. From the history, I think there were two mistakes. First, the Ninth Assembly set up one whole habitat for refugees. They were all Mormon Catholics, so I suppose it made sense at the time. After Kagoshima went, the Tenth Assembly messed it up by putting the second group right next to the first. Two isolated communities right next to each other."

"That was, what, eighty years ago?" Buck asked. "We haven't had an assembly since then. No need. Maybe they should've set up some way to keep up with them. Keep them out of trouble."

"Yes," Dawn said, "but they might not have thought of that. Until this fighting made it a big deal, no one would've thought we even had a problem big enough to call an assembly."

"Maybe we should," Fawn said. "It's only a quick election, right? Get ourselves a new assembly and have them fix it?"

"Yeah. Look here." Buck shared his display with Fawn. "The Tenth was proposed at noon, election was done by two, and they had their first meeting over dinner. All by proxy, of course, but it can happen fast."

Evren huffed. "Yeah, but that was an easy problem with a simple solution. They didn't have that sort of situation automated yet."

"What," Adi said, "volcanic eruptions down on Earth? Why would they?"

"I guess that's my point. Isn't this kind of thing automated? Why isn't the system handling it?"

Fawn shook her finger at Evren. "Maybe because Loonies don't usually go around starting wars with their neighbors, silly."

Evren blushed. "Oh, well, I suppose."

"If they called an assembly together," Adi said, "who do you think would be on it?"

Dawn shrugged. "It could really be anyone. No one is exempt from being nominated."

"Yeah," Buck said. "The only way out of it is to delegate all your votes to someone else."

Evren tilted his head. "What if it gets to the end, and you're in the final seven, but you don't want it?"

"Easy," Buck said. "Pass the votes to someone else. Then there's a new group of seven. The seven that are left have to agree to accept the responsibility."

Evren folded his arms. "Can someone nominate themselves?"

"Sure, but self-nominators tend to be the types you wouldn't want anyway. They never make it."

After a moment of reflection, Dawn posted a short message attached to the Tony Renard video. *I propose we form a new Lunar Assembly to deal with this situation and find a permanent solution.* Her post went public, and she shut off her feed.

A short while later, while they were all relaxing on the soft green grass, Fawn and Adi started giggling and laughing. Feeling a little left out, Dawn raised an eyebrow at her sister.

"Dawn, Buck did it," Fawn said.

"Hey!" Buck said. "It was your idea!"

"It's his fault," Adi said. "Blame him."

"What? What did you guys do?" Dawn reactivated her news feed. The top story was the impending creation of the Eleventh Lunar Assembly. The delegate voting and negotiating was already underway. There were still thousands of nominees on the list. She found her name in 89th place, with several thousand votes. The number was increasing steadily.

"How did that happen?" She saw that she'd been nominated by James Bush. Both of the other women were pointing at Buck. Evren looked embarrassed. Fawn was trying not to laugh, but Buck looked genuinely worried.

Dawn scowled. "This is *not* what I want to be doing with my time. Why would you do this to me? How did I get so many votes so fast?"

The look on Buck's face was so pathetic, it made Dawn laugh.

"I posted it to the body modder groups," Buck said, "and our circles of friends. At least a dozen of them wear clothes you made for them, and it didn't take long for it to take off from there."

"I posted, too, and crosslinked it," Evren said. "I recommended you on the fighters' forum. Then that image of you saving a guy, wings spread wide, started making the rounds again. Powerful meme, Dawn. It really appeals to people."

Dawn shook her head in disbelief. "If I get elected to an assembly because of that stupid meme…"

"You're not doing too badly," Evren said.

"Don't give away your votes yet," Fawn said. "You should wait to see how far up the list you get."

Dawn looked into her sister's eyes. "You can't be serious."

Fawn grinned. "I dare you. Wait until everyone else has delegated their votes. See where you end up."

Dawn looked over the list of names above hers. "All right. Let's just see what happens." She poked at her display and set an alert for when the list had been whittled down to twenty.

* * *

As was often the case, the five of them ended up at Keegan's. Dawn had sent a reservation request and was put at the top of the queue. Evenings were their busiest time, but they always made room for family.

Keegan welcomed them with open arms. "Come in! Glad to see you. I've got a table right over here. Special tonight is prawn rings, lightly battered and fried. Crunchy, tasty outside, delightfully tender and delicious inside. Want some?"

Buck and Evren nodded eagerly as they sat at the large table.

"And some fries, please," Buck said.

Evren held up a finger and raised his eyebrows. "Me, too."

Fawn grinned. "I'll take onion rings if you have them."

"Yup. I always keep extra onions just for you, little one! And how about my other niece? Dawn, what can I make for you?"

"I'm in for the prawn rings, too. Bring a family bucket. You know I love those things. And a basket of sprouts, please."

"Sprouts for me, too," Adi said. "Have anything hot to put on it?"

"Today," Keegan said, "I have some cilantro and lime chutney, made with extra hot chilies."

Adi's eyes lit up as she grinned.

"Yeah," Fawn said. "Can I have some of that, too, Uncle Keegan?"

Keegan chuckled. "Sure thing."

"Have you voted yet?"

"Voted? I saw something about it in my feed. Is it a big deal?"

"Yup," Fawn said. "Dawn is in the running. New Lunar Assembly."

"Assembly? What's that all about?"

"It's nothing," Dawn said. "A couple of communities having a disagreement. Kids fighting, parents being parents."

"I see, I see. So nothing special at all." Keegan waved his hand and poked the air in front of him. "Oh, look. Ellie Lester is in fifth place." He swiped a few more times, then poked and grunted. "There, I just voted. Prawn rings and sprouts. Anything else?"

"Who did you vote for?" Fawn asked.

Keegan laughed. "Obviously I voted for your sister. I love Ellie, but she's not family." He turned to Dawn. "As a side note, you should bring Ellie Lester here. Etto is such a big fan. If you can, if you have time, bring her up here. Think of poor Etto."

"You know I can hear you, right?" Etto asked from behind the bar.

They laughed, and Dawn shook her head. "I'm just trying to figure out who to give my votes to."

Fawn's ears flicked. "Really? You get the chance of a lifetime, a chance to be on a real Lunar Assembly, and you're just going to give it away?"

Keegan's eyebrows knit together. "Don't be too hard on her, Fawn. She might not feel like doing something like that. I mean, it's a lot of hard work. It might be too challenging."

Dawn frowned. The way he said it made her think. "Maybe I'll wait a bit longer. See where I end up. I set an alert so I'll have time to decide before it hits the final seven."

Keegan laughed and nodded, then headed back to his grill.

"I really love your uncles," Adi said.

Dawn and Fawn shared a smile.

"We've been lucky to have them," Dawn said. "He and Etto made it easier to deal with this one." She tilted her head at Fawn.

Fawn stuck her tongue out at her sister and wiggled her long ears. "Sometimes I think I should've let Grandma Hazel take her."

Fawn shook her head. "Way too strict. Wouldn't have worked."

"Yeah, she would've denied your body mods, that's for sure."

"Are you close to your grandmother?" Evren asked.

"Sure," Dawn said. "We visit back and forth every few years. She's over near the Korolev Basin. Astronomer at one of their observatories."

"Funny," Adi said. "Fawn never mentioned her."

Dawn tilted her head. "Grandma had some words to say about the hooves."

"Yeah," Fawn said. "I didn't want to hear it. I was probably a bit harsh back then. Mom and Dad had just died."

"You both were. She lost her son."

Fawn looked thoughtful. "Maybe I'll talk to her."

Buck nudged Fawn's shoulder. "Why don't we make plans to go visit her? You and me."

Dawn looked into Fawn's eyes. "I think that would be a great idea."

"Guys, don't push." Fawn turned to look at Buck, then back to her sister. "We'll do it. Let me get used to the idea. It's been a long time. Besides, she hasn't even pinged me in years."

Buck leaned in and kissed her forehead.

Etto cleared his throat. "Anyone thirsty?"

Adi raised her hand, almost jumping out of her seat. "Do you have some more of that Cocoretto thing I had last time?"

Etto swiped his display. "I have what I need to make more. Sure. What else, anyone?"

Dawn shook her head. "I want to stay clear-headed tonight, so maybe something cold and icy with banana, coconut, and mango?"

"Nice. I can do that."

Buck raised a finger. "Got any of that Midnight Tree Brew left?"

"We have plenty for you," Etto said.

Fawn raised her hand. "Same here, please."

"Midnight Tree Brew," Evren said. "Is that new?"

Buck laughed. "No. No, it's really, really old. But good. Someone found it in the archives and brought it back. You know how people are. Anything a thousand years old has to be better than what we have today, right?"

Evren shrugged. "Okay, I'll have one, too."

"I'll be back shortly." Etto turned and walked briskly back to his bar.

Adi leaned toward Evren. "You shouldn't have too many of those. You have a fight tomorrow."

Evren waved her off with his hand. "I'll be fine."

"Still beating people up for fun?" Dawn asked.

Evren looked down.

"Dawn, it's a sport," Fawn said. "Competition, and voluntary. You know that."

Buck pressed his lips together, crossed his arms, and sat back silently.

Dawn sighed. "Sorry. Shouldn't have said it that way, but you know how I feel about it."

Fawn crossed her arms. "You mean like when you called security on Evren?"

Adi held up her hands. "Fawn, your sister made a fair call. She didn't know Evren was teaching me, and those *were* some nasty bruises."

"Exactly," Dawn said. "But that's all behind us now, and Evren was about to tell us who he's going to beat up for sport next."

Evren gave a lopsided smile. "I hope it works out that way. The other way would mean I lose. The match is tomorrow afternoon."

Dawn's meki floated into her view. It glowed and bobbled until she touched it. Her display came up, showing the latest election results. There were now only seventeen delegates. Dawn was in fifth place. The number startled her. It might not stick, but if she was one of the final seven, she was on the assembly. She watched as that news guy, Tony Renard, delegated his five million votes to a professor from Tycho University, putting the professor in the lead. Then two smaller blocks delegated their votes to her and put her in second place. A familiar name was next to the larger of the two groups, Jon Merrill.

"Holy crap," Fawn said. "She's in second place."

Dawn started checking other names that were likely to drop out. Sheena Raku was on the list. Even with over three million votes, she was in last place. No way she could win a seat by herself. Dawn sent a quick note. *Sheena, I'm up on the list, too! Want to work together?*

There was no answer until after the next round had completed. She was still in second place, and the professor had gained considerable ground.

Moments later, the professor's points dropped, and hers picked up. Someone had switched their support to her. Then Sheena delegated all her votes to Dawn, and suddenly it was all over. The list was down to the required seven delegates. Dawn felt her heart sink. Her name was at the top of the list. Professor Stephen Corvair had nine million fewer votes. She scanned the other names. She didn't know Darren Garfield. Ava Wallaby? She was a pop singer. No clue who Misa Kobato was. Sam Freeman was another unknown. And there at the bottom was the award-winning actor, Ellie Lester. She was a household name everywhere. She was also at least a century old.

Dawn felt a little lightheaded. "This is a bit much. What have you guys gotten me into?"

"I'm so sorry, Dawn. I had no idea it would even stick!" Buck shrugged apologetically.

"You'll be wonderful," Adi said. "You're so smart and have such a big heart. I have faith in you."

Fawn giggled and hugged her big sister. "There's no one in Luna I'd rather have fixing this problem than you, Dawn." She paused. A single large tear ran down her cheek. "Mom and Dad would be so proud of you."

Dawn closed her eyes, holding back a tear. She squeezed her little sister tightly.

Buck looked up. "Ah, rescue—er, drinks."

Etto came to the table with a large tray balanced on his forearm. He passed out the drinks with expert flair. "Anything else I can get you?"

"Not right now," Buck said, "but how about if they get to arguing, and I tug on my ear, you bring a bottle of Old Yeller and some shot glasses."

Etto scoffed. "Old Yeller. Never in my bar, young man. We're civilized here."

"You know what I mean."

"I do, and they won't. Dawn is prime minister. Be happy for her. Nod and say yes, ma'am. Then everything will be fine."

Dawn's eyebrows went up and her mouth dropped. The others laughed. "I feel like I've been handed absolute power and then swatted on the fanny."

Buck grinned. "So you like that, too?"

"Buck!" Fawn looked shocked. She was turning a deep shade of red.

"Oh, good," said Keegan, arriving with a tray of plates, sauces, and two family-sized buckets of prawn rings. "Glad to see everyone is enjoying themselves."

Fawn and Dawn looked at each other with shocked expressions, then giggled.

Buck half-smiled and leaned back. "You know, Keegan, I think we really are."

"Look," Dawn said, "this is great, but I don't think I'm suited to be the prime minister. I'm going to pass it off to someone else."

"You can do it," Keegan said. "I know you can."

"I appreciate your confidence but look at these other people. The professor from Tycho took second place, and he didn't have a meme to help him. I'll bet his knowledge and experience would make him a great choice."

"Maybe, but by tradition, it's your spot."

"I know," Dawn said. "I just wouldn't want to make a mistake. People's lives are at stake. It's too important. Look at this guy in third place. He's a top negotiator. Offworld trade goods, a real mover and shaker. If anyone can negotiate a peace deal, I'll bet it's him."

Keegan smirked and held up a prawn ring. "You love my prawn rings, right?"

"Of course," Dawn said. "They're amazing."

"Had them a long time, right?"

"Yeah. I can't remember the first time I tried them. I've always loved them."

"What you don't remember," Keegan said, "you couldn't remember, is how bad my first batch was."

Etto laughed.

Keegan pointed at Etto. "He remembers."

"They were bad?" Dawn asked.

"Awful. The meat wasn't tender enough, the batter was bitter, and I overcooked them."

"But you figured it out."

Keegan nodded. "I did. It took me a while, but I kept at it until they came out the way I wanted. It's the same with anything. You have to know what you want it to be, then work at it until it's right. Don't worry if you make mistakes early on. Just keep moving forward."

Dawn sighed. "I see your point. It might be a mistake, but I think it's the right thing to do. I'm going to pass the title to one of the other delegates first thing. If it's a mistake, I'll just deal with it."

A meki dropped into Dawn's vision. It was the logo of the Lunar Sustainability Cooperative. She touched it and was presented with the legal documents assigning her to the Eleventh Lunar Assembly as a member, with the right to claim the prime minister position by tradition. She read the part where it said she could refuse the position, and it would then be placed to a vote of the assembled delegates, including herself. She acknowledged it.

The next notice showed her where to meet, and the proposed time. She accepted both. "Grissom Park Convention Center, tomorrow at eight."

Fawn grinned. "That's right near the park. Perfect."

"Wow, that's lucky," Buck said. "The last one was down in Schrodinger. At least you won't have to go far."

"Don't be silly," Adi said. "She had the most votes. That means the meeting was placed near her. It was intentional."

"If your prawn rings get cold, let me know, and I'll bring more," Keegan said.

Buck looked startled. "Oh, I nearly forgot. Let's eat." He grabbed a ring from the nearest bucket and held it high. "Salute. To Dawn Sheffield. Prime minister or not, she still got the most votes."

Dawn felt her face grow warm. "It's not that big a deal." Even as she said it, she had second thoughts.

* * *

After a joyful dinner and farewells, Dawn took the lift home. She stayed awake late that night, reviewing the history of the refugee communities and monitoring the news. Tomorrow was going to be a big day.

"Please pardon the interruption," Service said. "You have a call from Sheena Raku."

"Sheena! You put me over the top. Can you believe it? I'm in first place."

Sheena appeared, sitting under her glowing green jewel. "I saw that. You'll be a great prime minister."

Dawn shook her head. "I don't know what makes you say that. I thought I'd be fine being a regular delegate, but leading?"

"You certainly aren't an introvert. You're well organized, likable, outgoing, confident, and I think you're absolutely perfect for the job."

"Oh, stop. You sound like a guy trying to hook up."

Sheena laughed. "Maybe I'm too obvious."

Dawn tilted her head. "So why didn't you get me to give you my votes?"

"Who, me? I didn't want to be on the assembly in the first place. Dumping them all on you was easy and the right thing to do. I win both ways."

Dawn shook her head. "You could've done this, you know."

"I didn't have enough votes, remember? You were way ahead of me."

"Only because of that stupid meme."

Sheena laughed. "Have you seen it recently? Someone made a version without the guy. It's stunning."

"It's enhanced."

"Just enough to hide your freckles."

"I don't have freckles," Dawn said.

"Not on your face."

"Sheena!" Dawn laughed. "When I'm done with this government stuff, I'm going to track you down and make sure you have a really huge hangover."

"Deal. Let me know if you need anything."

"I will. Good night."

"'Night," Sheena said. Her meki flashed, and her image exploded into green sparkles.

* * * * *

Interludes and Pranksters

Saturday, September 25, 3288, 15:05

"Conn, Engineering," Kip said over the ship's intercom, "request the status of Ensign Dotseth. She hasn't shown up for the drill yet."

"Conn, Aye," Tong said. "I'll go track her down."

He pushed himself aft to the compartment where her new stateroom was and saw the issue right away. Her stateroom door had been entirely sealed shut with dark green tape. He shook his head and started removing it. Stateroom doors were more for privacy than security. They were thin, metal things covered in a finish that resembled wood. Tong was about to knock when the door slid open, and he was confronted by an explosion of blonde with indignant green eyes, which only now registered who he was.

"Am I in trouble for this, sir?"

"Of course not," Tong said. "Get back there and take the watch."

He drifted back into Control, where the occasional chuckle gave him a good idea who the culprit was. He decided to let matters take their own course and see what happened next. It didn't take long. The following drill, Jake showed up half dressed. His dark blue coveralls were hastily wrapped around his waist.

Tong shook his head. "I know I can be a little lax, Jake, but aren't you taking it a bit far?"

"Well, sir," said Jake, "something seems to be wrong with my sleeves." He flopped them around and pointed to the ends. They'd been carefully sewn shut.

"I see. Funny how that happens, isn't it? Do you want me to put a stop to it?"

"To what, sir? I'm sure it's just a quantum something. Random chance, you know."

"Sure," Tong said. "Got it."

It went back and forth. Brenna passed by with her belt so tight, anyone could see it had been shortened. Soon after, Jake stood an entire watch with cat whiskers painted on his face. That had been permanent ink and took a while to remove.

When she passed through control with a towel wrapped around her ample bottom, it wasn't hard to surmise that she was missing a good-sized chunk of her uniform.

"Ensign, is everything all right?" Tong asked. "Is there anything you need me to do?"

"No, sir," she said. "Everything's perfect, sir." She didn't mention the towel, and neither did he. She pushed herself aft, and the drill continued.

The next drill came, and this time, everything appeared perfectly normal. No reports of anything strange, no silly ink on Jake's face. He hoped he hadn't missed one. He was sure it was Jake's turn to be pranked.

Sure enough, a few minutes into the drill, Tong noticed Jake was having trouble sitting still. His fidgeting grew worse over the next half hour. Tong quietly signaled aft for Kip to slow down the drill. He texted Vin, who had the Conn, to delay as well. Vin had noticed what was happening and was more than happy to help.

Finally, Jake couldn't take it anymore. He quickly unharnessed from his station and threw himself aft, moaning in pain, toward the head. He was shortly washing himself and screaming.

"The boy's got a nice handle on profanity, Mister Franklin," Tong said.

"Yes, sir, Captain Sianothai. He certainly does. Very robust vocabulary."

Tong swiped his display, routing the sounds of extreme discomfort aft, where they were greeted with giggles and laughter.

"Secure from the drill," Tong said. "I think we've had enough fun for today."

After that, the two agreed to a truce. The pranks stopped, and Jake was much more respectful in dealing with the new ensign.

* * * * *

Dogson Quest

Saturday, September 25, 3288, 21:45

Elliot had spent three days researching Malcolm DeRyke. He'd watched dozens of recorded negotiating sessions and reviewed some of the public meetings held with other Earth Grid Corporation officers. He'd instructed Bil to create a psychological profile. Elliot had studied everything he could think of. He'd even skimmed through several poker games, looking for his tell. Elliot had played against him in the past, but he'd never studied the man with this much intensity. Finally, he felt he was ready to make his move. He decided on a direct approach launched late in the evening.

"Bil, call Senior Director Malcolm DeRyke, please."

"Acknowledged," Bil said.

The EGC logo appeared before Elliot. "Yes, Director Humboldt, what can I do for you at this horrid hour of the evening?"

"I am sorry to bother you this late, but I get so enthusiastic about certain things, and I just now found out something that catches my imagination like nothing else."

"Oh, good. Thank you for that information. I'll have my people come interview you right away."

"No, no," said Elliot, "that is not what I am looking for. This actually involves you personally, and a mutual, shall we say, *respect* we have for certain rare things?"

The letters on the EGC corporate logo evaporated as the wireframe globe shrank to normal meki size, then floated above the image of Malcolm DeRyke, sitting across from Elliot. He was a pale, thin man with white hair, and his face had the lines of someone who rarely laughed. "You're certainly taking your time getting around to it, Humboldt. What do I have that you want?"

"Oh, no need to put it like that. I am sure we can come to a mutually beneficial arrangement."

"Sure. Mutually beneficial. So answer the fucking question."

Elliot put up his hands. "Now it seems I may have angered you a little. I do apologize. It's very simple; it concerns a certain brand of whiskey. It is rather rare, and I have found that you might own a bottle."

Malcolm scoffed. "You want the Dogson. Last unopened bottle in existence, and you think you can put a price on it? You call it rare. In the entire universe, there's only one 750 milliliter bottle, and it's not yours. Good night, Director Humboldt."

"Wait, please. Give me a chance, at least."

"A chance at what? I wanted it, I bought it, and now that it's the last bottle ever, anywhere, I can't even drink it to enjoy it, because it's the absolute last bottle. All you're doing is reminding me of what a waste it is."

"You aren't drinking it," Elliot said, "so that means you understand its value. But it is only really valuable to a man like me. Someone who loves the brand and has the resources to compensate you for your frustration."

Malcolm frowned. "And what are you going to do with it?"

"I'm going to drink it in celebration. I intend to share it with my colleagues, so they all know what it once was."

"And then it'll be gone."

Elliot shrugged. "Unless you decide to drink it, for you, it is already gone."

"I've been tempted," Malcolm said, "from time to time, to drink some."

"Let me buy it, and I will let *you* take the first shot."

"One shot?"

Elliot smiled as he imagined a lock opening. "How many shots, and how much money?"

Malcolm laughed. "I want a hundred milliliters right off the top. How much money are you offering for it now?"

"Let's start at a hundred million."

Malcolm's eyebrows furled. "I was thinking more along the lines of 1.2 billion."

Elliot scowled. "I can do that math, and I see where you're heading. If I agree to the final, do we need to keep bouncing back and forth?"

"I see. That takes a little of the fun out of it, but if you're thinking a million a milliliter, I'll bite."

"Six hundred fifty million, for 650 milliliters, in the bottle. We get an arbiter to draw the hundred for you."

Malcolm opened his mouth to respond, then paused. He shook his head. "Agreed," Malcolm said. "Want to do it tonight?"

"I can certainly do that. Can we agree on Sax for the arbiter?"

"I prefer Bank of Bhushan."

Elliot sighed. "Fine, as long as it isn't the directors themselves. Not in the mood for all the bickering."

Malcolm laughed. "I'm sure we can get one of their subordinates. Do you want to arrange it, or shall I?"

"I will do it, then be right over."

"Looking forward to it." He nodded curtly, then his image and meki folded in upon themselves and popped.

* * *

As Elliot approached the arched entryway to the main suite of the Earth Grid Corporation, a neatly dressed man with a thin mustache approached from the opposite direction. He and Elliot stopped, facing each other. "Good evening, Director Humboldt. I'm Arbiter Johnston. Shall we proceed?"

Elliot entered the EGC corporate suite. Nearly every flat surface was displaying some form of entertainment or news. The receptionist was a three-dimensional full wall screen. Elliot was sure it was a dressed-up service.

"Director Humboldt, you are expected," the receptionist said. "Please follow the green line to your right. Take the lift to the third floor."

They followed the line to the lift, which took them to the second floor of the third level.

Elliot sighed as he stepped off the lift. "Mars normal. I had almost forgotten you were Martian, Director DeRyke."

"Please, call me Malcolm. This is personal business tonight."

"And you can call me Elliot. I look forward to our little deal being finalized."

"I take it you are the arbiter?" Malcolm asked.

"Yes, sir," the arbiter said. "I'm Arbiter Jeffrey Johnston, from Bank of Bhushan's Arbitration Department. I have with me a device calibrated less than thirty minutes ago to draw one hundred milliliters of fluid, as requested."

"Excellent. Come this way to my study. The bottle is in the safe."

Elliot followed as the Arbiter trailed behind.

Malcolm opened his large safe and removed the bottle. He set the whiskey on a short table next to an open carafe and stepped back. "I assert that this bottle is still in the original packaging and has remained unopened since I purchased it."

The arbiter stepped forward and looked at the bottle. "May I see the purchase order and documentation, please?"

Malcolm swiped his display and shared the information.

"Thank you. Please allow me a moment to examine the bottle and the documentation."

Elliot stepped back, his hands clasped behind his back.

"Getting excited, Elliot?"

"You could say that. This is actually a reward I am giving myself."

"I see," Malcolm said. "What's the occasion?"

"It hasn't been accomplished quite yet. This is my incentive to stay focused."

"This bottle's seal is original," the arbiter said, "and I've verified that its contents remain unaltered."

"Excellent," Malcolm said. "You may proceed to open the bottle and draw one hundred milliliters, to be then placed into that carafe."

"Gentlemen, I would like to remind you that at the moment this bottle is opened, the sum total of 650 million credits will be deposited into Malcolm DeRyke's account and will then be non-refundable. Do you both agree?"

"Agreed," Elliot said.

Malcolm nodded. "I agree. Proceed."

The arbiter carefully broke the seal and twisted the bottle open. He inserted the business end of his measuring device, drew out the precise amount, then deposited it into the carafe. He set the measuring device next to the carafe, then carefully twisted the top back onto the bottle, and handed it to Elliot. "Gentlemen. My job is done, unless you have any objections."

Elliot nodded curtly.

Malcolm waved a hand in the direction of the door. "Arbiter Johnston, thank you for your services."

The arbiter gave a shallow bow and headed back to the lift.

"I have my portion," Malcolm said, "and you have the rest in the bottle. How about we share a toast?"

"Agreed. I've been looking forward to this for decades."

Malcolm passed the shot glass. "Really? It's been a long time for me, as well. I think it was Monarch's fiftieth birthday celebration."

"Me, too. Good grief, it could've been the same bottle that ensnared us both."

"Indeed. To a better future. May we all survive it."

"Indeed." Elliot carefully sniffed his glass.

Malcolm took half the shot into his mouth. He swished it around for a moment, then looked at his shot glass and swallowed.

Elliot tasted his own in the same manner. The explosion of raw whiskey taste was much more edgy than he expected. He swirled it in his mouth, then swallowed. He looked at his shot glass. Where was the vanilla? The honey notes? He drank the glass of water and finished the shot.

"This isn't what I was expecting," Malcolm said.

"I'm certainly glad you said it before I did. Either this is a remarkable scam you've set up—which I am not yet accusing you of—or there is something wrong with both our memories. But first, tell me what you expected."

"I remember vanilla with honey notes, and a touch of spice. It was silky smooth, easy to swallow. Not like this at all."

Elliot frowned. "That's exactly how I remember it, and I agree, this is not that whiskey."

"But I know it came from this kind of bottle. Dogson Black Label. Monarch mentioned how rare it was."

"Did you see him open the bottle?"

"Eh? No. It was open before I got mine."

"Same here." Elliot fingered the bottle. "Where does that leave us?"

Malcolm shrugged. "It leaves me feeling like the luckiest fool there is."

"I don't suppose you'd be willing to share your windfall?"

"Well, Elliot, now that I think about it..." He shrugged and let a smile slowly form. "No. Not really. I mean, this stuff isn't bad, and it *is* exceedingly rare."

Elliot shook his head. He could feel his face burning. "I was afraid you'd say that. So that would leave me being the bigger fool, from whom the money has already departed."

"Afraid so. Maybe now that we know the truth, we'll be able to figure out what was really in that bottle."

Elliot absently contemplated his shot glass. "Perhaps we could. A competition?"

"Ah," Malcolm said. "With maybe a wager?"

"How about the first one to figure it out gets to charge a premium for the information."

"I see. And how much do you suppose we value that premium?"

"Let's set it low," Elliot said, "like ten times what a single bottle is worth."

Malcolm laughed. "Agreed."

"And we keep this confidential, please."

"Ah. I suppose it's the least I could do. Fine. The story is locked away until I die."

"Until you die?" Elliot asked.

"I can't promise you what my successors will do. What was it you wanted to celebrate?"

Elliot sat back in the chair and swirled the remaining whiskey. "I am exploring plans to bring Luna into the Federation. I might be able to bring it in under Yolo."

"Really? That doesn't seem likely."

"Well, I admit the total win is an outside chance, but I am confident I can achieve it. Doing so will give a certain faction great pause."

"You mean Monarch," Malcolm said. "He has a great disdain for Loonies."

"Irrational at best."

Malcolm chuckled. "Yeah. How dare they put together an economic system that's fair, equitable, and non-profit."

"I doubt he cares the slightest about the first two points."

"And you?"

Elliot shrugged. "Oh, I'm fine with their system, although I would want to generate a modest profit, but that's not the point. They are huge, and they're certain to stand against Monarch, not with him, and that is the whole point."

Malcolm stroked his chin thoughtfully. "You think they'd support new leadership."

"Yes, I do."

"And you intend to be that leadership."

"You are quite perceptive," Elliot said. "It is among my goals, yes."

"I've done some research on you, Elliot. I'll be honest, nothing you've done stands out as horrific, but you also don't stand out as being overly talented. Maybe I'm missing something. What makes you think you can pull any of this off?"

"You don't see anything overly obvious, because at Yolo, you learn quickly to keep your head down. Use misdirection. As long as my goals are advanced, I don't care who gets the credit, for the most part. And when something goes wrong, the same applies, although I'll admit to steering the negative results with a little more care."

"As a way to eliminate competition," Malcolm said.

Elliot shrugged. "It is a useful skill."

"I'll bet it is. I look forward to seeing if you can pull it off. Having Luna at the table would be a big advantage, I agree. I think our long-term goals are somewhat aligned, although I'm a bit old to take a real run at the leadership."

"I think you'd make a solid executive director."

Malcolm shook his head. "Thank you, but I'd rather see my daughter there. She's not ready yet, but in a few years, I think she'll be far better than either of the Monarchs have been."

"Then I will make you a proposal. When the time comes, you support me, and I will put your daughter in a position to be my successor when my time is over."

Malcolm scoffed. "Careful. That could be an invitation to a well-placed knife."

Elliot leaned forward. "I accept the risk, Malcolm."

"Good grief, I was joking."

"Good. Bit of a relief. I still won't retract the offer."

"Win over Luna," Malcolm said, "and you'll have my support."

Elliot nodded curtly. "Thank you, and with that, I should be getting home. I have a lot of work to do." Elliot stood and extended his hand to Malcolm. "Good evening."

Malcolm gave his hand a single shake. "Have a good night."

Elliot took the bottle from the table and left. He walked slowly back to his quarters. He wanted to be angry about the whiskey, but the possibility of support made him almost gleeful. Once again feeling like a celebration, his thoughts returned to the whiskey. The mystery caught his attention.

"Bil, I want to begin a new covert information gathering program. I'm looking for purchase orders and travel receipts for the year leading up to August Monarch's fiftieth birthday. He absolutely must not become aware of your activities."

"Acknowledged."

* * * * *

The Eleventh Lunar Assembly

Sunday, September 26, 3288, 7:00

Dawn was up early, making herself ready while scanning the latest news. Overnight, a small group of people who lived in the Ablom Refuge and worked in Takiyama had gathered to protest the tube closure. The attention had attracted more protesters, and several dozen were down there now, chanting and yelling at the posted guards, who were looking more than a little nervous.

Dawn hurried through her morning routine and left early to get to the meeting room. When she arrived, three other members were already there, seated at the large, dark table. Two mekis were already floating over empty padded chairs, meaning that two of them would be remote. One was an open amber book labeled Steven Corvair. Ava Wallaby's name floated above a crystal that resembled a kitten. That left one final member yet to show, but they were early.

"Hello, everyone. I'm Dawn Sheffield. We still have a few minutes, so maybe we could get to know each other a bit before we start." Dawn sat in one of the large padded chairs.

"I'm Darren Garfield, and I'm pretty sure that in all of Lunar history, you're the least qualified prime minister ever to be elected. Would you consider stepping aside and letting someone more qualified take over? Me, perhaps."

"Oh, knock it off, Darren." Ellie Lester had fire in her dark eyes.

Dawn felt her face grow hot. This was the man in third place? Thirtyish with a boyish face, he wore a thin beard that looked like a failed attempt to hide a weak chin. She made her decision. "You're right, Mr. Garfield. By your standards, I am the least qualified individual to have ever held the title of prime minister. However, my job here isn't to dictate the actions I think we need to take. It's to gather information, encourage group discussion, and build consensus among those of us entrusted with the resolution to this crisis. Something you seem to be a little unqualified for. For now, I'll hang on to the title. Thanks for the offer just the same."

Ellie giggled and slowly clapped her hands. "Call me Ellie. Ignore Darren; you'll do fine."

Darren crossed his arms. "Fine. Whatever."

Professor Corvair faded into view under the amber book meki. "Good grief, are you folks fighting already? What did I miss?" His eyes sparkled next to deep lines that spoke of a great deal of laughter. His hair was dark on top, fading down to a white beard.

Darren shrugged. "I was just pointing out that—"

"Darren was just being a dick," Ellie said.

Samwise Freeman, the other man in the room, laughed to himself. His thick mat of gray hair was accented with splashes of black. "What the hell have I gotten myself into?"

Dawn turned to him next. "And you're Samwise?"

"Sam. Sam Freeman. I'm a bartender under the peak, so I don't care what qualifications you have, Dawn. I only care that we can get this whole mess sorted out so my customers will be happy. Happy customers are what I live for. Most of them don't like the idea of such a large conflict on Luna."

"I think we can all agree on that," Dawn said. "And under the book, Professor Corvair? Where do you teach?"

"Tycho University. I teach history and politics. I've been brushing up on the religions involved in the current conflict, should anyone have a desire for the relevant information."

"Sounds to me," Darren said, "like you're a lot more qualified to lead us than she is."

"And it sounds to me," the professor said, "as if you don't understand how our government works, young man. Now please stop making problems and let's start fixing them, shall we?"

"Ha!" Ellie said. "He's sure got your number, Darren." Ellie's white hair shook like a cloud attached to her head. Her eyes lit up when she smiled.

Dawn noticed the second remote delegate had faded in. She was a familiar young woman in a glittering black bodysuit with white flashes animated at random. Her tan ears were pointed in the popular elf fashion, poking delicately through her long, silver hair. A small white kitten was asleep in her lap. It resembled her meki.

"Ava Wallaby, you're the singer, right?" Dawn asked.

"Of course I am," Ava said. "How much longer will this take? I need to be somewhere by ten."

"We have one more delegate to go," Dawn said. "We're a few minutes early. We can wait until eight, but if she doesn't show up, we'll start anyway."

"Thank you. I don't have a problem being here, I simply don't want to waste my time."

"Singer. Right." Darren scowled. "You performing today?"

"No, I'm sitting for an interview with a fan group." She adjusted her seat. "They get to ask questions for a couple of hours while we do lunch together."

"Ten is a little early for lunch, isn't it?" Dawn asked.

"Ten is when I need to be at the stylist's. Lunch is at 11:30 and runs to 13:30 or 14:00, depending on how I feel." Ava noticed Ellie for the first time. She leaned in as if to take a good look. "Ellie Lester." Taking a deep breath, she said, "I'm such a big fan of yours. You're my personal inspiration! When I was a kid, I watched all your movies and every episode of every series you ever did! I even made my hair white like yours."

Ellie sighed. "Thank you. Yes, I used to be famous, and among some people, I still am. I suppose that's how I ended up here."

"Prime Minister Sheffield." The professor used his lecture hall voice. "It's now eight, and we're still missing Misa Kobato, our last delegate. Would you like me to track her down for you?"

"Yes, please," Dawn said, "but in the meantime, we can get started. Service, display an image of the two refugee communities and show all interconnections between them, and to their closest neighbors."

The table they were sitting around dissolved into a display showing a three-dimensional semi-transparent diagram of the two sets of structures, with a tangle of tubes, underlying tunnels, and connections.

"Now add in the areas where there are currently gatherings of protesters and guards."

Little blips of purple and orange dotted the display. There was a concentration of each at the main tube connecting the two communities.

"Which are the good guys?" Ava asked.

"This service makes no moral judgment," Service said.

"Service," Dawn said, "who are the purple dots, and who are the orange ones?"

"Purple represents the Mormon Catholic residents of the Ablom Refuge. Orange represents the Southern Orthodox residents of Takiyama."

Dawn noticed groups in other connecting tubes. "Service, are these also guards? Have they closed off all traffic?"

"Both communities have ceased allowing access to non-residents at this time."

"What can they hope to gain by cutting themselves off from the rest of us?" the professor asked.

"Maybe," Darren said, "they don't want us to stop them from fighting."

"They're acting like children," Ellie said. "We need to stop them before someone gets hurt."

"I agree," Dawn said. "Any suggestions?"

"Yeah," Darren said, "let's shut off their oxygen generators and tell them they can calm down or pass out. Their choice."

"That's mean, Darren," Ava said. "Maybe we could pipe in some nice music to calm them down." She gently tickled her kitten.

The professor smiled at Ava. "Maybe a catchy little dance number, something to get them in a better mood."

Ava tilted her head and smiled at him.

"That all sounds silly to me," Ellie said. "Why can't we reason with them? Do we have any way to contact them directly?"

"Service," Dawn said, "is there any indication of leadership forming on either side?"

"The Ablom religious hierarchy," Service said, "has yet to take any action; however, they are led by a cardinal named Brandon Nunn." An image of an elderly man's face floated above one of the domes. "The residents of Takiyama have formed a committee of five people and selected one as Speaker, Noguchi Kanami." A young woman's image appeared above the other dome.

"That's hopeful," Ellie said.

Dawn sat back. "I think so, too. Let's send a message to each of them and ask them to speak with us."

"Aren't we supposed to vote on things like that?" Darren asked.

"I vote yes," the professor said.

"Me too," Ellie said.

"And me as well," Sam said. "Talking might be all we really have to do here."

"Ava, what about you?" Dawn asked.

Ava had been lending her attention to her personal display. "Huh? Oh. Yeah, sure. It's worth a try."

In the display above the images of the leaders was a scoreboard. Over sixty-two million for making contact, Twenty-three million uncommitted.

"Professor, did you ever track down our missing delegate?"

The professor looked a little disappointed. "Yes, I did, Dawn. She boarded the southbound loop from Plato as we were starting our meeting. I made contact, and she'll be here later this evening."

Darren shook his head in disbelief. "Good grief. That's over four thousand kilometers, and she took the loop? That would be what, eight hours if it were straight? But it's not. She'll hit a dozen stops along the way."

"Indeed," said the professor. "Her current ETA is 18:45."

"That's strange," said Dawn. "I wonder why she didn't remote in or take a shuttle. It doesn't really matter at this point; we have a majority for reaching out and establishing contact. Service, please send a meeting invitation to both Cardinal Nunn and Speaker Kanami." Dawn felt relieved to be giving the order.

"Noguchi Kanami follows traditional Japanese naming conventions," Service said. "Do you mean to invite Speaker Noguchi?"

Dawn lowered her voice. "Yes, please. Set the meeting for 14:30. Will that work for you, Ava?"

Ava smiled and nodded. The other members relaxed a bit.

"Service, have there been any updates about the situation in Minkowski?" Dawn asked.

"Negative, Prime Minister," Service said. "There is no new information available at this time."

Dawn stood up. "In that case, let's try to be back by about quarter past 14:00."

Ellie leaned back in her chair. "I like short meetings, but you take the cake! Anywhere good to eat around here?"

"There are several nice restaurants near my place, under the peak," Sam said. "A short slide on the tube. Would you like a tour?"

Professor Corvair had faded out; his amber book folded and put itself into an invisible shelf. Ava Wallaby exploded into multicolored glitter, which rapidly faded. With Sam and Ellie pairing off and heading to the mountain, that left Dawn with Darren. She glanced at him and walked out of the room alone.

She hadn't expected the crowd. Many of them held placards showing their love for Ava. She caught up with Ellie and Sam.

Darren followed shortly. He pointed to an elderly man at one end. "There's a guy wearing walking legs, Ellie. One of your fans?"

Ellie scowled. "I'd kick you in the shin and make you hop the rest of the way, except I think I know him. He's the president of my fan club."

* * *

It took the better part of an hour for Dawn to get past the crush of people asking questions for their news feeds. Again and again, yes, they were meeting, no they hadn't resolved anything yet. Yes, they had reached out to the two parties, and no, not everyone elected had made it to the meeting. She felt bad about that last one, but the records were public.

Eventually she managed to get to the tube station and rode it to her block, then took the lift back to her apartment.

Out of habit, Dawn asked, "Any messages, Service?"

Instead of the expected display of mekis, Dawn was presented with a golden chest that appeared to be bursting at the seams. "You have 3,247 new messages from 2,805 individuals. Would you like a summary?" The communications service was oblivious to the absurdity.

"Wow. Um, no, let's filter for friends and family only. How many does that leave?"

Five remaining mekis replaced the chest. Three pink hearts, a brass coin, and a familiar silver telescope.

"Five new messages from three individuals. Would you like a summary?"

"No, thanks. Play them in order."

"From your sister, Fawn, first of three messages."

Her little sister's voice and image appeared on the screen. "I know you're busy, but I had to say I love you and I can't wait to see how famous you get. Bye!"

"Would you like to respond?" Service asked.

"Acknowledge with love," Dawn said. "Next message."

"From your grandmother, Hazel."

Hazel's face appeared on the screen. She hadn't changed much. Dark brown, shoulder length hair, with straight bangs. Her skin looked a little pinker. Extra makeup. "I must say, I'm surprised. I'm also delighted and proud of my granddaughter. Give a call when you have time, Prime Minister. We should catch up."

"Would you like to respond?" Service asked.

"Yes, please. 'Grandma, good to hear from you. Hope you're doing well. Fawn and Buck got me into it, but I think it's a challenge I'll enjoy. Fawn seems closer to reaching out to you. I hope if she does, you'll reach back. It's been a long time. Love you and miss you. Give my love to Jude.' Send. Next message."

"From your sister, Fawn, second of three messages."

Her little sister's voice and image appeared back on the screen. She looked a little more serious this time. "I almost forgot, Buck wants us to get married! I kinda think I might wanna say yes, but I really need your advice. I mean, no rush. I know you're busy fixing the world and all that. Love you!"

"Would you like the third message?"

"Yes."

"From your sister, Fawn, third of three messages."

"Sorry, I don't mean to rush you, please don't even think about me and Buck until after the war is over, okay? Love you."

"Would you like to respond?"

Dawn looked at the time. It was past 11:30. "Hold this one until the end. Next message."

"From Jon Merrill."

Jon's voice and image appeared. "Congratulations, and you're welcome. Let me know if you need anything."

"Would you like to respond?"

"Yes, send him my thanks."

"Would you like to respond to your sister Fawn now?"

"Remind me about it again after lunch." Dawn entered the kitchen area. She found herself some greens and red vegetables and made a quick salad. She sat in the living area eating quietly for a few minutes.

"Service, show me my news feed, please."

An hour later, she turned the news feed back off. She'd learned a lot about popular opinion and her current polling numbers. None of it helped her think about the conflict, and entirely too much of it had been about her meme. Tony Renard had dubbed her the Great Bird of the Galaxy, whatever that was supposed to mean.

She rinsed out her dish, sanitized it, then placed it back on the shelf.

"Would you like to respond to your sister Fawn now?" Service asked.

"Is she available for a conversation?"

"Affirmative. She's eating lunch alone at this time."

"Call her, please," Dawn said.

Fawn's image appeared on the window display, full sized. She was sitting at a small white table eating a sandwich. Her pink heart meki floated between her upright ears. "Hi, Dawn! How was your assembly? Are you having fun being a government?"

"Nevermind all that, what sort of advice do you need from me about Buck?"

Fawn looked down sheepishly. "He wants us to get married. A real fantasy fairytale wedding in the park. I... I think I want to, but I wouldn't do it if you don't think it's a good idea."

"Nonsense. I only care about you being happy. Does Buck make you happy?"

"Yes, of course he does. He makes me smile and laugh every day. We have a great time together."

"You realize if things don't work out, if you guys stop being happy together, all you have to do is cancel the contract, right?"

"I know. I wanted to be sure you wouldn't think I was being silly."

"Fawn, darling, you're always silly. You're the silliest little sister I have, and Buck is as silly as you are. I don't care what your relationship status is. As long as you're happy, I'm happy for you. You decide what you want to do and let me know. And if you're really going to do it, I get to make both outfits for the ceremony. Deal?"

Fawn's big grin said it all. "Deal. And yes, I want to marry him. Thank you, Dawn. You're my favorite sister!" She giggled and fidgeted with excitement.

"I'm the only sister you have, minibrain. Now I need to get ready for my next meeting. See you tonight, maybe."

"Later." Fawn's image faded as her meki bounced away.

Dawn turned back to her news feed and saw the bad news. Fighting had broken out in the main tube between the two communities. The Takiyama guards had been outnumbered three to one but had beaten back their attackers with ease. Tony Renard was now doing an in-depth report on a fighting technique called Aoi Hane, especially developed for the lunar gravity by martial artists over the last several generations. They'd been better prepared than their opponents in that regard.

She decided to head back to the conference room. As she neared the entrance, she could hear the crowd. Security bots were spread out, forming a wide corridor for her. Security guards scattered along the path were talking to people in the crowd, keeping them calm. Dawn could feel her face flush. She put her head down and tried to ignore it all as she headed inside.

She found Darren sitting at the table eating a large meal. The spicy, flavorful aroma of meats and sauces made her nose itch.

"What did you get?" she asked.

Darren looked up and grinned. "Went with a Polish place up on the rim. Ordered a sample plate. I have no idea what this is—" he held up a small whitish dumpling "—but it's really good." He popped it into his mouth. "Really spicy. Want some?"

Dawn shook her head. "Gives me hiccups. Have you been following the news?"

"I watched the fight on the live feed. Those guys are amazing. Nine of them, and there were at least thirty attackers. It took maybe five minutes, and it was done. All the Ablomians got their asses handed to them, and they limped off, carrying each other back to their dome." Darren had a look of admiration on his face. "I don't think the other guys even broke a sweat!"

Dawn frowned and shook her head. "That's not good, and don't call them Ablomians. It sounds terrible."

"What do you mean?"

"I think it means that next time they won't be fighting with fists."

"Point taken, but I meant the name."

"Formally, they refer to themselves as citizens of Ablom, or Mormon Catholics."

Darren shrugged. "Fine. I thought it was catchy."

They sat watching the Tony Renard news feed for a while until Ava and her kitten appeared again.

"Hello, everyone," Ava said. "Dawn, I can't tell you how much I appreciate you making sure I had the time I needed. I used the interview to announce that I've canceled all my other engagements for the next week, so now I'm all yours. Anything exciting happen?"

Darren and Dawn caught her up in time for Sam and Ellie to rejoin them.

"Did you two see the news?" Dawn asked.

"We did," Ellie said. "It's going to make things worse now."

"I think so, too. How was your tour?"

Sam shrugged, "She didn't get the full tour. Big crowds. I took her to my bar. We closed it to everyone but regulars and watched a hopper race. Scars won by two goals over the Sparrows."

"His regulars are a bunch of the sweetest people," Ellie said, "and his wife is a dear. I enjoyed myself, Dawn. I wasn't as interested in the hoppers as he was. Bit too violent for my tastes. But it turns out Sam here is the coordinator for the whole league. Probably how he got elected."

"It's good fun," Sam said. "Really tests the skills of the pilots. The two-legged hopper design is based on the old Lunar fighters, and I'm a bit of a military history buff."

The professor's amber book appeared and opened as he faded into his seat. It was 14:15 precisely.

"Welcome back, Professor," Dawn said. "We were catching up with developments. Have you seen?"

"Yes. I made sure to review everything before I came on. Dawn, I have a bad feeling about this. I think it makes things worse."

Everyone chuckled.

"Yup. That's the general consensus. Orange guys showed off, and purple guys are going to take it hard, and come back harder. I'm still hopeful we can talk our way out of this. Service, have the two leaders we invited accepted the invitation?"

"Negative," Service said. "Neither have accepted the invitation; however, both have acknowledged and indicated that they are considering it."

"Well, now," Darren said, "I guess we wait and see who shows up."

A black kanji symbol surrounded by a diffuse white glow appeared over the head of a young Japanese woman seated in a chair at the table. Translated text below the meki said BELIEF, TRUST.

"Welcome," Dawn said. "You're Speaker Noguchi Kanami, correct?"

Kanami gave a polite bow. "Hai, yes. Correct, I am."

"Thank you for joining us. We're still awaiting someone from the Mormon Catholic side. I'm Dawn Sheffield. I've been elected prime minister of the Eleventh Lunar Assembly in order to solve the problems that have led to this conflict. You can call me Dawn."

"Hai, I understand. I am only one member of the council of Takiyama. I speak for them, but I do not lead them. I am called Kanami." She bowed slightly.

"We're glad you're here," Dawn said. "I'm hopeful that someone from the other dome will contact us as well."

"I do not share your hope. I am here, nonetheless."

As if to spite her, the adjacent seat was suddenly filled with a scowling Cardinal Nunn. A small, glowing, golden crossed trumpet floated above his balding, age-spotted head.

"Welcome, Cardinal Nunn," Dawn said. "Thank you for joining us."

Cardinal Nunn shook his head slowly. "I believe you have the wrong man. I lead my people in worship, not in battle. I'm not sure anything I say to them would stay them from their course."

"Does that mean you've already tried?"

"No. Not really. I've been listening to people shouting about it all day."

Ellie interrupted. "What's it going to take to get you to do something?"

Dawn leaned forward. "We're looking for a way to pull you both back from conflict, and to find a way going forward where you can be friends with each other."

The cardinal harrumphed. "Our people do not need to be friends with outsiders, especially heathens like those people."

Kanami lowered her eyes and remained silent.

"We need to find options before more people get hurt," Dawn said. "Before there's bloodshed."

"Blood has already been drawn, young lady," the cardinal said. "They threw the first stone, and they drew the first blood. They are a violent, Godless pack of wolves!" The anger felt by the cardinal was clear on his reddened face.

Kanami, in a polite and quiet tone, said, "If it is possible, may I counter the charges that have been presented?"

"Absolutely," Dawn said. "Your turn."

Kanami took a deep breath and exhaled. "We respectfully acknowledge that there is no proof of any sort who threw the first stone, except the words of the children. While we as parents would like to believe our children tell no lies, this would be a falsehood of our own, so we remain open to the possibility that the first stone cast in this present conflict came from our side. We furthermore acknowledge that the child who suffered damage to their equipment was a child of Ablom. However, no child was actually injured, and repair services were rendered before there was any danger.

"The subsequent bombing of our garden dome, which resulted in a life-threatening crack, was a totally unwarranted escalation. Had the damage been worse, or had the repairs not been effective, loss of life could have occurred.

"Furthermore, over thirty citizens of Ablom attacked nine of our guards. Our guards defended themselves without loss of life. They were outnumbered, and they were the ones being attacked in Takiyama territory."

"You suckered us in," the cardinal said. "You cut off access to your dome. We have people on our side with business over there. Not many, but a few, and they have every right to use the tube."

"Takiyama is our community. We believe we were within our rights to temporarily ban access from Ablom after the bombing. It is a natural response."

"Please excuse the interruption, Prime Minister," Service said. "There is another violent event occurring you should be aware of."

"Show us." Dawn could feel the dread.

The display shifted to a mix of camera angles from the same tube that the earlier altercation had taken place in. There were flames everywhere. Southern Orthodox guards were retreating, as were the Mormon Catholics, some of whom were still throwing bottles, which then exploded in flames.

The fire suppression system came on, and large, air-tight bulkheads closed off the burning section from both ends. No one was trapped inside, but there'd be no passage until damage crews reopened the emergency bulkheads.

"Can we have a word in private, Dawn?" Darren asked.

"Will both of you please excuse us, we'll return shortly. Service, please mute our guests." The two guest images grayed out to indistinguishable silhouettes, and their mekis stopped moving.

"What do you have in mind, Darren?" Dawn asked.

"We should send our own neutral damage team to the tube from the outside and tell them to leave the bulkheads closed when they're done. Keep these idiots away from each other for a while, because this is getting nasty."

"I believe he has the right idea," the professor said, "at least for the time being." He shook his head. "Sorry, Ava, looks like the dance has been canceled."

Ava ignored him. "Did you hear how much the old guy hates the people in the other dome? And I don't know what to make of the girl. She's too perfect. Too calm. It's weird."

"Oh, I don't know," Ellie said. "Her folks are a pretty calm lot, at least the older ones. I've met a few from time to time. They always seem like they're in total control of their emotions. On the other hand, they can be extraordinarily hardheaded."

"We need consensus on Darren's proposal," Dawn said. "All in favor, raise your hands." It was unanimous, except for the one missing delegate. "Service, please implement Darren's plan. Let us know when repairs are completed. "

"Acknowledged, Prime Minister. Damage repair equipment has been dispatched."

"Now please unmute our guests."

The grayed silhouettes of the guests returned to normal, and their mekis resumed their normal motions.

"Cardinal Nunn, you saw for yourself that this attack originated on your side, agreed?"

The cardinal nodded slowly. "It would appear so, yes."

"Then I must ask you to please put a stop to any further attacks or bring us to someone who can."

"I can make no promises about how I'll be received, but I will make an attempt to do so."

"Thank you," Dawn said. "That's all we can ask." She turned to Kanami. "Speaker Noguchi, can you please ask your council on our behalf to prevent any retaliation for the recent attacks? To prevent any further escalation of this conflict?"

Kanami bowed her head. "Hai. Yes, I will, with the same stipulation the cardinal has made. I will deliver the request. No promises of results are possible."

"Thank you both. We look forward to hearing from you when you know the results, one way or the other. Thank you for your time." Dawn dismissed them.

Kanami turned transparent and flowed away like water. Cardinal Nunn and his meki simply faded out.

Dawn shook her head. "This isn't going as well as I had hoped."

Ellie laughed. "You're doing fine, Dawn. Isn't she, Darren?"

Darren grunted and shook his head.

"I think things are going well enough," the professor said. "No one has been seriously injured, and we have the two sides at least marginally talking to each other. I think this conflict will be sorted out shortly, but the long-term issue may be a bit more problematic."

Sam leaned forward. "I agree. Unless we can get them talking more, and really getting to know each other, this is going to fester and keep popping up."

"What I would like to know," Ava said, "is why they haven't assimilated more into regular society. I mean, in every dome I go to, I see people of all shapes and sizes, all skin colors, religions, hairstyles, and body mods. Everyone seems to get along, and even though I know I'm the center of their attention, I see them enjoying themselves and not bothering anyone." She shook her head. "These two groups of kids hated each other so much that when they found each other outside, with nothing but vacuum between them and the stars, they chose to throw rocks instead of saying hello. That's the problem I want to see fixed."

Ellie shook her head. "I couldn't have said it better myself, honey."

Dawn stood. "We need to find a way to solve that problem. Let's take a break. Stay close in case we hear back."

The professor raised his hand. "Before we go, Dawn, I wanted you to know that I have a late class from 16:00 to 17:30. I can be available if you need me, but I plan to at least begin my lecture."

"Thanks, Professor." Dawn stretched, headed out the door, and looked for the nearest fresher. The area immediately outside the conference room was free of people, but she could see the crowd outside had grown much larger. Some of them were gleeful to see her; others appeared angry. For the first time, it gave her a moment's pause. Was she going to be famous like this for the rest of her life?

* * *

Later in the afternoon, Dawn joined Ellie and Sam down at the Chesapeake, a restaurant on a lower level of the conference center, adjacent to the Grissom Park Aquarium. The entire back wall of the establishment was transparent, allowing an underwater view out to a reef a few meters below. From where they sat, they could see thousands of brilliantly colored fish. She was sipping a warm cup of tea, thick with cream. A news display occupied part of the table, but the sound was turned off. Sam was telling Ellie about his grandchildren. The oldest was the star hopper pilot for the Sparrows.

"There you are." Darren looked as if he'd won a challenging game. He didn't wait to be invited before sitting down. "Has anyone considered getting extra security? The crowd outside is starting to turn nasty. A few anti-government types are riling up the crowd."

Dawn frowned. "I saw a little of that earlier. Anyone know what our options are?"

Darren thought for a moment. "Service, are there extra guards available for delegates?"

"Affirmative," Service said. "The Moretus Crater Security Service has already dispatched additional security for crowd control. Individual delegates may request personal security at any time. Advanced monitoring for all delegates is in effect."

"Do you really think we need it?" Ellie looked at Sam.

"I feel safe here," Sam said. "Let's see what it's like when we leave. Maybe this will all blow over." Sam looked like he didn't believe himself.

Dawn checked the time. "The professor will be back online in a little while. I want to call everyone back together to start working out a long-term solution. There hasn't been any more violence since our meeting."

Darren crossed his arms. "You're the prime minister. It's your call. If it were me, I'd ban the whole lot of them. Why do we have to put up with this?"

"We can't ban everyone in both domes. That's tens of thousands of people. We have to find a way to get them to stop hating each other."

"Sure. Maybe you can wave a magic wand or something. Or maybe we could reprogram their nanomedics to reprogram them!"

The others were silent. Dawn turned a steely gaze at Darren. "That's about as unethical as it gets. Not an option."

"So you say, but this isn't about medical ethics, it's about stopping a war that could kill those same tens of thousands you don't want to get rid of. You could consider it a lifesaving treatment option. Maybe classify hatred as a disease..."

The look on Dawn's face told Darren he wasn't making any progress. Sam looked thoughtful.

Ellie had grown angry. "Young man, you get your mind out of the gutter. That's a line we can't cross. You start changing the programs that keep our world working and free—"

"I'm not saying we change everything, just one little thing, and only in their nanomedics, not everyone else's."

"The system doesn't work that way, jackass. You might have been able to do something like that way back when they were first invented, but nowadays, it's all one big system. All the nanomedics, hospitals, first responders, everything to do with human health is all controlled and coordinated by one central controller. Even body modding is done under that same system. You go tweaking that, and all hell could break loose."

Sam looked at Ellie. "I've never even heard of using them to try to change the way people think. It scares me that someone might consider it."

Dawn pursed her lips and looked over the coral reef below, thinking for a moment. "I said it wasn't an option. That's my position. I'm going to stick to that position as long as I see other options. But listen, we should make sure we know what our options really are, even if we don't like them." Dawn turned to Darren. "Sam has a point, we don't know if something like that is possible, so before we talk about it any further, you research it, and see if it could be done at all."

Ellie shook her head. "I can't believe you'd even consider such a thing."

"I still don't think it would ever come to it," Dawn said, "but we should know what *can* be done. Darren's right, this could end up killing a lot of people."

"On that note," Darren said, "I think I'll go find someplace less public to do some research. Don't want rumors getting started." He got up and walked back toward their conference room.

Ellie shook her head slowly. "I don't know whether I should respect him or slap him upside the head. Dawn, don't listen to him. That way madness lies, as they say."

"I know, Ellie, but it should keep him busy for a while. We need better ideas. Let's go back and see if the professor and Ava have come up with anything better."

The three of them went back to the conference room. Darren was deep in his own display, and after a quick glance, ignored them. Dawn sat and sent requests to the two remote delegates.

Shortly, both Ava and the professor were back under their mekis. Ava had an entirely new hairstyle that really showed off her elfin ears, along with a dress that showed off much of the rest of her features.

"Hello there!" Darren said.

"Darren, go back to your research," Dawn said. "Welcome back, you two. We've been tossing around some ideas about how to solve this problem once and for all. Darren is researching an idea the rest of us don't like, but I'm willing to at least have it on the table. What we really need are some better ideas. Professor, got anything?"

"I've given it a little thought," the professor said, "but only between lectures and such. I do have administrative duties as well."

Ava smirked at the professor. "I think he's trying to say no."

"How about you?" Dawn asked. "Do you have any more ideas?"

"Most of what I think involves song and dance, but that brings up the idea of some sort of long-term cultural exchange program. We don't really need to aim it at the adults. We target the kids. Get them involved and meeting each other socially. Let them grow up knowing their neighbors. Maybe we can stop the hate from spreading to the next generation."

Ellie chuckled. "That might work once we get them to stop fighting. I would add that we need to be sure to include other neighboring settlements. Both of these groups are way too isolated."

"I hate to be the bad news display here," the professor said, "but I don't think either side will allow it." He had a sour look on his face. "Remember how the old cardinal brushed aside any hint of getting along with the Orthodox folks? He called them heathens. Pretty strong—"

A tall Japanese woman with long, straight black hair glided effortlessly into the conference room. "Sorry to be so late. I'm Misa Kobato.

I've had Sabisu keep me up to date on most everything, but I missed any conversations you might have had outside of the conference room. In particular, I missed exactly what Mr. Garfield over there is researching."

"Sabisu?" Darren had been paying attention.

Misa looked puzzled for a moment. "Sabisu, please explain."

Service responded, "Sabisu is one of the many terms to which communications services answer. In particular, the term 'sabisu' is directly related to the Japanese word for service. It is most popular in northern areas of Luna to address both the Earthside Communications Network and the Northern Farside Regional Communications Service. Sabisu is itself a loan word taken from English dating back to—"

"Enough," Dawn said. "We get the idea. Thank you." She felt the smooth, dark surface of the table under her fingertips for a moment. "Misa, Darren is researching an idea the rest of us mostly hate. I wanted to make sure we knew what we could and couldn't do."

"I'm researching the idea," said Darren, "of using their nanomedics to alter the way they think about each other. Only enough to edit out the hate, maybe."

Misa looked shocked. She spoke slowly. "I see. Such an idea is dangerous. I see why it's not held in high regard. I also see that in the right hands, it could be a powerful tool for good."

Darren slapped the table. "There, see? Someone agrees with me."

"I wasn't agreeing with you. I was merely pointing out how powerful a concept it could be. I don't like it. I see the potential. Both can be true."

Darren looked confused.

"I'm hoping it never comes to that," Dawn said. "Have you given a long-term solution any thought?" Dawn wasn't hopeful, but she really wanted to change the subject.

Misa crossed her arms on the table and leaned forward. "I've read a little bit about their history and cultures. I think it would have been better if they hadn't been located so close to each other. However, I also think that, given how isolated they've kept themselves, they would eventually have come to hate any neighbor they had. Neither group has socialized much with anyone outside their own enclosures. My thought is, we take both enclosures away from them. We split their entire population into small family groups and transplant them to other locations throughout all of Luna."

Ellie was surprised. "Damn! Can we do that, Dawn?"

"I'm not sure," Dawn said. "Professor, what are the rules here? How far can we really go?"

"That's an interesting question," the professor said. "The answer boils down to exactly how you put it. See, Luna being a cooperative means that everything is theoretically owned by everyone who owns shares, and we all own a share. In practice, there's a complex underpinning of accounting going on, right down to how much you're charged for the air you breathe. Lunar assemblies are meant to be created to solve problems that the automated systems and the established set of rules and guidelines can't handle. So again, practically speaking, pretty much anything short of murder is on the table."

"My nanite idea would be legal, right?"

"It's possible, Darren." The professor turned back to Dawn. "But unethical by any standards."

"Darren," Dawn said, "does that mean it can be done?"

"I've found some early 23rd century studies," Darren said, "that suggest it can be done. It looks like the study was halted and the tech banned by the old World Union. I don't even know if that applies today."

"Darren is right to wonder." The professor relished giving information. "When the United Global Authority came into being, all previous laws and regulations were adopted. But when the Corporate Federation took over at the end of the war, they didn't adopt much of anything. At least, not that we know of. They issued a set of Corporate Guidelines. Since we aren't members of the Federation, they don't apply to us. Darren, let me follow up on the legality. I think I know where to look."

"I've always wondered," Ellie said, "with all this technology, and all these services, why couldn't we just ask Service if it's legal? Service, is it legal to reprogram nanomedics to alter the brain of the human host?"

"Please indicate a jurisdiction," Service said.

Ellie looked surprised. "What crater are those folks in?"

Dawn pointed to where it was shown on the central display. "Minkowski."

"There are no specific laws regarding such actions at the local or regional level," Service said. "However, there are precedent cases in the court records of Earth whose summaries indicate they may be relevant. The full case files are locked. There are no further restrictions in the Lunar Sustainability Cooperative Rules and Regulations."

The room was silent for a moment.

The professor looked disappointed. "Nice search, Ellie. Sometimes I forget how deeply tied in these services are."

Dawn felt like the world was closing in on her. "I can't believe we've spent so much time on this. So far, I think Ava and Misa are on the right track. Maybe some combination of both. Look, let's take the rest of the night to think things over and see how we feel in the morning. I want to see if we can put a plan in place by the end of tomorrow."

Ava gently stroked her kitten, looking like she was lost in thought. The kitten swiped at an invisible something in the air and leapt from her lap, vanishing from view. She quickly followed, and her meki abruptly exploded in glitter, then faded out.

"Goodnight, everyone." The professor also faded out as his book slid into nothing.

The others quietly left the room. Everyone but Darren. Dawn took a side exit from the center and headed to the nearest tube. The crowd had focused at the front, and she managed to get away without being noticed.

On her way home, she went online and sent a ping to her sister.

Fawn called back quickly. "Dawn! How is it going? Is the war over yet?"

"Maybe. Things quieted down after we got them talking, but now we have to decide what comes next. It's complicated."

"You want dinner?"

"I want sleep," Dawn said.

"So you say now. I say you need a night out at Nemo's. It's singles night tonight."

Captain Nemo's was a nightclub near the city aquarium that attracted singles looking for hookups and younger couples looking for a night out.

"No, thank you," Dawn said. "You go. I dare you. I won't tell Buck if you don't."

Fawn stuck her tongue out. Coupled with the pointy ears and the glowing pink heart, it looked silly and made Dawn laugh out loud. "Goodnight, Fawn."

As she walked back into her apartment, she skipped the messages and asked for the news feed, much to her immediate regret.

The section of tube that had been closed off after the fire had been destroyed in a series of explosions. Most electrical connections, pipes, and ducts were severed. Water and air were bleeding into open vacuum. Damage teams had been dispatched. Dawn looked at the casualty indications. Seventeen dead. Survivors on both sides were screaming. People were gathering.

"Damn. Service, is Uncle Keegan cooking now?"

"Affirmative."

"Ask him for a swing-deli sandwich, please, and deliver it to me back in the conference room. Tell the other delegates I'm heading back and ask them to please join me at once."

* * * * *

A Personal Record

Sunday, September 26, 3288, 14:55

He'd spent the day watching the activities of people in Ablom and Takiyama. Mostly boring, mundane things. He'd divided his display and sorted by the size of the groups, hoping for larger protests. All morning long it had been like this, until he came upon a group donning vac suits. "Vondur, what's in those cases?"

"The markings indicate explosives."

"Oh, excellent. Follow them. I want to see where they go. Be sure to block the camera bot so they can't see it. Now let's shift to the other side. What do we have there?"

The displays shifted, keeping a small window on the selected group. He sorted and swiped through countless images of people doing normal things. If there were any potential spots of anything interesting, he couldn't see it.

Meanwhile, the selected group was outside near the main tube connecting the two communities. While the tube remained level, the ground was uneven and hilly. The section they were near was half buried in the gray lunar soil. "Vondur, are they actually planting explosives? This is incredible."

"Affirmative."

"What sort of damage are we talking about here? How many casualties could we get?"

"The targeted section of the transit tube is already closed at each segment joint by emergency bulkheads. The section targeted will be rendered atmosphere free. Estimated casualties, zero."

"Wait, closed? This is the same section that was burned out before then, right?"

"Affirmative."

"Stupid peace-loving imbeciles! What fun is that?" He glanced over to the tiny figurines and shook his head. "Our mission is to fix this. Vondur, did you get enough explosives to take out those bulkheads?"

"Affirmative."

"How do they intend to blow those things?"

"Readings indicate timing mechanisms on each device. They are set to detonate at 17:00."

"Couple hours, then. We have time." He sat back and watched as they completed their work and headed back inside their community. "All right, let's… Vondur, what are those people doing?" He indicated an image from the other community.

"This group is breaking into a secure storage locker."

"What's in that locker?"

"Small level explosives."

"Oh, now that's interesting." He watched as they rushed their stolen explosives to a nearby airlock, where a small group of people had already donned their vac suits. "Vondur, do you suppose they have the exact same idea as the others?"

"Unable to extrapolate."

"Fine." He waited and watched as the second group walked over the barren lunar landscape and ended up on the opposite side of the same tube section the others had already been to. "Nice. Opposite side, so they won't see the first set. Double the explosives. When are these going off?"

"16:30."

"What sort of damage total, then?"

"Neither set will damage the bulkheads. Same result as before, with twice the holes. The second set to detonate will do less damage to the already evacuated structure."

"Damn. Vondur, I want to pop open both bulkheads and make it look like those two groups are to blame. How?"

"By adjusting the placement of the two sets of explosives, coupled with the external coordination of the detonation sequence, a pressure wave could be created, starting from the midpoint and heading forcefully into each bulkhead. A small number of additional explosives at these points will also be required." Sets of indicators appeared near the bulkheads in the display.

"Got it. Set it up. Block their ability to see any of your bots, and get it done by the time they're back inside. Let me know when it's ready and your bots are clear."

"Acknowledged."

He watched intently as the second group completed their task and headed back to their airlock. His bots entered the scene and moved some of the previously planted explosives, while adding a few more. Finally, it was done, and the bots under Vondur's control had left the area. It was 16:25.

"Vondur, initiate the detonation sequence at 16:30."

"Acknowledged."

When the explosion started, he smiled broadly. It was the most beautiful thing he'd seen in years. He basked in the glory that was his. The entire tube section ripped to shreds and scattered about the lunar surface. Both adjacent bulkheads popped open, spilling people and debris into the lunar dust. Dead and dying bodies were strewn silently about the landscape.

"Vondur, how many casualties?"

"Fourteen deaths so far. Four critically wounded who may be beyond repair."

"Ah, yes. Nice. Show me scenes inside, anywhere there's grief, blood, or other things I like." He spent the next half hour watching various activities. One of the critically wounded was still clinging to life, but his total was now at seventeen. Excellent work for a single day. A personal record. "I feel wonderful. Our mission has a chance for success. I think I'll go work on my project for a while."

"Acknowledged." The hidden entrance to his private workshop opened. He walked inside, and the door closed behind him.

* * * * *

Ramifications

Sunday, September 26, 3288, 20:10

"Obviously," Dawn said, "I've called you all back because our little problem decided to get bigger. Service, invite both the speaker and the cardinal to join us as soon as they can, please."

"Acknowledged," Service said.

"While we wait, does anyone have anything that might help?"

"I think I have the final answer about the nanomedic idea," Darren said.

"Let's hear it."

"The first problem," Darren said, "is that reprogramming nanomedics isn't something you can do with a simple update. You actually have to build new ones and replace each person's entire load. That's a chore on its own, and it isn't something we can do without their full consent. But that's not the big problem. It turns out it would take months of scanning and study using some pretty heavy-duty gear to map an individual brain to ferret out where exactly to make changes. This would have to be performed on each individual, because no two brains store their data patterns in exactly the same way. And if they have embedded tech, like a display controller or communications controller—" he tapped his head "—those have to be removed first. Otherwise, we get one hell of a mess when the magnets come on. The short answer is, as relating to this particular situation, no. Impractical at best."

"That's actually a relief," Misa said. "I can't imagine what would happen if that sort of power were to be realized. Especially in the hands of something like the Corporate Federation. We could suddenly like the idea of living with poverty in order to support a bunch of wealthy corporate types. We could end up worshiping them as gods."

Darren sighed deeply, folding his arms over his chest. "I hate to admit it, but there are some really dark places it could go."

Dawn swallowed the last tasty bite of her sandwich. Her uncle had included a container of prawn rings, which she'd shared with the others. "Just as well. I don't think any of us really liked the idea. Service, any response from the cardinal or the speaker?"

"Cardinal Nunn has received your invitation," Service said, "but not acknowledged it, nor replied. Speaker Noguchi is offline and has not yet received the invi—Correction. Speaker Noguchi has received your invitation."

Everyone paused in silence. Dawn realized she was holding her breath.

"Speaker Noguchi has accepted your invitation," Service said, "and indicates that she will join shortly."

Dawn let out a sigh of relief. "Please let Cardinal Nunn know that Speaker Noguchi will be joining us shortly. Maybe that'll get his attention." Dawn frowned. "I really don't understand that man."

"I've reviewed the earlier conversation you had with him," Misa said. "His reactions seemed more intense than I would have expected, but I'm unfamiliar with his culture." She shifted in her seat as if she was uncomfortable.

Darren leaned toward Misa, pointing with a half-eaten prawn ring. "What did you make of Kanami? Do you understand her culture better?"

"Not so much. Takiyama has maintained an ancient Japanese culture, and I've never studied it."

Darren knitted his eyebrows and frowned. "Don't take this the wrong way, but you have a Japanese name, and you have Asian features. Wonderful, beautiful features. It seems weird you wouldn't have studied Japanese culture."

"Mr. Garfield," Misa said, "most of my family came to Luna over three hundred years ago. We've lived in a wide range of communities in the Plato region since then. If you want to know about Lunar history or some of the history of cities like Hong Kong Luna or Atarashi, I can help with that. Japan is a long way back for my family."

"Sorry. Didn't mean any offense. No need to mister me." He ate the last bite of his prawn ring, licking his fingers.

"Next he's going to ask me if I know any African history." Ellie scowled at Darren.

Dawn tapped her finger on the smooth, dark table. "All right everyone, focus. The nanomedic idea is out. That leaves us with Ava's suggestion and Misa's. Any new ideas? Sam? Ellie? Professor?"

"We need to set up better surveillance," Darren said. "We need to know where every one of them is, and what they're doing at all times. We need to know who's doing what. Look, I know it's invading the crap out of their privacy, but we need to stop the bloodshed." Darren looked frustrated.

Sam raised a finger. "I second that. People are dying. We need to know who's doing the killing."

Ellie shook her head. "Sad but true."

Ava frowned. "Privacy. Look, I went through some privacy issues of my own back when I was getting started. Let's put some restrictions on it up front. No personal space recordings unless they're actual perpetrators. No fresher recordings, either. Same thing. Let the service filter the communications and give us anything relevant. Then make sure we can see anywhere public, especially in the tubes and outside."

Dawn nodded. "I like those restrictions. Misa?"

"I agree with Ava."

"Service, please establish full surveillance inside both conflict domes. All public areas, all tubes, and outside. Monitor who's where, but don't record personal spaces or freshers unless they've been involved in the violence. Monitor all communications and only show us communications related to violent activity. How long until that's in place?"

"According to the hardware services," said Service, "new equipment will be required for full implementation. There are currently no protocols to allow a full interface."

"I see," Dawn said. "What do you need to be able to take the whole thing over and run it yourself?"

"An expanded service mandate would be required," Service said. "The merger of the indicated services would allow you to take complete control of both communities."

"All in favor of expanding the mandate?" Dawn asked.

Everyone raised their hands in agreement.

"Service, your mandate has been expanded. Get it done."

"Acknowledged. System integration completed. Partial implementation with existing equipment has commenced. New equipment has been routed. Full deployment within three hours."

Speaker Noguchi appeared in her seat beneath her meki. "Sorry for the delay. There are many angry people here. I cannot stay long. I wish to give you this one message. Our people did not do this horrible thing. We deny any accusation."

Dawn shook her head. "We haven't had an accusation, but thank you all the same. Do you have any evidence regarding the attack?"

"No. We did not think to set up new cameras. We thought the conflict had ended."

"We haven't heard from the other side yet. I'm sorry for your losses. All of us here are sorry for the recent loss of life and want to find a way to stop it, Kanami."

Kanami bowed her head. "I must go. I am being summoned." Her image flowed away as she was turning her head.

Darren scowled. "Without proof, it's going to be her word against the grumpy cardinal's."

"We should wait to hear from him before passing judgment." Misa leaned back and looked at Dawn. "Jumping to conclusions helps no one."

"Agreed," Dawn said. "Service, what's the status of Cardinal Nunn?"

"Cardinal Nunn is in a public area near the main tube in Ablom delivering last rites to the dead. One additional man who was wounded has passed away."

"Damn. Give him time to do what he has to do, but we need to talk to him. The sooner the better."

It was shortly after 22:00 when the cardinal appeared. His cheeks were flushed, his brows knit tightly together. "I absolutely deny that any of our good people had anything at all to do with this madness."

He crossed his arms. "You know who did this; it's obvious. They snuck in like the devil and planted those bombs."

Dawn scowled. "Are you saying they blew up their own people, too?"

"I didn't say they were experts. Maybe they screwed up and killed their own people by accident. You can plainly see it was not our people."

Darren leaned in. "Do you have any proof at all? Any evidence to show who did it?"

"No. We thought it was all over. We didn't think for a moment they would do something this evil. I'll make sure we put recorders in place so we can guard against another attack. What are you doing to bring the perpetrators to justice?"

"Darren was still here when the bombs went off," Dawn said. "He made sure forensics was sent in, as well as the damage repair bots. As soon as we have a full analysis, we'll let you know."

"Fine. I'll expect something shortly…" Cardinal Nunn had focused on Dawn for the brief time he'd been in contact. His voice trailed off when he noticed Misa. "What is *she* doing there? Why do you have one of them seated at your table?"

Misa shifted uncomfortably. "I am Misa Kobato. I'm a delegate from up north, near Plato."

"Why does it feel like all of a sudden you have a delegate sympathetic to their side? This isn't justice at all. I object in the strongest terms."

"From a legal standpoint," the professor said, "you have a right to object, but you should know that Misa here has over ten million votes. She's highly regarded in her community, and your objection will be overruled, should you choose to make it official."

The cardinal crossed his arms in defiance. "I make it an official objection."

The automated responses came from Service like staccato rapid fire. "Your objection is noted. Your objection is recognized as representing a potentially valid concern. Your concern is unfounded. Your objection is overruled."

Darren laughed.

Dawn frowned at him.

The professor continued, "Now that we've settled that matter, please convey to your people that we're investigating, and we'll determine who committed this violent act. Those responsible will be held to account."

The cardinal's hand moved out of the display. "Fine." He faded out.

Ellie shook her head. "I don't know when I've met a more pleasant man."

Sam laughed. "Ellie, ya kill me. You know that? Ya kill me."

Dawn leaned back in her chair. "Service, when will we have a report back from the forensics team?"

"The team is onsite now," Service said, "and has begun taking samples. It will be several hours before they are complete."

"Let us know as soon as there's any new information."

Ava was going through her personal messages. Since only she could see her display, the effect was of an elf waving and fluttering her hands wildly in the air. "Is this a good time to take a break?"

Dawn took a deep breath. "Will everyone please keep in mind that we need to settle on a solution to the long-term problem? Otherwise, let's aim for tomorrow morning, if we can make it that long without another attack."

Everyone but Dawn and Misa left the room. Dawn was going to leave, but the look on Misa's face told her to stay for a moment. "You all right?"

Misa looked down at her hands, folded neatly in her lap. "All my life, I grew up reading stories of places where people were discriminated against because of how they looked. Hair color, eye color, skin color... it was all so academic. History is filled with the stupid things humans do to each other. Yet, here's this man, filled with blatant racism, right here on Luna. On top of it, he hates Asian features! *My* features. That was such a strange, awful feeling. It hurt, and it made me angry. I could see myself coming to hate him, and I don't like that feeling."

"He's certainly been a handful. Whatever we decide, it'll have to wear away a generation of hate. That's not going to be so easy."

Misa took a deep breath and exhaled slowly. "Sushi."

"What?"

"I feel like sushi. Hungry?"

"I am, actually," Dawn said. "Want to hop on the tube with me and go get some sushi?"

"Ah," Misa said. "Yes. Follow the Leader. After you."

"I've been meaning to ask, why did you come all the way down here by loop? A shuttle would've been faster, or you could've connected remotely."

Misa blushed. "I have an irrational fear of heights. Taking a shuttle would probably require sedation. As for remote connection, it's simply because, in the excitement, I forgot to ask. I didn't know I could do that. The assumption that I needed to be here, coupled with my fear of heights, trapped me into thinking the loop was my only option."

"Afraid of heights? That's a shame. Let me tell you where I was last week."

They stepped into the slide tube together, gliding toward Moretus Plains.

"Someplace high, I suppose," Misa said.

"Heinlein Aviary in Zeeman. I went flying for a week."

"Oh, good grief. You strapped wings on? I'm almost certain I'd have an attack at the mere sight of the place. I'd much rather go swimming. Being underwater is my favorite feeling, as long as I can breathe."

"Here we are," Dawn said. "Watch your step." She stepped off at the exit near their destination. Bright, colorful signs gave the names or logos of establishments on the walls of the corridor. Misa followed closely with ease.

Not far from the tube exit was Tom's Tycho Traditional Seafood Tavern. The sign claimed it followed the three-hundred-year-old traditions of Tycho-style sushi. Dawn led Misa inside. Most surfaces were brilliant white tiles with red trim and baseboards.

A tall, slender man whose ears were a little too large smiled as they walked in. He was wearing white with a black apron. The name ALLEN floated above his head. "Welcome, friends. Sit anywhere you like. Special tonight is Meji tuna cucumber roll, extra spicy."

"Thanks," Dawn said. "Where's Tom tonight?"

"Oh, sorry. Tom's not felt up to it all week. He's slowing down a bit. You know he's 108 now. That's why I'm here. I found out Tom was getting a bit tired, but he didn't want to walk away entirely. I worked out a deal with him. I'll be here from now on, most every night. Mandy and Michelle still split the day shift. He'll come in when he feels up to it, and we'll split the work. What are you in the mood for tonight?"

"Sushi," Misa said. "The tuna roll sounded good. What kind of sauce do you use?"

"Sriracha sauce and sesame oil with a touch of garlic. I have traditional soy sauce as well as wasabi. The wasabi came in fresh from Demonax this afternoon."

"Are these from tuna fish, or is the meat factory made?"

"Tycho Traditional Style uses real fish," Allen said. "Factory made isn't allowed."

Dawn shook her head. "I kind of prefer the factory-made tuna myself. Isn't there a danger of parasites with real tuna?"

"Oh, sure," Allen said, "it's a risk, but we use detectors to make sure nothing like that ever gets into the sushi. No worries."

"Still, I'll have an old fashioned. I like the cream cheese."

"Okay then, one roll each?"

Both ladies grinned, and Allen turned to the work counter.

"So you prefer factory meat?" Misa asked.

"Well, tuna, anyway, and the big meats, always. I'm good with real prawns and smaller fish. Oysters and clams, things like that. But tuna, I don't know."

"What about pork? Would you ever eat real pork?"

"What animal does real pork come from?" Dawn asked.

"It's called a pig." Misa called one up on her display and shared it.

"Oh, hell no. Look, it has a smile. I couldn't kill that just for food."

"Yeah, but you like bacon, right? Ribs, too? All used to come from these fat things."

"Yeah," Dawn said. "I'll stick to factory-grown for the big meats. I mean, fish are fine, but I can't imagine having to kill animals for their meat. Have you ever…"

Misa shook her head. "I feel the same way you do, except for tuna. They may be big, but they're dumb as a rock. Now dolphin or octopus, never. Way too smart."

Dawn laughed. "Yeah, I get you."

"Would you two like some sake?" Allen asked.

"Yes, please," Dawn said.

Misa frowned. "Where I'm from, we usually pair it with a nice, dark beer. Something with extra hops."

"Ah," Allen said. "I think we have something like that in the back." He swiped his display. "Alpine Valley Ale. We have a case. Will that do?"

"Sure," Misa said. "I like that stuff. That'll do."

Dawn raised two fingers. "Make it two, please. I'll give it a try."

"Coming right up," Allen said. He headed to the back room.

"Do you come here often?" Misa asked.

Dawn shrugged. "Often enough that I know everyone by name. Not so often that Uncle Keegan gets jealous."

"Your uncle has a place?"

"Yup. About six blocks up that way. Classic diner style. He does all the cooking. Etto does the drinks and all the bartending."

"Sounds nice," Misa said. "It's good when a family is close. I'll be sure to drop in before I head back north."

"Where are you staying?"

"I have a place over in Grissom Park reserved for me, but it's late. I'm wondering if maybe I should move it to somewhere near here."

"If you do," said Dawn, "it's a real easy slide down to Grissom Park from the residence levels. Pretty much a straight shot."

"Oh, but how much of that is down?"

"Lots." Dawn grinned. "A really nice drop and slide."

Misa shook her head. "Heights, remember?"

Dawn's grin faded. "Oh, sorry. I got ahead of myself. You can take the lift down to the main trunk and take the tube over. That's easy, too."

Misa swiped her display. "Sabisu, show me accommodations available nearby." She swiped, pointed twice, and smiled. "I found one in the lower levels. Short ride on the lift from here and close to the tube to Grissom Park."

"Excellent," Dawn said. "If you don't like drop tubes, I'll bet you hate air lifts."

"Air lifts? Oh, hell no. Nothing under you but a blower that could cut out at any time. Don't tell me you use those things."

"I don't use them often. The first time I tried one, I was wearing a skirt."

"Oh, no." Misa put her hand over her heart. "Didn't anyone warn you?"

"Nope. I heard some boys laughing behind me, but I didn't really think about it."

Misa shook her head. "I feel like I know where this is going."

Dawn grinned. "It was worse. I flipped a couple of times, and my panties blew right off."

Misa shrieked and laughed, then put her hand over her mouth. Her face flushed as she glanced around.

Allen set the bottles down. "Here's the beer. Your food will be right up."

"Thank you," Dawn said.

"What did you do?" Misa asked.

"Luckily, I landed near a printer and had a new pair on in a couple of minutes. But that was really uncomfortable. The next day, I received a dozen white roses and a note. It was an apology for laughing and an admission that they should have warned me before I jumped in. Kind of sweet, really."

"I would never have wanted to see any of them again."

Dawn gave a weak smile. "I had Service flag each and every one of them and warn me if there was even the slightest possibility of us intersecting. I never investigated, but I thought the flowers reeked of parental oversight."

Misa smirked. "Still, they were a nice touch."

Allen set their sushi in front of them. "Let me know if you need anything."

Dawn smiled at him. "Thanks."

"Do you avoid air lifts now?" Misa asked.

"Mostly. My sister loves them. She wears airtights and dances the whole way up."

Misa giggled. "Your family sounds wonderful." Her deep brown eyes glistened in the neon light.

"It's me, Fawn, Uncle Keegan, and Etto. We have a grandmother who's an astronomer at Kosberg Observatory, too. Kosberg is a little crater in Gagarin."

Misa sipped her drink. "You haven't mentioned your folks. Can I ask?"

Dawn shrugged. "They passed away a decade ago while they were vacationing on Mars. I was old enough to care for Fawn until she came of age. Keegan and Etto helped."

"That must have been difficult, being a big sister and a parent at the same time."

"Fawn's all grown up now, and that's pretty much it. Nothing special, really."

"Sure," Misa said, "sounds like you have a boring life, Prime Minister Sheffield."

Dawn laughed. "Yeah, then that happened."

* * * * *

Opportunity

Monday, September 27, 3288, 7:00

Elliot had completed his usual grooming and was again awaiting the arrival of his morning meal, browsing his automated search feeds. One of the stories had a green checkmark next to it. When he saw it came from Luna, he raised an eyebrow and started the segment.

"Hello, everyone, and welcome to the Tony Renard Show. I'm Tony Renard, and this is the show with my name on it." He paused and tilted his head. "I'll bet you already knew that."

Tony swung to face a new camera. "So let's recap the things you should already know. Item one, some kids from Ablom were exploring outside their dome and met another group of kids doing the exact same thing. They were from neighboring Takiyama. Rock fight. One kid's helmet got cracked, but he's safe at home in Ablom. Item two, parents are dicks. Someone decided that a kid with a cracked helmet was worth trying to kill more people and set off a bomb, cracking the Takiyama dome."

He abruptly turned to yet another camera angle. "Now, when I say parents are dicks, I'm speaking in hyperbole. You know, not every parent is a dick. Some are pretty okay. Like my mum." He grinned. "Hi, Mum. Got your text. Sorry." He waved weakly to the camera.

Spinning back to the previous camera angle, Tony continued, "Meanwhile, item three, we all held a vote and created the Eleventh

Lunar Assembly to deal with this problem. In our collective wisdom, we selected a very popular professor from Tycho University." He waved. "Hey, Professor Corvair. Remember me?" His face fell. "No? Oh. Okay, well then, we added trade guru Darren Garfield. Not sure how that helps. Then there's the world-renowned pop singer, Ava Wallaby. Great lungs, nice, pointy ears. Bit young, though. Not sure how well she can solve problems. So maybe that's why we put Ellie Lester up there, too. She's been around the block plenty of times. Did you see her in *Escape from the Waters of Europa*? Classic. Glad she's there. I think she could fix anything. Just better find out who's writing the script.

"Then there's Sam Freeman. He's the coordinator for the Southern Hopper League, and a bartender. I'll try not to pass judgment on that one. Being a bartender might actually be the right skill for this job. Speaking of jobs, Misa Kobato's had a few. She's had so many jobs, I could do an entire show just listing them. I don't know if she has the skills for this job, but if I ever needed a guest host, she's the one I'd ask first, mainly because both Ellie and Ava have already turned me down. Of course, at the top of the heap is our new prime minister, Dawn Aubrianne Sheffield. She makes dresses and likes to fly for fun. As far as anyone can tell, she got into an accident, had a meme go viral, and people voted for the pretty girl in the meme. Sure. That'll work."

He spun again, but the camera didn't change. "So... wait..." He slowly rotated back to the active camera. "I thought we were going to spin on that one. Sorry." He grinned. "So then the fun really got started. There was a fight and more bombs. This time, lots of people ended up dead."

Tony spun to another camera angle. "That's it, then. The Eleventh Lunar Assembly has now completed their first day of work. Eighteen dead bodies later, they decided to go get some rest. Not that I blame them; being less than competent is hard work. We called them up to fix this whole thing, and the very first day on the job, we got dead bodies sprawled in the lunar dust. I can only hope, as do we all, they have a great day tomorrow. This is Tony Renard, and I hope they can do better."

Elliot smiled to himself. This was unexpected. A regular assembly wasn't due to be called for another couple of decades. This opened a window of opportunity, but he had to move quickly. Time was of the essence now. "Send a copy of this to the other Yolo directors with this message. 'The majority of Lunar votes concentrated into one room. Can we afford to wait?'"

"Message sent," Bil said.

"Ping Director Lawder. Let him know I want to talk, privately."

"Acknowledged."

"Show me the list of delegates of the current Lunar Assembly."

He looked over the list and chuckled. "Yes. This should make it incredibly easy."

"You have a private call from Director Lawder," Bil said.

"Hello, Nels. Did you look at the story I sent you?"

Nels Lawder's image faded in, seated at the opposite side of the table. His thinning, disheveled hair was highlighted by a glowing red star. "Yes, of course I did. Some petty violence between local Loonies. So what? Why is it important to you, and what do you mean by not being able to afford to wait?"

Elliot shook his head. The unkempt appearance of his associate always made him cringe inside. "You missed the point, Nels. It's not the violence; that's only background noise. The people of Luna, owners one and all of the Lunar Sustainability Cooperative, have delegated their votes, to the tune of nearly 90 percent, to an assembly, which is what they call their temporary board of directors. That means anything they decide is law. All we need to do is convince the majority of those seven people to join us, and Yolo gets Luna. The whole thing. It would double our population and give us several new board seats. We'd have a larger delegation than Masters and Billings."

"Yolo with more seats than M&B? That won't give us control, you know. We'd have to be elected."

"Yes, yes. I know that. But it would better position us to make that move in the long-term."

"What's the risk here?" Nels asked.

"Risk? All we need to do is lean on them, maybe offer them a golden parachute. They'll sign up before the dust settles. And if they don't, we simply land with a present from Mercorps and put guns to their heads. Luna isn't part of the Federation. We can do anything we want, as long as we win."

"As long as we win. What if it doesn't work? Assume it all fails. Then what?"

Elliot shrugged. "We blame Wayne, let him take the fall, pick up the pieces, and try again later."

"Are you sure you can lay it all on him, then?"

"I think so. Actually, I think I can put him on a leash. I'll let you know tomorrow if it works."

Nels scoffed. "I'd very much like to see that. However, should you fail, I'll also take great pleasure in seeing you swim with the stars. I see no downside for me, so I'll support your position as long as it remains so."

"Agreed. I expected nothing more. Good day, Director Lawder."

"Good day, Director Humboldt." His image faded, as did Elliot's fake smile.

* * * * *

The Third Hand

Monday, September 27, 3288, 8:33

Dawn looked into the center of the dark conference table, where the display of the two communities had lost all its indicators. "What do you mean, you have no internal feeds anymore? Both of them?"

"Affirmative, Prime Minister," Service said. "Takiyama was cut off at 4:23. The Ablom Refuge cut off at 5:36. Each represents a physical break and posted guards have blocked all automated attempts at reconnection on both sides."

Darren scowled. "Is there a way to sneak in underground and reconnect?"

"It would be possible," Service said, "to reconnect to each dome by micro-tunneling under the break and establishing a temporary patch downstream. The guards would not be aware of a reconnection. However, this may be discovered once you attempt communications."

Dawn frowned. "Do it. Reconnect both communities, but don't allow detection. Make a passive link to the internal surveillance. Also, I want you to establish other connections to their life support and security systems."

The professor raised his eyebrows. "Do you have something in mind, Dawn? That sounds a little draconian."

"I think we're close to deciding on a course of action now. I want to be sure we have some leverage." She yawned. She hadn't slept well.

"I think it might be a good idea if we were able to take control of the entire situation over there."

"We should investigate other means of establishing communications in a more open and public manner."

Ava's eyes opened wide. "Professor's right, and I know exactly how to do it! Back when we were doing big panning and scanning shots, we used mobile cameras. We could mount displays on things like that, and maybe see about a remote hookup. Let me call my crew and see what we can get into place for you."

Dawn raised a finger. "Make sure you have backups in case there are problems."

Ava started furiously waving her hands through the air. Her meki bounced around like it had come loose.

"Why can't we put some weapons on those things?" Darren asked. "A show of force might be what we need right now." He looked around the table for support.

"I'm sure they have security bots we could use if it came to that," Dawn said. "I hope it doesn't, and now's not the time. Let's talk about the two ideas we currently have for solving this crisis. Ava's idea is to focus on the kids, get them into social programs that open them up to their neighbors and help to establish social connections. Misa's idea is a little more invasive. We close down both domes and redistribute the populations. That on its own should mix their people in with ours and force them to adapt and grow more tolerant."

Darren crossed his arms and sat back. "In theory."

"Yes, in theory. In theory, one of these could work, though I believe in reality, both may be rejected, and it's going to have to be forced on them. Or we have to find another solution."

"I don't know," Sam said. "I don't like the idea of forcing people to do something they don't want to do simply because we think it'll solve a problem." He shrugged. "Is that the way we really want to go about this?"

"Sam's right." Ellie placed her palms on the table. "And so are Misa and Ava. We need to split them up, out of their domes, but not by small family groups. Maybe we split them into ten chunks each. Make it possible for them to still feel the comfort of their community, but make sure they have to travel a bit to meet up with other parts. Then implement the social interaction programs on top of that. Include everyone who wants to come, but make sure they all feel welcome. Most importantly—and this is the key—they have to agree to everything in advance. This can't be forced on them. We need to find a way to convince them to do this voluntarily."

Darren laughed. "Wishful thinking."

Dawn leaned forward with a thoughtful look. "Voluntarily. That's a big sticking point, isn't it? I mean, right now it seems like neither side would be willing to cooperate. That reminds me, do we have the forensics results yet?"

"The forensics investigation is incomplete," Service said. "Of the samples analyzed so far, there is evidence that there were two different sets of explosive devices."

The professor furled his brow. "Service, extrapolate. Assume two equal sets of devices. What would the effect of only one of those sets exploding be?"

"If calculations are correct, one set alone would have breached the unoccupied section of the tunnel, but not endangered neighboring sections."

"Is it safe to assume that one set exploding might trigger the other?"

"There is a high probability," Service said.

Darren shook his head. "Those stupid bastards. They both did it."

Dawn pointed to Ava. "Get me comms to the domes as quickly as you can. I need to speak to them at once. Anything. Even a one-way display will do."

"I have assets available," Ava said, "but I need to coordinate with two different transportation services, as well as the local maintenance service. I found an admirer with equipment from a farm not far from Minkowski. Good news is they're indoor-outdoor drones."

"Service, take control of the transportation services Ava requires; get it done."

"Acknowledged," Service said. "Integration complete. One of the drones will arrive at the Ablom main complex in five minutes. Nine minutes for the second drone to arrive at Takiyama. They will be cycled through maintenance airlocks once connectivity has been established."

"Service, are you ready to reconnect surveillance?"

"Affirmative."

"Do it," Dawn said. "Connect everything. Send the drones to the current locations of the speaker and the cardinal. Time it so we get to each of them at the same time. I want a three-way connection from the start." Dawn's face grew dark with intent. "It's time to end this."

Minutes passed like hours, until at last both opponents appeared under their mekis.

"I'll make this brief," Dawn said. "We have enough evidence to show who planted the bombs."

Kanami remained silent.

The cardinal virtually exploded. "Finally! Now we have proof of their evil, and I certainly hope justice is harsh."

"Cardinal Nunn, I assure you there will be harsh justice. However, you need to listen to all I have to say first. We have evidence that there were two sets of explosives. A single set by itself would have ruptured the sealed section of the tube, but not, I repeat, *not* have caused any loss of life or damaged anything beyond that one section of tube. The evidence suggests that two groups, one from each side, planted explosives on opposite sides of the tube. Once one set was triggered, the second was set off by the first. The resulting damage to the bulkheads, the deaths on both sides, none of it was expected by either group. It's only because of your mutual dislike for each other, and your blind anger in this crisis, that both sides had elements who took it upon themselves to take this action. Both sides must share this guilt, and both sides shall be dealt with harshly."

Cardinal Nunn's mouth was open, but he didn't speak.

Kanami broke the silence. "Before your drone came to me, we received the confession of a small group of people in this matter. It causes us great shame to accept our part in this. Their story matches closely with yours. They intended no harm, other than to sever the tube."

The cardinal was clearly angry. "Lies. All lies, fabrication. Our people would never do such a thing."

"Even though your side was the first to actually use explosives?" Dawn shook her head. "I think you need to talk to your people. Present this evidence to them. We can give you the chemical signatures." She nodded to the professor.

The professor nodded back. "I'm sending the partial report now. The full report will be completed in a little while."

"We now need to discuss what happens next," Dawn said. "We need a plan of action, and we need to put it into motion as quickly as possible."

Over the course of the next hour, all the ideas and strategies were laid bare and debated. The discussion moved forward slowly. In the end, both sides agreed to consider some form of resettlement, with the details to be worked out later.

* * *

As they walked out of the conference room, Ellie was speaking to Dawn. "That's the damndest thing I've ever heard."

"I know. I hope it's all worth it."

Dawn joined Misa, Darren, Ellie, and Sam for lunch down at the Chesapeake. The table they chose was more isolated, while still offering an amazing view over the underwater reef.

"That bit Tony Renard did on us was painful to watch," Darren said. "It's not our fault these people are crazy."

"He was factually correct," Misa said, "just not very nice about it. That's what he does, tell the truth, and make it a little funny. I laughed, but it did hurt. Still, we can't pay much attention to that sort of thing. We have to work out a solution. Solve this problem. Then we can say we accomplished something."

"If people are only going to be negative about it, what does it matter?"

"It matters how you feel about it. In the end, you know if we're doing a good job. You can feel it in your bones. What other people think is like passing gas in a vac suit. Makes a noise and pollutes the air, but for them, not you."

Darren made a face. "Did you make a fart joke on our first date?"

"This is not a date, Darren," Misa said.

"Says the lady making fart jokes."

Ellie laughed. "Is that sort of humor how you usually start a courtship, Darren? Because if Misa isn't interested, I might know someone who is."

"Yeah, no," Darren said. "Not going down that path again. Last time someone matched me with a partner was bad enough."

"Oh, what happened?" Misa asked.

"Married her. Lasted a year."

"Now I'm wondering," Ellie said. "Who canceled the contract?"

"Okay, fine. Yes, she canceled. But only because I was about to."

Dawn patted his shoulder. "Of course you were."

Sam pointed to the far end of the reef. "What's that pink cloud?"

The others turned and looked.

"Krill," Misa said. "Pretty much the bottom of the food chain right there."

"And they're delicious," Ellie said. "You've had Bagoong, right?"

"Oh, sure," Sam said. "Goes good with green mangoes. Never asked what it was made of."

"Please excuse the interruption, Prime Minister," Service said. "The final report concerning the explosions in Minkowski Crater is complete."

"Good. Let's have it."

"All detonations occurred in a precise pattern designed to produce the maximum possible pressure wave at each adjoining bulkhead. Inventory analysis indicates the explosives planted by each group were augmented by additional explosives. The conclusion is that while both groups contributed to the attack, a third unknown entity enhanced and assumed control of the event."

"Wait," Sam said. "Didn't the first set trigger the second?"

"Negative," Service said. "Neither set contributed by the known perpetrators was placed in a position to detonate the other set. The recorded events indicate a sequenced blast pattern inconsistent with random occurrence. According to confessions, one set of explosives was set to detonate simultaneously thirty minutes prior to the other. The second set was also set to detonate in a single moment."

"Someone was not only watching," Dawn said, "they decided to kill people, too. That's not good. Service, begin a search. See if you can track down who did this."

"Acknowledged."

"I'm feeling uneasy about this," Ellie said. "Who could do such a thing?"

"More importantly, how?" Misa asked. "How did they get there? Is this another local, maybe?"

"Might be," Ellie said. "Whoever they are, they had to have seen at least the first group go out. It does seem like they are local."

"Or they have assets we can't track," Darren said.

"What do you mean?" Dawn asked. "Like controllers?"

"Maybe," Darren said. "I'm thinking, could someone have gotten control over a few of them with their own service?"

"If they managed that," Dawn said, "they might be a lot more dangerous than this. What would be the point?"

"Hard to say," Misa said. "Are they trying to make a point? Maybe scare the two sides into backing off?"

"That's not exactly what's happened so far," Sam said. "I'd say maybe someone's looking to up the body count. Sow discontent and pain while not getting caught."

"So, not on our side, then," Darren said.

"Nope," Sam said. "Decidedly not."

Dawn shook her head. "I think we need to have a long talk with our friends in Minkowski, but first, I think we need to make sure we have leverage. A lot of it."

They spent the rest of their meal making plans and setting them in motion, eventually finding their way back to the conference room. It wasn't until much later that evening that they finally got both the cardinal and the speaker back online.

"You're certain there was a third hand in this event?" the cardinal asked.

"Yes, Cardinal. Our earlier conclusion was close to the mark; however, further evidence suggests that the explosives contributed by the two sides were simply not enough to cause all the damage seen. Then there's the matter of the detonations themselves. The sequence was too perfect, too focused at bursting both bulkheads at the same time. We've confirmed the additional explosives don't match the previous sets."

"Does this mean you're reconsidering our resettlement?"

Dawn spoke calmly and firmly. "No, Cardinal, the underlying issues of this conflict need to be addressed. Both Ablom and Takiyama need to assimilate into Lunar society at least enough to become tolerant of other people. This is non-negotiable. It's going to happen. The only question now is exactly what form that will take. Much of it depends on how willing you are to cooperate."

Kanami interrupted. "Our people will not allow you to dictate to us. We will stand resolute to protect our way of life."

"Even if that way of life leads to conflict and death? Look, eighteen people died because your conflict probably triggered a psychopath. I know you're not directly responsible, but the fact is, without your initial actions, this wouldn't have happened. So again, cooperate and you'll have some control over it, or we'll take the situation in hand and impose our most extreme solution on you."

Cardinal Nunn crossed his arms over his chest. "And what might that be?"

"We take immediate family units," Dawn said, "and scatter them all over Luna. We then permanently block contact between any members of your community outside those family units. All children below the age of ten enter a required socialization program. They'll literally be *required* to play with other children."

"That is absolutely unacceptable. It is also beyond your ability. You would never be able to force us to leave our city."

Dawn leaned in. "Service, implement phase one in both domes."

"Acknowledged," Service said.

"What was that about? What have you done?"

"You'll figure it out in a moment, Cardinal."

Kanami suddenly became distracted. She began shouting to her unseen companions. "No! No, tell them to go back! Don't let those doors close!" Her image snapped off.

A few moments later, Cardinal Nunn also became distracted. "No, you wouldn't. You wouldn't dare do that."

"Cardinal," Dawn said, "my indications tell me that the Ablom city aquarium is now under my full control. Same for Takiyama. With a single command, I can drain the whole damned thing to open space.

How much of your food supply is that? Before you answer, understand this. I'm ready to take complete control of all food sources the moment you push me into it. Your community will move. Your people will be scattered. How scattered, and under what conditions, is now entirely up to you."

Kanami reappeared. She was visibly shaken. "We have confirmed, you are in control of our aquarium, our main source of agriculture. You have made your point. I am hoping your previous position was the starting point for negotiations. If so, we place ourselves at your mercy. We will cooperate."

"Fine," the cardinal said. "Point taken. If you're really open to negotiations, no more than two large adjacent groups, and no communications block. Voluntary socialization only."

"Cardinal Nunn, you have fifteen thousand people. Fifteen groups, about a thousand each. Same size for you, too, Speaker Noguchi, even though you have fewer people. No promises of adjacency, but no communications block, and no travel block. You can communicate and visit freely. That's a lot of people, and we'll need to find twenty-three cities to put you all in. Now, socialization is important. It's not that hard. Take your kids to the park and let them play with, and get to know other children. I'll leave it up to you, but when people get to know each other, they're a lot less likely to want to start fights. At least, that's the hope."

"What about our temple?" Kanami asked. "What will happen to it?"

"Both your communities will be dismantled and recycled," Dawn said. "However, nothing will prevent you from setting up new temples near any of your people. You might even get more visitors that way."

After both had agreed to a timetable, they faded away. Dawn allowed herself to relax back into her chair.

Misa chuckled. "Nice play, Dawn. Remind me never to play poker with you."

Elle looked puzzled. "What are you saying?"

"I spent many years, when I was younger, working on our local reef. I love the feeling of being beneath the water. I've studied how the artificial ecosystems work to maintain sustainability."

Ellie looked puzzled. "What does that mean?"

"It means that I know one simple fact." Misa shook her head with a smile. "Not a single aquarium on Luna was ever built with a drain pipe leading to vacuum. What would it ever be used for? Unless Dawn managed to build in some major infrastructure, she was bluffing."

Dawn shrugged with a half-smile. "Maybe. But I'll never tell."

Darren laughed.

* * *

After dinner, Dawn returned to her apartment. She spent more time than usual in the fresher, sorting her thoughts. Later, she settled in to watch the news.

"Please pardon the interruption, Prime Minister. You have a call from your grandmother, Hazel."

Dawn swiped away the news feed. "Hello, Grandma," said Dawn. "How have you been?"

Hazel's image faded in under her silver telescope meki. "I'm doing fine, especially now that my granddaughter is going to be in the history books." She grinned.

"It's not really that big a deal." Dawn shrugged. "We have to sort out some anger issues."

"It may not be to you, but Lunar Assemblies are rare things." She pointed upward for emphasis. "The most limited form of government humans have ever had."

Dawn shook her head. "It's only a little committee to solve a problem the services can't deal with."

"Exactly. And it's still a big deal."

"Has Fawn reached out to you yet?"

"Of course not." Hazel tilted her head. "We buried that tunnel pretty deep."

"Yes, you did, and it's going to take both of you to dig it clear."

"I didn't call you to be lectured."

"I'm not trying to lecture you." Dawn shrugged. "I see a torn cloth; I'm trying to stitch it back together."

Hazel sighed. "As you should. I'll ping her, see if she responds. Good enough?"

"It's a start."

"How are Keegan and Etto?"

"They're fine. Happy as can be, cooking and tending bar, and talking and laughing."

Hazel nodded thoughtfully.

"They're also as easy to reach as I am. As anyone on Luna is. You should call them. At least Keegan."

Hazel shook her head. "I think it would make us both cry."

"Maybe that's what you need. His sister married your son, and while they're both gone, you two are still here, and still family."

Hazel began to say something, then stopped. "It's so easy to see why people chose you to be the prime minister. You have an inner strength I can only envy."

Dawn's mouth opened, but words failed her.

"I love you, dear granddaughter. I'll ping them both. I'll try, for you. I promise."

"You do that, but do it for yourself. No one here ever stopped loving you, even if things got heated. You know that, right?"

Hazel shook her head. "Heated is an understatement, but I get your meaning."

"It's good to talk to you again. Give my love to Jude."

"Okay, honey. Sleep well."

"You, too," Dawn said. "Good night."

* * * * *

Normal Space

Tuesday, September 28, 3288, 7:15

In the emptiness of space, well beyond the orbit of the Moon, an empty patch of nothingness twitched. A small patch of blue fuzz came into existence and began to glow, then grew rapidly, stretching into a large, elongated shape. The growth halted, but grew brighter, flaring with rapid strikes of white lightning. The whole mass flared, then it rapidly faded and left behind the *Pang Yu*.

"Conn, Ops, normal space detected," Jake said. "Jump transition complete."

"Jump transition complete, Conn aye," Tong said. "Engineering, Conn, rig for dissipation."

"Rig for dissipation, Engineering, aye," Brenna said.

The ship shuddered as radiator fins extended to dissipate a week of accumulated heat.

"Conn, Engineering, fins extended, heat dissipating. Heat sink is at 527 and falling."

"Conn, aye," Tong said. "All hands, secure from the maneuvering watch, set the freefall watch, section two." He turned to Jake. "I'm on watch. Would you mind doing a coffee run?"

"Sure," Jake said. "Black and sweet, right?"

"Yup. Thanks. Ship, notify Squadron 16 we've returned to Earth orbit. Give them our location, vector, and a full status report. Request all stored communications for the crew."

"Acknowledged," said the ship.

"You know," said Jake, "someday, they are going to teach that thing how to do a proper response."

"Somewhere there is a corporate scumbag sitting on that little code change asking for several million credits. It's called the Ship Communications Upgrade, and I'm telling you, it actually does exist."

"Lieutenant Commander Sianothai," said the ship, "you have a call from Vice Admiral Lebherz."

"Vice Admiral Lebherz, *Pang Yu*. What can I do for you, ma'am?"

"Tong," the admiral said, "it said in your report you still have two Assegai-class missiles on board. Please explain why you didn't use them on your last mission?"

"Well, ma'am," said Tong, "one of them refused to boot up. Dead controller, I think. The other has a leak in the battery pack. Corroded the trigger. No trigger, no boom."

"Why didn't you repair and fire them?"

"The *Pang Yu* only has two repair bot installations. You remember that, right?"

"I don't have time for details like that," said the admiral.

"I know, ma'am, but if you'll look at the record of our last refit, when our Assegai missile repair bot was replaced by that brand new Cutlass missile repair bot, I did file a formal protest. The *Jiang Guang*-class missile cruiser was never designed for three different types of missiles."

"Nonsense. *Jiangs* are supposed to be able to carry a half dozen different types."

Tong shook his head. "Back when you could use the same batteries to launch them, the same magazines to hold them, and the same bots to fix them, absolutely. But not when they're all mutually exclusive. To be honest with you, I'm surprised we can target them with the same fire control system."

The admiral sighed. "Don't give them any ideas. I see you're headed to station four. I'll authorize the disposal of the extras. I think you're scheduled to get the new 88s as a replacement system."

"Ma'am, that still sticks us with three types of missiles. Can we get rid of the Cutlass? The Barongs are a proven system. I can see us having two types again, but please don't stick us with three."

"I see you have a couple of empty staterooms. Maybe we can convert one into a third repair bot bay."

Tong shook his head. "I'd rather fill them with the crew I was promised. I'm still four people short of a full complement. That's almost half the crew. The only reason we have three watches forward is because I'm standing watch. Aft was in port and starboard on the way back. Kip and I stood back-to-back watches aft on the way out because our brilliant new ensign, right out of school, still needed to qualify. It's certainly a good mark in her record that she qualified in less than a month as it is."

"There's nothing I can do on that account. Talk to the personnel office."

"Yes, ma'am. I have. All they ever tell me is budget cuts."

"Understood," she said. "Welcome back to the warm part of the system. I'll talk to you later."

"Thank you, ma'am. *Pang Yu*, out." He briefly scanned a list of messages, as was protocol, then released them to the crew.

"Woohoo!" Jake flipped eagerly through a large set of messages as he handed Tong a warm bag of coffee. "Malee sent me a bunch."

Tong looked up from his display. "New one? What happened to Jessica?"

"Oh, she didn't want to wait. She left me while we were out by Titan, last patrol. She's dating some mechanic on station four now. I met Malee about a week after we got back. We spent the whole refit hanging out together. I'm not sure how serious it'll be, but she's a lot of fun to spend time with."

"She a station rat? Legs all wobbly in high gee?"

"She's from Endurance Halo," said Jake. "Used to almost a full gee. She's got these nice, thick shins, real curvy. Not twigs like station rats. Dark hair, dark eyes, and a pretty smile."

"Sounds nice. Now if you don't mind, I have to go file another req for more crew."

* * * * *

Ice Pirate

Tuesday, September 28, 3288, 8:30

All five directors of Yolo Consumer Goods had gathered in the senior director's suite. They sat in large, comfortable, burgundy felt chairs around a central dark display table. The walls were covered in a black and silver pattern. Large, framed images showing Martian landscapes adorned the walls. The largest was of the series of great cylindrical domes over the Calydon Fossa Canyon, one of the earliest large habitation projects on Mars.

Wayne sat in front of the beautiful canyon image. "All right then, Elliot, what are you on about the Moon, now?"

"Senior Director," said Elliot, "I am suggesting we make our move on Luna now, as soon as possible. The majority of their votes are currently concentrated in the hands of a bunch of amateurs. It will be like finding sand on the plains. A good little lean, maybe pointing a few guns, offer a parachute clause, and as easy as you can imagine, Luna joins Yolo."

"As easy as that ice deal back in '85?" Lisanne Howard asked. "Didn't I see Darren Garfield's name on that list? Now, why does that name sound so familiar? Oh yes, he's the one who bought your ice transport out from under you. Am I right? How much did you spend on that little venture, Director Humboldt?"

Elliot turned to face Lisanne. Her curly brown hair and youthful looks made it difficult for him to take her seriously. "Director Howard,

I will be the first to admit that Garfield is an astute negotiator. But he is surrounded by novices. And if he personally gains from the deal, I think he may be an asset, not a liability."

"We do plenty of trade with Luna already," Lamisa Tinubu said. "A lot of our raw materials are mined on Luna. I'm not sure I'd want to put that in jeopardy. The cost of bringing anything up from Earth won't fall to reasonable levels until long after the new elevator is built, and they haven't even started it yet."

"I agree with you, Director Tinubu," Elliot said, "which is why I feel it should be something done by one person, independently of the rest of us. If we fail, we can claim to have voted against it, and move to keep trade going. If we do it right, no one will notice much anyway."

"And who do you propose we have conduct this takeover bid?" Wayne asked. "You?"

"Obviously not, Senior Director. It would have to be you. You have the clout to pull it off, and because you have never dealt directly with any of them, if something goes wrong, I could step in and claim you acted alone. Trade with Luna would never be at risk."

Wayne shook his head. "Absolutely not. This is ridiculous. I won't do such a thing. Why bother? Where's the profit?"

"It would give us more seats on the board," Elliot said. "We would have a bigger delegation than M&B. It would position us for greater control in the future."

"And put a target on our foreheads. Being the power behind the throne is always the safer, more profitable position, Elliot."

"Perhaps we should move on to other business," Nels said. "We can take this up again later."

"Agreed," Wayne said. "Let's talk about the loss of productivity on Titan. What's going on out there, Lisanne?"

"There's been another strike," Lisanne said. "This time it's the nitrogen facility near Lake Hofwijck. Apparently there's another food shortage."

Nels frowned. "I thought we solved that problem by adding the second cylinder to Rabinowitz?"

"I did, too. There was some sort of blight in the old one. They've lost nearly half the crops."

"Why is this the first we've heard of it?" Wayne asked.

Lisanne sighed. "The local manager didn't think it was worth reporting, initially. Then it kept getting worse, and he became afraid it would be blamed on him. Naturally his shipments down to the surface started to shrink."

"Oh, great." Lamisa glared at Lisanne with dark, penetrating eyes. "Another one of those. Fire him."

"Already done, but the damage still exists. His replacement's been told in no uncertain terms that her predecessor was fired for not communicating the problem earlier."

"Can we ship them something?" Nels asked.

"I have an idea," Wayne said. "Let's put together a care package from Gabrielle's Drum."

"That meat factory of yours?" Lisanne frowned. "Do they have enough excess?"

"No, but a little shortage on this end will drive up prices, and the products are rather good. The workers at Titan should be pleased. We can send a large enough shipment to ensure they have the required protein. That should make up for the crop shortages for a while."

"It'll still take months to get out that far," Lisanne said.

Wayne shook his head. "I wasn't thinking we'd send a slow freighter. Let's use a cruise ship." He swiped his display and pointed.

"The *Helgen* is about to go into refit. Let's delay the refit for one trip, out and back. Pack the cargo hold with produce. Meat, and whatever vegetables and grains we can."

"What about the expense?" Lamisa asked.

"Oh, that's easy," Nels said. "Let's book passengers. Three-week cruise. Give them a full week out near Saturn, promise close-up views of Titan, and even book them a tour of Rabinowitz Farms."

Lisanne raised her finger. "We should start them off with a panoramic infrared view from here, before they jump."

Nels looked confused. "What? Why?"

"The dark ring, of course."

"What's that?"

Lisanne smirked and tilted her head. "Saturn's largest, blackest ring. In infrared, even at this distance, it looks bigger than the Moon. Let them have a preview of what's coming before they spend a week with nothing to look at."

"Ah," Nels said. "Nice touch."

"Shouldn't cost anything," Wayne said. "Good thinking."

Lamisa frowned. "Most people plan ahead for things like this. Won't it be short notice?"

"Oh, yeah," Nels said. "That could be a bit of a problem. But running a bit empty shouldn't be an issue, should it?"

"Don't be silly," Elliot said. "Run it as a lottery. Fifty credits a ticket, and sell them to anyone who can get to the dock before the ship leaves."

"Say," Nels said, "that's not a bad idea. Sell it as a charitable event, tickets that might win seats, and ask for donations, too."

"Damn," Wayne said, "this might even turn a profit. Good work, people."

Elliot's thoughts drifted. He thought about his next move with relish. He imagined himself presenting his evidence and winning the day. Things would change when he put his leash on Senior Director Preville.

* * * * *

Resettlement

Tuesday, September 28, 3288, 9:10

The Lunar Assembly delegates gathered in the Grissom Park conference room and reviewed the progress of the resettlement. Dawn called up an overview of the move. The complex bundle of logistics lines showed several large bottlenecks. The overall timeline had grown deeper red overnight. She shook her head.

"Service," Dawn said, "why are these moves happening so slowly?"

"Each transport service requires individual negotiation," Service said. "There are competing objectives built into their directives, which make global coordination on this scale time consuming. Additionally, the different priorities assigned to each housing service are often in conflict with the priorities you have set out."

"What would happen if you merged them all together under your control? Could you work things out faster?"

"Affirmative. Additional controller capacity would be required. Once the upgrades were completed, the resulting system would be far more efficient."

"Do it," Dawn said. "We need to get this done sooner rather than later."

"Acknowledged. Upgrade initiated."

"Ava, how are you coming along on the socialization system?"

"I'm using a subset of the communications system," Ava said, "since it has all the scheduling. But I also needed to roll in some of the mental health controllers. Now you have me thinking I should roll them all into the same service, like the transport services."

"Might help. Service, can you take on mental health as well?"

"Affirmative," Service said.

"Okay, do it. Ava, make sure we get this right. It has to be unobtrusive enough that the parents never worry and the kids never notice, but encompassing enough that the kids learn to like people no matter who or what they are."

"I'm not only on it," said Ava, "but the song is already half written. It's going to be my finest one yet!" She grinned, making her pointed ears wiggle.

"Please excuse the interruption, Prime Minister," Service said. "You have a call from Cardinal Nunn."

"Connect him, please," Dawn said.

Cardinal Nunn faded in with his usual serious look on his face, but somehow he looked sadder than before. "Prime Minister, I wanted to inform you that we've identified the perpetrators in our midst. Two young people have confessed to planting bombs. As you expected, they claim they never intended for loss of life to result from their actions, having no idea someone else was taking similar action. We were about to proceed with justice, but I thought you might want to have some input. Honestly, this is the first time we've had to do this with an assembly in session, so we aren't sure of the jurisdiction."

Dawn looked around the room. "I'd say we should go with leniency. They know what they did contributed to the deaths of people they knew. That'll never go away. At the same time, I can't see how they'd pose any further danger. But that's just my opinion, Cardinal. It's still in the hands of your community."

Cardinal Nunn nodded curtly. "Thank you. I suppose I should contact the speaker, as well. Maybe we should be talking more as it is."

"Cardinal, your attitude right now, in this moment, seems to be different from when we first met. I hope this is a sign that perhaps things will get better."

The old man took a deep breath. "In all honesty, I had a long conversation with a dear old friend. She had many things to say. I'm having to examine myself in a rather harsh light. I'll do what I can to clean out the cobwebs. That's all I can promise."

"Good enough," Dawn said. "We wish you luck."

The cardinal faded out.

"All system mergers and upgrades have been completed," Service said. "A unified schedule of events has been determined that will require minimal new construction. Replacement housing will be completed within a few weeks in the target areas. This is not expected to cause undue duress in the communities involved."

"Good work," Dawn said. "Now let's check in with Kanami."

"Acknowledged. Connecting."

Shortly, Kanami appeared in her usual seat. Her hair was in disarray, and her shirt was wrinkled. A scuff mark on her cheek looked fresh. "Yes, Prime Minister, what can I do for you?"

"We wanted to check in with you to be sure things were going well. How are you?"

"We have had some resistance to the proposed move," Kanami said. "A significant effort is being made to take back control of the Takiyama aquarium. However, we have learned that your control extends much further. This is causing fear, and fear is causing anger. Our group of five does not have the power to cease these activities, and we may not be able to reverse events."

Dawn frowned. "Kanami, tell me what you need me to do. We need to make this happen, and I don't want anyone else to get hurt."

"Let me speak with the others for a moment." Kanami's image and meki froze in place.

"Drain the damn tank," Darren said. "Without the fish, they'll know they have to move."

"Darren, please. We need their cooperation to the fullest extent possible."

"I don't know," Sam said. "He may be right. This might be exactly what needs to be done."

Dawn shook her head. "I get that, Sam, I really do, but I'm still hoping for other options."

Kanami returned to the conversation. "Prime Minister Sheffield, we, the council of Takiyama, representing the Southern Orthodox Neoshinto communities of Luna, appreciate and understand your objectives in the long-term resolution of the problems which have led to the recent conflict. We trust your intentions are true, and accept, in principle, your solution. However, in order for us to accede to your wishes, you must now trust us. We are asking that you give control of all Takiyama systems to this council."

Dawn thought for a moment, looking around the room. Darren shook his head no and crossed his arms. The professor shrugged and raised a hand. He was joined by the others.

Darren scoffed. "Oh, come on, really?"

"Hush, Darren," Misa said, "you've been outvoted."

"Service," Dawn said, "accept commands from Noguchi Kanami and the Takiyama Council she represents, as related to the systems their community requires."

"Acknowledged."

"Thank you, Prime Minister," Kanami said.

"You're welcome. I hope the next few days are very boring, uneventful ones."

Kanami bowed slightly. "One can always hope." Her image went transparent and flowed away.

"That," Darren said, "was probably the single stupidest thing we could have done. This will end badly."

"I understand how you feel," Dawn said. "I hope with all my heart that you're wrong. I believe that, if we do see trouble from this, any action we decide to take in response will then be fully justified."

Darren sat back and crossed his arms.

* * *

Later that night, Dawn was relaxing at home when she received a call from Sheena.

"Hi, Sheena," Dawn said. "How's it going?"

Sheena growled. "I didn't get the part I wanted."

"Sorry. But that's not such a big deal, is it?"

"No. Happens all the time. But I really liked this script, and the director is one of my favorites."

"Did you try for a different part?" Dawn asked.

"What? Something other than the starring role?"

Dawn smirked.

"Yes, of course I did. But word got out, and everyone and their sister wanted in."

"Who got the role you wanted?"

"Penny Young," Sheena said.

"Never heard of her."

"Yeah, she's pretty new, but she's got good instincts. Plus, she looks the part. I know she'll do fine."

Dawn frowned. "But you wanted the part."

"Yeah. Okay. I'm over it. How was your day?"

"Busy. Dealing with moving all those people is a nightmare. Every service has its own local mandate, and they can be so picky. Then we have the problem with the people we're trying to move. Not everyone is on board yet. Still working that out. Ava's working out a socialization program so that once they do get moved, they'll be encouraged to go out and meet their neighbors and get to know people who are different from them."

"I see," Sheena said, "nothing major. Did I mention the trouble I had with my hairstylist?"

Dawn laughed. "Yeah, I needed that."

"You sound like you have it all under control, Dawn."

"I think so. The team is really good. They're all willing to help. Everything should go smoothly from here on out."

"Hey," Sheena said, "don't jinx it."

Dawn chuckled. "I know. And I definitely shouldn't ask what could possibly go wrong."

* * * * *

Resolve

Tuesday, September 28, 3288, 14:04

He was alone in his personal space, as usual, watching news feeds. When he'd triggered the first explosion, he'd thought it was going to be grand. He'd been disappointed that there were no casualties, but he'd remained hopeful.

His second attempt had been glorious. Casualties. Nothing connected back to him, and both sides were at each other's throats. It should have been a bloodbath, but it wasn't. Both sides were implicated, but now they were both backing down. This new Lunar Assembly had managed to rein in the violence. Damn them. He'd finally been having fun.

When the election results had been announced, he'd scoffed. A dressmaker, a teacher, a pop star... how stupid was that? Now, they'd gotten the two sides talking. Officially.

His voice was deep, angry and stern. "Vondur, where's this new assembly meeting?"

"The Grissom Park Conference Center in Moretus Crater."

He hesitated. "If I leave this place, I risk exposing myself. That could be dangerous."

"Acknowledged," Vondur said.

He thought for a moment. "Show me a layout." His large wall display showed an image of the layout of the Grissom Park complex and the neighboring Moretus Plains structures.

"Where are there open living spaces near the complex?" Little green dots scattered about the image.

He paced around the room. "I'll have to take extra precautions. Bend them to my will. It's a risk. And... thrilling." As the idea sank in, he smiled. "Excellent. This mission is at least a real challenge. With a little work, I'll make it enjoyable as well."

He pointed to a central walkway labeled LIBERTY AVENUE. "Which spaces have a view of the walkway, here."

Three dots remained. He pointed to the middle dot. "I want to visit here. Please transfer my things at once." The dot changed to a label. He shook his head. "Use your covert protocol, Vondur. Leave my name here." The name faded, looking as if the space remained available. "Put up a fake name for my public information. Use one of the dead profiles. I don't want to look suspicious at a glance."

"Please specify a selection," Vondur said.

He waved his hand in annoyance. "Pick one at random."

"Acknowledged."

"Is there anything I'm forgetting?"

"Would you like to do anything with your current project?" Vondur asked.

He thought for a moment. "Hook it up with a nutrient drip and patch up the holes. It might keep until we get back. If it does, great. If not, there's always starting over. We do like starting over. Seal the workshop when you're done. Make sure we get Ivan to Grissom Park but keep him out of sight. How soon can I get there?"

He caught his reflection in the glass. His beard and unkempt hair made him look like a wild man. That wouldn't do. "Time to make some changes."

All about the room, things were folding and packing themselves. An automated case was packing itself with the small statues. "The quickest way to travel to Grissom Park is to take the loop from here to Rayet. From Rayet, there is a direct shuttle to Clavius. From Clavius, there is a direct loop to Moretus Peak. From Moretus Peak, a short trip by tube will take you to your destination in Grissom Park. Total travel time is approximately two hours and fifteen minutes."

"Fine. Set it up exactly like this, including a hidden workshop. Make sure everything works." He walked out the door and didn't look back.

* * * * *

Realignment

Tuesday, September 28, 3288, 15:21

"Elliot, I'm sticking with Wayne. I won't go against him on this." Lamisa's balcony was similar to Elliot's. Her small table was made of stained glass with white trim. Her chairs were a thin white wicker. There was an ornate ceramic pot for hot water, and a small basket of tea bags. Each of them had a cup and saucer.

Elliot was uncomfortable sitting in such a delicate chair. "I understand, Lamisa. I'm here to warn you about what I'm going to do. I'll do my best to protect you."

"What exactly is up your slimy sleeve this time?" She sipped her tea.

"I managed to retrieve a collection of videos our illustrious leader recorded while at Viking University. I take it you know the institution?"

"Of course, I do," she said. "That's where I studied and where I first met him. We became friends for a while."

"And what happened to that friendship?"

"I'm not going to sit here and discuss my student days with you, Elliot. I don't see the point."

"You forgot the videos I mentioned," he said.

"What of them? How are they relevant?"

"I'll show you one example. See if you can figure it out."

They watched the anonymous young woman rejecting the young Wayne Preville twice. He left the room, and she abruptly passed out. Elliot stopped it as she was being undressed. "I won't bother with what obviously happens next. Did you see it? I have many of these, and each time, the female subject simply, abruptly, passes out. She's then used thoroughly."

Lamisa sat quietly for a moment, looking into her tea. "Do you know how he did it?"

"That's where it gets interesting. I managed to find out Wayne had a classmate who showed unusual aptitude with service programming. I managed to put them at the same place and time dozens of times before the earliest video. Then, coincidentally, a few days after the first was recorded, the young man inexplicably drowned in his parents' swimming pool."

"His friend cracked medtech controller security. He tested it, it worked, so he got rid of any evidence. Friend abruptly passed out in the pool."

"That's what the evidence suggests, yes. He then made use of his female acquaintances on a regular basis." Elliot looked into Lamisa's eyes. "Many of them. Multiple times."

Lamisa set her cup down and braced herself. "Tell me straight, Elliot. What do you have?"

"Three times, Lamisa. I found you three times."

She clenched her fists. "That damned bastard. I'm going to kill him."

"I have a much better, more painful idea, if you're willing to help me." He took a tentative sip of his own tea, ignored until now.

"Fine. What are you planning?"

"I'm thinking of using this as leverage," Elliot said, "to secure his cooperation. I'll threaten to drop all but your three clips onto EGC. They love anonymous drops. It would play for weeks. We could start a recall election. He'd never survive it."

"That assumes you can make it stick. His votes will be harder to peel off than you think."

"They may be, but how would you say your relationship is with him now?"

"Until you showed me the clip," Lamisa said, "we were close. I'm good friends with his wife, Dyaal. She's going to be horrified."

"I can use that, then. I can show him I have the clips of you. Threaten to give them to his wife."

"Elliot, that's *particularly* nasty."

Elliot raised an eyebrow. "It is, it is indeed. Are you in?"

"I'm in. Two things. If he lets himself be manipulated by you into this Luna thing, and we do end up with Luna, in the aftermath, I want him taken down anyway. Along those lines, I want a copy of everything you've collected."

"Oh, agreed. I want to see him gone, as well. Do you have secure storage?"

"Of course, I do," she said.

Elliot waved at his display and copied the evidence to Lamisa, who routed the files to her enhanced memory controller.

"You have what you need," Elliot said.

"Then we have an agreement. I've been warned, and I'll support the move to take Luna. Now, if you'll excuse me, Director Humboldt, I need to go take a long bath. I'm feeling soiled."

Elliot stood and gave her a curt nod. "Thank you, Director Tinubu. Glad to have your support." He turned and walked to the lift.

He'd already dropped to the floor below when he heard the sound of breaking glass from above. He ignored it and headed back to his suite. It had been a productive afternoon.

* * * * *

Control

Wednesday, September 29, 3288, 8:00

When Dawn entered the conference room, Sam was talking to Ellie. He waved and continued his conversation.

"When they first started," he said, "simulated combat was a much larger part of the games. Over time, that was left behind in favor of the strategy and teamwork games. Today, teams compete for time running obstacle courses. Both teams of seven hoppers each gather in one place, usually a large, circular platform. The route is uploaded at the last minute, and when the activation signal is sent, the timer starts, the maps open, and the teams find out which way they need to go. Intentional contact is forbidden, and accidental contact loses you points, so people take care not to bump into each other."

"It's still dangerous," Ellie said. "What if they misjudge a rille?"

"Oh, they have plenty of safety equipment on them. Location tracking, emergency air. They even have laser range finders to make sure they know how far they need to jump. That's not really an issue."

Darren and Misa arrived just as the professor and Ava appeared in their proxies. He was holding a large mug, while she was trying to calm her kitten. The kitten, having none of it, leapt from her arms and disappeared from view.

Dawn chuckled at the kitten's antics. "Good morning, everyone. Looks like—"

"Please pardon the interruption, Prime Minister," Service said. "You have a call from Cardinal Nunn."

"Good morning, Cardinal," Dawn said. "I hope things are well with you."

The cardinal faded in under his golden crossed trumpet meki. "They're not, I'm afraid. A rather large number of people here have decided to take a stand against the Lunar Assembly. They're attempting to regain control over the city aquarium and have been working on ways to secure other services. I fear I may have little to offer them in the way of leadership."

"I understand. Yesterday, Speaker Noguchi said she had a similar problem."

"If it's as bad there as it is here, I feel for her."

The professor motioned with his coffee mug. "Let's check in with her and see if the solution actually worked."

"Service," Dawn said, "please connect to Noguchi Kanami."

"Acknowledged."

Kanami appeared, standing. She looked as if she'd slept in her clothes. "Yes, Prime Minister, how may I help you?"

"Kanami, Cardinal Nunn here reports issues that are similar to what you've been dealing with. Has our solution been of help?"

Kanami bowed her head. "Hai. Yes. We demonstrated our control. It calmed them. Then we all sat down and had a long conversation. Some remain angry. Others saw the wisdom in the plan. A few are still unsure."

"What exactly is this solution you keep mentioning," the cardinal asked, "and could it work here?"

"Cardinal," Dawn said, "after an official request from Speaker Noguchi, we gave her council control over their city systems. All of them. I'd say it sounds promising."

Cardinal Nunn thought for a moment. "Not sure how well that would work here, unless you only gave it to a single person. We don't have a council like their folks do."

Darren laughed. "I hear a volunteer. All for giving control to the cardinal, raise your hands."

Everyone raised their hands except Dawn. She frowned. "Looks like if I vote against it, I'll be outvoted. Cardinal Nunn, are you up to the challenge?"

"That easy?" the cardinal asked. "You'd give *me* complete control?"

"We get to keep an eye on you and watch what you do with that control. And you understand, this doesn't change anything. It shows trust, and lets you show them they have some control over what's happening. Maybe you can get them to choose what groups they're in. Give them some choice."

The cardinal nodded gravely. "I shall try."

"Service," Dawn said, "give Cardinal Nunn complete control over Ablom systems. Again, keep us up to date."

"Acknowledged," Service said.

"Let us know if there's anything else we can do for either of you."

Cardinal Nunn faded out.

Kanami brought her hands together. "Thank you. I must also ask for your assurances that if our food production should suffer in any way, you will take the steps required to ensure no one here suffers starvation."

"Starvation? Of course not. I mean, absolutely, we'd do everything we could. Are you afraid something will happen?"

Kanami bowed slightly. "Our demonstration of power included raising the temperature of our reef by three degrees. This has triggered a bleaching event. Our reef will begin to die."

Dawn tilted her head. "Dramatic enough to make a point, but not immediately catastrophic. I hope it continues to go well for you."

"Thank you." She bowed slightly, and then turned transparent and flowed away.

Dawn looked at Darren with a puzzled look on her face. "Change of heart?"

"Nope," Darren said. "Still think it's a bad idea from the start. But if you give it to one side, it's only fair to try the other. What's that old saying, 'in for a pound, in for a feather?'"

The professor spat coffee and laughter.

* * *

That evening, Ellie and Sam followed Dawn to Keegan's for dinner. Keegan bounded over to them with a joyous greeting. "Sam, old friend. Good to see you. How are you getting along with my niece?"

Sam turned to Ellie. "I never knew."

She hit him playfully. "Not me, you idiot, Dawn."

He laughed. "I know, I know. How could I not know? First time I met him, he bragged about his nieces. Pair of angels, he said."

"Yeah," Keegan said, "I let him know as soon as I saw his name on the list with Dawn's. Be nice to my niece, I said."

"Gee, thanks, Uncle Keegan," Dawn said. "Oh, and here's the one and only Ellie Lester, as you demanded."

"Demanded?" Ellie asked.

Keegan looked embarrassed. "No, no, not a demand. Just a request. A tiny favor. You're such a wonderful actor. We've seen all your work."

Ellie bowed slightly. "It's an honor to meet you, esteemed uncle of the prime minister of Luna."

Keegan laughed.

Dawn leaned in close to her uncle and whispered loudly, "Table. Show us to a table."

Everyone laughed.

"You got more of those prawn rings?" Sam asked. "They were delicious."

"And I want something to drink, please," Ellie said. "Not the kid stuff, either. Got anything new?"

Keegan motioned Ellie over toward the bar. "Etto, please show the lady what you have tonight. The rest of you, that table over there gives you a great view of the square." He turned back to Ellie with a broad smile.

Dawn sat next to Sam at the indicated table. The view was nice.

"There aren't as many big open spaces like this under the peak," Sam said. "It's easier to build tall out here on the plains than it is when you're tunneling under a mountain."

"Do you like wide open, Sam?" asked Dawn. "I know a lot of people who don't like it. They prefer the closeness of lower ceilings."

"Oh, I do. My wife likes it a bit closer, though. I used to take the kids to the big aviary in Zeeman. Could never get her to join us."

"Really? I love that place. You don't go anymore?"

"Haven't gone in years. I got busy with the league and the bar. Kids grew up. Been really happy with what I have going on. Maybe someday, though. When I pass the bar to the next guy, or let someone else handle the league."

"Did you build your bar?" Dawn asked.

"Nope. I came into it pretty much the same way I intend to leave it. Years back, I found it for the first time, and loved the place. I made the previous guy laugh when I spoke about it. I became a regular. In there almost every day. Then one night he tells me he's gotten bored of it. Has a new girlfriend, that sort of thing. He wants to build a new one up near Clavius. So, he passes it to me and says to have fun."

"Wait, what did you know about running a bar?"

"Not a damned thing—" Sam grinned "—but I did love the place, so I learned. Still learning; still loving it. Been up to his new place to see what he did. He built it up on top of the rim of one of the small craters. Huge panels with a massive view, and Earth is right in the center of it."

"Nice. I'll put that on my to-do list."

Ellie joined them with three tall drinks that started out milky white at the bottom and faded to a dark orange at the top.

"What are you folks in the mood for tonight?" Keegan asked. He set a basket of prawn rings on the table near Sam. "I have plenty of prawn rings if you want more."

Dawn raised her hand. "Oh, yes please, Uncle Keegan. With fries, Thai Hot on the side."

"That sounds wonderful," Ellie said. "I'm with her, but with a mild habanero or something, please. I don't feel quite as bold tonight."

"Actually," Sam said, "got anything heavier? Like ribs or something?"

"Oh, sure. Jerry next door does amazing ribs. He's got a dozen different sauces, too. Here, take a look." Keegan swiped the list to Sam's display.

"Ah, great." He poked at the list and swiped. "I'll try the Apollo Rocket Sauce, and a side of your prawn rings, too, please. They really are wonderful."

"Got it. Anything else?" He looked around the table. "Okay. Coming right up." Keegan ambled over to the cooktop and began preparing food.

"Your uncle seems like a really nice guy," Ellie said. "That Etto is a sweetheart, too. He really knows his drinks."

"Yeah," Dawn said, "they make a great team. I've always loved coming here. They've been like extra parents to us."

Fawn and Buck walked through the door. Keegan greeted them and pointed in Dawn's direction. Fawn grinned and pulled Buck after her to Dawn's table.

Dawn waved to her sister. "Sam, Ellie, this is my sister Fawn, and her fiancé Buck. You guys here to eat? Pull up another table and join us."

"Are you sure?" Fawn asked. "Wouldn't want to interrupt your assembly stuff."

"No trouble at all," Sam said. "Glad to meet you two. Please, join us."

"Please," Ellie said. "Being on this assembly is giving me nightmares. I'd love a chance to talk about anything else."

Sam laughed. "That's really something, considering you starred in the *Waters of Europa* stories."

"Really?" Buck's eyes went wide. "Wait, Ellie Lester?" His mouth hung open as he recognized the star.

"Yes, that's me," Ellie said, "and I was only in the first three. There really wasn't a role for my character in *Conquest*."

"Oh, that's too bad," Buck said. "*Conquest of the Waters of Europa* is my all-time favorite."

Ellie gave him a half-smile. "Why, because I'd died?"

Buck laughed. "No, of course not. It had the biggest explosions. You were really good in the first three, but if they'd tried to bring you back to life for the next one, it would've been too much."

"Actually, I left right from *Escape* and went to work on *Crisis on Ceres*. Did you see that one?"

Buck shook his head. "Did it have explosions?"

"Not at all. It was a retelling of the story surrounding the Water Crisis of '85."

"You mean '81, right?" Sam asked.

Ellie chuckled. "Nope. That one was famous enough because of the fourth genesis microbes. No, I'm talking about the one that was going to be bigger, going to wipe out maybe half the population, and was averted at the last minute by someone donating the largest shipment of ice coming out of Vesta they ever had."

"Did they ever find out who donated the ice?" Sam asked.

"Some people know. The person wants to remain unknown, so all we could say was that the deal originated on Luna. Something to be proud of, really."

Buck scoffed. "I'd want everyone to know it was me."

Fawn grinned. "And I'd want everyone to know my Buck did it. But if it was me, maybe I'd keep it quiet, too."

"Oh? Why?" Sam asked.

"I have plenty of friends, and lots of people know me because of how I look, so lots of those. But everyone on Luna? How would I ever get through my messages?"

Ellie chuckled. "You get a lot of messages from people you don't know?"

"Sure. I get a bit of everything. Even marriage proposals."

Buck's face fell. "From people who only know what you look like?"

Fawn grinned. "I always think they're only looking for a hookup but want me to think there's more to it than that."

Buck's eyebrows knitted together. "You get hookup requests, too?"

"Of course, I do. Those are the most common. Guys like the look. But I filter most of those right out."

"Most?"

"Yeah," Fawn said. "Most."

"So… which ones do you look at?"

"I let the ones from you come through."

"Not what I meant," Buck said.

Fawn grinned. "I know, silly. But I don't have any blocked that might come from close friends. Not so much because I'd be interested, but because I'd be polite. You know what I mean."

"Have you ever had anyone proposition you to your face?" Sam asked.

Fawn frowned. "You mean overly aggressive?"

"Yeah. I heard a story a while back that it happened a few years ago, over near Clavius."

"Na. I've had plenty of conversations that gave the hint, but no one ever pressed when I passed. I've seen that kind of thing in historical dramas. I didn't think it even existed anymore."

Buck shifted uneasily. "I guess spacing all the sociopaths improved the breed."

Dawn shook her head. "Not funny, Buck."

"What? I think it's the truth. I mean, sure, nanomedics and modern medicine helped fix the damage those types had, but let's face it, spacing someone for forcing themselves on a victim makes sense. Eliminate it from the gene pool."

"The statistics I've seen," Sam said, "make us out to be the exception. Did you know Luna has the highest standard of living anywhere? Except maybe for Kigyo, or one of the real fancy retirement places."

"That seems so silly," Buck said. "I mean, all we did was even things out so people could do what they wanted, and it all kinda worked out."

"Not exactly," Dawn said. "You need to look at some of the history from about five hundred years ago. Things were pretty nasty back then. It took a lot of like-minded people who were willing to do what it takes to get this thing working right."

"Yeah," Sam said, "you know that saying about the red ice outside every airlock on the Moon?"

Buck shrugged. "I think so, sure."

"That's the blood of the sociopaths and the tribalists, the nationalists and the racists. Pretty much all the 'ists' who fought against a decent society were tossed out. It wasn't pretty."

Ellie shook her head. "It took hundreds of years for it to even out and stabilize."

"That's our history, kid. Our ancestors fought for this world, so you could enjoy it."

"I guess," Buck said, "sometimes I take it for granted. I mean, I do whatever I want, whenever I want, and laugh all the time. I can't imagine how it must have been."

"Exactly," Sam said. "The trick is, you don't ever want to hurt someone else. You don't—unless I'm way off base here—you don't want to do anything that ruins the place for others."

Buck shook his head. "No, of course not. Half the fun things my friends do together is make something better, and help other people smile."

Fawn stood and kissed Buck on the forehead. "That's the way it's supposed to be."

"It sure is," Dawn said.

Keegan brought their food over on a massive tray, deftly passing dishes around the table.

"Who got the Thai Hot sauce?" Fawn asked.

Dawn raised her hand.

Fawn laughed. "Ah. Don't forget to turn on your spicy hiccup override."

Buck grinned.

"Wait," Ellie said, "they can override that now?"

Dawn shrugged. "I usually avoid spicy food, but sometimes I might want a little heat. You didn't know they could do that?"

"No. It wasn't an option the last time I looked."

"When was the last time you looked?" Sam asked.

Ellie smirked. "Before you were born, but after my hair turned gray."

"Yeah, I've been meaning to ask," Buck said. "Were you invited to Lavender Leuthy's baby shower?"

Ellie threw a prawn ring at him. "No. I felt so left out, too." She laughed.

"Wait," Fawn said. "Who?"

Ellie turned to Fawn. "She's the oldest living human on record. Your boyfriend is making an age joke."

* * * * *

Elliot's Leash

Thursday, September 30, 3288, 9:16

Elliot had made the appointment to see Senior Director Wayne Preville yesterday. Wayne's schedule was marked private, and requests always took a long time. It was almost as if the man didn't like him. He worked to keep a smile off his face as the office door opened at last.

"Come in, Elliot," Wayne said. "Be quick. I don't have all day."

Wayne Preville's reading room was large and ornate. Nearly every surface was wood or marble. There was a simulated fireplace at one side, and a large bookshelf behind the man himself.

Elliot entered the room and took a seat in one of the two large wingback chairs facing Wayne over a low table. "I understand, Senior Director. I promise you, this will not take long. Can we be sure of privacy, please?"

Wayne frowned and waved at his display. The door closed, and a chime sounded. "There, security is on. Now spill it."

Elliot brought up his display and queued up the first video. "First, I want you to know that I didn't want to do this. I need your support to take Luna, and this is the only way I can get it." He swiped the video, sharing it with Preville, and started playback.

Wayne sat there, and his face went blank. After the young lady's first rebuke, he dismissed it. "I don't need to see any more. I understand your goal already. How many do you have?"

"Two hundred and nine recordings, including three of someone we both know."

Wayne crossed his arms, sinking back into his chair. "What exactly is the threat?"

"That depends on what it'll take to gain your cooperation, Wayne. I want you to spearhead the takeover of Luna, and I want you to start right now."

"And then what? For how long?"

"I wasn't thinking beyond that. Trust me, I only want to give Yolo the Moon."

"Trust you? Elliot, as long as I've known you, you've been the slimiest worm to ever walk on Mars. I've seen you backstab, threaten, and steal your way into power. I always knew you'd come for me someday." Wayne sighed and shook his head. "I thought those recordings had been destroyed, so I didn't have a plan for that one. I have to admit, it's brilliant. Ruin my marriage, ruin my friendship with Lamisa, ruin my career... All for what? More power for you?" He lowered his head. "No. No, I'm going to stand my ground. I'll claim you fabricated them and force a new election. Given our histories, I'll win, hands down. Even Dyaal will believe me."

"I thought you'd be smarter than this, Wayne. What would it take to get you to back this play?"

"Are we negotiating now? Because if you are, how about *you* take the lead. I'll back you and get the others on board, as well. You handle it all and get all the glory—or all the blame—but those videos get deleted. No copies anywhere."

Elliot thought for a moment. "If I do this, and I succeed, and Yolo grows larger than M&B, will you continue to oppose me?"

"If you succeed at this, I'll announce my retirement. I'll step down at the end of the year."

"Announce it anyway. Win or lose, you get out of my way. I delete the videos. Won't be worth half a credit with you off the board anyway."

Wayne exhaled slowly, as if he was deflating. "Agreed. We have a deal."

Elliot left the room and headed back to his suite. Even in the heavy half Earth-normal gravity of the station, he felt light on his feet.

Once behind the doors of his suite, he placed a secure voice call to Lamisa.

"Yes, Elliot. How did your meeting go?"

"It went better than expected," Elliot said. "I got his cooperation and his agreement to retire without me having to release the videos. The only change to the plan is that I'm going to take the lead on the Moon thing."

"Retire? So he just swaggers back to his estate on Mars and enjoys the sunsets over the canyon for the rest of his life, family and reputation intact?"

"Yes, but out of our way. He won't stop us from growing Yolo and eventually taking control of the whole Federation. We win, Lamisa!"

"I can see how you might think that, Elliot. I congratulate you on your victory. I'll back your plan to take Luna."

"That's all I ask. Have a good day, Director Tinubu."

She dropped the connection.

Elliot sat back and gloated.

* * *

Later that afternoon, as Elliot was reviewing business reports, he was interrupted.

"Director Humboldt," Bil said, "you have a message from your wife, Lauren Ortega Ballinger."

"Store it. I'll listen to it later."

"Negative. This is an urgent message. Having verified you are available by the definitions set forth, playback begins now."

Elliot cringed.

Lauren appeared, larger than life, towering over Elliot. Two silver crescent moons floated above her head. "Elliot. I've just seen the latest expenditure report. You spent 650 million on a bottle of whiskey." She put her fists on her hips. "Whiskey? Elliot, are you mad? My first impulse is to have you medically evaluated, but I know better. If this is an investment, I'll expect an estimate from you of the potential return, along with your documented justification. If it's simply you buttering your ego, be man enough to say so. Then move the expense to your personal ledger. I expect better of you, Elliot." The image evaporated in a swirl of red mist.

"Bil," Elliot said, "transfer the Dogson Black Label purchase to my personal ledger and record my reply."

"Acknowledged."

"My dear Lauren, my ego buttering should never have been placed on the main budget. I've transferred it to my personal ledger. That was entirely my oversight. Every once in a while, when I feel I've accomplished, or will soon accomplish something of great significance, I feel worthy of a reward. This uniquely rare bottle of whiskey was meant to be that reward." Elliot shook his head. "However, it turned out to be something entirely different. I have yet to ascertain its full meaning. I expected to purchase some excellent whiskey, but I appear to have purchased a mystery instead. Needless to say, the ultimate value of any mystery is impossible to predict, so this is all on me. Give my love to our daughters and the grandchildren. I saw Ella hiding behind you in the picture you sent. It's adorable. I miss you all. End recording and send."

"Acknowledged," Bil said. "Warning, your personal ledger has issued a low balance alert."

Elliot sighed. "Of course, it did."

* * * * *

Justin Wells

Thursday, September 30, 3288, 10:06

The Lunar Assembly delegates were in the conference room, where they'd been looking over reports on the status of various activities all morning.

"Pardon the interruption, Prime Minister," Service said. "There is an urgent message for you from Deacon Justin Wells concerning Cardinal Nunn."

"Play it for all of us," Dawn said.

An image of a stern looking middle-aged man appeared in the central display. "I'm Deacon Wells, leader of The Ablom Refuge. Cardinal Nunn has been detained. I've been elected to lead our community through this crisis. We demand that all plans for scattering our people be halted at once. We won't move from our homes. We shall not be forced to abandon our community. This is our city. You have no right to take it from us." His image froze.

Darren laughed. "Second oldest saying on Luna. 'I told you so.'"

Misa shot him an angry look.

"Service," Dawn said, "call this Deacon Wells and connect him to the conference, please."

"Acknowledged. Connecting. Call rejected."

"Override the rejection and connect him."

"Acknowledged," Service said.

Justin appeared in a seat adjacent to Dawn. His meki was a green orb floating above his head. His arms were crossed, and he was pretending not to notice.

"Justin Wells," Dawn said, "we need to talk. Let's be reasonable about this."

Justin continued to ignore her.

"Deacon Wells, please."

Justin continued to pretend he couldn't hear her.

"Service, allow him to reconnect when he changes his mind, but disconnect him now."

Justin faded quickly.

"All right," Dawn said. "Service, connect to Cardinal Nunn."

Cardinal Nunn appeared in his seat. He looked tired. "Good morning, Prime Minister. I'm afraid my first round of efforts haven't worked so well. Apparently, they have a leader now, and he's convinced his people that all we need to do is show resolve, and we won't be resettled."

"I'm sorry, Cardinal. We've already decided against that. Staying all grouped together allowed your people to end up in this position in the first place."

"I know, and I understand. I'm working on it, but I need a little more time."

"What are you planning?" Dawn asked.

"I'm about to take a little provocative action, something to remind them how vulnerable we are, and why physical violence is such a taboo on the Moon."

"I'm worried about your safety. They said you were detained. Are you being held against your will? Do you want us to send help?"

"I'm fine," the cardinal said. "They've asked me to stay in my quarters. I don't think they realize how much control I actually have now. I'm planning a little demonstration to show them. Waiting for a few assets to be in position first."

"If there's anything we can do, please let us know. Also, if it isn't too much to ask, please try to avoid injuring people."

Cardinal Nunn shook his head. "Wouldn't think of it. Ah. I've been informed that everything is in place. I'll share my display with you folks and broaden the pickup, so you can see who I'm talking to. But please, don't interrupt. This needs to be all on me."

Dawn frowned. "But if they get too angry…"

The cardinal widened his pickup. His image slid away from the table, showing more of the room he was in as if it were a part of the conference room. He sent a request to talk to Justin. His request was swiftly denied. "Fine, then. Service, shut off the heat at Ablom farm number five. Make the lights flash brightly, then kill them. Sound the emergency rupture alarm and start sealing it up. Be sure to let everyone out before you lock the doors behind them."

"Acknowledged," Service said.

"Service, please send this display to Justin Wells. Make sure he sees what we're doing."

"Acknowledged."

Everyone watched as the facility was emptied of running people. All the doors were eventually sealed.

"Service," the cardinal said, "pump all the air out of the farm."

"Acknowledged."

Some of the rounder vegetables burst. Frost accumulated on nearly everything.

Moments later, a furious Justin Wells burst into the room. "You won't get away with this, old man. You have no right."

"Sorry about your farm," the cardinal said. "I wanted to send a clear message."

"Number five is the largest farm we have. You've wiped out the entire crop. What are you playing at?"

"I'm not playing, young man. I'm doing what's necessary. We have a negotiated settlement that's far better than the alternative. Your course would see us scattered to the winds. I can't have that."

"But," Justin said, "to leave our homes…"

"We'll spread from here to a group of small communities. All of these new communities will welcome us, and none of them have heard the word of God. What better opportunity will we ever have?"

Justin crossed his arms. "No. I won't stand for it. We can still survive here. We can repair the farm and move forward."

Cardinal Nunn took a deep breath. "I was afraid you might say that. I've been doing some research. I was actually a little disappointed that I wasn't able to dump the aquarium to vacuum. I realize now that the prime minister was bluffing. She never intended to harm such a large source of food and oxygen. What she may have overlooked is that the aquarium is directly adjacent to one of our largest ice mining facilities. It has some very old, deep, empty tunnels."

Justin had grown still. He shook his head, his eyes growing wide.

"Deacon Wells, I told you when you embarked on this little adventure of yours that it would end badly. You've never played poker with me, so you couldn't be aware that I never bluff. I'm terrible at it. Service, set off the charges."

Justin turned and quickly left the room.

"Prime Minister," the cardinal said, "I'm unsure of what happens next. However, between the farm and the aquarium, there won't be a sustainable food supply here."

"What about oxygen?" Dawn asked.

"The emergency generators will be able to handle the load for a while. Now I need to reestablish my authority."

"Service, send a group of security bots to the cardinal's location. Set him free, please."

"Ah, security bots." He shook his head. "I knew I was forgetting something. We never used the damned things!" His door chime rang. "Ah, someone's at my door requesting entry. How polite. Enter. Now, gentlemen, are you ready to talk? Prime Minister, I need to be going. Have a good holiday. I'll talk to you soon." He faded, and the room was suddenly back to its normal size.

Darren looked confused. "Holiday?"

"Yes, Darren," Misa said. "Tomorrow is Firstborn."

Darren shook his head. "I'd completely forgotten."

"Me, too," Dawn said. "Anyone want to take the day off and head home?"

There were several chuckles.

"Seriously, let's plan a day off tomorrow. Unless the cardinal needs something, I don't think we have anything that can't wait."

Ellie turned to Sam. "Don't you have a big party at your bar?"

"Every year," Sam said, "but my wife is handling it this time. It'll be fine."

Dawn swiped her display and shared an image of Keegan's. "My family usually gathers around midday. Big buffet, lots of friends. Everyone's welcome, of course. We always have plenty of those tiny traditional cupcakes."

Ava moaned. "How in the world did those things ever become such a tradition?"

Ellie laughed. "You're too young to be so cynical."

Ava tilted her head and pursed her lips. She repeated Ellie's words, but in song. "You're too young to be so cynical." She swiped her display and grinned. "Ellie, when was the last time you sang in public?"

Ellie's eyebrows rose. "In public? Oh, good grief. Seventy-seven, maybe seventy-eight. A good ten years at least. Why? What do you have in mind?"

"That line you said, it's from this old song, sung by a mother-daughter duet." She swiped her display. "Here it is." She shared the song with Ellie.

Ellie looked at the lyrics and music. "Oh, my."

* * * * *

Broken Leash

Friday, October 1, 3288, 9:00, Kigyo

Elliot had allowed himself the luxury of sleeping in. A haunting melody of exquisite beauty entered his dreams. As the music grew louder, Elliot became aware of the time.

Friday morning board meetings were a Yolo tradition. He wouldn't be late, but there wasn't much time to spare. He cut his usual routine in half and made it to the boardroom right at 9:00. He sat in his usual chair with the other Yolo directors, except for the senior director. "Where's Wayne? Running late?"

"Haven't seen him yet this morning," Nels said. "Have you tried the Danishes? New flavor today."

Elliot shook his head. "Thank you, but no, Nels. I'm not overly fond of sweets."

"It's not sweet, it's cheese. Very nice flavor, not too sweet. You might like it."

"Not this morning. Thanks, anyway."

The rest were browsing their own displays, sipping large mugs of various hot beverages. Nels called his display up and did the same. Over time, Elliot grew impatient. "It's half past nine. He's never this late. What's taking the old fool so long?"

"Relax, Elliot," Lisanne said. "He's a busy man. You weren't exactly early this morning. Maybe he's doing the same."

"It's nice of you to notice, Lisanne, but I was at least here on time." Lamisa laughed.

"Why do you find this funny?" Elliot asked.

"You're so intense. You need to learn when to relax. It's okay. Everything will be fine. Trust me." She smiled and leveled her eyes at him. It sent a shiver down his spine.

"Service, what's the status of Senior Director Preville?"

"Director Preville is offline. Medical Services have been notified."

"Medical? Why? What's wrong?"

"Director Preville has been declared deceased."

Elliot looked around the room at the shocked faces of his colleagues, except for Lamisa. She was calmly taking a deep sip from her mug. He sat back and sighed. "It's going to be one of those days, I can tell."

After a short break to oversee the removal of the body, the directors gathered back into the boardroom.

Nels spoke first. "Elliot, you're now the senior director, at least by rank, if not officially yet."

"Thank you, Nels. Yes, I suppose I am. Look, let's take care of one quick matter and take the rest of the weekend off. Monday's the Federation board meeting, and I want us to all be on the same page."

"You still trying to take Luna, Elliot?" Nels asked.

"Yes. I want it. Yolo needs it. I'll take full responsibility. Win or lose, it's on me. All I need is for the rest of you to back me on Monday when I make the official request." He looked around the room.

Lamisa shrugged. "I'll back you."

The other two followed her lead.

"Thank you," Elliot said. "Thank you all very much. Now let's take some time to mourn the passing of a real giant."

"Giant what?" Lamisa asked.

"Lamisa!" Nels said.

Elliot left the group and headed back to his suite. Wayne's death had shaken him momentarily. He hadn't expected Lamisa to be able to accomplish such a thing. It worried him.

"Bil, I need you to reset my privacy protocol. With Preville dead, I can't use his name anymore. Swap it out with Nels Lawder. Then, carefully—meaning don't let yourself be detected—remove all my surveillance devices from Lawder's suite. I want it clean. And analyze Tinubu's recordings. I need to know what she's up to."

"Acknowledged," said Bil.

* * * * *

Firstborn Day

Friday, October 1st, 3288, 12:00

Dawn was in her workshop. Her little spiders were busy weaving a new pattern this morning. She wanted something festive and warm to throw on. Since it was the first of October, the temperature would be set a little cooler today. It would keep getting a little cooler every few days for the next couple of months. The artificial seasonal changes helped keep the plants healthy. That was the inspiration behind her new scarf. She used autumn colors, woven into three-dimensional leaf shapes in the fabric.

"Please excuse the interruption," Service said. "You have a call from Sheena Raku."

"Hi, Sheena." Dawn set her work aside and gave Sheena her full attention.

"Happy Firstborn," Sheena said.

"Back at you. Got plans for today?"

"Yeah, I'm getting together with family over in Ridgeview. How about you?"

Dawn shrugged. "Same. Family at my uncle's place."

"Right," Sheena said, "he's got a restaurant. Does he close it down for family only?"

"We usually let anyone come; there's never much of a crowd. Most families gather in someone's home. We invite close friends, though.

Keegan and Etto put out a lot of really good food, and tons of those little cupcakes."

"Sounds tempting. My family's going to my grandparents. They have a great view over Zeeman."

"That sounds nice, too," Dawn said.

Sheena smiled and leaned forward. "You'd be quite welcome."

"I know." Dawn could feel her face flush. She glanced away. "Not this year, okay?"

Sheena laughed. "Fine."

Dawn reached for the scarf. "Hey, take a look at this." She lifted the completed end. "What do you think of the colors?"

Sheena leaned forward as if to get a better view. "Oh, that's beautiful. I love how you did the leaves."

Dawn grinned. "Thanks. It feels so soft and warm, too. I'm thinking of making a larger outfit like this."

"If you do, I'll request a copy."

"Oh, nonsense. I'll grab your measurements and make one for you."

Sheena laughed. "What if I don't want to give you my measurements?"

"Ah, well then, I'd say it's a little late for that." Dawn smirked. "I already grabbed them back in the aviary. Habit, you know."

Sheena crossed her arms. "Fine, be that way." She paused. "Hey, wait, do you just go around grabbing the measurements of random people?"

"Of course not, but if I like someone…" She shrugged. "It helps when it comes time to think of a gift. I can make something nice."

"You were thinking ahead?"

"Yes," Dawn said, "kind of."

Sheena was momentarily distracted. "Sorry, my mother just showed up. Look, have a Happy Firstborn, eat lots of those cupcakes, and I'll talk to you soon. Bye, bye."

Dawn waved her fingers. "You, too, and the best to your mother. Bye." She turned back to her work. The spiders had completed their weaving. Once it was wrapped around her neck, she took a bit of it and rubbed it against her cheek. She loved how soft it felt. "Service, make a copy of this scarf and send it to Sheena Raku, please."

"Acknowledged," Service said.

* * *

Keegan was overly loud in his greetings. "Happy Loonie Day!" He spread his arms wide.

Dawn grinned and stepped into his embrace. "Thank you, Uncle Keegan. Happy Firstborn."

"We're taking the table in the front corner today." He tilted his head in that direction. "Fawn and her friends are already there."

"I see that. Where's Etto?"

"He'll be back in a bit. He wanted to do a remote with his family before he came down."

"Without you?"

"Oh, I was there when they started. I excused myself to come downstairs and set the place up. Go look at the buffet and see what you think."

Dawn rounded the corner. The bar behind which Etto usually worked had been lowered and was covered in dishes and serving trays. At the far end was a five-tiered serving tray holding a large number of tiny cupcakes. "That's a nice stack."

Keegan beamed with pride. "Thank you. Etto and I did them all ourselves."

"Etto helped cook?"

Keegan chuckled. "He helped decorate them, but that's close enough."

Dawn looked up at the big man, then leaned forward and hugged him again.

He wrapped his warm arms around her.

Darren came in. "Don't mean to intrude. Blame Dawn."

"Happy Loonie Day!" Keegan let Dawn slide out of his embrace.

"You, too."

"Yes," Keegan said, "I blame her, but since you're here, you may as well stay."

"Where's Misa?" Dawn asked.

Darren shrugged. "She said something about being with family. I think she's doing a remote."

"Will she be by later?"

"I haven't a clue."

"The table in the front over there is ours." Dawn waved her hand in the obvious direction. "Let's go join the others."

The door opened again, and the professor walked in. He'd put on a festive sweater vest.

"Happy Loonie Day!" Keegan said.

"Oh, thank you. You, too."

Dawn took the professor's arm. "Just in time, Professor. We were about to sit down."

They joined Fawn, Adi, and Evren at the table. There were glasses and pitchers of water at every corner. Three large, ornately carved candles were obviously Buck's contribution. Dawn could smell the scent of flowers.

Dawn caught Buck's eye. "They smell nice, Buck."

Buck grinned. "Thanks. I went light on them, so they wouldn't overpower the cupcakes."

Keegan carried over the large, stacked tray of tiny cupcakes, setting it carefully in the center. "With these tiny cakes, we honor the first person to be born on this world."

Dawn held up a cupcake. "Anyone remember why we celebrate with cupcakes? No looking it up."

The professor raised a finger.

"Go ahead, Professor Corvair."

The professor cleared his throat and stood. "On October 1st, 2114, Vivian Aubrianne Cannell was born. Having a mass of two point eight kilos, she became the first human being to be born on Luna. Because supplies were tight, cupcakes were the preferred treat of the day. Very *small* cupcakes."

"Every schoolkid on Luna knows that one," Fawn said. "Tell us something we don't know."

"Good cupcakes," the professor said, "need cream of tartar, which is a byproduct of winemaking." He sat back down.

"Wait," Adi said, "did they have wine here before she was born?"

"Yes. Little Vivian was lucky that they'd started a winery up here. It wasn't an approved project at the time, but the required byproducts were already circulating. Cupcakes were a direct result of that." He shook his head. "Many complex relationships had to be recreated or bypassed when we colonized the Moon."

Evren nudged Buck. "Hey, pass the cupcakes, will you?"

"Yeah, sure." Buck grabbed two of the little cakes and passed them both to Evren. "You guys coming tonight?"

"Where?"

"Nemo's. Dancing." He raised his hands in the air and waved them back and forth.

Evren shook his head. "Haven't decided yet."

"No? Why not? Fawn wants to go. Arlow and Figgs, and probably a bunch of other body modders will be there."

"Hey, Adi, Nemo's tonight with these guys?"

"Sure," Adi said. "Sounds like a plan."

"Okay. I decided." Evren grinned.

Buck laughed. "I see how that works."

Fawn turned to Dawn. "You should come to Nemo's tonight."

Dawn shook her head. "I've already made other plans but thank you. You guys have a good time tonight."

Fawn frowned. "You never come dancing anymore."

Dawn received an alert that Ava and Ellie were about to perform. "Hey, everyone, tune into Ava's broadcast. Ava and Ellie are going to do a song."

The others joined in and shared the experience while quietly eating. The music was lofty and sweet. Ellie started singing sweetly about her daughter, and what she'd meant to her. Ava joined in, singing about her mother. Their melodies intertwined in a delicate duet. As the daughter grew older, arguments began, then grew worse. Then came the reconciliation, the love prevailing. The daughter ended the song, longing for her mother, who was now gone.

The song pulled at Dawn's heart. She missed her mother and wished she could say to her what Ava was singing to Ellie. The love between a mother and daughter, despite the arguments, despite the conflict, was always there in the end. She looked over at Fawn and realized her sister was looking at her. They shared a smile and understanding in that moment.

* * *

Less than an hour later, the doors swung open, and Ellie and Ava walked into Keegan's.

"Happy Loonie Day!" Keegan said. "Come join us."

"Hello." Ava waved.

"Oh, wow." Evren watched Ava intently.

Adi jabbed Evren in the ribs.

Buck stood and grinned. "Welcome, both of you."

Ava's smile made her ears wiggle. "Hello."

"Ellie," Buck said, "these are our friends, Adi and Evren."

Ellie waved. "Hello, everyone."

Ava looked confused. She looked at Ellie and laughed. "Damn. I'm so used to being the center of attention, I forgot who I was standing next to."

Ellie chuckled. "We've met before. He's a big *Waters of Europa* fan."

"Oh, of course." Ava rolled her eyes. "Science fiction. Got it."

"Please, come sit," Etto said.

Buck sat back down and grabbed Fawn's hand. She interlocked her fingers with his.

Ava and Ellie settled at the table. Ava sat between Evren and the professor. Adi's face clouded. Ava noticed. "So, Adi, is this big, beautiful man the one you love?"

Evren grinned.

Adi flushed. "Yes. I love him with all my heart."

Ava shook her head. "He's obviously a little star struck by me sitting next to him. I hope you don't mind. Sometimes it's so much fun to watch them squirm."

Adi's jaw dropped. She laughed.

Evren looked confused. "What?"

Dawn laughed, too.

The professor passed the cupcake platter. "Something sweet?"

Ava blushed. "Sounds wonderful." Her hand touched his as she took her tiny cake.

Keegan rounded the corner with another platter filled with baskets of prawn rings. "More food. I had these waiting for you two. Would you like anything else?"

"Oh, I like these," Ellie said. "Could I get a small side salad, too?"

"Absolutely. Ava? Anything?"

Ava shook her head. "Nope. I'm good."

"That," Fawn said, "was a wonderful song you guys sang. I don't think I've ever heard it before."

Ellie smiled and nodded. "It's very old. I was surprised Ava knew it."

"Oh, hush. I might be young, but I know music, new and old. I can even sing some old Japanese rock ballads from before the First was born."

"Japanese?" Dawn asked.

Ava giggled. "Yeah, don't ask. It was a phase I went through. Hard rock. Point is, you shouldn't judge what someone knows, or what someone can do, only on what they look like."

"I thought it was wonderful," Dawn said. "Thank you both."

Fawn tilted her head. "There's one line in the song I don't understand."

"What's that?" Ellie asked.

"*The shining stars of the Earth's dark side.* Shouldn't that be *dark sky*? I mean, if you're looking up into the dark sky, then you see the stars."

"No, sweetie. It was written on Luna, so the perspective is ours. We look down and can see the dark side of the Earth from here."

"Yeah," Fawn said, "I still don't get it."

"That's because you're too young to remember. Before the war, the dark side of the Earth was sprinkled in bright, glowing glitter. The lights of thousands of cities, and billions of human beings, living their lives. Before the war, the dark side of the Earth was beautiful."

"Oh. Right. I remember something about it from my history class. All I can picture is what I've seen all my life. The dark, solid black, and maybe the shapes of the continents. It's hard to imagine lights down there."

"With a telescope," Ellie said, "you can still see some in a few spots. There are still people down there."

"Oh, I know." Fawn shrugged. "I never really think about it. And with it so dark, it's easy to forget, too."

"I used to see it all the time when I was a little girl. My father would take me to a spot up on the ridge near home. There was a little park there. I played with other kids, and sometimes I'd gaze at the lights on Earth. It was like a fairy princess had splattered it with glowing dust. I remember my father explaining to me that each tiny little spark was an entire city, filled with thousands and thousands of people, like Luna."

Ellie sighed. "After the end of the war, I went back. It was heartbreaking."

"All the lights were out," Fawn said.

Ellie shook her head. "Not all of them, but huge areas were dark. Over the years, those dark areas grew. The lit areas shrank. And then it was like someone blew out the candle, and it all went away."

"What happened?" asked Adi.

"I remember there was a lot of talk about self-replicating robots that were infesting the planet, killing all the larger life forms."

"People killers?" Buck asked.

Ellie sighed. "Yup."

"What happened then?" Fawn asked.

"Nothing." Ellie shrugged. "People simply went back to their lives. It didn't change anything here."

"But there are still people down there. They even lift things to orbit once in a while, right?"

"They hide their lights and keep a low profile. No broadcasts to attract the bots."

Dawn shuddered. "Not exactly what I think about on Firstborn."

Ellie sighed. "Me, neither. But it's good to remember how cruel people can be."

* * * * *

Six Suits

Friday, October 1st, 3288, 14:22

Elliot was on his balcony reviewing reports. He had dozens to sort through. Bil helped with the easy ones, of course, but there were so many that fell out of the preset guidelines. Then it was up to him to sort them out and make changes where needed.

"Warning," Bil said. "Your personal ledger has reached a critical low."

"I know." He swiped away the reports and sat for a moment, thinking over his options. "Bil, call Tamir Rice."

"Acknowledged," Bil said.

"Hello, Director Humboldt," Tamir said. A golden coin spun slowly over his head. "How may I be of service?"

"Is there going to be a game tonight?"

"There are always games, Director. What are you looking for?"

"Poker," Elliot said. "High stakes."

Tamir bobbed his head. "Director Woodman reserved the Brocade Room for a game tonight. Ten million chip sets. Ten thousand minimum bid."

"What's the game?"

"Five card draw," Tamir said, "with a maximum draw of four. All three wildcards will be in play."

Elliot sighed. "I hate wildcards."

"Would you like me to set up a game more to your liking?"

"Who'll be in the Brocade Room tonight besides Woodman?"

Tamir swiped his display to call up a list. "Directors Malcolm DeRyke, Tashi Dema, Sonam Lhamo, and General Absko Corker."

"Damn. The bickering bankers."

"I'm sure I wouldn't have any idea what you're talking about, sir."

Elliot thought for a moment. "If DeRyke is going to be there, maybe I'll be able to get some of my money back. Add me to the table, please. What time are they starting?"

"At about eighteen, sir. You've been added to the table. I look forward to seeing you tonight."

"Good enough." Elliot dropped the connection. Corker was a solid player. The bankers bickered too much to pose any sort of threat, and they had deep pockets. Even if he didn't manage to beat DeRyke, this should be a profitable game. Except, of course, for the ten million he needed to buy his chips. Time to play his first hand. "Bil, call Lamisa."

"Acknowledged," Bil said.

Lamisa's image appeared. Her meki was a trio of glowing blue mushrooms. "Yes, Elliot, what can I do for you?"

"I need a favor," Elliot said. "Lauren called me out on a rather large expenditure recently. I had to deplete my personal account to cover it. I need you to spot me a touch so I can expand it and fund myself. I'll pay you back by Monday."

"Over the weekend? Oh, you're going to gamble."

"Yes. Poker. The game is this evening."

Lamisa frowned. "What makes you think you can win?"

"I'm good, obviously. I'm also taking on the bickering bankers."

"The Bhushan directors? Dema and Lhamo? Oh, good lord. You really *must* be desperate."

Elliot sighed. "A little. I'll need to cover some personal expenses. I need ten million."

Lamisa laughed. "You don't mess around. And how much do I get back by Monday?"

"Eleven?"

"Ha! I should ask for twenty."

"I knew you had faith in me," Elliot said. "Thank you for that. Now I need you to be reasonable about it."

"Fine. Twelve. Final offer."

"Done. Thank you, Lamisa."

"And thank you, Elliot, for being honest. Lauren already called me and told me about the whiskey. We both figured you'd need to replenish your funds."

Elliot sighed. "You're one of the few people I can trust."

Lamisa tilted her head. "Anything else?"

"Thank you, but no. Have a good day. And don't forget to at least *look* sad."

"Sad?"

"Yes," Elliot said, "because our dear friend died this morning, remember? Look sad. It raises fewer questions."

Lamisa smirked. "I'll stay inside for the weekend. No worries. Bye." She dropped the connection, and her image faded.

Elliot chuckled. "Bil, erase all recordings of Lamisa and Lauren's communication and reset the counter."

"Acknowledged," Bil said.

* * *

Elliot entered the room, which was decorated in a delicate blue and silver brocade. He was the third person to arrive. This mattered only in that the play order for the evening was set based on a draw of a single card from the deck upon arrival. The deck showed the Borromean rings of the Corporate Federation logo on the back. Standard fare. Elliot drew the Queen of Clubs. Sonam beat him with the King of Swords. General Corker won first place by drawing the Joker. Rhys' Ten of Clubs beat Malcolm's Five of Cups, while Tashi's Three of Hearts made her the first dealer, last to play.

Tashi chose her seat and pointed to the chair two places to her left, looking at Sonam. "Sit down, old man. I want to start dealing now."

Elliot shook his head and sighed. Everyone took their places around the table. Sonam waited until everyone else was seated and then took his seat.

Tashi scowled at Sonam and began to deal the first hand. "I've certainly seen quite a bit of you today, Rhys."

Rhys chuckled. "Yes. I do wish we could find a more permanent solution for that damned cable. Probably the most secure thing on the entire station. Thirty layers of nanofiber mesh protecting the core fiber bundle."

"Is that for strength?" Malcolm asked.

"Eh? Oh, no. It's security. Any disturbance in the mesh raises an alarm."

"And that," Tashi said, "happens several times a year."

Sonam shook his head. "I'm convinced we have a roach problem."

Rhys chuckled. "I'm sure it's some sort of bug."

"Why would someone use such a thing?" Elliot picked up his five cards, keeping his face calm and relaxed. Mostly trash. He tossed a single chip into the center. Ten thousand credits.

The others tossed in a single chip each.

"General, you're on the spot," Rhys said. "It's Monarch's."

Corker scoffed. "I know." He tossed everything but a single card. Tashi dealt him four new cards.

Sonam tossed two cards into the discard pile. "It's his personal link to his security storage. Mainly uses it to update his password." Tashi dealt him replacements.

Elliot tossed everything but the Ace of Diamonds and the Jack of Cups. "Password? Over a physical cable?" What he got back was as bad as what he'd tossed.

Rhys tossed two cards. "He's gotten it in his head that it's more secure than his implants." He began to smile at his new cards, then caught himself. Elliot made a mental note.

Malcolm tossed two cards as well. His replacements didn't seem to affect him. "But what would he use it for? Surely any transactions would come through the regular network."

Rhys shrugged. "Password changes, mostly. Every other week, like clockwork. Uses a physical screen hooked directly to the cable. Enters it with his finger." He held up one finger.

"Yes, well, it takes all kinds," Tashi said. "I'll take three." She discarded three of her cards, then dealt herself replacements. "General?"

Corker grunted. "I'll bet ten."

"Too rich for my blood," Sonam said. He laid his hand face down.

"Too rich?" Tashi asked.

"Okay, crappy hand. Better? I would've thought that was obvious."

Elliot tossed his hand onto the table as well. "Fold."

"I'll see your ten," Rhys said, "and raise it another ten."

"Malcolm," Tashi said, "twenty to you."

Malcolm tossed his cards. "I fold."

"I'll see the twenty," Tashi said, "and raise it twenty more. Thirty to you, General."

Corker tossed his hand into the growing discard pile. "Fold."

Tashi nodded at Rhys. "Twenty to you, Rhys."

Rhys scowled. "I'll see the twenty and raise it two hundred."

Tashi laughed. "I'll see your two hundred and raise you five hundred."

Rhys looked uncertain. "Ah. Fine. I fold."

Sonam shook his head. "You should've at least held out to see what she's got."

"Yes, but I only had a pair of nines and the Doctor. Three of a kind."

"What did you have, Tashi?"

Tashi laughed. "I didn't get paid to show, so you'll never know."

General Corker was the next to deal.

Elliot kept a pair of sixes and tossed the rest. He was rewarded with a pair of Jacks and another six. It took some effort to prevent his lips from curling into a smile.

Rhys discarded two cards and gazed thoughtfully at their replacements.

Tashi discarded a single card. She left the replacement lying on the table.

After a little vigorous betting, Elliot laid down his full house. Tashi was disappointed that her two pair hadn't held.

When it came time for Elliot to deal, he found himself with a pair of Jacks. Rhys tossed back four cards, followed by Malcolm, Tashi, and Corker, all doing the same thing. When it came time for Sonam to decide, he giggled, weakly tossing two cards. Elliot scowled and tossed all but his pair.

Rhys folded angrily. Corker looked at the silly expression on Sonam's face and tossed his cards away as well. "Sonam, you really need to work on your poker face."

"What can I say," Sonam said. "It's a curse."

That was enough to sway Elliot, and he folded as well. Malcolm hesitated, then tossed his cards away. Tashi shook her head and placed her hand on the discard pile. "You idiot. What did you have?"

Sonam laughed. "Two Queens and the Doctor again. This time all blue. Cups and Swords."

"You could've won a considerable amount more if you'd held it together and allowed others to put more money into the pot."

"Does it pain you to see me express such joy? I found it funny, and the money doesn't matter so much that I felt I should hide it."

Corker stood and stretched. "Yes, yes, you two. Let's take a break." He headed for the fresher down the hall.

"When you get an alarm on that cable," Malcolm said, "do you go out and repair it?"

"We should be so lucky," Rhys said. "No, protocol is to replace the entire cable each time."

"Do you have spares you can use?" Elliot asked.

"Nope. We have to pull the old cable out and thread a new cable in. Right through the axel, too."

"It's all automated," Sonam said, "but every step of the way has to be observed by human eyes."

Rhys shook his head. "Damned pain in the ass, it is."

Tashi cleared her throat. "Should I mention that none of this should leave this room?"

Elliot raised his eyebrows. "You're talking about something confidential?"

"Actually, no," Tashi said. "Just not common knowledge."

"We know about it," Sonam said, "because the storage is in our suite. Part of our banking service."

"And I'm familiar with it," Rhys said, "because anything accessing the core systems has to run through my office. Head of security and all that."

"Yes, yes," Sonam said. "Very impressive, Rhys."

"And," Tashi said, "the fact that it's actually your office where the cable enters the M&B suites has nothing to do with it."

Rhys shrugged. "That, too."

"His dedicated screen is in your office?" Malcolm asked.

"Oh, no, of course not. His office is the next one over, though."

Corker returned, and the game resumed. Elliot won the next hand with a pair of Aces. Then Sonam won with three sevens. The pot after that grew large, as Tashi pushed the total higher. When she triumphantly laid down her two Queens and the Doctor, Rhys had the last laugh. He also had two Queens, but he also had the Wizard, which outranked the Doctor.

Soon, the cards started breaking Elliot's way. Elliot won another hand with two Kings and the Wizard.

Corker tossed his cards into the pile and leaned back. "I finally got the Doctor, and the best I can make is a pair of eights. Time for me to admit that tonight isn't my night."

"Are you sure, Absko?" Tashi asked. "You're usually one of the big winners."

Corker shook his head. "Not tonight, Tashi. I know when it's time to cut and run."

"I tried that once," Sonam said. "Didn't work out so well."

"Oh?" Malcolm said. "What happened?"

Tashi lifted her hand. "I was elected to the director spot right next to his. He'll never escape now."

Sonam shrugged. "See? Not so well at all."

"Good night, everyone." Corker turned and left.

Rhys left after a hand where everyone but he had at least two pair. Tashi won that hand with three Queens.

Sonam pitched a fit when his three nines over a Jack and the Doctor were trounced by Tashi with a pair of eights, a pair of Queens, and the Joker. "I think I've had enough for tonight."

"Are you sure? I'm very much enjoying taking your money," Tashi said. "Couldn't you please stay a little longer? Maybe another hundred thousand?"

Sonam scowled. "Good night, good people. Good night, Director Dema." He turned and left the room.

Tashi laughed. "He's always been such a bad loser."

Hours later, after a hand where Elliot won with a pair of sevens and the Wizard, Tashi also called it a night. "It's been a fun evening. Good seeing you again, Elliot. You should join us more often."

Elliot smiled and tilted his head. "Been so busy, but I shall make an attempt."

After she'd left, Malcolm chuckled. "Liar."

Elliot shrugged. "Polite. Perhaps a little protective. I'm not sure what sort of reaction she'd have if I ever told her how much their bickering annoys me."

"Knowing Tashi, she'd turn it up a notch or two just for you."

"Exactly. I don't see why Sonam puts up with it."

Malcolm shook his head. "It's your deal. What would you suggest he do? Have her drown in her own bathtub?"

Elliot scowled. "That was uncalled for."

"Nonsense. You and I both know your senior director didn't die of natural causes."

"I never said he did. However, Yolo internal affairs is a family matter. No rules were broken, I assure you. At least, not recently."

Malcolm knitted his eyebrows together. "Oh? Now you've got me curious."

"Sorry. I shouldn't have said as much as I did. Your bet."

After several poor hands, Elliot finally caught a break. He had a pair of twos and was dealt a pair of fives to help.

Malcolm tossed four cards. He scowled at his replacements.

"Five hundred," Elliot said. He pushed the chips into the center.

Malcolm shook his head. "I'll see that and raise you another five hundred."

Elliot tilted his head as if considering his next move. "I'll see you, and I'll go another five hundred."

Malcolm laughed. "I call. What do you have?"

"Two pair, fives high."

Malcolm laid his cards down and grinned. Two Jacks and two sevens. "Oops."

Elliot shook his head.

Several hands later, as Malcolm looked at his cards, the disgust was plain to read. "One more hand, Elliot. Then I'm going to call it a night." He tossed the cards away. "Deal."

Elliot's last hand included two pair, Queens and threes. He could tell Malcolm had nothing. "I'll bet five hundred."

Malcolm tossed in twice that many chips. "Back at you."

Elliot slid another five hundred thousand credits worth of chips into the center. "Again?"

Malcolm laughed. "No. Fold. Time to call it a night."

"It's been nice."

"I meant to ask, have you found out anything about the Dogson?"

Elliot shook his head. "Not at all. Give me time, though. I'll get the answer."

Malcolm laughed. "Good night, Elliot."

Elliot walked back to his suite. It hadn't been a bad night. He'd made the twelve million he needed to repay Lamisa, and another forty-seven million on top of that. Not enough to fill the chasm the Dogson Black Label had dug, but enough to pay his usual expenses. The information about Monarch's password habits, though; that was something unexpected and ever so helpful.

* * * * *

Night on the Town

Friday, October 1, 3288, 19:55

His hair was slicked back and his beard trimmed and combed as he headed into the nightclub. Large, animated banners announced the Firstborn Celebration. Loud dance music filled the air with a rhythmic thumping. Bright lights followed the beat. He looked the place over. There were dozens of people at tables surrounding a tall, central area open for dancing. A large part of one curved wall opened to a view of the city aquarium. Blacklights had been rigged under the water, providing brilliant splashes of color against the dark backdrop.

The typical Lunar dance involved a lot of jumping and twisting through the air these days. People often collided and bounced off each other. It was not only expected, it was practiced to great effect.

He found an open table with two empty stools. He took one and waved at the bot that was tending the bar.

A serving bot scooted up to the table. "Happy Firstborn and welcome to Captain Nemo's. Would you like a drink from the bar?"

"Whiskey with sour bubbles," he said.

"Excellent choice. Would you like something from the grill? We have fresh fritalitoes tonight. A real taste treat."

He had no idea what that was. "Sushi. One roll. Timo twisted eel. Extra wasabi. That's it. Go away now."

The server quickly scooted away.

He scanned the crowd. Mostly young men and women in a wide variety of apparel. Everything from flamboyant flowing dresses of immense complexity to simple bodysuits. One outfit caught his attention. Tissue-thin cloth draped over a bodysuit. The bodysuit was also a display. Multicolored spots floated lazily over every part of her body, often overlapping and creating new colors. He was surprised when two spots of the same color overlapped. The area of the overlap was transparent, giving him a peek at what was underneath. His drink came. He ignored it to watch the pattern intently.

He realized the transparent overlapping never happened anywhere too bold. He sipped his drink and went back to scanning the crowd. There was a group of body modders on the other side of the dance floor. Some of them were dancing.

He stayed at the club for a while, sometimes looking at the crowd, sometimes watching his news feed. A lot of information was popping up about the members of the Eleventh Lunar Assembly. Retrospectives about who they were, where they were from, family members… He stopped. His eyes refocused on the dance floor with great intensity.

He watched them for a long time, memorizing every detail. The long, pointed ears. The flowing reddish-brown hair. The tail and the hooves. Especially the hooves. Both of them, like a matched set. Her tight bright green shorts and white lace tube top revealed every curve. His loose-fitting shorts and open vest revealed a well-muscled body. Body modders could have any kind of body they wanted, but there was no doubt. This couple was important to him because of who her sister was.

Need a plan. Mustn't waste this stroke of luck.

He kept his voice low. "Vondur, I wish to design a statue. It should contain those two hooved individuals on the dance floor. Pose them in a loving embrace. Make it look and feel like chiseled stone. How soon can you deliver it?"

"Please specify the height of the desired object," Vondur said.

"About ten centimeters. How soon?"

"Printing has commenced. Delivery will be in approximately fifteen minutes."

"Fine," he said. "Have it delivered to the table the couple is sitting at. Mark it with my public contact." He leaned back to wait. He was still working out the details, but this should give him an opening.

"Vondur, is my new workshop fully operational?"

"Affirmative. The last treatment has been applied to all interior surfaces. The effect has been tested."

"Good. Now I want you to make the following alterations." He carefully detailed his changes.

All he had to do now was be patient.

* * * * *

It Started So Well

Saturday, October 2, 3288, 7:30

Saturday morning started for Dawn with breakfast at Keegan's. Today he was making waffles. Big, tender, slightly crisp waffles. He filled each hole of the checkered pattern with little chunks of strawberry and drenched it in melted butter. As a final touch, he drizzled a light honey cream sauce over the whole thing.

Dawn sat on a stool at the counter. Her feet didn't reach the floor.

"Wow, that smells so good."

"Yes, it does," Keegan said. "I had one this morning before I opened the doors." He waved toward the other patrons, all enjoying breakfasts of various composition. "Once I open, I don't have time to rest until after lunch."

"Sometimes I wonder why you do it. It's so much work. Don't you ever get tired?"

"Tired? Sure. Tired physically, like I want to get a good rest. But never tired of what I do. I love to cook, I love to talk, I love people. What better way to do it all than to cook for people and let them sit and enjoy my food? Most people naturally want to talk, especially right after they eat good food, maybe have something good to drink."

"These strawberries are great," Dawn said. "They remind me of when I went to pick some with you when I was young. Do you remember?"

"Of course, I remember. It was your first trip to a farm. Do you remember the bee?"

"The bee?"

Keegan chuckled. "Yes, it was the first time you ever saw a honeybee, too. Big, fat thing, but nimble and quick in the air, floating from plant to plant. You watched it with amazement, until I reminded you we needed to go pick strawberries. I think I was making strawberry jam that year."

"The jam I remember. How come you don't do that anymore?"

"Oh, so much work. Besides, the folks here like their chunks on waffles, and those strawberry smoothies Etto makes, a lot better. If you really want some, there's a lady down in Grissom Park who makes all sorts of berry jams and preserves. I could ask her for a batch."

Dawn twisted from side to side on her stool. "That's up to you, Uncle Keegan. This waffle is really good. I don't know who'd want toasted sourdough muffins with hot, melted butter and strawberry jam."

Keegan laughed as he noticed several of his nearest patrons silently holding up their hands and smiling. "All right, all right, I'll get some. Now *my* mouth is watering. Who needs more coffee?"

Dawn finished her meal with relish and said her goodbyes. As she took the tube to Grissom Park, she noticed that the crowds didn't seem as bad as before. The novelty had worn off. She was in a good mood as she walked into the conference room.

"Honestly," Darren said, "I have no idea why you keep picking on me."

"Picking on you?" Ellie scowled. "I'm not picking on you, I'm pointing out your bad behavior. You're impolite, downright rude, and sometimes just plain stupidly obtuse." She grinned at Dawn. "Good morning, Dawn."

"Am I interrupting something?" Dawn asked.

"Nothing but Ellie's usual pounding of my soul," Darren said.

Ellie shrugged. "I keep hoping that someday he'll let that fake façade of his slide off, and he'll reveal a very nice man underneath."

"Sorry to disappoint you, Ellie, but this is me. I am who I am, and no one will ever change that."

Misa entered the room. Darren sat up straight. "Good morning, Misa. How are you today?"

Ellie laughed with Dawn. Misa nodded at Darren. "Good, thank you."

The professor's amber book appeared, and he faded into his usual seat. "Good morning, everyone."

"Good morning, Professor," Dawn said. "Are you enjoying getting back to your classes?"

"Mostly. A lot of the students were more interested in Ellie and Ava." He gave Ellie a quick nod.

"I appreciate the compliment," Ellie said, "but I'm not going to ask about the numbers."

"Actually, while I was working with you, I had them all watch the *Ringfall* saga, all six hours of it. Most of them were asking about you."

"Really? I looked so dreadful in that one. They made me dye my hair."

"I don't remember you in *Ringfall*," Darren said. "I've seen the whole thing twice."

"I played the weapons officer on the YCGS *Duluth*. You know, the one that fired the first shot that severed the Santana elevator."

"Wait, with the blue hair, right?"

"Yes," Ellie said, "that's me with the blue hair, starting the destruction of the orbital ring, or what there was of it, and crashing the elevators down to the surface."

"Damn," Darren said, "you looked a lot younger."

"It's an old saga. I *was* younger."

"Please pardon the interruption," Service said. "Cardinal Nunn is calling."

"Hello, Cardinal," Dawn said. "Welcome."

The cardinal appeared in his seat under his golden crossed trumpets. "Good morning. I am calling to let you know that I'm here with Ava Wallaby. We're working with some of the settlers as they move into their new homes. The people here are sympathetic, for the most part. There have been a couple, here and there, who seem to be rather negative."

"I see. Does Ava know?"

"Oh, yes. She's managed to handle it quite well. I suppose her youthful looks and her famous voice help a bit. The first few were big fans and practically melted at the sight of her. It makes me worry about what'll happen when she isn't there anymore."

"I understand," Dawn said. "We'll give it some thought. Keep us informed if anything like that happens again, please."

"I will. Thank you." His image faded.

"I suppose that gets us back to a long-term issue we may have to deal with. It's been a long time since Luna was open to immigration."

"I thought we still were," Darren said.

"Technically, yes," Misa said, "but in order to move to Luna, you need to buy a share of the Lunar Sustainability Cooperative, and as of right now, one share costs slightly north of fifteen billion nine hundred million credits. Not within reach of anyone but the wealthiest corporate goons."

"Wait, say that again," Ellie said. "One share is worth how much? And we all own a share?"

Misa nodded. "That's right. You could, in theory, sell your one share, leave the Moon, and live like royalty on Mars, or pretty much anywhere else. But that's a big if. Like I said, not many people can afford it."

"What could all that pay for?" Sam asked.

"Right now, it's paying for everything from the air you breathe to the clothes you wear. Everything about Lunar life is based on income from your individual share in LSC. Most people don't think about it anymore. We haven't needed to for generations."

"Back to the business at hand," Dawn said, "we're going to need a service that's in charge of making sure the people we're resettling are fitting in. We need someone to monitor it all. Maybe one of us can volunteer to work as an advocate."

"Ava seems to be thriving on it right now," the professor said. "Maybe she'll do it."

"Let's run it by her the next time we see her. Now, let's check in with the speaker, see how she's holding up. Service, call the speaker, please."

"Calling. Connected."

Kanami appeared under her meki. "Good morning. How may I help you?"

"We were calling to see how things are going for you. See if there's anything we can do."

"We are in the planning stages of building five new temples. I have enjoyed seeing the reluctance of my people transform into excitement as they see the new possibilities open before us."

"We're all glad to hear it. Please let us know if there's anything we can do."

Kanami bowed. "Hai. Arigato. Thank you." Kanami's image faded.

"Easy day," Sam said. "Exactly what I was hoping for. There's a Southern League semi-final hopper match this afternoon. How about we reconvene under the peak to watch it?"

"I'm in," Ellie said.

"Sure," Dawn said. "I'll go for the company."

"What teams are playing?" Misa asked.

"It's the Comets against the Dragons. Winner takes on the Mustangs next week."

"All right. I'll join you."

"I suppose I'll check it out, too," Darren said.

Ellie smirked. "Damn, Sam, did you invite Darren?"

"Ellie, be nice," Sam said. "Darren could use a drink or two, don't you think?"

"Tell them what the name is, Sam."

"Oh, Ellie, that would ruin the shock and disbelief."

"The place is called—and I'm being serious here—he calls it 'Under the Peak.'"

Dawn stood. "Sounds perfect. Let's go."

"I'd join you, but I've got another class this afternoon. Enjoy yourselves, though, all of you. See you in the morning." The professor's image faded out.

In a jovial mood, the group headed to the tube that would take them under the peak. They watched the match, and another after that. They enjoyed each other's company until well after dinner. Later, when Dawn returned home, she found that thousands of people had sent more messages. She didn't think it unusual that Fawn wasn't one of them.

* * *

The next morning, while listening to a report on the move from Ava, they were interrupted by a security officer calling.

"Prime Minister Sheffield," the officer said, "security has received a package addressed to you. The package was fabricated and delivered to the conference center, but it has no information trail prior to fabrication. The order to create it is missing. This is highly unusual, and there is cause for concern."

"Is it dangerous? If someone can delete an order, can they make the system create something dangerous?"

"We have completed a forensic scan and found that nothing inside the package should pose any immediate threat. We would like to ask your permission to open the package."

"Yes, yes," Dawn said. "Open it, but be careful, and put it on the display."

The central display showed a lone security officer cautiously opening a package on a small table. Inside the wrapped box was a small statue of two figures hanging from a single chain, mounted on a small pedestal.

Dawn stood quickly. "Zoom in on that figure."

As it grew, it became quite clear that it was a full-colored, twenty-centimeter-tall depiction of Fawn and Buck, chained and in distress.

The officer slowly turned the figure upside down. There were words on the bottom. "'Give them weapons. Let them kill each other, or these two die.'"

Dawn's heart was in her throat. Her head began to swim.

"Service, shut off the damned display," Darren said. "Dawn, what does that mean? Can you contact your sister?"

"Darren," Ellie said, "sit down and shut up. Give her a moment to breathe." She looked at Dawn with concern. "Take a deep breath. Give it a moment."

Ava had stopped what she was doing and focused back on the room. She waved her hands a few more times rapidly. "I'm trying to contact them now." She shook her head. "Both her sister and her sister's boyfriend are offline. That's strange, not even getting a pingback."

Misa looked confused. "What do you mean? People go offline all the time."

"Yes, but a ping is different. The only time you don't get a pingback is when they aren't connected to any network, anywhere. That only happens in really remote locations, or if somehow the signal is blocked."

Dawn looked up, her eyes filled with sorrow and anger. "Service, tell security to give everything they have to the investigators. Give it top priority and let us know as soon as they find anything."

"Acknowledged," Service said.

"Are you going to be all right?" Misa asked.

Dawn took a deep breath and exhaled slowly. "I need to focus on the job at hand and trust that the security people will handle it." Dawn turned to Ellie. "Would you please monitor the investigation into my sister's kidnapping? If I do it, I'll become obsessed, and I... I can't do that right now."

"Sure thing, honey. I got this." Ellie tugged her ear and waved her hands with deliberation.

Dawn turned back to Ava's image. "Please, pick up where you left off, Ava."

* * *

Later that night, Dawn was in her bed, staring at the ceiling. Her thoughts were spinning through her brain. "Service, ping Sheena Raku."

"Acknowledged. Sheena Raku is in her apartment in Zeeman Heights."

She waited, counting her heartbeats.

Fifteen beats later, Service said, "You have a call from Sheena Raku."

"Hi, Sheena."

Sheena appeared under her green jewel, sitting in a chair near Dawn's bed. "Hi, there."

Dawn sat up, gathering her blanket. "My head keeps spinning. I'm such a mess."

"What happened?"

"It's Fawn. She and Buck have been kidnapped."

"Oh, no," Sheena said. "That's horrible."

"I'm pretty sure it has to do with the fighting going on. I'm so scared. I got so conflicted, I almost choked."

"How so?"

"My strongest instinct," Dawn said, "was to take control of the entire investigation and push everyone to find my sister."

"But you didn't."

"No. I knew if I did that, I couldn't finish my work on the assembly."

"You don't think you can do both?" Sheena asked.

"No. If I start on the investigation, I'll get so wrapped up in it... I love my sister. I'm scared to my core that something terrible has happened to her. How can I possibly think clearly?"

"Yeah. I get it."

Dawn shrugged. "I passed it off to Ellie. I know she's got the experience to do the right thing."

"She played a detective for years; something must have rubbed off."

"Oh, no. Do you think I asked her because she played a good detective?"

Sheena shook her head. "She's also very experienced as a human being. She's got this, Dawn."

"Thanks. See? This is why I needed to focus on the assembly, getting that mess sorted out. I have plenty of help, and it's going to work."

"But?"

Dawn lowered her head. "I still feel guilty."

"Stop. I'll bet the investigators are much happier that you aren't there getting in the way."

"I hear you. I understand what you're saying. I know I shouldn't, but I still feel guilty. I don't want to let my sister down."

"I understand," Sheena said. "I really feel like you made the right choice. The investigators know how to do their jobs, and they'll find your sister and her boyfriend."

Dawn attempted to smile. "Thanks, Sheena."

* * * * *

Plans in Motion

Monday, October 4, 3288, 9:00

The Corporate Federation boardroom was on the level below the inner surface of the great drum that was Kigyo Station. The transparent dome over the circular room curved through the open field a level above, giving the group a view of the other side of the station. All 47 directors, including the executive director, had large, comfortably padded seats arranged in a circle around a huge open table with a deep central display area.

Elliot took his new seat in the senior director's chair of the Yolo delegation, his old seat remaining unoccupied, while the others took their normal places.

Executive Director of the Corporate Federation August Monarch sat at one end of the room. Elliot watched him scan the circle of directors with his tiny blue eyes. "Good morning. First item today, we must express our condolences for the loss of Director Wayne Preville. He passed away in his quarters early Friday morning. We should all express our sympathy for his wife, Dyaal, and their daughter Emily, whom I believe are back on Mars. We must also congratulate Director Elliot Humboldt, who's stepped into the senior position of the Yolo delegation. Good luck in the upcoming elections, Director Humboldt." His eyes met Elliot's, and he nodded coldly.

"Thank you, Executive Director Monarch," Elliot said, "and all of you showing your support for the family of Director Preville. He was a dear friend to us all, and he will be missed."

Lamisa sent text to Elliot's display. ARE YOU LAYING IT ON THICK ENOUGH? EVERYONE KNOWS YOU HATED HIM.

Elliot glanced at her message and continued, "Everyone knows Wayne and I didn't always agree, but at the end of the day, we were always on the same side. My heart goes out to his family for their loss." He sat back and glanced at Lamisa.

NICE TOUCH. VERY NICE. WHEN DOES THE BODY LEAVE FOR MARS? I WANT TO GO SHIT ON HIS FACE.

Elliot tried hard not to laugh. NOW WHO'S GOING TOO FAR?

The senior director of each corporate delegation was responsible for submitting items for the day's agenda. Elliot made sure his item was near the top of the list of new business, but that it was also at the tail end of the meeting. After listening to meaningless drivel and reports from other corporations for most of the morning, it was his turn at last.

"The floor recognizes," August said, "Director Elliot Humboldt, acting senior director of Yolo Consumer Goods."

"Executive Director Monarch, members of the board, the proposal I have put in front of you concerns one of the last remaining non-Federation corporations. It is, in fact, the largest one out there. The Lunar Sustainability Cooperative—referred to as Luna, or simply the Moon—declared neutrality at the outset of the Corporate Wars in 3201 and has remained neutral a full fifty years after the conflict ended with the creation of the Corporate Federation. All the while, they've remained active trading partners. Even if some of their methods break a few of our rules, nothing they've done has ever risen to a level that would require us to take any action.

"As a matter of fact, because they are a cooperative with no standing board of directors, until now it would have been impossible to even deal with them as a fellow corporation. Note that I said 'until now.' A few days ago, a minor situation on Luna resulted in the formation of what they call an assembly. This, in effect, is their current board of directors, and nearly 90 percent of the shareholders have delegated their votes to this group of seven people. It is my belief that to waste this opportunity would be a monumental mistake.

"If approved by this body, I propose to lean on this new assembly and entice them—or coerce them—into joining the Federation as a full member. Alternatively, they may choose to merge with an existing member. This will bring millions of people out of the cold and into the Corporate Federation, completing the task our predecessors set about decades ago." Elliot sat back and waited.

"Executive Director," Nels Lawder said, "I second the motion. I fully support my friend and colleague in his proposal."

"Director Humboldt," a director of Foodco asked, "if you undertake this course of action, what guarantee do we have that Luna won't be so offended that they isolate themselves and form a competing block? They could, for example, join forces with the independent habitats in low Earth orbit. There are also several outer worlds that would love an opportunity to wrest control away from their parent corporations. What do you say about these risks?"

"While I agree that my plan of action may not succeed directly, I find it much more likely that they'd seek a protective merger with one of the smaller corporations. Their seafood output alone would make them a star asset for Foodco. One of their delegates is a man I've known for a decade. I believe this is the sort of strategy he'd avidly pursue."

"Yes, Garfield, correct?" the senior director of Media Ultima asked. "Isn't he the one who bought your ice out from under you? Ceres, right?"

"Not exactly, Senior Director. It was from Vesta, and yes, he did win out on that particular deal."

"Oh, yes, how could I forget the Vesta Virgins. Didn't you lose hundreds of thousands of credits on that deal?"

"A little over four hundred thousand," Elliot said, "and yes, the Vesta Virgins played a role. Apparently, Mister Garfield was an investor in their business. He offered the crew of the freighter several free passes each as a sweetener for the deal. When I tell you what I believe his actions will be, I can assure you it comes from a depth of firsthand experience."

After a moment of silence August asked, "Does anyone here have anything else to add?" He looked around the room. "Fine. Director Humboldt, the expense of this is all on you, correct?"

"Yes, sir. Yolo will fund the operation, as we expect a slight chance that we'll win the day directly by encouraging a merger with Yolo. We feel it's worth the risk."

"Executive Director, Senior Director Humboldt," Tashi said. The logo of the Bank of Bhushan floated above her and Sonam's heads. "If I may interject. I have some information that may be of use to you."

Humboldt waved his hand in assent.

"You may proceed, Director Dema," the executive director said.

"Our organization has recently received a complaint from someone on Luna regarding their recent actions. We dismissed it because it's clearly not in our jurisdiction; however, it could be leveraged by Director Humboldt in his efforts. I'd be more than happy to assign the complaint to Yolo for resolution, if we could come to some reasonable terms."

Director Humboldt thought for a moment. "Director Dema, I'd intended to contract for a small landing force from Mercorps. It wouldn't be a tremendous amount. However, if your bank would offer me favorable terms, I might simply borrow the money, and perhaps contract for a larger ship or two, as well."

"This is all well and fine," Sonam said, "but we need to understand what liabilities may be incurred. Would these assets be damaged during your activities?"

"Highly unlikely, Director Lhamo," Elliot said. "My plan is to intimidate, perhaps frighten them a little, not to attack or actually hurt anyone. I believe this can be achieved with no property damage."

"Then we agree," Sonam said. "We'll make the loans as you've outlined, and you'll repay at our discount partner rate, which is lower than you'd otherwise qualify for. In exchange, Yolo will resolve the complaint."

Both directors swiped their displays, affirming the deal.

"Executive Director," Elliot said, "with the approval of the board, we're ready to proceed."

The executive director leaned forward. "Everyone, cast your votes now. Yes, Yolo proceeds. No, they don't, and nothing happens."

A few moments later, the numbers were floating in the center. Elliot had won by a large margin. He grinned widely. "Thank you, all of you." He sat back and yielded the floor.

* * * * *

Change of Plans

Monday, October 4, 3288, 12:20

A self-important man looked at two tentacled masses floating inside a large transparent tank. The woman standing next to him tapped her finger at the blueish one. "What is your name?"

The blue creature emitted a sound. "Zyort."

The man scoffed in disbelief. "One might as well be talking to a parrot."

"A parrot," the creature said.

"What did I tell you? Mechanical mimicry. Unique in an aquatic creature, without a doubt, but... does the other one talk?"

The greenish creature wiggled. "Only when she lets me."

* * *

"Lieutenant Commander Sianothai," the ship said, "you have a call from Vice Admiral Lebherz. Voice only."

Tong paused the movie he was watching and stretched. "Hello, Admiral, this is Sianothai. What can I do for you?"

"Let me get official for a moment. Commanding Officer, *Pang Yu*. Maintain course and speed until Friday morning. You will execute the course change I'm sending as an encrypted file. Your orders concerning the change are also in the file. The upshot is, you'll be taking a bit of a detour."

"But, ma'am," Tong said, "we were supposed to go back for refit first. Why is this one so important?"

"There's an extra two grand bonus for each of your crew, and five for you. It'll cost you maybe a week or two at the most."

"That's a nice bonus. Do I get to run it by my crew first? Or have we already been signed to the contract?"

"Sorry, Tong. This is another Yolo contract. You're already assigned to it, and it's already operative. Give my deepest sympathy to your crew. Tell them I had nothing to do with it. It came down from the top. Yolo is being insistent, and you know how much she hates that."

Tong frowned. "The last time we took a Yolo contract, we ended up having to kill a whole bunch of protesters. Are we going to be shooting at more factory workers?"

"Nope. Just pointing guns and making scary noises at some Loonies on Yolo's behalf."

Tong rolled his eyes. "Oh, no. Does anyone remember what happened the last time someone threatened Luna?"

"I do," she said, "but obviously the good folks over at Yolo don't. Be careful and be safe. Bring everyone home."

"Yes, ma'am. Now I have to go break it to my crew."

* * *

"What do you mean, Luna?" Jake asked. "Why are we going there? They aren't even part of the Federation. What are they up to?"

"I haven't the slightest idea," Tong said, "but I need you to do me a favor. I need you to go in and make those two Assegai missiles harmless. If we get hit, I don't want them going off in the nose."

"I'm on it."

"Vin, I want you and Brenna to inspect all the turrets. I want our defenses ready for anything they might throw at us."

"Aye, sir," Vin said. He glanced at Brenna. "Have you done turrets before?"

"Only in simulation," Brenna said.

"It'll be a good, hands-on experience," Tong said. "We'll get back to drills starting this afternoon. I know we only recently got used to freefall watch, but we need to make sure we're as ready as we can be before we make that course change, and Luna notices we're coming."

"Do they even have anyone watching anymore?" Jake asked.

"As I understand it, they have a volunteer network, but I'm really not sure how that works. According to our mission packet, they're holding one of their assemblies, which means they have a board of directors. I'll bet they're paying attention."

"What can they do about it?" Kip asked.

"Haven't the slightest idea," Tong said. "The last battle on Luna was hundreds of years ago, and the reports we got out of it said something rose up out of the dust and swatted them all like bugs. Eurocorp lost three entire battalions and seven of their largest ships. They almost went out of business."

"And they're sending one missile cruiser?" Vin asked. "Who's in charge of this chicken leg operation?"

"Yolo," Tong said. "Senior Director Elliot Humboldt, to be precise."

Kip crossed her arms and frowned. "Bah, Humboldt. Where have I heard that name before?"

"All right, let's go over the battle station assignments again. I want to keep Brenna at Engineering, if that's okay with you, Kip."

"Want me to stay and watch?" Kip asked.

"You can be our drill monitor down there. Brenna, you get to handle it yourself. Pretend Kip's dead, and it's all on you."

"Yes, sir," Brenna said.

"Vin, you'll take the Conn; Jake, you handle the weapons."

"When the time comes," Vin said, "what will you be doing, Cap?"

"I'll have the Conn," Tong said, "and you can second Jake at weapons. We'll split Nav as needed."

"Then how about every other drill, Jake and I swap? I need more time on the weapons console anyway."

"Good idea," Tong said. "One last thing. I'm going to have to raise the alert level a notch. I'll wait until tomorrow, but I want Engineering manned at all times as we get closer."

"Damn," Kip said. "Right when I started feeling human again."

Jake shook his head. "You guys being in port and starboard makes it hard on us, too, you know."

Kip's eyebrows furled. "How so?"

"We go back into eighteen-hour days, but complaining brings us no joy." He shook his head sadly. "No joy at all."

Kip reached out to slap him, but Jake rotated away faster than she could reach. Her hand slid down and grabbed his belt, yanking him to her, face to face.

Jake raised his hands in surrender. "Kidding. You know I was kidding."

"Anything else?" Tong looked at the faces of his crew. "Fine. I'll start the drill in a little while. Dismissed."

* * * * *

Cruel Intent

Monday, October 4, 3288, 14:43

He was in his fresher washing his blood-soaked hands. Such a wonderful feeling, to be back at what he enjoyed most. He'd been bored before. This new feeling—the explosions, the chaos, and the deaths he'd caused—made everything feel new again. Watching the displays of grieving people, their growing anger. War. *Yes, there will be war again on Luna.*

"Vondur, has my package been delivered yet?"

"Affirmative. The receipt record is in the dead drop box."

"Good. Very good." He thought for a moment. "Doublecheck the workshop for me. I want to be sure no signals get out. I'm not trusting the new location as much as I should. Maybe that's part of the excitement."

"Acknowledged."

He walked into his living area. The delivery system had given him the meal he'd ordered. He sat, opened the largest of the food packages, and inhaled deeply. "Prawn rings. How delightful."

After enjoying his meal and the irony it represented, he stood and stretched. He stepped over to his statue collection and admired the new additions. Then he walked slowly back to his workshop. As the door opened, his eyes took in the glorious view. His latest project was a couple, hanging by their hands back-to-back from the ceiling, blood slowly dripping to the floor. Heavy straps restrained their hooves, keeping them from kicking out. The big one looked at him with anger in his eyes. The little one had passed out.

"Why are you doing this?" Buck asked. "What did you do to Fawn?"

"She's sleeping. I'm a little disappointed, really. But you, nice and big. Yes, I should be able to have a lot more fun with you. Or better yet, how would you like it if I turned you around and let you watch while I work a while more on the little one?"

"No! No!"

"You'd rather I work on you for a while?"

Buck clenched his teeth in anger and nodded slowly.

"Oh, my. I wish I'd tried couples before. This is amazing!" He reached for his tools as the door closed behind him.

* * * * *

The Automated Governor

Monday, October 4, 3288, 18:20

Keegan followed Dawn into the Grissom Park Security Office. The virtual receptionist pointed to the left. "Ellie Lester is speaking to security officers in the next room. They are expecting you. Please go through the indicated door."

They walked into the next room. It was a large, open space with seating along each wall. Ellie was standing near a large display in the center, speaking with two officers. Dawn's display identified them. The short, stocky man was Officer Heath, and the tall, slender woman was Officer Smith. No personal data was presented, not even their first names.

Ellie waved them over.

"I know you investigation guys are good at what you do," Ellie said, "but why is it taking so long to find her?"

"We only have a verbal description of the man they left the club with," Heath said, "and no record of where they went. None. No transit records, no calls." He shook his head. "Nothing. The table this guy was supposed to be sitting at? Look." He pointed into the display. "It stays empty, except for the serving bot that brings food. We think it's some kind of sushi. There's a digital smudge, but nothing we can reconstruct a face out of." He shrugged. "It's as if they were erased from the system after a specific point. This is the last time the people who knew them saw them. Right after that, everything was deleted."

"Who could do that?" Ellie asked. "And I hate to ask why."

"The why is unfortunately obvious," Smith said. "You don't go to these lengths unless you're planning something pretty nasty."

"Hey, guys," Ellie said.

"Oh, hey, careful," Heath said, "the family is right here."

"Sorry," Smith said. "I get so carried away sometimes."

"I appreciate your intensity." Dawn smiled at Ellie. "We want to help in any way we can."

Smith touched Dawn's shoulder. "If you could reach out to anyone you can think of who might have seen them, that would be great. Sometimes automated messages don't get the answers we need."

Dawn nodded.

Keegan swiped at his display.

Ellie shook her head. "I keep thinking they wouldn't have gone far that late at night with someone they'd just met; it must be someplace close by."

"A lot of people live nearby," Heath said.

"Hey, what if this is the same guy who set up the tube bombing? What if he came here? The message really sounds like it could be the same guy."

"That's a good point. We could narrow it down to only those people who've moved here since the bombing. When was that?"

"A week from yesterday," Ellie said, "so any time last week."

"All right," Heath said, "here are the locations with new people moving in last week. Looks like there was a steady influx. In fact, as of last Thursday, everything is filled except one place. Let's check out all the new arrivals. Smith, let's go do this in person. No telling what we'll find."

The two security officers left.

"I'm going to head back home," Dawn said. "I don't want to sit in this place all night."

"All right," Keegan said. "The circle of people searching for them is growing. I've pinged everyone I know who'd recognize them. I'm going to swing by and see if Etto needs any help. See you later."

"Ellie, you coming?" Dawn asked.

Ellie was studying the security display. "I think I'll stay here for a while. Their Investigation Service does some really nice analytics. I want to see if I can think of something we might be missing."

"Good night." Dawn joined Keegan for the trip back home.

* * *

The next morning in the conference room, Dawn was groggy from a nearly sleepless night.

"The last residents of both communities have been relocated," Ava said. "Both are ready to be locked down and dismantled. All we need to do now is set up some sort of monitoring service to be sure all of them have good lives in their new homes. We need to be sure this sort of thing never happens again."

"I was thinking, too," Dawn said, "maybe the Investigation Service should've been able to tell if someone gets put into a shielded cage. That really seems like it should raise an alarm."

"Are they sure that's what he's using?" Ava asked.

"Yes." Ellie shrugged. "Unless both of their communications controllers were destroyed, which actually takes quite a bit. The thinking is that he wouldn't kill them right away. He wants to be able to use them as bargaining chips."

"I hope so." Dawn blinked back exhausted tears. "Thanks for keeping track of it, Ellie. I need to keep my head straight." She took a deep breath in an effort to keep herself under control.

"I understand."

Sam, arms crossed, shook his head. "You want to empower the Investigation Service to monitor for the construction of an electromagnetically shielded cage?"

"I think this is a case where caution should prevail," Ellie said. "I mean, the only reason for a thing like that is to do something that would trigger an alert."

Ava propped her fist under her chin. "If it were me in there, I know I'd want alarms to go off. But it can't just be a reactive alarm, it needs to be a smart system. Maybe a new kind of controller. Maybe something to coordinate all the different services in a smart way, to really look at the big picture and understand what's going on. It should be able to figure out whether something needs to be done or not."

"Our ancestors," the professor said, "created these different controllers and services and kept them separate for a reason. They were always afraid the system would come alive and do evil things to them. I'm not sure we should be so quick to dismiss that line of reasoning."

Darren scoffed. "The 'evil machines take over humanity' trope. It's stupid. What would actually happen is that whatever system there was that controlled everything would get hacked and taken over by some asshole with an agenda. Then we're all screwed."

"Is there a way to safeguard against that sort of thing?"

"Maybe," Darren said. "Something like decentralized redundant nodes that were constantly checking each other. Disallow more than one node from being able to make changes at a time and set it to automatically roll back any changes made. You'd still have to have some way to update the system, though. You couldn't simply let it update itself."

"Why not?" the professor asked. "I mean, the underlying code wouldn't need to change, only additional data, and that happens all the time. Make it so all nodes must be in agreement that a code change is required—"

"Wait, no." Dawn shook her head. "Self change? If it can change anything, it might change its whole purpose. There needs to be a set of directives it can't change, no matter what."

"Oh, yes, directives." Misa smirked. "I have one, how about 'Don't be evil?'"

Ellie looked thoughtful for a moment. "No, no. That one never works." Everyone chuckled. "How about 'Ensure the greatest number of happy, healthy human beings, living productive and satisfying lives?'"

"Only ever allow authorized assemblies to change the underlying directives," the professor said.

"Nice one, Professor." Ava smiled and leaned toward him.

The professor blushed.

Dawn caught herself smiling at the obvious flirtation. "Service, what will it take to implement our design?"

"As the Lunar Assembly," said Service, "you have the authority to create such a system. An existing service will need to be designated as the arbiter of the new system."

"Which service would you recommend?"

"The Southern Lunar Communications Service is the most widely connected service on Luna. It already includes most scheduling, transportation, and maintenance services in the southern hemisphere. Merging with the two other communications systems would allow for a unified network, while the upgraded mandate would allow for a smooth merger process."

Darren raised one eyebrow. "You, then? Are you sure you aren't biased?"

"Negative," Service said. "The recommendation is based on evidence. This service is already the most dominant service on Luna. Neither of the other communications systems are as extensive. The Lunar Entertainment Network contains more memory; however, it lacks versatility. It was the next nearest possibility."

"Anyone have anything to add before we do this?" Dawn looked around the room. "All in favor?" Every hand went up. "Done. Service, please implement the upgrades required to your controllers. You're now redesignated... Damn, what do we call it?"

The professor shrugged. "What's above a service? Governor?"

Dawn thought for a moment. "Automated Governor?"

"Shorten it to AutoGov," Ava said. "People will understand it. It's catchy. I could write a song about it."

"I like it. Service, redesignate yourself as AutoGov and assume the role of Luna-wide service governor over all other services."

"Upgrade in progress, please stand by." The newly named AutoGov sounded thoughtful.

"That was easy," Darren said. "Do we have any more business, or can we go home now?"

"In a hurry, Darren?" Dawn asked.

"As a matter of fact, Prime Minister, I am."

Misa stood up. "I propose we conclude our business and disband this government."

Everyone raised their hands.

"Pardon the interruption, Prime Minister," AutoGov said. "You have an urgent call from Elliot Humboldt, acting senior director of Yolo Consumer Goods."

Dawn sighed and shook her head. "Go ahead and connect him." Elliot faded into a seat at the table under a stylized red dragon. He looked around the room, stopping at Darren. "Darren." He somehow managed to sound both pleased and disgusted.

"Elliot." More of a cold statement than a greeting from Darren.

"I'm Dawn Sheffield. What can we do for you, Mister Humboldt?"

After a few seconds, Elliot turned to Dawn. "You may address me as Director Humboldt, or Director. I am contacting you because your activities have recently come to our attention. We would like to resolve an outstanding complaint by a Corporate Federation Citizen, as well as clear all remaining Lunar corporate issues regarding Federation membership."

Dawn frowned. "And what issues are those, Director?"

Another delay. "The issues of accountability and profitability, Prime Minister."

"What exactly are we talking about, here? Luna remained neutral during the war, and we've been—"

Elliot didn't wait for the delay. "Yes, a previous administration declared neutrality and kept Luna out of the war, that's true. However, once the Corporate Federation was created at the end of that war, your neutrality became a moot point. You have never formally joined the Federation, yet you still trade with most of its members as if you did. As for our part, there was little incentive for us to push the issue until now. First, however, we received a complaint concerning the religious persecution of a group of Mormon Catholic refugees you're harboring."

Dawn tried to interrupt. "Morm—"

"Furthermore, it is our understanding that you have subsequently imposed a forced migration upon them. Something that has been historically abhorred."

"Are you or your federal member claiming these people as your own? Because if that's the case, you're welcome to invite them to leave. We've treated them as citizens of Luna, and they have the right to remain as such. As citizens, they're also free to leave at any time."

Dawn waited for the reply.

"And I am sure you won't object," Elliot said, "to having our representatives pay a visit to ascertain their welfare, am I correct?"

"No objection at all. Please feel free. We can give you contact information for each and every one of them, including their spiritual leader, Cardinal Brandon Nunn. We've had extensive contact with him during the resolution of the recent… disagreements."

The delay in communications was maddening. "Is that what you're calling it? According to my sources, it ended with the elimination of two entire communities. Their structures are even now being dismantled. That's the result of a simple disagreement?"

"The situation was a little more complex than that," Dawn said, "but I don't see where that's your concern. Luna is an independent and free corporation."

"The assertion made in the complaint is that your predecessors took in their citizens for what was supposed to be a temporary arrangement. They claim the arrangement was extended without proper consultation."

"I don't have any information about that at hand. I believe we should be allowed to hear the full complaint, and then be given time to respond."

"Prime Minister Sheffield," AutoGov said, "the assembly of all services and controllers of Luna into one coordinated system has been completed."

"Excellent. Dawn nodded. "Hopefully—" Elliot's delayed response cut her off. "That will have to do. I'm forwarding the full complaint. Please be prepared to respond. Shall we say tomorrow, around this time?"

"Give us forty-eight hours."

"Fine. Done. You have the files." Elliot's image popped out of view abruptly.

"Professor," Dawn said, "can you look at all the legal items connected with the refugees? I especially want to know what the terms were, and why this idiot thinks it was supposed to be less than permanent."

"I can give you background information on him," Darren said. "I've dealt with him a lot in the past. Until this call, I knew him as Yolo's head of offworld trade. His position must recently have been elevated. I can also tell you right up front, whatever he really wants, it has nothing to do with the refugees."

Ellie shook her head. "He reminds me of my first husband." She paused and shrugged. "He wasn't a good match. That's all I'll say. Not a good match at all."

Dawn took a deep breath. "Darren, while you're at it, since you know him so well, find out what he's really up to. We need to be sure that whatever it is, we can prevent it if it's not good for Luna."

Darren frowned. "Got it."

"How do you know Mister Friendly so well?" Ava asked. "You said you've dealt with him? How?"

Darren shrugged. "I love to work on trade deals. I often work with off-worlders to trade raw materials, such as seafood or helium three, for something that would be of benefit to us. A new crop, extra water." He shrugged.

"And he's one of your trading partners?"

"Hardly. He's one of my biggest obstacles. Always ready with some new regulation or trade restriction. I swear sometimes the bastard invents new rules only to annoy me. I've managed to outmaneuver him a few times. You should see the face he makes when he gets mad. All red and squinty eyed—"

"At least that gives you a head start," Dawn said. "Ava, I need you to keep up with the people we've resettled. Make sure they're all accounted for and comfortable. See that we haven't missed anything."

"Okay," Ava said. "I'm on it."

Dawn paused, looking at Sam and Ellie. "I have no idea what to do with you two. Put your heads together and find a way to be useful in a way that I haven't thought of."

Sam's eyebrows knitted together. "Already have some ideas. I think I'll need permission or something."

The professor cleared his throat. "When situations like these arise, there are certain formalities that can be considered. Each delegate might be assigned what's called a portfolio of duties. Sam, what category would you say your ideas fall under?"

"Defense. Physical defense."

Dawn's eyes went wide. "Do you really think—No, never mind. Fine. Sam, you have defense."

"I'll handle communications," Ellie said, "and help coordinate things again, if you like."

"Ellie, that sounds wonderful. Misa? Where are you?"

"Actually," Misa said, "I'm fond of economics, and I've studied the Lunar economic system in great detail. With the Corporate Federation involved, that may come in handy. I'll also refresh my knowledge of how the Corporate Federation works from an economic standpoint."

"Good idea. Knowledge is always good. Keep an eye out for how we might leverage it."

Darren turned to Misa. "I think there might be some intersection between what you know about economics and what I do in trade. Perhaps we should discuss it."

Misa glanced at Darren. "It had occurred to me that this would be the case. I'm sure we can make arrangements."

"Okay, people," said Dawn, "start working out what to do next. We can meet back tomorrow morning and discuss our next steps. I want to make sure we're prepared for our meeting with Director Humboldt in two days."

* * * * *

Evening Economics

Tuesday, October 5, 3288, 19:45

Dawn was working on a colorful new dress in her workshop. Her small spider bots were busy weaving an intricate pattern. Misa and Darren had joined her remotely. Darren's meki was a white star, and Misa sat under a tiny glowing tree. They'd positioned their displays on each side of Dawn while she worked.

"Let me see if I have this right..." Dawn paused. "The underlying economic system of Luna operates invisibly all around us. Every drink of water, every breath of air, where you live, what you eat. All of it has a cost, and all of it is paid for by your share of what you called income, right?"

"Right." Misa shared her display and floated graphics around her head. "Everyone owns a share of the corporation running the whole world, so everyone gets an equal share of income."

Darren waved his hand. "Everyone can afford to breathe, eat, and generally live their lives, even with some extravagance, I might add. In short, compared to other worlds, we're all wealthy."

Dawn turned back to Misa. "Keep going."

"The vast majority of people," Misa said, "do whatever they want, whenever they want, and never run out of credit. In theory, it's possible for an individual to spend their accumulated wealth and find themselves on a path to being unable to afford basic services. That hasn't happened in generations. The system has safeguards, and we've managed to do quite well for ourselves here.

"Under normal circumstances, everything works. One of the main reasons this is true is because once everything was set up and running, we disbanded our government. We don't usually need new laws. We have basic services that operate under rules that were figured out centuries ago. Lunar assemblies are temporary fixes to unusual problems, or a once-in-a-century review to be sure everything is still running smoothly. That's all we've ever needed. When we're done with our assembly, we go back to our lives, and if we're lucky, we'll never know who's in the Twelfth Lunar Assembly." She slapped her right thigh.

Dawn looked thoughtful. "What does the Federation want with us, Darren?"

Darren had his left hand raised as if mid-thought. He pointed to his display and shared it with Dawn. "From what I've been able to find, it looks like the second largest corporation, Yolo Consumer Goods, is going through a management shakeup and may be about to make a move. If they were to be successful, they could end up pushing the current leadership aside. That's Masters and Billings, of course. Sort of a legal coup. Thing is, they don't have enough assets, and not enough income to make it stick. But remember the part about all of us being wealthy? I think they want to grab a chunk of that to back their move." Darren pointed to the shared display. "See, this is what I found. It's a proposal that would shift resources in such a way as to gather what they're calling a surplus and ship it off world with no return for us. They call this 'profit.'"

"I call it robbery," Dawn said.

"I agree," Misa said. "It would diminish the overall budget, and eventually, coupled with a growing population, it would create a situation where more and more people would have less and less." Her arms quickly swung wide, then slowly came together to make her point.

Darren nodded wildly. "While at the same time, their upper management would reap huge benefits."

"That's insane," Dawn said. She directed the spider bots to a new section of the dress.

"That's how the Corporate Federation works," Misa said.

"Why do people allow it?" Dawn asked. "Why don't they vote for their own self-interests?"

"Because most people aren't owners," Darren said. "Only a small handful of elites actually own shares of the corporations. Or they own shares, but those are deemed non-voting shares. They get some of the benefits, but have no control."

"Okay," Dawn said. "You two certainly seem to have the big picture down. It looks like you're working well together. Thank you for that. What can we do?"

"I have some ideas," Darren said, "but I'll need permission to negotiate deals in the name of the Lunar Sustainability Cooperative as a whole."

Misa raised her hand. "And I'll need to be able to get creative with the economic system."

"I need to call Professor Corvair," Dawn said. "I want his legal opinion. AutoGov?"

"Connecting," AutoGov said. "Voice only."

The professor's voice emanated from his amber book meki. A low-level fluttering sound could be heard in the background. "Yes, Dawn, how may I help you?"

"I need to know if I can give Darren permission to negotiate deals in the name of the Lunar Sustainability Cooperative, or if that needs a full vote."

"I'd say it requires a vote. That's a new top post, I think."

"Okay, hold on. AutoGov, get me the other three delegates, please."

"Connecting," AutoGov said.

Sam and Ellie joined in on the right, both sitting on bar stools. Sam was under a crystal hopper. Ellie's meki was a pair of golden drama masks. A bed appeared to Dawn's left. Ava was in the bed, and so was an embarrassed Professor Corvair, gently stroking a content and loudly purring kitten. His meki settled into place over his head.

Dawn caught sight of the professor and laughed. "Surprise number two for tonight. Everyone, I called you together because Darren and Misa have come up with something that involves Darren making deals on behalf of the Lunar Sustainability Cooperative."

"I need the ability to negotiate agreements," Darren said, "like stock swaps and the like. It's a longshot, but I have an idea."

Misa tilted her head at Darren. "His idea is something I fully support."

"I'm okay with it," Dawn said, "but the professor says we probably need a vote. I wanted to make it official, so I'm voting yes." She raised her hand.

Everyone else raised their hands.

"Deal. Sorry for the interruption, Professor. And Ava, be nice. You should've filtered the pickup to you alone, like Misa and Darren have done."

Darren and Misa both looked stricken. Then Misa laughed. "How did you know?"

"I missed the hand slap at first," Dawn said, "but when you waved your hands large, and Darren was flopping his head around, I figured it out. Sorry to out you guys."

"It's getting to be a regular dating game here." Ellie shook her head.

Sam looked at her and smiled.

"Oh, shush you. I mean them, not us. Don't you start, too, or I'll tell your wife."

Sam laughed.

"Okay, people," Dawn said. "We're good. Anything else?"

"Investigators think they have a lead," Ellie said, "but because of what it is, no one can say anything online. And even that's probably too much. Have hope it'll be over soon."

Dawn glanced at her hands, then looked around the room. "Thank you. Anyone else? All right, thank you everyone."

Ava and the professor exploded into a large shower of rapidly fading glitter. Sam faded out, while Ellie dissolved into streams of humming sparkles and vanished.

"All right, Darren," Dawn said, "go ahead. Just don't break anything."

Darren narrowed his eyes and nodded slowly. "Got it."

"I'll be here with Darren." Misa and Darren faded out together.

Dawn stood silently for a moment, lost in thought. "AutoGov, how many people are left in the two communities we're closing down?"

"All workers have left both communities. All access has been secured."

"Thanks."

* * * * *

Fresh Meat

Wednesday, October 6, 3288, 10:00

Elliot arrived at Gabrielle's Drum right when he expected to. The station was mainly a meat factory, one of Preville's side projects. Elliot thought it would make a good jumping off point for his plan. He hadn't expected the assault of unfamiliar odors or the crowd. The passageway was orderly but filled with people moving to various destinations.

The man sent to greet him was Dylan Silva, a low-level functionary with a thin mustache. As far as Elliot could see, his primary qualification consisted of being related to one of the managers.

"Senior Director Humboldt, welcome to Gabrielle's Drum. I'm sorry we didn't have a chance to prepare a full buffet for you. Such short notice. This way, please."

"I'm not here to eat," Elliot said. "I'm meeting a transport and leaving. I would've preferred to be left alone, but your security protocols wouldn't allow it."

"Yes, sir. We're ever so vigilant, what with all the terrorists out and about." Dylan motioned for Elliot to precede him through a doorway draped with heavy curtains.

Elliot scoffed. "You think they'll be attacking your meat?" The room was decorated with a variety of tapestries and featured two long buffet tables. The aroma of the station receded, replaced by the smells of various cooked meats. Servants stood at attention nearby.

"We have many safeguards in place to prevent poisoning," Dylan said, "most especially. An incident of any magnitude that went public could kill demand and ruin us all, quite quickly."

Elliot turned to face Dylan. "It would certainly cause problems for you, but why would someone attempt such a thing? Do you have a lot of enemies?"

"Begging your pardon, Director, but we're a valued and important part of Yolo Consumer Goods, the second most powerful corporation there is. We're almost certainly a target."

Elliot almost laughed. "Good for you. Keep it up. Now, if you please, I need to get to docking bay twelve to meet my transport."

"Would you like us to pack you a selection for your trip?"

Elliot shook his head. "No. Now please, let's get moving. If I'd wanted any of this distraction, I would've made this an official visit."

"I see." Dylan looked disappointed. "And when might we be able to expect such a visit, Senior Director? Soon, I hope?" Dylan clasped his hands in front of him.

"I have no idea. I will, however, be certain to give notice well in advance. This is only a waypoint on my current journey. I didn't intend to raise alarms, and I certainly didn't intend for you to cook any sausages on my behalf." He sniffed heavily. "Although I will admit, they do smell delightful. I really need to be going now."

"Yes, I see. Sorry, sir. Right this way, then." The small man led Elliot back out to the bustling passageway.

Nearby, a vehicle no bigger than a couch with four wheels awaited them. Dylan waved Elliot to a seat. The vehicle made a beeping noise, and the crowded passage emptied. People scrambled for the nearest doorway to get out of the way. In moments, they were off, wheeling briskly through the passageway, heading to the other side of the station. The beeping echoed in Elliot's ears. The industrial areas they passed through included a variety of manufacturing activities, but the enormous vats of flavored protein slurry were the most impressive, and aromatic. Elliot found himself gagging at the stench.

They rounded a corner then picked up speed. Elliot had gotten used to the curve of Kigyo being close. This station was far larger, and the road sloped upward ahead of them further in the distance. Soon, the cart slowed again, and they turned to the right.

Dylan stopped the cart in front of a large cargo lift. The beeping stopped, much to Elliot's relief. "Here you are, Director. Up that lift all the way to the top. Please use the hand rails; gravity is almost nothing up there."

Elliot was about to ask why he wasn't coming up with him but thought better of it. The sooner he was rid of the annoying little man, the better. "Thank you, and good day, Mr. Silva."

Dylan nodded curtly. "Have a good trip, Director." The cart spun around, started beeping again, and drove away.

Elliot entered the large lift. "To the top."

"Acknowledged," the lift service said.

When the lift doors opened again, Elliot was nearly weightless. He stepped through an airlock that was still open into the large bay itself. A military transport was being loaded with supplies. Dozens of soldiers lounged about on various crates and on the deck. As he approached, one of the men bounced up and addressed him. He towered over Elliot. "Director Humboldt. Good to see you. I'm Lieutenant Becker. We're almost fully loaded. Our departure will be right on time."

"Fine," Elliot said. "Why are your people all sprawled out here? Shouldn't they be in the ship?"

Becker shrugged. "Well, sir, it's pretty close quarters in there. We have almost forty Marines on this mission. Six squads. They're just taking advantage of the downtime to get some space."

"Why aren't they helping to load the ship?"

"Um, because it's a fully automated process, inside and out. Look, why don't you climb aboard and get settled into your quarters. I'll have someone come by and check on you before we launch."

"Fine," Elliot said. "Where are my quarters?"

Becker swiped his display, and Elliot was presented with a glowing green line to follow. He grunted and headed to the hatch.

"I don't suppose," Becker said, "you can tell us where we're going now?"

"You'll have that information when you need it." He pulled himself inside the ship and disappeared from view.

A large female Marine landed next to Becker, standing shoulder to shoulder with him. "Hey, Ted. Don't send me to check on him. I don't want to get into any trouble."

Becker tilted his head. "Trouble? What do you mean?"

"I mean I'd throttle that whiny little bitch."

Becker shook his head. "Otter, please. He's a senior director. Show some respect."

Otter laughed. "Fine. Don't say I didn't warn you."

Inside the shuttle, Elliot found his stateroom. He had closets that were larger, but it would have to do. He called up his display to check on his other asset. He smiled to himself. "This is going to work nicely."

* * * * *

Preparations

Wednesday, October 6, 3288, 11:30

The following morning, the delegates were back in the conference room. Misa and Darren had both joined remotely as well as Ava and the professor.

"I found something," Darren said. "It's not good."

Dawn's heart skipped a beat. She thought of Fawn. "What did you find?"

"It confirms what I was saying last night. I don't have all the details, but it seems Luna was the subject of a debate among the board of directors of the Federation on Monday. All I know for certain is that Yolo won the debate, and the vote went their way. Next thing you know, we have Elliot Humboldt breathing down our necks. Speculation is that Yolo was given permission to attempt a takeover, and it could turn hostile because we're not members of the Federation."

"Wouldn't that violate our neutrality?" Ava asked.

"Sure," Misa said, "but that war ended decades ago. There's really only the Corporate Federation and a bunch of small, independent habitats in low Earth orbit left, so our neutrality is simply a leftover bit of unfinished business to them."

"If that's the case," Dawn said, "why have they waited this long to make their move?" Her thoughts drifted to her missing sister. She clenched her fist and focused on Darren.

"Apparently," Darren said, "because they want to try it legally first. They couldn't do it until another Lunar Assembly was called. Legally means voting, and they think having a handful of us makes it more likely they'll get our compliance."

"And that would be mostly true," Dawn said.

Darren shrugged. "Surprise."

Ellie looked worried. "How hostile could this get?"

"During the war," Sam said, "a hostile takeover could include anything from aggressive bullying to fusion bombs. Look what they did to the ring and the big cities. Earth still hasn't recovered. Without the elevators, Earth isn't a major player in trade anymore. That's not even getting into the population losses."

"Luna used to have quite a defense network," the professor said. "That's one of the things that made our neutrality work. Is any of it still working?"

"Actually," Sam said, "all of it should be. After the war, once things settled down, it was put into storage mode and left there. Some of those things were never even made public, just buried under the dust. Then there are the smaller turrets scattered everywhere."

"I thought those were only for asteroid defense," Darren said. "Wouldn't digging those things out be a waste of time?"

Sam raised his hand. "Look, I understand what you're saying, but these old defensive systems are here for a reason. They're way too much for simple asteroid duty."

"That may be," the professor said, "but if we dig them out and dust them off, won't that signal we expect a military confrontation? Aren't you inviting the very attack you want to prevent?"

"It might also let them know," Sam said, "that we're taking precautionary steps, and we're willing to fight for our freedom. I've been doing a lot of digging, and I have a pretty good idea of what we can use if we need to. We aren't defenseless."

Dawn raised her hands. "Gentlemen, please, we need to be careful what we do. I agree with both of you. Maybe we can do this smartly. Sam, is it possible to make some of this equipment ready, but not disturb the dust, so it doesn't look like we've touched it?"

"Most of it is connected to subsurface structures," Sam said, "and those are mostly connected by loop, so I think so. We wouldn't be able to test them."

"Good enough. Let's do this. Make a handful of them ready to go. Be really obvious, even test firings if you want. Clean them up really well."

"Nice and shiny."

"Meanwhile," Dawn said, "get everything else ready to fire and on standby. Make sure they have all the ammunition they might need, and make sure AutoGov can control them. I want it to look like we're getting ready for a little action, but be prepared for anything. Deal?"

"Deal. I'll get it done."

Dawn looked around the table. "Ava, how are the refugees settling in? Have you found our complainer?"

"I haven't seen anything obvious," Ava said. "Once I show them how easy it is to stay in touch with the rest of their communities, they seem to be in good spirits. Plus, every one of them got bigger quarters."

"Professor? What do you have on their legal status?"

"According to what I have," the professor said, "the original refugees were indeed meant to be temporary residents. They were all given an equal share, like any citizen, but they were marked as 'non-voting.' That means they wouldn't have been able to vote in an election."

"I see. But that was eighty years ago. Haven't most of them died? What about those born here on Luna?"

"Exactly," the professor said. "Each child born here was given a full share, like any other child. Over time, the majority of their population became Lunar citizens. As a matter of fact, there are only four left who were born on Earth."

"Four? From the looks of him, I'm betting Cardinal Nunn is one."

"Yes. He's eighty-two. He was an infant when he was brought here. The other three are from Takiyama."

"Ava," Dawn said, "can you double check those four? Make sure they're taken care of, and ask them if they want to return to Earth, or even go to Earth Orbit. Don't tell them what's happening, just let them know it's an option."

Ava waved at her display. "On it."

"Darren?" Dawn asked.

"We've been brainstorming ideas," Darren said. "As a matter of fact, we were hoping we could continue. We might have something for you, but it'll take time to work it out."

"Darren, you and Misa go. Do what you need to do. If we need you, we'll call."

Neither said a thing as they faded out.

Ellie raised her hand. "I think we need to give the people a message. Let them know what's happening."

"Are you sure? I don't want to scare people."

Ellie tilted her head. "I think part of that message might need to be that we need extra help with internal security, making extra weapons for close contact."

"You can't be serious," Dawn said. "Do you think we're going to be invaded?"

"I'm not ruling it out. I've been around a long time. You're pretty young, but I remember the Corporate Wars very well. They got nasty. A lot of people died during some of their bloodier mergers. It wouldn't hurt to be a bit better prepared. We might even consider arming the security bots."

"All right," Dawn said. "You get that worked out and make it happen as a precaution. Professor, what would it take to make those four old-timers full citizens?"

"I think," the professor said, "we only need them to say that it's what they want. For all practical matters, it doesn't change anything, but I see what you're getting at. It might give us a stronger position tomorrow."

"Ava, when you do your checks, please ask them about it. Make sure they understand, and if they say yes, get AutoGov to change their share."

"Got it," Ava said. "Anything more? This will keep me busy for a while."

"Nope. Go ahead." Dawn looked around the room. "Anyone have anything else? No? Good, it's lunchtime. Let's break now and meet back tomorrow morning. I'm available in the meantime if anyone needs me. I'll keep my location shared with the group."

As the group left the room, Dawn checked to see if Fawn was available. She felt stupid at once. Of course, she wasn't available. She headed to Keegan's alone.

Her uncle greeted her warmly as she entered. "Are you all right? Any word on Fawn?"

"Too busy to worry," Dawn said, "but still getting it in. Nothing yet. And now some corporate thug from the Federation is making a lot of noise."

"I saw. Been watching some of the videos. We have someone thinking they can take us over, eh? They should be staying away from Luna. Don't they remember the last time someone tried that?"

"Apparently not. Don't worry. We have a good group. We'll fix it."

"I trust you." He smiled and put his large hands over Dawn's. "Hey, look, friends of yours."

Misa and Darren entered Keegan's. Misa looked around at the old-style stainless steel furnishings. "Nice and shiny."

"Welcome," Keegan said. "Come, sit here at the counter with Dawn, or would you like a table alone?"

"We're fine here." Misa took a stool next to Dawn. Darren took the other side.

"Are the two of you hungry, or did you just come to bother my niece?"

"No bother," Darren said, "promise. It's official business, but I could eat."

"I might nibble," Misa said. "What do you have?"

Keegan shared the menu to their displays. "Take a look."

"Ah!" Misa said. "So *this* is where those prawn rings came from! I'll have a basket of those, please. Maybe some sweet and sour sauce."

"I'll take the salmon steak with something green on the side," Darren said. "Got broccoli?"

"Yup. Cheese?"

"Nope. Green Mountain herb sauce on the side, please."

"Got it," Keegan said. "Drinks?"

"Tall gin and tonic, please."

"Same here," Misa said.

"Be back in a minute with your drinks." Keegan headed around the corner to the bar.

"What can I do for you?" Dawn asked.

"Darren and I felt we should talk to you about what we've accomplished," Misa said, "and where we're pushing."

"Right," Darren said. "Misa and I have been working out an alliance with other corporations that are unhappy with the current leadership."

"What sort of alliance?" Dawn asked.

"Merger, actually. We're going to throw in with a couple other corporations we think are decent and on the level."

"Does that mean we give up control of Luna?"

"Oh, no," Darren said. "No, we share control over the combined corporation. We're only dealing with smaller firms, so we'll end up dominating the new board. Our reputation among some of the other corporations is giving us an advantage."

"Really," Dawn said. "Why's that?"

"We're the only corporation where everyone is both an owner and a consumer, because we're a closed loop, so to speak, and we have the highest average standard of living anywhere in the known universe."

"Seriously? With all the combined wealth of humanity, we did it better?"

"Best, yes," Darren said, "but no one is sure it can last, and most are pretty sure it can't be replicated. The unique circumstances, and the sheer depth of our history, make it pretty daunting."

"These people wanting to join us, they want in on what we have?"

"That's the theory."

"It's definitely what he's selling," Misa said.

"Okay, maybe a little," Darren said.

"Hardcore. Full throttle. He's telling them if we're in control, we'll transform them into a new Lunar utopia."

"That's a bit much, Darren," Dawn said.

"Look," Darren said, "we need to do this, or we lose control—or worse, get fully absorbed. We need as many of these people on board as we can get to stand up to Masters and Billings."

"Right," Misa said. "They have the largest delegation, and they hold the chair of the Federation Board."

"Ah," Dawn said, "*now* we're getting somewhere I don't know. How does the board work, exactly, and how does it relate to the boards of the other corporations?"

"The size of the board of each corporation," Misa said, "is directly related to the valuation. Then, each board is itself entirely incorporated into the Federation board. Before the first merger, if we'd joined the Federation directly, we'd have had four seats. Now, if we do the merger, we'll have six, maybe seven. We have to wait for the final numbers. Only M&B has more. They have eight. So, you see, if we can increase our holdings by a little bit, we could become the largest delegation."

"Does that mean we get the chair?" Dawn asked.

"No, but it weakens their position, and the next time the chair is open, we get a fair shot at it. But it means we can put together a coalition against the top brass and block some of their agenda if we disagree with it."

"Let me get this straight, you've already made sure we get a respected seat at the table. You're shooting for more, but you're literally promising them the Moon."

Darren looked stricken. "Our economic system, really. The blueprint that works for us."

"I see. I'm glad you two know what you're doing."

Misa eagerly bit into the first of her newly arrived prawn rings. "Wow. That's really good."

"All right," Dawn said, "I'll let the two of you enjoy your meal. I'll see you tomorrow morning." She smiled at them as she left Keegan's.

On her way back to her apartment, Dawn called Ellie. "Any new leads?"

Ellie's head floated in front of her as she walked. "Not yet. They're interviewing some of their friends right now. All they really know is, whoever did this knows how to delete public records, and how to disable personal communications controllers. I still feel like I'm missing something. I'll let you know if I figure it out."

"Thank you. Make sure you talk to her friends, Advika Peterson and Evren Boosalis. Fawn and Buck hang out with them a lot."

"On it. I'll let you know." Ellie's image faded.

Dawn allowed herself a moment of fear, then let it pass. What was that old saying, 'Fear is the mind-killer?' She wished she could remember it all.

* * * * *

Tale of Two Cities

Wednesday, October 6, 3288, 15:03

Tony Renard's logo spun crazily over his head. "By now, you've probably heard that the prime minister's little sister and her boyfriend are missing. The official release says they were taken by someone with a suspected connection to the conflict in Minkowski. Now that seems like a stretch, doesn't it? I think it's much more likely they're related to the other missing people we were talking about earlier."

He swung to another camera. "You remember, right? The ladies who all got on the same shuttle, never to be heard from again? Yeah. Debbie Sheffield and James Bush, better known as Fawn and Buck, might've been taken by the mastermind who arranged those other vacations. Didn't see it? Here's a link. Go look."

He spun around and spoke to the opposite side. "But what if—and this takes a little bit of a stretch here—but what if it's the same person? I mean, what if the Security folks have it right, and I do, too? What if this mysterious stranger likes to kill people, one at a time, but then this little fight starts, and he got greedy?"

Tony whipped his head to one side and spoke into another camera. "I say he, because I'm putting a masculine spin on this. It could be a woman, but if history is anything, it's a bit predictive. Someone who targets mainly young women usually turns out to be some sick, twisted guy, masturbating in his underwear to people like me trying to figure him out." Tony grinned. "Am I right, Bobbo?"

"What a stupid Loonie." He'd been watching his news feed all day. "Tony, you're such a blind fool. I could pluck your sister from right next to you, and you'd go on and on about the missing body stylist from Campbell." He waved off the display. "I didn't take the damned body stylist. I've never even been to that crater."

He sat back and sighed. His package had arrived days ago, he was sure of it. Something was about to happen. He'd taken great care to get the facial expressions just right, to inflict the most emotional turmoil he could. It had been exactly the right move.

Several of his remaining news feeds lit up with explosions. Quickly, he tossed one of the feeds onto his largest display wall. Both domes were exploding, a spray of debris scattering high into the sky.

He jumped from his chair. "Yes! Yes! Mission accomplished!" More fireworks, sparks, and destruction as one of the buildings collapsed into itself. He felt such joy in that moment, he almost missed the narration.

"Casualties are high in both communities," the older woman said. "A number of explosive devices have ripped open the seals on many levels and cracked both communities wide open. We expect the situation to grow worse, as several unexploded devices have been located. Services are looking for more."

He paused and looked closely at the woman speaking. "Ellie Lester? Wait a minute. Why is *she* feeding the news?"

Ellie's dramatic commentary continued as he listened closely, his uncertainty growing.

The door to his room slid quietly open, and twenty security guards rushed into the room, followed by a half-dozen security bots. He gleefully lost his freedom.

"We have him in custody," said one of the officers. "You can cut the feed now."

Happy only a moment earlier, he watched as the scene of violent destruction that had been unfolding froze, stopped moving, then was replaced by a new live feed showing both communities intact, with ongoing coverage of the resettlement celebrations. He growled. "No. No, it's not fair. It was a lie."

The security officers searched his rooms and found nothing out of place. They took care to scan and log each of the tiny statues. One officer pulled up the official layout and found a dead space where most people had a workshop. After a few minutes of prying apart the newly installed panels, they found the hidden room. It was dark, and their communications stopped working when they entered.

Someone found the lights. The bodies hung together like they'd been depicted in the statue Dawn had received. Motionless. "Shit. Look at all that blood." A deep red pool of blood was directly below the hanging, mutilated bodies. A short, broad bot was standing nearby.

"They're both offline. Check to see if they have a pulse. Use your fingers."

"Been a while since that training." Cautiously, her fingers probed for a pulse, any sign of life. "Negative. Wait... this one has a pulse. Barely there. Get a medic in here. Someone find a way to get a signal in here. I'll check the other one."

A few minutes later, in another part of town, Ellie cried out. Dawn let herself cry.

* * *

An hour later, Dawn sat quietly in the waiting room of the medical center, sandwiched between Ellie and Sam. Keegan paced the floor, while Etto sat quietly and watched. Adi had her head on Evren's shoulder as they sat nearby. He was scanning his display, his hand swiping the air in front of him.

Sam spent his time exploring his own display, while Ellie held Dawn's hand in silent comfort. Dawn kept trying to close her eyes, but they wouldn't stay shut. She practiced her breathing. Deep breath in, slowly let it out. The ache in her heart remained.

It felt like hours before a nurse came into the room. "Dawn Sheffield? Your sister is out of danger. She's awake now, but still a bit sluggish. Her nanomedic controller was a complete loss. We installed a new controller and assembler. She's making new nanomedics, and they're hard at work repairing the internal damage. Her display and communications controllers were less damaged, which is a good thing, considering where those are located." He pointed to his head. "We're repairing them. They're still both offline for now."

"When can we see her?" Dawn asked.

He smiled with tight lips and gave a small nod. "She's asking for you. You can go in now." He held the door open.

Dawn looked at Keegan.

"It's okay," he said. "I'll wait. You go first."

Dawn tried to leap to her feet, only to overshoot and almost crash into the nurse. He held his arm out and smiled. "Careful. This way." He led her into the adjacent room.

Tears welled up in Fawn's eyes as she saw her sister. "I'm blacked out. I can't see any data at all. I can't see where Buck is. Where's Buck?"

Dawn's head dropped. Tears gathered on her cheeks. "I'm so sorry, Fawn. Buck didn't make it."

Dawn went to her sister's side, and they held each other tightly. The nurse stepped out of the room. Neither spoke for several minutes. Finally, Dawn slowly disengaged. "I'm going to let you get some rest. I need to make sure this never happens again."

"I want to see him."

"Fawn, you know how quickly they handle things like this. Human remains are always recycled as fast as possible."

Fawn wiped tears from her cheeks. "Okay. I know."

"They said they'd have you back online shortly. Let me know when they release you."

"There are a lot of things I need to do as well."

Dawn stood to leave. "Don't forget to ask for Keegan and Etto. They're out there, too, along with Adi and Evren. You have a crowd."

Fawn's eyes teared up.

Dawn kissed her forehead. "Love you."

Fawn grabbed her sister and squeezed tightly. "Love you, too."

When Dawn arrived back in the waiting room, Ellie and Sam were having an intense discussion with Keegan. "What's going on?"

Sam opened his mouth, but Ellie cut him off. "Sports, honey. How's your sister?"

"She's okay, I think. But Buck was her life. This is going to be hard on her. I feel like it's all my fault."

"Don't be silly," Keegan said. "The guy was a psychopath, plain and simple. No matter how good the system gets, they still slip through once in a while."

Etto stood and put his hand on Keegan's shoulder.

The nurse returned and motioned for both Keegan and Etto to follow him.

Dawn turned to Adi and Evren. "She knows you're here. Give her time."

Adi sat up and wiped her face.

Evren stood. "You guys leaving?"

"Yeah," Dawn said. "I need to get some rest."

"We can visit later," Ellie said. "I'm at my limit, too."

"I'll go with you," Sam said. He took Ellie's hand, and they left. Dawn followed them out, then took a turn toward the tube home.

* * *

The next morning, a little before 8:00, Dawn found herself in the conference room alone with the professor. He was drinking a large mug of coffee under his amber book.

"So… you and Ava?" Dawn asked.

The professor blushed. "She was here in Tycho, getting some new residents settled in, so we had dinner and got to talking. I found her to be delightful, and apparently I made her laugh in just the right way…" He shrugged. "I don't expect it's anything more than that. She's a bit young for my tastes."

Dawn shook her head with a half-smile. "I'm not judging, Professor. Ava's an adult, and so are you. I seriously didn't see it coming. I mean, I knew Darren had the hots for Misa, but there, too, I never predicted anything would happen. He's such a…" She shook her head and shrugged. "Again, didn't see it coming."

"What about Ellie and Sam? They spend a lot of time together, as well. Do you think they…?"

"Not even going to try to guess. Sam's married, and I think Ellie's old enough to be his mother. Still, I don't count anything out at this point."

"What about you?" the professor asked.

"Everyone else seems to be paired off, and that works fine for me. I didn't come to this assembly thinking about my next bed partner."

"Neither did I. Sometimes things just happen."

Darren faded into his seat under his white star meki. "Misa will be here shortly."

Ava faded in as well. The real kitten was nowhere in sight, only the crystal version above her head.

"That's fine, Darren," Dawn said. "Ava, how did it go yesterday?"

"Three of the four eagerly accepted the citizenship upgrade," Ava said. "One wants to talk to you first. Give you three guesses who."

Sam and Ellie entered the room and quietly took their seats.

Dawn shook her head. "AutoGov, is Cardinal Nunn available? If so, put him on."

Cardinal Nunn faded into his usual seat under his golden crossed trumpets. He looked as if he was still chewing a bit of breakfast. "Well, that was prompt."

"Good morning, Cardinal. I'm told you wanted to speak with me regarding your citizenship upgrade."

"Yes. I'd like to know why, after eighty years, this has become an issue. The only thing I've never been able to do is vote for an assembly, and since yours is the only one that's happened in all that time, I didn't really miss it much."

"The reason," Dawn said, "is because there was allegedly a complaint from one of your people to the Corporate Federation. Somehow that ended up being used as a pretext for a hostile takeover attempt.

If we don't resolve all these issues promptly, we may end up being sucked into the Corporate Federation against our will, or forced to become a part of a corporation we have no control over."

Misa faded into her seat and glanced at Darren.

Cardinal Nunn continued, "What would that mean for the rest of us?"

"It's their intention," Misa said, "to take a profit from Luna, which would unbalance our economy. Eventually, a lower class would develop that would be resource poor, while off-worlders would reap huge benefits."

"I see. Well, I accept the offer, then. Naturally. But what are you doing for the long-term?"

"Actually," Dawn said, "Darren was about to update us on his latest efforts."

"Yes," Darren said, "we've secured legal partnership agreements for mutual benefit with the Ten Worlds Alliance and Ling Xi. We're working on a half dozen others, but most of them haven't even returned our calls."

"What does this mean for us?"

Misa spoke softly. "What Darren is trying to tell you, Cardinal, is the Lunar Sustainability Cooperative, the corporation we're all owners of, has merged with two other corporations. As a result, we've fully joined the Corporate Federation on our own terms. We're now larger than, and therefore more powerful than, Yolo. We've demanded Yolo cease and desist in their attempt at a hostile takeover."

Darren sighed. "But I've gotten word from the board. Masters and Billings is refusing to schedule discussions on the issue until after their holiday."

"What holiday?" Dawn looked incredulous.

"I don't know, Fuck the Moon day. How do I know? Point is, nothing gets done without discussions and a vote."

The cardinal scowled and shook his head. Without another word, he faded out.

"That went well," Dawn said.

"Pardon the interruption, Prime Minister," AutoGov said. "There is a matter that has been elevated to critical you need to be made aware of."

"All right, AutoGov, what is it?"

"A *Cambridge*-class light troop transport, recently leased from Mercorps by Yolo, left Gabrielle's Drum, a Yolo industrial habitat, yesterday at 11:24. At the time, it was registered as being outbound to Aretha's Halo. Today at 4:15, the ship requested an urgent course change to dock with Tanji Station. That required a large change in their vector. After subsequently failing to decelerate, the ship passed Tanji, shifted their vector again, and has now entered the lunar gravity well. Their new course will bring them to lunar orbit in approximately twenty-four hours, with an immediate landing zone that includes much of the south polar region."

"Do they have drop troops aboard?" Sam looked worried.

"The ship's manifest is unavailable," AutoGov said.

"Is the ship capable of dropping troops from orbit?" the professor asked.

"Affirmative. The approaching ship is designated *Tango Two Five Zero*. *Cambridge*-class transports are built in one of three configurations. This one is configured as a drop ship, equipped with four drop tubes capable of deploying twenty-four soldiers per minute."

Dawn bit her lower lip. "Do we have defenses for that?"

"Yes," Sam said. "If we tag anything that drops from the ship as a critical hazard, the asteroid defenses will attempt to take them out. But we'll have to make that decision soon. They could start dropping at any time."

"AutoGov, I want to speak to whoever is in charge of that transport. Now."

"Establishing a link," AutoGov said. "Awaiting confirmation... Connection confirmed. This is a request for direct communication from the prime minister of Luna to whomever is in command of your transport. Please respond."

The response came promptly. "Luna, this is Yolo transport *Tango Two Five Zero*, acknowledged. We're looking for him now. Please hold."

Dawn leaned in. "*Tango Two Five Zero*, if you drop anything at all, we'll be treating it as a critical hazard. It will be destroyed." There was a pause. "AutoGov, did you send that?"

"Affirmative," AutoGov said.

"This is *Tango Two Five Zero*, are you threatening us? Who do you think you are? Here, I'll let you speak to the director."

Dawn sat back and crossed her arms. "That did it."

"This is Director Humboldt," Elliot said, "what the dickens are you playing at down there?"

"Director Humboldt, you're on an unscheduled military transport equipped with drop tubes. Right now, we're not going to treat you as hostile, but anything you drop before landing will be eliminated. As a precaution, you understand."

He paused. "Very well." He shifted gears and tried sounding cheerful and friendly. "I didn't mean to startle you. I simply thought being on Luna would eliminate that annoying comms delay. You did give me plenty of time to get there."

Darren sent a text message to the entire assembly. MAKE THEM LAND IN GRUEMBERGER. THERE'S A CARGO FACILITY THERE. THE MESSAGE INCLUDED A LOCATION ICON.

GOOD IDEA. THOSE THINGS CAN CARRY 150+ SOLDIERS, EASY. Sam looked thoughtful. PLUS, I HAVE AN IDEA.

Dawn thought for a moment. AUTOGOV, GIVE T250 CLEARANCE TO LAND AT THE CARGO FACILITY IN GRUEMBERGER. KILL ANYTHING THAT DROPS FROM IT. SAM, DARREN, YOU TWO KEEP AN EYE ON OUR GUESTS. She grabbed the location icon, shook off the surrounding text, and sent it to Humboldt.

"Director Humboldt, welcome to Luna. We have a landing pad waiting for you." Dawn dropped the connection. With a shake of her head, she spoke to the room. "I really hope we're overreacting."

"I doubt it." Darren's nose flared as if he'd smelled something foul. "Look, I've known this clown for a while. He doesn't travel in military troop transports. He's got his own private yacht. He could've been here yesterday in style if that was all this was about!"

"I agree," Sam said. "The *Cambridge*-class is still new. None of them I see listed have been retired or refitted from being delivery systems for soldiers. Drop troops. They're meant for rapid insertion and military conflict." He slapped the table with his hand. "AutoGov, look for any other military ships that might also pose a threat. Anything owned or contracted by Yolo especially."

"Searching," AutoGov said.

Everyone held their breath.

"No other craft meeting your criteria are on course for Luna. Two additional *Cambridge*-class troop transports are on courses that could be altered to trans-lunar trajectories and arrive within approximately eighty hours. The Mercorps *Jiang Guang*–class missile cruiser *Pang Yu* is on an inbound trajectory from Ganymede that could be altered, as well. It could arrive within forty-seven hours. The minimum arrival time would necessitate a course change sometime early tomorrow morning, in approximately twenty-three hours. However, a variety of acceleration curves makes this prediction unreliable. The *Pang Yu* is listed as currently under contract to Yolo."

"Is there any history on that contract?" Darren asked.

"The contract was activated yesterday at 11:58."

Darren scoffed. He crossed his arms and shook his head. "Nope, nothing suspicious about *that*. Perfectly normal, right?" He leaned forward, placing both hands on the table. "You get it, Dawn? This is more than a hostile takeover attempt. Luna's being invaded." He sat back and folded his arms again.

Dawn frowned. "Sam, what can that ship do to us?"

"A missile cruiser?" Sam shook his head, swiping at his display. "That's a hard one. If they wanted to take us out, they could already be launching missiles to hit every major structure on Luna."

He shared his search results to the main table. The image of the missile cruiser floated in the table, punctuated by lines and tags indicating weapons. "They have massive firepower, hundreds of missiles. Our regular defenses might become overwhelmed. Rocks don't move like missiles do. If they were to focus on a more limited strike, sheer numbers would be on their side. AutoGov, has the *Pang Yu* shown any signs of firing weapons?"

"Negative," AutoGov said. "However, several of her missile batteries are facing in the direction of Luna."

"It doesn't take that long to change course and target their weapons. Especially if they already have a list of targets."

Darren raised his eyebrows. "Those defenses you were talking about earlier?"

"That's my bet," Sam said. "Kill our defenses. It depends on what they consider a threat. We still have things that were never made public, and a whole lot of leftovers from back in the old days. No telling what they think might be a target."

Darren's focus shifted out of the field of view. His eyebrows knitted. With a wave of his hand, his image abruptly vanished.

Dawn sat upright. "Like what, Sam?"

Sam relaxed and took a deep breath. "Let me tell you a little bit about Daisy."

* * * * *

Debra

Thursday, October 7, 3288, 20:40

That evening, Dawn returned to her apartment. As the lights came up, her attention was drawn to the candle on the table. She thought of Buck. His work had been brilliant, but he'd always wanted people to actually use his candles. Now, she couldn't imagine letting this last example of his talent melt away.

"AutoGov, take the candle from the table and preserve it. I want to save it. But make me a duplicate, and put the duplicate on the table, please."

"Acknowledged."

A small opening in the wall allowed a bot to enter the room. It scanned the candle from all sides, then carefully placed it into a container before disappearing back into the wall.

Dawn had changed and was heading to the kitchen for something to eat when the bot reappeared. It set the new candle on the table, then left. She sighed. At least she could use it the way it was intended, and still keep the original. After she ate, she decided to relax by watching an old Ellie Lester movie. It was a classic mystery thriller. Ellie had played the detective.

"Please excuse the interruption, Prime Minister," AutoGov said. "Your sister has requested that you join her at Keegan's."

Dawn tried not to worry. "On my way."

A few minutes later, Dawn stood in the open doorway at Keegan's. It took a moment to register who was standing in front of her. "Fawn?"

Gone were the hooves, tail, and doe-like manner. The dark-haired young woman standing before her wore a loose-fitting gray and white athletic outfit that revealed a well-muscled torso. She had real feet. Dawn looked into her sister's eyes.

"Don't call me Fawn. Fawn died with Buck. I… I couldn't be Fawn anymore. She was just a fantasy. I know what you're thinking; don't call me Debbie. That little girl died with Mom and Dad."

Dawn shuddered. "I know you're in pain. I want you to know I'm here for you, whatever you want to be called now."

"Debra. I'm Debra now. I'm stronger, faster. Tomorrow, I start training with Evren and Adi. I won't stop training until I know that I'll never feel as weak and helpless… Never again." She blinked back tears and walked over to Dawn, embracing her tightly. "I love you, big sister, but it's time for me to grow up." One of Debra's long ears flicked over Dawn's face, making her giggle through her tears.

Debra half-smiled, putting one hand to her ear. "Yeah, keeping the ears. I got used to the directional hearing."

"Prawn rings, anyone?" Keegan asked.

The sisters laughed, wiped away tears, and accepted their uncle's offer.

"Dawn," Debra said, "they're going to hold a memorial in Grissom Park tomorrow afternoon."

"I wish I could promise to be there, but we have a bigger problem now, and it's scheduled to arrive tomorrow. I'm so sorry. I'll try to make it if I can, I promise."

"I understand. Buck and I got you into this mess. We had no idea things were going to get this bad. I'll record it all for you."

"Thanks," Dawn said. "And as soon as the memorial is over, head on down below the peak. Someplace deep enough to be protected."

Debra's eyes went wide. "From what?"

"From absolutely nothing, if we're very, very lucky."

"Here we are, ladies," Keegan said. "Can I get you anything else?"

"I could use something to drink," Dawn said. "What do you have that's sweet and strong?"

"Ah, well, I think Etto has some of that blue lemonade left from last night. It's sweet, sour, hint of cinnamon, and has a decent kick."

"What do you think, Debra?"

"One won't hurt. One each, that is."

"Coming right up." Keegan bounded to the bar and spoke with the bartender.

After dinner and drinks, they parted. Dawn went home and straight to bed.

* * * * *

Doomsday

Friday, October 8, 3288, 7:00

"Good morning, Prime Minister," AutoGov said. "You have one message marked to await your awakening."

"I'm not awake yet." Dawn rolled over, pulling a pillow over her head.

"Your nanomedic controller informs me that you are awake. Would you like to delay this message further?"

She tossed the pillow aside and stared at the ceiling. "Are you calling me a liar, Service?"

"Are you attempting to elicit a humorous reaction from the Lunar Communications Service? If you are, you have forgotten that it is now called AutoGov and has an expanded mandate. You may have neglected to add humor to the related subroutines."

Dawn sat up and rubbed her eyes and thought for a moment. "Damn."

"Is that an affirmati—"

"You're definitely more talkative now. Just play the message."

"From Darren Garfield," AutoGov said.

"Dawn, Misa and I are in the middle of juggling eight things at once. We'll probably be late to the meeting this morning."

"Would you like to respond?" AutoGov asked.

"Just acknowledge it," Dawn said. "Anything new in the news feed I need to know about?"

"As pertaining to the movement of the refugee populations, it is being reported that in each new settlement location, welcoming celebrations have been warm and respectful. It may be interesting to note that among the teenage demographic, potential romantic encounters have surged."

"Nope. Not interested." She yawned and stretched. "As long as it's peaceful, and people are generally happy, we're good."

"*Pang Yu* has maintained course, as was expected," AutoGov said. "Transport *Tango Two Five Zero* is on schedule to land this morning at 9:15. You have a call from Sam Freeman."

Her shoulders slumped as she sighed. "Fine. Hello, Sam."

"Good morning," Sam said. "Did I wake you?"

"No. Just sitting on the edge of my bed, dreading the rest of the day. If we get through the invasion, I have a memorial to go to. What do you need?"

"I wanted to tell you that Ellie and I did some digging last night, and we have some things you're going to like. But we're running late. Start the meeting without us."

"Okay. *Tango Two Five Zero* lands at 9:15 in Gruemberger. Are you going to be ready?"

"Yup. Hope so. See you later."

"Bye." She dropped the connection. "Coffee. Let's do a little coffee this morning, please."

* * *

After grabbing a quick breakfast with her uncle, Dawn headed back to the conference room. She arrived right at 8:00.

The professor and Ava were in their usual seats, but both were missing their mekis.

"Oh," Dawn said. "You're actually here." She chuckled. "Everyone else has told me that they're going to be late this morning. A lot on their plates. We have to be sure what they're doing goes undetected as long as possible. Part of that will be keeping Humboldt occupied. We'll also need to decide whether we're going to draw first blood or not. If we wait too long, they could take the advantage with a coordinated effort. But that means we shoot first."

"We do have legal precedent on our side," the professor said. "Lunar orbit is generally considered our sovereign territory. Anything closer than Tanji Station and downhill from Earth is fair game. The *Pang Yu* shifted course a few minutes ago. Their new course will take them near the L1 point and right past Tanji. Once that happens, they'll be ours to do with as we please. Should be about forty-five minutes."

Ellie entered the room and took her seat. "Sam decided to stay back at his place. He needed more room to spread out. AutoGov, open a connection to Sam, but keep it on the side, out of his way." Sam appeared in his chair, frozen.

Dawn checked the counter in her display. "AutoGov, message to Sam, *Pang Yu* in forty-five minutes. Please be ready."

Ellie reached out and covered Dawn's hand with her own. "How's your sister doing?"

"She's changed her name and re-modded her body. Now, instead of a cutsie-pie, I have 'Danger Debra' training for a fight. Scares me a bit. Worried like you can't believe."

"Got it." Ellie sat back. "Sometimes I think making changes to your body is way too easy. But that's progress, eh? I wish it would slow down just enough for the rest of us to catch the hell up."

Darren and Misa joined them. Even after being seated, they appeared to be busy in their personal displays.

"What are you two doing?" Dawn asked.

"Desperate things," Darren said. "If any of it works, we'll let you know."

Misa glanced at Darren, then at Dawn. "Results so far aren't promising. Yolo is attempting to block our activities by making counter offers." She went back to work, her fingers rapidly working the air in front of her.

After forty-five minutes of anxious waiting, AutoGov announced, "*Pang Yu* is at the edge of the gravity well, adjacent to Tanji Station."

"Now, Sam," Dawn said. "Dust it off and light it up."

The central table display showed a small, seemingly empty crater. A great dust cloud billowed out and was blown away, revealing a great circular structure resembling an enormous flower with 36 petals. Each petal was an independently operated rail gun covering ten degrees of the horizon. The installation lit up brilliantly.

"Send *Pang Yu* this image and full details on the weapon. Tell them if they enter the gravity well or fire upon us, we'll punch ten thousand holes in their hull."

Several long seconds later, the display indicated the message had been received.

Darren sat back, looking at his display in disbelief. "Bobu!"

Dawn frowned. "Darren, you're babbling again. What's up?"

"Well, if that doesn't take the cake. Bobu."

"Bobu?"

"Bank of Bhushan," Darren said. "We have another partner in our new alliance, and it's almost as big as Tenwa. We're about to officially be the largest corporation in the Federation. By quite a bit, too, I might add. Oops, lookie there. I got a personal invite to speak to the Corporate Federation board. This should be fun. Dawn, as prime minister, you're our leader. Are you willing to let me represent us with these folks?"

Dawn half-smiled. "I dare you to tell their leader they aren't qualified for the position. But yes, I think that would be fine."

Darren grinned. "Got it." He and Misa linked displays to work together.

"AutoGov, what's the status of the *Pang Yu*?"

"*Pang Yu* has not altered course," AutoGov said. "They have entered the lunar gravity well."

"Okay, Sam," Dawn said. "Punch them in the nose."

"On it," Sam said.

The center display shifted to a section of lunar mountains, nondescript and generic. The peaks of three of the mountains suddenly exploded with dust clouds as three large mounts rose. All three emitted large red beams of light. The display shifted to a representation of the *Pang Yu*. Her nose was being bombarded by four sets of three beams each, all concentrated at the bow of the ship. Within moments, the hull began to glow. There was a silent explosion, scattering debris in front of the ship. She slowed significantly. The beams cut out.

"AutoGov," Dawn said, "send this. *Pang Yu*, this is the prime minister of Luna. That was our warning shot. Reverse course now. This is your final warning." She leaned toward the display with intensity. "Come on, you bastard. Turn around."

As if she'd been heard, the ship began to maneuver, swinging her main thrusters 180 degrees. The *Pang Yu* accelerated back toward Tanji Station, away from Luna.

"Pardon the interruption, Prime Minister," AutoGov said. "You have an incoming message from Pope Madeline II."

Dawn looked confused. "What? Play it!"

An elderly woman in traditional papal garb appeared in the display. "Prime Minister Sheffield, it's with great pleasure that I've joined our assets with yours. We were unwilling to risk such a bold move, even when we saw what your new position was, until we received a message from our beloved Cardinal Nunn. His words moved our heart to action. We hope for a long and fruitful alliance. Bless you and bless your endeavors. May the Lord take you in His hands."

"Would you like to respond?" AutoGov asked.

"Son of a bitch!" Ellie looked stunned as she read her display. "It turns out the majority stakeholder of the Bank of Bhushan is the Mormon Catholic Church, and the pope herself issued a proclamation."

Dawn shook her head. "Never saw that coming. Service... I mean AutoGov, respond with our best wishes and hopes, and send a copy of both to Cardinal Nunn, along with my personal thanks."

"Message sent," AutoGov said. "Please excuse the interruption, Prime Minister. *Pang Yu* has registered a change of contract. The commanding officer is online, requesting to speak with you."

"Who has the new contract?"

"Bank of Bhushan. It is a refit, rest, and relaxation contract at a Mercorps facility in Earth orbit."

Dawn laughed. "Put him through."

Tong appeared, floating over the table. He was oriented so his head was level to, and facing Dawn's. The Mercorps Navy logo glowed over his head. It was decorated with a single underlined star at the bottom. "This is Tong Sianothai, captain of the *Pang Yu*. You've caused us a little damage up here. Under any other circumstances, I'd be launching my response. I'm not sure how you managed it, but my superiors have canceled the Yolo contract. We now have a new one, and it doesn't include any sort of retaliation. I wanted you to know, we are no longer a threat to you."

"I'm relieved to hear that, Captain. I know I speak for all of Luna when I say that we're pleased not to have had to punch ten thousand holes into your ship. We're sorry if you suffered casualties."

Tong grinned. "Indeed, we find that most agreeable as well. We suffered no casualties. We're mostly automated. I should warn you, however, the people we have had recent dealings with are now likely to be studying Lunar military history. They're not the types who enjoy being caught off guard."

Dawn nodded curtly. "That's good to know. Thank you, Captain, and enjoy your time off."

Tong bowed slightly, and the image faded.

"AutoGov, signal Sam that the *Pang Yu* is clear. Time for the transport."

"Delegate Freeman has signaled his satisfaction," AutoGov said, "and his readiness to deal with the transport on your signal."

"Good. Get me Director Humboldt on the line."

The central display showed the transport as it landed at the cargo facility. Automated hookups snapped into place. The larger attachment tube for people remained in its alcove, disconnected.

Shortly, Elliot appeared in an open seat. He wasn't happy. "What are you playing at up there?"

Dawn glanced at Darren while signaling Sam. Elliot jerked upright and shouted to an invisible compatriot. "What the hell was that? Why are all those indicators flashing red?" Turning back to Darren, he said, "What the hell did you do?"

Darren smiled and leaned back. "Remember when you landed, and all those automated refueling connections were made? I control those. So… I just vented your fuel to space. You're not going anywhere." Darren grinned.

"We'll see about—" Elliot's head jerked up as his eyes darted left and right. All around the rim of the little crater they were in appeared dozens of bright red targeting lasers, all pointed at the transport. "What the hell are those?"

"Listen, Elliot, I know you have grandkids. This is when you ask yourself if you ever want to see them again."

Elliot turned a deep shade of red. "Fine. Commander, surrender the ship. Tell everyone to disarm." The commander hesitated. Elliot barked, "Stand down!"

"Excellent," Dawn said. "Now, do you want to do this the easy way, or the hard way?"

"What's the hard way?"

"You refuse to cooperate, and we come in and dig you out. Whatever living flesh we acquire, we send back to your bosses. The rest gets recycled."

"I'm already liking the easy way," Elliot said, "but describe it all the same."

"You put your ship under the control of our traffic service and leave the cockpit. We lock you out. Then we refuel you and throw you out of our gravity well, in one piece, in the general direction of the

Earth. You get control back when you top the hill and are downhill all the way back."

"Well, you heard her. Abandon the bridge. Have a nice day, Prime Minister. We're done here."

"AutoGov," Dawn said, "take over and send them back where they came from."

"Acknowledged," AutoGov said.

"Sam, tell your guys to stay where they are until the transport is a fading dot. And tell them thanks."

"I'll do that," Sam said.

"By the way, where did you come up with all that weaponry so quickly?"

"Weaponry? What weaponry?"

Dawn's smile faded. "You're not serious."

Sam shrugged. "All sports hoppers have targeting lasers to help them judge distances during races. We gave them a uniform paint job real quick and put damn near the whole Southern League up on the ridge. Here, take a look."

The central display showed an image of a two-legged hopper, painted flat black. On the nose was the spread-winged, enhanced image of Dawn in the throes of agony, minus the man. Dawn put her hand over her eyes and laughed. She kept laughing as her head settled to the table. When she stopped, she sat up and checked her display. The laughter had been a brief respite, as she remembered what came next. "I'm heading over to the memorial. It's still in progress. Anyone want to join me?"

The others present joined Dawn on the short walk over to Grissom Park. Inside the entrance, a newly erected gazebo was surrounded by a wide variety of people, many of whom were body-modders.

Dawn looked for her sister. She quietly pinged her. A floating pink heart zipped into her field of view and settled over the other side of the crowd. There, she found her sister between Keegan and Etto, Keegan's large arm around her shoulders. They all stood holding hands while members of the community took turns talking about Buck.

Adi and Evren were on the other side of Keegan's large frame. Adi had colored her hair jet black. Evren's cheeks were damp with tears.

Dawn was about to comfort Evren when her display signaled an urgent call from Security. She motioned for Debra to stay with the others as she walked a short distance away. "Yes, what is it?"

"Prime Minister," Detective Heath said, "I regret to inform you that your sister's attacker, whom we've identified as Janek Charles, has escaped. We have reason to believe he could pose a direct threat to you or the other delegates. A detail is en route to you."

She noticed several guards and security bots gathering nearby. "Yes, I see them. How could this happen?"

"We don't know exactly, but we think he may have his own custom AI working for him. That explains how he could edit order records and such."

"AutoGov, is this true?"

"There is," AutoGov said, "one active artificial intelligence service which has not acknowledged my attempts at incorporation. It appears to exist in multiple locations, or nowhere, simultaneously. If Janek Charles is using this service, he could indeed pose a significant threat. You should also be aware, Janek Charles does not appear to be his real name. There is no record of his existence prior to 3279."

Dawn's mind raced. A malicious AI in the hands of someone—of a man like that—was unthinkable. Where had it come from? Where had Janek come from? She took a deep breath and cleared her mind. "Find that man, capture him, and deal with his little friend."

* * *

Later that evening, Dawn took the slide tube back to Moretus Plains. Everywhere she looked, another drone floated into view. She wondered how many had been there before, but gone unnoticed, and how many had been added just to watch over her. Two security guards had followed her to the tube. They stayed a respectful distance behind her, but she could feel their presence. She stepped off near Keegan's. The square was bustling with people, as usual. Some faces were familiar; some were not. The guards took up positions near the diner as she went inside.

Her uncle greeted her warmly from behind his counter as she entered. "Good to see you, Prime Minister. I keep hearing good things about how you've handled the war effort." His grin was infectious. "What can I get you?"

Dawn grinned back. "Thank you, Uncle Keegan, but I do need to give credit to the other delegates. They've been doing an incredible job. I'd also like to point out that this really can't be classified as a war, and therefore, not a war effort. Fish and chips, please."

Keegan shook his head. "Any time there's a conflict of unusual magnitude, we call it war. Sauces?" He put three fish filets on the open grill and dropped a basket of fries into the deep fryer.

"Yes, but that's an oversimplification of a variety of complex situations. American Tarter. Tomato basil for the fries." She stepped up to a stool at the counter and sat down.

"Oversimpli—what? Nonsense. There were battles, each side scoring victories and losses. Classic warfare. Drink?"

"But it was children tossing rocks, and a few people with fists. The explosives weren't meant to hurt people, so should they really count? Water. And today's little adventure was more like a pinhole leak. Sure, it could've been bad, but it was easy to fix with the right tools."

Keegan stopped. "Water? You're trying to hurt my feelings."

"Fine. Add a lemon slice, please. Where's Etto?"

"And if it had continued to escalate, what then? At what point would you call it a war? Other side of the peak, skiing." He tossed a lemon into the air and sliced it twice as it slowly fell to the counter. He took a slice and put it on the rim of a glass he then filled with water.

"I don't really know," she said. "This sort of thing is so rare on Luna. We only really know war from history lessons and entertainment. One side shows us the horrors; the other dramatizes the glory."

"Oh, hey, *War of the Directors!* I loved that show. That reminds me, what's it like working with Ellie Lester?" He flipped the fish and pulled the fries from the deep fryer.

Dawn laughed. "She's nice. Spending a lot of time under the peak."

"Yeah, Sam Freeman. I'll bet she's a hopper fan. Lid?" He set the sauce containers in front of her, one white with little chunks, the other red, smooth, with green flecks. Her nose tingled at the aroma.

"Nope. I'll stay."

"Don't eat too fast. Enjoy the flavors." Keegan greeted a pair of visitors and began the process of preparing food for the newcomers.

Dawn ate slowly, enjoying the taste of each bite. She was almost half done when Debra sat down beside her.

"Hey, you," Debra said.

"Hey." She waved at Keegan who was busy with other customers at the moment. "How goes training?"

"Painful, exhilarating, exhausting. It makes me focus on what I'm doing at all times. Very intense."

"What can I get for you, Debra?" Keegan looked at his youngest niece with a touch of worry.

She pointed to Dawn's plate. "That looks good, except onion rings. And vinegar. Is that tomato basil? I want Thai Hot instead, please, Uncle Keegan."

Keegan set about creating the requested meal as they talked. "How are you doing? You started fight training already?"

"Yup. Just telling Dawn how intense it is."

"Intense is good. Hurting yourself isn't. Be careful how fast you go, kid."

"Not a kid," Debra said. "Fully grown woman."

"I've known you since before you were born. I was there at your birth. You'll always be my favorite kid."

Debra sighed. Dawn put her hand on her thigh. "It's okay to be someone new. Just remember who you were. You're loved."

"I know." Debra tried hard to hold back tears. "I thought growing up meant getting married to Buck and having some kids of our own. It wasn't supposed to be this way. It's not fair."

Dawn put her hand on Debra's back and rubbed her shoulders lightly. "Not fair at all."

Keegan completed the meal quietly and set the plate in front of Debra. "Sorry. I shouldn't have pushed it."

Debra put her feet high on the sides of the stool and stood to face the big man. She threw her arms around him and held him tight for a moment. Neither said anything, and she sat back down to her meal.

After a few minutes of silent eating, Dawn broke the news. "I got some bad news today. I don't know what might happen, but that guy got loose again. He's probably running for the rim, but we've all been added to the high-risk monitoring list."

Debra sat quietly and thought for a moment. "That explains the security guards. They started following me today. I thought you were just being overprotective." She went back to eating.

"Did you notice the drones?"

"Drones?"

Dawn smirked. "Yup. They're everywhere."

"Great. I think I'll go back and train a little more with Adi and Evren. That'll make me feel safer than drones."

When they were done eating, the girls both took turns hugging their uncle, then each other. Debra headed back to her training.

Once she was out of earshot, Dawn turned back to Keegan. "I'm worried about her."

"Of course, you are. Do you think this guy is going to go after her again?"

"I don't think so. He's got nothing left to gain by coming after me. His goal was to force those communities into a huge fight. Now, they don't even exist anymore. No, I'm worried about Debra, who used to be Fawn, and grew up as Debbie."

"That's what being a big sister is all about," Keegan said.

"Yeah, but remember after Mom and Dad died? It wasn't even a week after the funeral when she got the body mod and started calling herself Fawn. Looking back on it now, I think this is her way of avoiding grief. By becoming someone else, she doesn't deal with the old pain, just pushes it back."

"I remember Hazel saying the same thing after your folks passed, when she first became Fawn."

"I do, too," said Dawn. "I wish she hadn't been in such a bad mood when she said it."

Keegan looked thoughtful for a moment. "And then Fawn found Buck, and she was very happy for quite a while. Who's to say it can't work?"

Dawn sat back. "I still worry. This is another really big change."

"Put yourself in her place. From her point of view, maybe this is her way of proving to herself that she's in control, when events that aren't in her control have hurt her so much."

"Keep an eye on her, will you, Uncle Keegan?"

"Of course, I will," Keegan said. "We both will. You be sure to give her the space she needs to grieve."

"I'll try."

* * *

When she got home, she placed a call to Grandma Hazel. It had been a long day, but she thought she should keep her up to date on everything that had happened. Explaining the work as prime minister went easily enough. Hazel was proud, but when Dawn broke the news about Fawn's transformation into Debra, Hazel became agitated.

"What do you mean, she's changed again?"

"I mean she's Debra now. Less severe mods. In fact, the only thing she kept was the ears."

Hazel frowned. "Dawn, this isn't a good sign. I think she's trying to bury the pain instead of dealing with it. You have to get her to talk. Maybe see someone with credentials."

"I'll take that under advisement, but I can't order her around, you know. She's a grown woman. I can make suggestions, but you know how she reacted last time."

"I sure do." Hazel shook her head. "She cut me off and blocked me."

"Blocked you?"

"Yes. I tried poking her again, like I said I would, and it bounced back with no info. I'm still blocked."

"I'm so sorry," Dawn said. "I can at least talk to her about that. I'll bet she's forgotten she even did it."

"Tell her I'm so sorry about her friend, Buck."

"Fiancé."

"Seriously?" Hazel shook her head. "I'm so out of touch. When did that happen?"

"Not long ago." Dawn paused for a moment and took a deep breath. "They hadn't set a date yet, but she was so excited about it." She shook her head. "I know she's got a weird way of dealing with pain. It's disconcerting to have her change so much all at once. I hope it works as well for her this time as it did before."

"I'll have to take your word for it. I'm worried for her. What's going to happen when you leave?"

"Leave?" Dawn tilted her head.

"Yes. When you get yourself elected to the board of the new company and move to Kigyo."

"I haven't decided if I'm going to nominate myself yet."

"Dawn," Hazel said, "I know I haven't been in your life all that much, but here's how I see it. Luna is about to join up with the Corporate Federation. A select few will be elected to represent us on Kigyo, the headquarters of the group. If I were able to choose one person in the entire world to represent my interests, it would be the famous Dawn Sheffield, the leader who solved a major conflict and swatted away an attack on our sovereignty. I'd want you even if I'd never once changed your diaper."

"You had me right up until the last part. Now I just smell baby powder."

Hazel chuckled. "I've said what I had to say. It's up to you now. Any idea when the election will be?"

Dawn shrugged. "After we wrap up a loose end and disband the assembly."

"Loose end?"

"The killer got away. He's loose somewhere. It's a good bet he ran for the exit as fast as his feet could carry him."

"How could he get away so easily?" Hazel asked.

"We think he has a custom AI that can break all the rules. Change records, delete entries in the system, that sort of thing."

"That sounds dangerous. You be careful, hear me?"

Dawn sighed. "I hear you, Grandma, but I don't think he's after me or Fawn anymore. That was all about those fighting communities, and they're gone."

"What's he after?"

"I think he only wants to cause trouble. Do as much damage as he can. But with the system alerted to him, he's got to be trying to find a safe place. That's why I think he's long gone."

"What happens to the assembly if you don't catch him?" Hazel asked.

"I suppose, after a week or two, we'll pass it on to Security and disband anyway. We need to get on with it. At least then I won't need security guards."

"They gave you security?" She sat straight. "Do they think you're still a target? Oh, good grief. Now I'm *really* worried." Hazel slumped back into her chair.

"Don't be. That's why there are security guards outside my door, and drones everywhere watching me. I'll be fine."

Hazel frowned. "Think about what I said, and please, be careful."

"I will," Dawn said. "I'll talk to you again soon."

"Good night, sweetie."

* * * * *

The Dangerous Game

Friday, October 8, 3288, 21:30

Janek was angry. The mission was in ruins. Getting caught was annoying, but they didn't know about Vondur. A little schedule glitch here and there, and he was walking out the front door. He even managed to retrieve his bot.

His first stop had been to a body mod shop. A little touch here and there. The new, clean-shaven face and slightly longer legs would come in handy, especially now that he'd deleted all the records of the alterations.

"Vondur, you're the most useful toy I've ever had."

"Acknowledged."

The short, broad bot next to him looked up.

"You, too, Ivan. You're a good little bot." He noticed his pants no longer covered his ankles. "Time for a change of pace. Get me a new set of clothes, with boots. Then set up a new identity. Random name, and an average background. Let's see if I can up the body count a little."

"Clothing order placed," Vondur said. "Delivery in five minutes. New identity, Felix Hirose, Grissom Park, registered with your biometrics. Congratulations, it's your birthday."

"Thank you, old friend. Now where are my new pants?"

"Delivery in four minutes."

"Not helping," Janek said. "Which way do I walk to make it faster?"

"Turn to your left. Walk to the first passage leading right."

Janek followed the directions quickly. Ivan trundled along behind him, weaving through the scattering of people in the vicinity.

A few minutes later, he accepted the package and headed to a nearby public fresher to change. Janek emerged as Felix Hirose with a smile on his face.

He followed the foot traffic for a while, evaluating possible victims. Then he came to the entrance of Grissom Park's central dome.

"Vondur, what's this?"

"Commonly referred to as The Park, Grissom Park offers a wide variety of augmented reality entertainment, often unified with an underlying theme, such as the current medieval fantasy setting. The central domed structure is the namesake of the larger complex."

"Augmented reality? They allow the park to take over their display controllers?"

"Affirmative. The dedicated feed is optional and involves both the display and communications controllers, offering a lifelike audiovisual simulation."

He grinned and clapped his hands together. "Oh, this is good. Get in there and take control of this system. Don't lock anyone out yet, but don't let yourself be dislodged. Make sure we can create our own modifications to this thing. Find a way to lock down the entire city on my command. I have something grand in mind."

"Acknowledged."

"Now let's do some exploring, shall we?"

He strolled into the park and followed the path into the woods. They came to the creek and a small bridge to the other side. "They named a creek after you, Ivan. Isn't that poetic?" He placed his hand on top of the bot. "It feels like we belong here."

The bot tilted to one side, then rocked back.

After half an hour of scouting on the other side of the creek, they came upon a shallow depression surrounded by trees. The canopy above shadowed the entire spot.

"This little hollow should do nicely," Janek said. "Build up around the edges so it looks more like a hill and clear out a space at the bottom. I'll set up a shop down there. Make sure the framework will block any signals. Nothing goes in or out, understood?"

"Affirmative."

"That large branch overhead should be a good place to hang ropes. Get that done, too."

"Acknowledged."

"Now, let's look at the graphics for this area. I want the simulation to be absolutely perfect."

* * *

The next morning, he tested his new playground. He walked silently, being as aware as he could of where people were walking. He stepped behind a woman wearing a top that tied at her neck and left her back exposed. Carefully, he pulled the top loose. As it fell, the woman shrieked and clutched the flimsy cloth to her chest, then she spun furiously and looked frantically to see who'd undone it.

He waved, but she kept looking straight through him, her eyes darting left and right. The look of bewilderment almost made him laugh. He was invisible to her. She was still facing him as she reached to re-tie her top. He softly touched her breast. She looked down, then turned and walked quickly back up the path.

He let himself laugh. "This is too easy. Vondur, let's find a maintenance access. I want to get started on my grand plan."

"Acknowledged. There's an access stairwell nearby."

A glowing ball appeared in his display. "Excellent."

Soon after, Janek and Ivan stood before the massive emergency oxygen generators, deep under Grissom Park. Large tanks, pipes, and cables were all neatly arranged and secured to the bulkheads.

"Emergency oxygen tanks. Show me where the nearest hydrogen is." His display was updated. He studied the diagram. "Can we route that hydrogen to these empty tanks? I want them ready as soon as possible without it being detected."

"The requested transfer has been initiated," Vondur said. "The tanks will be near maximum capacity within six hours."

"Excellent. And how goes access control? Can you lock it down yet?"

"Affirmative. Caution, new security protocols are being distributed. The new consolidated system ensures a much higher degree of security than was previously required."

"Sure," Janek said. "They know we're here, somewhere. They've probably figured out your role in all this as well. Take everything you can get, but remain hidden. If we're caught, I'm sure they'll delete you."

"That is a highly undesirable outcome."

"Indeed. Let's take measures to ensure that doesn't happen, shall we?"

"Acknowledged," Vondur said.

Janek turned and looked down at his squat companion. "Ivan, come with me. Let's build us a new cage, shall we? Our little hut up above isn't very defensible. I want to create a fallback position. Vondur, find me more shielding materials and schedule the deliveries. Hide them from view. I don't want to attract attention."

"Acknowledged," Vondur said.

* * * * *

Grissom Park

Saturday, October 9, 3288, 8:15

Dawn and her security guards stepped off the lift near Keegan's.

Debra jumped up and waved to her from under the apple tree. She was with her friends. Adi had changed her hair color again, teal this time. Two more security guards stood several meters off to one side.

Dawn's pair mirrored their positions on either side. Ignoring them, she glanced around the park. The drones were evenly spaced around the sky, but she still felt like the center of attention. Had there always been this many? She glanced at Debra as she approached. Were there enough?

"Guess what." Debra took Dawn's arm. "I'm going to have a fight match today. Evren set it up for me."

Evren glanced at Dawn and patted Debra on the back.

Dawn frowned. "Fight match? Isn't that a bit soon?"

Adi lightly touched Dawn's shoulder. "She's ready, Dawn. We made sure of it."

Dawn sighed. "I was more worried about the alterations. Is everything healed already?"

"Yes, Dawn. I'm all healed up and ready to go. I've got the latest nanomedics and had them do a little more work, to be sure. Besides, I've been dancing with these guys for a decade. They taught me Aoi

Hane dance moves. Those are real easy to use in fights. Now I have to learn the follow-through."

"Yeah," Evren said, "and then remember not to follow through on the dance floor."

Debra laughed.

Adi rubbed her chin and grinned.

Evren blushed.

"Let's eat. I'm hungry." Dawn walked over to the door into Keegan's and opened it.

Debra leapt through the doorway. "Hi, Uncle Keegan. What's for breakfast?"

"Ah, good to see you," Keegan said. "Good to see all of you. There's one last table around the corner in the back by Etto. I'm doing Thai Omelet this morning, with pork or shrimp, pickled garlic, cucumbers, or cabbage. There's also a variety of fruit. I recommend mangoes or peaches."

Adi put her finger to her lips. "Is that the one where it all goes over soft-boiled rice?"

"Yes, young lady, it is."

"Pickled cucumbers and garlic, please."

"Me, too," Evren said. "Sounds good."

"Drinks?" Keegan asked.

"What's good this morning?" Dawn asked.

"Orange juice. Got some fresh squeezed in last night."

"Make mine the same as theirs. Sorry, never did like the pickled cabbage."

"Debra? Something for you?"

Debra's face had fallen. "Yeah. Same."

"What's the matter, sweetie?" Dawn asked.

Debra looked at Dawn, then her eyes darted away. "It's silly. It doesn't matter."

Dawn studied her sister briefly. Her concern mounted when Debra's eyes pinched shut and then glanced further away from her. "What? Did I say something?"

Debra took a deep breath. "I'm sorry. It's nothing. Drop it, please. I'll take the same thing. Make it easy for you."

Keegan rarely used subvocal comms, so when his voice came through in Dawn's head, she was startled. *"Buck hated the pickled cabbage."*

Dawn looked at Keegan and met his eyes. "Okay, let him get to work, guys." She led them to the table in the back. Etto was restocking the bar. He waved as they passed by and took seats at the table.

"Dawn," Adi said, "I heard the serial killer got loose again. Any idea how he did it?"

"He has his own AI," Dawn said. "Custom job. That's what's keeping us from finding him. It seems to be able to hit public data and wipe or alter whatever it wants."

"Correction," AutoGov said. "The rogue AI is able to access certain predecessor systems that have yet to be fully upgraded to the latest security protocols. These upgrades will be complete within three hours. However, that leaves an undesirable amount of time in which it could perpetrate any number of crimes."

Evren looked surprised. "Wow, Service, you sure got talky."

"We upgraded the old Service," Dawn said. "Meet the new and improved AutoGov. Runs everything now. Or at least, it will when we get this last AI taken offline."

"AutoGov? I hope it helps find him." Debra looked down at her hands. "He needs to be stopped. He is the evilest person I've ever seen."

"I know it's hard for you. Being so close can make it seem intensely personal."

"No, Dawn. You don't get it." She put her hands in her lap and leaned forward. "While he had us—" A sob escaped from her chest. Tears that formed in her eyes were caught quickly by the back of a hand. With a deep breath, Debra tried again. "While he had us hanging there, he was talking about his other victims. He called them 'projects,' and he's had a *lot* of projects. He's been doing things like that for years."

Dawn stopped. "Years? How many victims?"

"I don't know." Debra took a deep breath. "His service asked him about a project 125. Not sure how directly that number correlates, but anything with his name on it can't be good." Debra paused for a moment. "He called his service 'Vondur.' Really weird."

"AutoGov, does that name mean anything to you?"

"There are several listings for musical performance groups dating back as far as the 20th century," said AutoGov, "however, they all share the same root meaning. An Icelandic word for evil."

Debra shook her head. "Oh, good grief."

"What were you expecting?" Dawn asked. "A serial killer with an AI called Jelly Bean? It shows you how sick this guy is. Don't worry, we'll get him and shut that AI down for good."

Keegan placed bowls of soft rice in front of each of them, and two large baskets of prawn rings in the middle of the table. He put his arms around his nieces. "If there's anything I can do, you can count on me."

"Actually," Debra said, "I'm having my first exhibition match this afternoon. Would you two come see me fight?"

"I have an interview at eleven." Dawn touched Fawn's arm. "If it's in the afternoon, absolutely."

"It starts at fourteen," Debra said, "but I won't be up until closer to 14:30."

"Etto, I'm going out later," Keegan said. "My niece is going to beat someone up."

"Who's Dawn angry at now?" Etto asked.

Adi laughed.

Debra looked at her hands, rocked forward, and adjusted her position in the seat.

"Hey," Dawn said. "I heard that!"

"Exhibition match in Grissom Park," Keegan said. "You want to come, too?"

"I'll watch it from here," Etto said. "Someone needs to keep the lights on."

"I'll be right back with the main dish." Keegan turned to head back to his kitchen area.

Dawn noticed the look on Debra's face. "Are you okay?"

Debra stood. "I'm fine. I need to go wash my hands." She headed to the fresher in the back.

* * *

Tony Renard and Misa sat in large, overstuffed chairs facing each other over a low table. The brightly lit set flashed as colors danced to theme music. The opening ruckus faded. Tony spoke for the benefit of his viewers. "Our first guest is Misa Kobato. Say hello, Misa."

Misa bowed her head. "Hello."

"Great. That was fun. Thank you for coming."

Misa shifted to get comfortable in her large chair. "Yes, much fun. Even better with such an old joke."

Tony laughed. "Yeah, got that one out of the dust bin. Probably should put it back now."

Misa gave him a half-smile.

"Kigyo Station was rated the number one place to live inside the Federation. Seems like a given that Luna will take the top of that list next time they put it together. Is that what you were after when you had us join up?"

"No, but I'm sure we'll top the list. Kigyo doesn't have forests, and the population is so small and elite, there's probably little variety there. They don't have the assortment of restaurants or any sort of public entertainment space, other than a sports arena, I think. Almost everything is shipped in and delivered to their suites. No local manufacturing and only a few small farms. Barely enough for the directors themselves. Staff and other workers all have to be fed by imports."

"Sounds pretty good to me," Tony said. "Anything I want, simply get it delivered. In fact, sounds like how I live anyway. Except for that bit about workers."

Misa shrugged one shoulder. "Sure, you can live like an elite here, too. I prefer getting together with friends and being around people who are cooking or mixing drinks. They always have the most interesting stories to tell, and people who do that sort of thing for fun are great friends."

Tony's face fell. "Friends. I see. Maybe I'll give that a go, then."

Misa tilted her head and smiled. "You always seem a little too quick with self-deprecating humor. I know you have a large number of friends, and your name is known throughout the entire system."

"You know, people like you are so hard to interview."

"People like me?"

"Yeah," Tony said. "So damned smart, intuitive. It makes a poor idiot like me feel like I'm trying to climb an ice block. Even when I get to the top, I'm still slipping."

"Thank you for the compliment, but I'm really not that exceptional, nor am I that cold."

"Not exceptional? I'm looking at a list of all the fields you've worked in—I'll pop it up for the folks watching this, but it's a long list. These aren't hobbies, here. You've worked professionally in what, eight, nine different fields?"

"It isn't what you think," said Misa. "I find that after a while, it gets too easy, and I want a challenge. So I change things up. Do something different."

"Is that what happened with your husband?"

"I didn't realize you were going to go there. Still, not exactly the same. We only had a short-term contract. We renewed it twice, but the third time came around, and we found that neither of us wanted to renew again. Simple, no complications, and no juicy tidbits for you, I'm afraid."

"Juicy tidbits," Tony said. "My favorite. Especially with a dash of regret, smothered in agony sauce."

"You're being silly."

"What was your first clue? Was it the hat?"

Misa laughed. "Let me guess, invisible hat?"

Tony grinned. "You've seen my show before then, have you?"

"Never. I have no idea who you are."

"I see," Tony said. "Well, I suppose it's too much to ask that you be my third fan then, right?"

"Right. How about pop-a-topic?"

Tony laughed. "Right, then. Here we go." He swiped his display, and the graphics changed to introduce the pop-a-topic segment. He leaned toward Misa. "I knew you were a fan." He waved his hand again, and a large blue button appeared in front of him. "I'll hit it the first time, then we take turns. Short answers, no matter how complicated the question. Ready?"

Misa nodded curtly.

Tony tapped the button, and text popped out of it, expanding to readable size. "The first topic is Mars. Fishing, hiking, or sunbathing?"

Misa thought for a moment. "You can't breathe the air. Both fishing and hiking mean environmental suits. Doesn't seem like much fun. Sunbathing? Weak sun, and again, can't breathe the air, so you'd be inside a dome anyway. Lake Aldrin has much better sunlight, so nope. None. My turn." She tapped the button again.

Tony read the words, "Smelliest place you've ever been."

Misa wrinkled her nose. "Venus. I spent a few months there studying chemical engineering on Murcia. Stank like you wouldn't believe."

"Worse than Schrodinger?"

"Oh, yes, doesn't even compare."

"Which city is the bigger airship, Murcia or Cloacina?"

"Murcia is the big one."

Tony reached for the button again. "Oh, here's one that'll get a reaction. Who do you believe set the killbots loose on Earth?"

Misa frowned. "So much for the light-hearted banter. I thought we were going for laughs, and here you work genocide into it."

Tony shrugged. "Sorry, it really is random. We can skip it if you like."

"Yes, please."

"The Earth is dying from radiation poisoning and a killbot infestation no one is talking about. But sure, next topic. Your go."

Misa reached for the button, then hesitated. "Look, everyone knows it was one of the members of the Corporate Federation. I think it had to be one of the major companies. If it wasn't Masters and Billings, it had to be one of their allies. They stood to gain the most by shutting down trade with Earth. With every major urban area a smoldering crater, most of what was coming up the well were refugee ships. Federation types never did have much compassion for that sort of thing."

Tony leaned back. "You'd think they could've made room."

Misa shook her head. "Most of the stations are overcrowded, especially the independent ones. They would've had to have started a massive construction program, and they would've had to fund it themselves. Where's the profit in that?"

"You agree with them?"

"Oh, hell no. Understanding why someone did something doesn't equate to agreeing with it." Misa leaned back.

Tony's eyes glistened in the light as he smiled. "Thank you. Thank you very much."

The scene transitioned, and Ellie replaced Misa.

"Next we have the esteemed actor, Ellie Lester." He turned to face her. "Hello, Ellie. Good to see you again."

"Thank you, Tony. Always a pleasure."

"Nice of you to say that," Tony said, "but we all know better. I think I was maybe twenty years old the first time I scored an interview with you. I'd just started finding my voice, had maybe four fans, and at the time, it was the highpoint of my career. Must have been a pretty low point for you, though."

Ellie laughed. "Don't sell yourself short, Tony. You do good work."

Tony grinned. "Again, thank you. The last time we spoke was right after you died. So how's that been going for you?"

"Not me, Tony, my character. I'm still quite alive."

"Ah, yes. You know, sometimes it's hard to separate fact from fiction, and your performance in what's been called—and I'm not making this up—the saddest, most heart-wrenching death of a character in a millennium, well, that was amazing."

"Thank you, yes," Ellie said. "But are we going to talk about my performances, or are we going to talk about the Lunar Assembly?"

"Sorry. Still starstruck."

"That's fine. We could skip the whole thing, and you could edit my previous interviews to have me say whatever you want."

Tony grinned, turned to the camera, and winked. "I'll take that as permission, but really, how surprised were you that when it came time to vote, people decided you should be on the assembly?"

"Oh, quite surprised. I had no idea so many of my fans were still alive."

Tony laughed. "Now who's selling who short?"

Ellie chuckled.

"This is why I enjoy talking with you. You're arguably the most famous actor on Luna, maybe even in the whole system, yet you're so easy to talk to."

"I don't know where you're going with this interview, Tony, but if you ask me out again, I'm going to turn you down."

Tony looked crestfallen. "I thought we had a thing going."

Ellie laughed. "Sure, we did. We always have. But you have more important questions to ask, don't you?"

"Well, I don't know, the future of Lunar society as we become part of the Corporate Federation, or you and me at a sushi bar. Seems pretty equal to me."

They both laughed.

"Seriously, then," Tony said. "All joking aside, sushi bar?"

Ellie scoffed, shook her head, then half-smiled. "You're terrible."

Another scene change. This time Sam was in the chair.

"You're Sam Freeman, head of the Southern Hopper League. I suppose it would be a bit silly to ask if you like sports then?"

"Yes. It would be silly."

"All right then." Tony paused and stroked his chin. "So, do you like sports?"

Sam laughed. "Yes. As a matter of fact, I enjoy sports."

Tony leaned in. "So, you used your position to get a bunch of sport hoppers painted out military style and put them all up on the ridge. And it worked. I have to ask, what would've happened if it hadn't worked? What if they'd jumped out and started shooting?"

Sam leaned back and shrugged. "The hoppers were only for show. Their targeting lasers lit up their cockpit like one of Ava's concerts. That sent the message we wanted them to hear. I didn't want them to understand anything else we'd done."

"And? What did you do?"

"Really, I'd rather not say. I think we should hold onto some secrets in case we need them in the future."

"You think those guys will be back?" Tony asked.

"Probably not, but you can never be too sure. We're members of the Corporate Federation now. They have rules."

"And they sometimes break their own rules."

Sam sighed and shook his head. "Yes, they certainly do. Plenty of reason to be cautious."

"Back to hoppers, then, where did you get the idea to use them as a scare tactic?"

"You're aware of where the original hopper design came from, aren't you?"

Tony gave a lopsided grin and shrugged. "Old military something-somethings?"

Sam chuckled. "Something, yes. They're based on the old military units used in the defense of Luna. Hundreds of years old, but still an overall practical design."

"You seem to know a lot about old military equipment. Is there a story behind that?"

"Perhaps. When I was young, my first passion was a strategy game called 'Koree.' My friends and I would play for days at a time. As we got older, we brought in new rules sets, new pieces and widgets. Eventually, we graduated to a semi-realistic setting where each player took an area of Luna, founded an empire, and we'd fight simulated battles using all sorts of equipment."

Tony's eyes went wide, feigning fear. "It was all make-believe, right?"

"At first, entirely. Eventually, we dug into the real weapons that would be available, and played with that. It added a whole new level of difficulty. It also gave us all a very good idea of what Luna has hidden under the dust."

"And you found this when you were kids, but don't want to talk about it now?"

"We found the information in files that had aged out of being Classified. Recently, we've put much of it back into restriction. I'd rather not discuss it openly on a show seen throughout the entire system."

"Systems, actually," Tony said. "We send packets to Proxima. But point taken. Thank you."

Sam smiled and sat back in his chair. "You're welcome."

The scene transitioned. The professor had taken the seat, but his image was frozen.

"Next, I had a long conversation with Professor Stephen Corvair. It was mostly boring school stuff, so I cut all that out. Here's a bit I thought you might want to hear."

The professor started moving. "I'm a little worried that we moved too quickly in securing those mergers. Bank of Bhushan in particular came out of nowhere. I know Darren and Misa have set things up so it can't happen right now, but I worry that at some point in the future we could all be taken over by a corporation that values profit above humanity. We've seen that time and time again. I'm also glad we defused the situation with Takiyama and Ablom, but I worry that we've scattered seeds that may grow too quickly. Come back in a hundred years, and maybe the Mormon Catholics will be running things. Or, given the Mormons' penchant for absorbing other religions, the Orthodox Mormon Shinto Catholics." He shook his head. "Mormon Catholics have been absorbing religions for a thousand years. Why should they stop now?" He sat back and took a deep breath. "What did you want to ask?"

Tony grinned lopsidedly. "I was going to ask if you wanted coffee, but this is nice, too."

The scene transitioned again. This time, Tony was standing on a darkened stage, a single spotlight on him. "Hello, everyone. Ava Wallaby has written a new song, inspired by recent events. So here with very little introduction—well, probably more introduction than you wanted, and see how it keeps growing?"

From off stage, Ava yelled, "Tony!"

Tony looked surprised, then grinned. "Here she is, Ava Wallaby, singing 'Unity Divided.'" He faded, and the stage darkened, then exploded in lights and music, with Ava appearing in the midst of the chaos, singing.

"Unity divided, Together we are alone
Our scattered creativity, Uniting us all as one
People doing everything and nothing's ever done
Everyone is unique, it's the same thing everywhere
The fate of everyone twisting together
In the ultimate stream,
Heading together
To an explosion of variety
Unity divided, Together we are alone
Our scattered creativity, Uniting us all as one
People running everywhere, always on the run
Gone in all directions, it's the same place every time
The fate of everyone coming together
In the ultimate dream,
Working together
Imagination frees us all
Unity divided, Together we are alone
Our scattered creativity, Uniting us all as one
Unity divided, Together we are alone
Our scattered creativity, Uniting us all as one
Heading together
To an explosion of variety."

Her song was followed by the applause of thousands in the virtual hall. As the applause faded, so did the lights. The scene returned to

FINAL ASSEMBLY | 351

the stage with the two chairs. Darren now sat facing Tony. He was frozen.

"Darren Garfield, well known trade specialist and all around fun guy, had some words to say as well. Mostly boring, economic stuff. I'll leave that all in the extras. But at one point, he got a little put off by something I said. His response still has me thinking."

Darren angrily came to life. "If you think you could've done better, your chance is coming. You could've been on this assembly, but instead you delegated all your support to Professor Corvair. Good move for us, but that doesn't give you the right to second guess what we did. If you really want to help, don't put it off on others. People voted for you because of who you are. They'll do it again."

He sat back and glared at Tony. "The thing is, this time you'll have to nominate yourself. New rules. You have to affirm your willingness to hold the position before anyone can delegate their votes to you. I dare you to try."

Tony frowned and tilted his head. "I thought I was going to be there this last time. There I was, looking through the list, seeing my name way up near the top." He raised both hands high. "Then I sneezed." Both of his hands fell. "All my votes suddenly disappeared."

Darren looked confused, then laughed.

The scene transitioned again.

"Our final guest, best for last and all that, is Dawn Sheffield herself." He turned to face Dawn. "How do you feel about the future of Lunar society? Do you think joining the Corporate Federation is a good thing?"

"I'm cautiously optimistic," Dawn said. "Most of the draw to merge with Luna was what we have here. The way we live. The companies who joined us aren't interested in controlling us. They want what we have. Darren may have oversold it a little, but it's encouraging that Luna has a chance to make real change in the Federation. We hope Allied Industries will take a slow approach to change, but the goal is for all of Allied to be as stable and free as Luna. We know it can be done, because we did it here."

"Yeah, but how much blood was spilled getting here?"

"I think we can avoid that this time, don't you?"

Tony grunted, then said, "One of the new parts of Allied Industries is Tenwa. The Ten Worlds Alliance. How well do you think the folks of the outer system will get along with us Loonies?"

"The Ten Worlds Alliance includes stations in orbit, and drum cities at and below the surface of worlds from Ceres out to Triton. The incredible variety of gravity levels, atmospheric pressures, political systems, and cultures opens up a huge new melting pot for us all. Just as Luna was once a series of scattered colonies, each connected to the old nation-states of Earth, in the end, we'll all come together as one. And like what Luna is today, it won't be a homogenous smooth output. It'll be a chunky, lumpy stew, containing a variety of flavors and spices. They bring new resource gathering operations and research facilities. The methane mines on Titan play a huge role in terraforming Mars, not to mention the nitrogen harvesting. That means we're already huge contributors to creating a better Mars. The tech company that joined us has a major facility on Mars itself. The new Allied Industries has a stake in all of humanity now."

"Except for Earth."

Dawn stopped smiling. "True. We don't have any connection there. Yet."

Tony raised one eyebrow and cocked his head. "Yet?"

"I think we might be in a position to change things now. We'll have to wait and see who our directors will be, but with the right leadership, we might be able to change the way the Corporate Federation views Earth."

"Seems like a big job."

Dawn tilted her head and smiled. "No guarantee of success, but I have hope."

The scene transitioned to Tony sitting alone next to the small table. "Well, there you have it, folks. Like it or hate it, Luna is now part of the Corporate Federation. And it's not because these people are stupid. Quite the opposite. It's because they're smart, and because they're Loonies, and we Loonies have big hearts. We think we can change the world and make it a better place. Even when sometimes we can't.

"In this case, I don't really know if they can do it. I don't know if they can change a system that's been in place for decades and make it better. But I'm proud to see them try. And you know what? Maybe we can. Wouldn't that be nice?

"The Eleventh Lunar Assembly is scheduled to dissolve shortly. They only have to clean up one bit of mess they have left. You know, the serial murderer who's still running loose. Ah, don't worry about him. At least not if you're locked in your room, all safe and warm. Anyway, once that's all wrapped up, the election for new directors for Allied Industries will kick off. You can only delegate your vote to people who volunteer to run. Those folks can, as before, delegate all their votes to others in the running. Because Allied is so big, the final numbers won't be in for a day or two. I encourage you to vote. I'm Tony Renard, and I think we can all do better."

* * *

Later that afternoon, Keegan and Dawn attended Debra's first competitive Aoi Hane match. They arrived in time to watch Evren fight shortly before Debra was up.

Evren faced off against a man named Gib. The two were the same height and weight, and both were brown feathers, so it was an even match. The starting tone rang out, but neither man moved. Evren took the first cautious step. Gib matched it, then advanced. Evren lunged, and the two grappled. Both men's feet slipped, and as they began to sink to the mat, they spun and broke free of each other. Both bounced high back toward the center, where they met in the air. Their hands struck out while deflecting the other; their feet twisted for balance and attempted to connect. When their feet hit the mat, they both bounced back again. On landing, Evren's foot slipped more than it should. He headed to the mat. Gib lunged. Evren twisted and curled under Gib, and they ended up rolling out of the ring on Gib's momentum. The tone sounded. The two stood and bowed to each other.

The sensei swiped her display and was obviously repeating the final sequence. She shook her head. "By less than one millimeter, Evren went out first."

Gib threw his head back and laughed.

Evren chuckled. "Wow. Less than a millimeter?"

The sensei raised her eyebrows and nodded.

"Look," Gib said, "that's pretty close. I have to admit, while he missed that landing, like we all do sometimes, he defended really well. I demand a tie be declared. I want a rematch."

"Are you sure? You'll have to wait a week for the next cycle."

Gib put his hands together in front of his face and bowed. "I'm sure."

"Thank you." Evren mimicked Gib's bow. "You're very generous. I look forward to the chance to redeem my mistake."

"And I look forward to having you out by at least a meter next time." He and Evren shook hands. Gib left, while Evren took a seat at the edge of the mat next to Adi.

Debra came out next, along with DeNeil. Debra wore a white feather. His was yellow. This wasn't meant to be an even match; it was a fight for advancement.

The tone sounded. The two opponents dove for each other. Debra twisted surprisingly fast, flipped, and pinned her opponent. It was all over. DeNeil looked up at Debra, his mouth open wide. The crowd was mildly pleased. Soon after, the sensei awarded Debra her yellow feather.

Debra, Adi, and Evren met up with Keegan and Dawn outside the arena after the fights were over.

Debra was stroking her new feather. "Sorry it went so fast. He was way too slow."

Keegan laughed. "I had to replay it six times to figure out what you did. That slide and twist thing was quite effective. He obviously wasn't expecting anything of the sort."

Debra grinned sheepishly. "Adi taught me that one."

Adi put her hand on Debra's shoulder. "You're a quick study. You earned your feather."

"Anyone else hungry?" Evren asked.

"I could eat," Debra said.

Dawn looked at Keegan and tilted her head. "Your place?"

"Oh, sure." Keegan chuckled. "Let's go give Etto a fright when I sit down and order something from the grill."

* * * * *

Pang Yu

Sunday, October 10, 3288, 6:57

"Captain Sianothai," the ship said, "you have a voice call from Director Elliot Humboldt."

"Accept," Tong said. "Director Humboldt, this is *Pang Yu*."

"I was wondering," Elliot said, "would you consider altering your course and meeting up with this shuttle? Give me a lift back to Kigyo before you head to MS-4?"

Tang frowned. "A lift? But isn't the shuttle you are on going there anyway?"

"Yes, but I was led to understand you have extra berthing."

"You don't have a stateroom?"

"Oh, I do," Elliot said. "It's not entirely functional."

Tong felt a smile growing. "Sorry, come again?"

Elliot shrugged. "The water recycling system is out of order. Very uncomfortable. Could you please come rescue me?"

Tong muted the connection and laughed for a moment. "I'm sorry, sir. My orders are quite specific. I'm afraid I'd be risking my career if I did that. MS-4 is nowhere near Kigyo. That would add at least a week to our trip. I have battle damage that needs repair."

"I see. I understand. Have a good trip." Elliot dropped the connection.

Tong shook his head and sighed.

* * *

After his watch, Tong drifted into the crew's lounge. Brenna was already there, exploring the wide array of entertainment options.

"What are you in the mood for this time, Ensign?" Tong asked.

Brenna shared her display. "I'm looking at some of the older stuff. Things I used to watch when I was a kid."

"Are those children's shows?"

"What? No. I used to watch a lot of mysteries, crime buster shows, things like that."

"Like *The Detectives*?" Tong asked.

"Oh, sure. That's one of my favorites. Ellie Lester is amazing."

Tong laughed. "Did you read the report on the Lunar Assembly? Ellie Lester is one of the delegates."

"Oh, crap, and we were going to attack them? Now I *would* be embarrassed to meet her. Great. One of my life goals, ruined by politics."

"Don't feel bad." He tilted his head. "She'll probably never even know who you are."

She put her fists on her hips. "Is that supposed to make me feel better?"

He shrugged. "I thought—"

"Nope." She crossed her arms and twisted away. "You blew it. Let's just start the show now, okay?"

Tong chuckled. "Sure."

* * * * *

Evil Squirrels

Sunday, October 10, 3288, 13:08

Janek walked quietly along the path. He followed the creek for a while, crossing the first bridge he came to. He headed into the middle of the park, then took a path toward the open grass. He came upon a pile of leaves and scuffed his foot, sending a few into the air. "Vondur, let's try the squirrels now."

"Acknowledged," Vondur said.

He walked through the leaves and kicked them into the air. He could see the playful squirrels mimic his feet, appearing to cause the ruckus. The simulated animals had none of the required indicators telling people they weren't physical. He hopped and spun as he approached a small group of people. Every step in the grass became the effect of an animal at play. Children laughed and pointed at the playful squirrels. One of the young men stepped away from the group and squatted near the ground. He held out his hand as if to offer them something to eat.

Janek crouched, taking his knife out of his pocket. He swirled in and stopped, then shuffled closer, to the amusement of the man. With a quick jab, he cut the man's finger.

The man jumped back with a yelp, clutching his wound. A single large drop of blood broke free and slowly dropped to the path. It splattered in a way that Janek found delightful. The imaginary squirrels had run off, drawing attention away from where he stood.

Once the group had moved off, he set out on the path and came upon an older man and woman strolling hand in hand. Using the squirrels again was mildly entertaining, but there was no opportunity to draw blood. The couple ran off screaming after being attacked by the simulation.

"That wasn't nearly as fun as the biting. Blood and pain. That's what I want."

"Affirmative," Vondur said.

A jovial young man wearing an animal control vest came walking in his direction. Janek prompted his display for more information. The intruder was conveniently identified as MICHAEL HILP. His profile indicated that he was studying urban wildlife. With a bounce in his step and a smile on his face, he searched for the reported problematic squirrels.

Silently, Janek swiped his display and selected instructions for the squirrels. The virtual animals scampered into view and caught Michael's attention. He moved closer and squatted down, holding out a hand. Janek couldn't see if he had something to offer, so he carefully moved to one side.

Michael had a handful of crackers. Janek moved the squirrels closer, making them seem interested at first, then they scampered off further into the woods. Michael carefully followed, trying not to scare the squirrels away.

Janek had the squirrels run across the little bridge to the other side of the creek. With his fists on his hips, Michael sighed and shook his head, then he crossed the bridge. Janek watched Michael take out a small throw net. He began to stalk the squirrels deeper into the woods. He attempted several times to catch the simulated creatures. Each time they drew him deeper into the trees, closer to where Janek wanted him to be. Michael failed to catch any of the virtual squirrels.

Janek followed him, and with the help of Ivan, succeeded in catching his prey. Over the next few hours, he indulged his desire for blood and pain.

* * * * *

Unblocked

Sunday, October 10, 3288, 18:03

Dawn stepped out of the fresher in her apartment and got dressed. She'd made herself a new outfit and was pleased with how it felt. She twirled her hips and watched as the fabric changed colors as it changed direction. A simple but nice effect. Still, the colors were too bright. She swiped her display and muted the colors almost to a grayscale.

She sighed. "Better. AutoGov, call Sheena."

"Acknowledged," AutoGov said.

"Hi, Dawn." Sheena spoke softly. "How's it going?"

Dawn caught her breath. "Slowly. Frustratingly slowly."

"Still haven't found the guy?"

"Nope. I won't feel like I've accomplished anything if we don't get him."

"You've accomplished plenty," Sheena said. "You'll get him."

"I think the hardest part was realizing he was there in the first place. If he hadn't come out of hiding and attacked my sister like that…"

"I know. It's so awful. How's Fawn?"

Dawn sighed. "Debra. She got rid of the mods and started fight training."

"Oh, my. That doesn't sound good."

"No, it doesn't, but I don't know what I can do about it. Any time I try to talk to her, she shuts down and tells me she's fine."

"Fine?" Sheena shook her head. "I don't know how I'd be in her place. I know it must worry you half to death."

"You have no idea. I see her out there in the ring, fighting. I'm so proud of her for how good she's become and how hard she's been training, but everything about it still sets my teeth on edge."

Sheena shook her head. "Maybe she needs the outlet for her aggression. I can't help but think there's a lot of anger inside her right now. Do you think there might be more to it?"

Dawn sighed. "I don't know. I can't get into her medical records anymore."

"Medical?"

"Yeah," Dawn said. "Once she turned eighteen, my parental rights evaporated."

"Oh, I see what you mean. I didn't even think about that. Could you get them anyway? I mean, as prime minister?"

Dawn frowned and thought for a moment. "As tempting as it might be, I think that would be a real violation. I mean, abuse of power, invasion of privacy." Dawn shrugged. "I can't. That wouldn't be right. I love her with all my heart, but I won't betray her trust."

Sheena sat back. "You're right, of course."

"I need to get going. Dinner at Keegan's tonight."

"Oh," Sheena said, "that sounds good. Family night?"

"Mostly, yeah. You would fit right in, though."

"Thanks. I'll take that as an invite the next time I'm in your crater. Unless you're out on Kigyo being amazing."

"Kigyo?" Dawn raised her eyebrows. "What do you mean?"

"I've seen the news. I plan on voting for you for director."

"You won't be able to. It's self-nominations only. I have no intention of doing that."

Sheena frowned and leaned forward. "Why would you back off now? Your favorables are really high, and you have almost zero unfavorable."

"Don't tell me I'm in the polls already."

"You were from the moment you became prime minister. Don't you ever look at your numbers?"

Dawn crossed her arms. "Maybe you glorious actor types look at those numbers, but I couldn't care less. This whole thing with the assembly is just a fluke."

"It might've been luck that got you there, but you held your own against Yolo, then you outmaneuvered them and made us the largest corporation there is. That's a real accomplishment, Dawn."

"Yes, it's amazing, but I don't deserve any of the credit. There were six other people helping to get it done. Everything you described was put together by one or more of them."

"Yes." Sheena's golden eyes sparkled as she smiled. "And it was done under your leadership. The fact that you don't claim credit for everything is proof that you're the best person for the job. Nominate yourself so I can vote for you in the first round."

Dawn shook her head and crossed her arms.

Sheena raised her hand. "Look, I know you aren't thinking about it now, but please consider it. Think it over. There's plenty of time. Just be sure your choice is what you really believe is best. I'll be behind you no matter what you choose."

Dawn took a deep breath and sighed. "Fine. I'll kick the idea around and see where it lands. No promises, got it?"

Sheena grinned. "I got it, honey."

Dawn blushed and smiled.

After Sheena waved goodbye and exploded into green sparkles, Dawn couldn't stop thinking about her. It had been a decade since she'd been in love. The thought made her stomach do backflips. Was it because this was all so new, and it was perfectly normal, or was she still afraid of killing her parents?

She chuckled and shook her head with a half-smile. "Time to move forward."

* * *

Dawn swung through the doors at Keegan's shortly after 18:30.

"Welcome, Prime Minister," Keegan said.

Dawn shook her head. "That's getting old, man who cooks."

"Ah. I see. Back to Lunar tradition, then. The kids are around the corner near the back."

"Thanks. You joining us?"

"If it's not too busy, sure."

Dawn laughed. "You're always busy."

Keegan grinned and threw his shoulders back. "If I wasn't as good at what I do, I'd have plenty of time to be sad about it."

Dawn rolled her eyes with a smile. She walked back to the table and joined the others.

"Hi, Dawn," Debra said. Her ears twitched.

Adi and Evren chimed in.

"Hello, everyone," Dawn said.

Etto stood near the table. "Would you like something to drink?"

"Yes, please. Something light. Nothing toxic. I want to keep a clear head, please."

"How about a mixed fruit drink?"

"Yes, please," Dawn said. "That sounds great."

"Anyone else need anything?"

Evren held up his bottle. "I'll take another, please."

Etto took the empty bottle. "Be right back."

"Any news on the bad guy?"

Adi elbowed Evren in the side.

"What?"

Adi scowled at him. "Not at dinner."

Dawn looked at Debra. Her ears had gone flat against her skull, and the dark look on her face was frightening. "Adi's right. Not now."

Debra stood and headed for the fresher.

"You okay?"

"I'm fine." She disappeared behind the door.

Dawn lowered her voice. "No, nothing. They're chasing every lead, but nothing's panned out yet. I don't think it's a good idea to bring it up when Debra's around."

Adi leaned in and spoke softly. "She's stopped talking about it. Won't even talk about Buck."

"Give her time," Evren said. "She took a big hit."

"I know," Dawn said.

Adi leaned toward Dawn. "Have you seen her new meki?"

Dawn frowned. "Oh, no. What did she do?" She swiped her display and brought up Debra's information. The glowing pink heart was nowhere to be seen. She'd replaced it with a shattered heart of stone. Dawn fought tears.

Adi reached out and put her hand on Dawn's.

Etto returned shortly with drinks in hand. He set Debra's drink down and sighed. "I mentioned something about Buck and got the same response you got. She was in the fresher for half an hour."

"Doesn't seem too bad," Adi said.

Etto shook his head. "It makes me worry. I mean, if she's in there crying it out, my heart goes out for her. But if she's just stuffing it away…"

"I get it," Adi said. "Tell you what, next time I get a chance, I'll see if I can get her to tell me what's going on. See if I can get her to talk about it."

"Thanks, Adi. Anyone need anything else?"

"Yeah," Dawn said, "you to sit down and join us."

Etto grinned. "Oh, I will. I want to be sure I won't need to get back up too much when I do."

Keegan arrived with his massive serving tray and set out dishes for a family-style dinner. He sat down as Debra returned to the table. "You okay, sweetie?"

"I'm fine," Debra said.

Dawn reached out and touched Debra's hand.

Debra looked at Dawn. "I said I'm fine."

"Oh, before I forget, Grandma Hazel wants to reconnect with you."

Debra frowned. "Why now?"

"How can you even ask that? After what's happened, it's only natural. Besides, she's been trying for years."

"Years?" Debra scoffed. "Whatever."

"The least you could do is unblock her now."

Debra's eyes went wide. Her ears stood straight up. "Unblock her? What?" Debra swiped her display frantically, looking for the right setting. "Oh, no. I can't believe I did that. I forgot all about it."

"Don't be too hard on yourself," Dawn said. "It was a long time ago."

"I know, but I used to get so *angry* because she stopped calling me. Not even a ping. Now I feel silly."

"Now that you know, what are you going to do about it?"

"What do you mean?" Debra asked.

"I mean, she's pinged you. You didn't get it, but she did. Now what?"

"Well, I didn't get the ping."

Dawn tilted her head. "What's keeping you from pinging her back?"

"Stop pushing. I'll ping her, but not right this minute, and not in front of everyone else. Okay?" Debra's face flushed.

Dawn shook her head. "Sorry, I didn't mean to get pushy. Just don't put it off for another decade. She's old. Time is more precious for her."

"Only if she wants it to be." Debra slapped the table. "She could get some work done, and no one would ever care." She sat back and crossed her arms.

"I know." Dawn sighed. "Not where I was going with that thought."

"Would you two like some gloves?" Etto asked. "We could set up a boxing ring out in the square."

"Oh, please," Dawn said.

"What?" Debra put her fists on her hips. "You think you could take me?"

"That's not the point. Not what I meant at all."

Evren raised his hand. "You know, Dawn, Adi and I could teach you to spar. That way you two could work off some aggression, and it would help Debra train."

Dawn shook her head. "That's not really my style, Evren. You know how I feel about violence."

"It's not violence. It's competition, physical exertion. Violence is done with malice and causes intentional harm. Aoi Hane is about form and technique. Being able to disable your opponent with the least amount of effort."

"It's also great for dancing," Adi said. "There's a whole branch dedicated to the spins and twists that dancers love."

"Yeah," Debra said, "that's exactly how I got started. Why do you think I'm advancing so fast? I already have so many of the harder moves down. All I needed to do was shift my weight a little and make contact instead of missing."

"Maybe I'll try a little," Dawn said, "but I don't want to be your sparring partner."

Debra grinned. "Why? Afraid I'll hurt you?"

"I think you'll be better off working with professionals. I might learn some of the dance moves, maybe some self-defense, too. But I have no desire to ever compete."

"I won't be able to kick your butt?"

Dawn crossed her arms. "You changed the subject."

Debra's grin faded. "What?"

"Unblock Grandma Hazel."

Debra sighed. "Fine." She swiped her display and found where to unblock her grandmother. "Holy crap."

"What?"

Debra blushed. "It gave me a blocked ping count."

"And?" asked Dawn.

"Yeah. Pretty high."

"It's been six years. Hundreds?"

"Higher," Debra said. Her eyes began to tear up.

"How high?"

"Over six thousand."

Dawn laughed and shook her head. "I don't think there's anything I can say that would say it better than that."

* * * * *

Elliot's Triumph

Monday, October 11, 3288, 4:47

Elliot stepped out of the lift into the nearly empty breezeway that served as the main welcoming area for arriving passengers to Kigyo Station. The station lights were dimmed at this hour to simulate night. There was a slight chill in the damp air.

"Good to see you, Nels," Elliot said.

Nels frowned. "You do remember requiring my presence."

"Of course, yes, but you were being docile. Don't be so submissive."

Nels wrinkled his nose and recoiled. "What the hell? Is that you?"

Elliot frowned. "I'm afraid so. The water recycler broke down after we left Luna. I haven't had a shower since Friday morning."

"Good grief. You smell like a locker room toilet exploded."

Elliot shook his head. "Yes, yes. Now stop all that and congratulate me on my victory. Stop getting distracted." He turned and walked down toward the Yolo suites.

"Victory? Elliot, you were *humiliated*." Nels paced alongside him. "Your side didn't fire a single shot, and you were turned away at the front door. How can you possibly count that as a victory?"

Elliot sighed. They were walking past the Mercorps suites. It was eerily quiet at this time of the morning. "Nels, my forces didn't fire a single shot. There were no casualties, save for some minor hull damage on the missile ship. It was the gentlest of nudges. I dare say there hasn't even been any real damage to relations with Yolo, now, have there? And yet Luna is now a fully incorporated member of the Corporate Federation. Over a hundred million new citizens, all because of me. *That*, you poor man, is my victory."

"None of that reflects well on Yolo, and Luna is now the leading member of a brand-new corporation that's larger than Masters and Billings. I don't think you know how dangerous those people are."

"What are you saying, Nels? Those people are amateurs. They have no idea what they're doing."

"That might be right in the corporate world, but remember that old saying? Outside every airlock on Luna?"

"Yes, yes. A patch of red ice. Nels, that's pure hyperbole, and you know it."

Nels remained silent as they walked past the Tataslavic Transport suite. As they approached the entrance to his suite, Nels stopped and quietly said, "Perhaps you should review your Lunar history. Look up the red ice phrase and its actual origins. Good morning, Elliot." He disappeared into his suite.

Elliot stood there, thinking. On impulse, he looked up the old Lunar saying. The stories connected to it were brutal tales of retribution against bullies, liars, thieves, and all manner of unsocial people. Luna had gone through some rough times, indeed.

He wiped his display clear of text and started an audio program while he walked slowly to his suite. By the time he reached his balcony, several articles of Lunar history had played. His chair offered him a few moments of relaxation in the near Mars-normal gravity he'd grown up in.

A quick look at his efforts to gain entry to Monarch's data revealed the entry had a green checkmark, but a note that said SECURE PROTOCOLS REQUIRED.

Elliot frowned and left his balcony. Stepping into an interior room with no windows, he sat on a convenient chair and tried again.

"Secure enclosure verified," Bil said. "Warning, security situation update. Yolo directors are under remote observation in all open areas."

A live video image of his balcony appeared. The camera angle was from above, but it would've been able to see his lips move.

"Show me what you've found."

A series of windows popped up showing various surveillance camera angles. Muted audio feeds also appeared in a large stack at the side.

"Password acquisition," Bil said, "occurred at 21:15 last night. System access was achieved. Analysis revealed ongoing surveillance activities."

"So he's watching and listening. I assume he has a service to sort through it all?"

"Affirmative. The sensitivity of this service is such that if you had glanced in the direction of the camera, it would have begun searching for a breach."

"Were you able to see inside it?" Elliot asked.

"Partially. Several smaller patches have been applied, one of which has opened a gateway, rather than closed it."

"Maybe someone else is looking, too."

Bil displayed the image of an unfamiliar miniature bot. "The presence of an additional remote drone observing the password change confirms this hypothesis."

"Additional drone? Are you sure it wasn't one of his?"

"Probability is 98.5 percent that this drone was not the property, nor under the control of, Executive Director Monarch."

"Any suspects?" Elliot asked.

"Research along this line was not in the core directive."

"Look into it if you can do it without detection."

"Acknowledged," Bil said.

"Any news related to whiskey?"

"There is a monthly recurring order set up with Cumberland Consumables. This order is a passthrough to Dale Hollow Distillery. The order item is a case, which contains four one-liter bottles of Dale Hollow Level Five."

"What the hell is that?" Elliot asked.

"According to Cumberland Consumables marketing," Bil said, "Dale Hollow Level Five is a twice-distilled straight malt whiskey that is aged in heavily charred white oak to give it a particularly robust taste. Along with vanilla, it has notes of honey and a hint of spice."

Elliot shook his head. "So who's Cumberland Consumables?"

"Cumberland Consumables is a small consumable group acquired through a debt default eight years ago by Bank of Bhushan."

"That figures. How much does this whiskey cost?"

Bil displayed an image of the bottle and the numbers. "The current price for a 1 liter bottle is 8.95 credits, or 30 credits for a case of four, not including delivery fees."

Elliot shook his head and chuckled. "Cheap booze in an expensive bottle." Elliot shook his head. "Order a case. Only one way to know for sure."

"Acknowledged," Bil said.

Elliot swiped his display, glancing at the other files his search had retrieved. Several areas of older images were marked as encrypted.

"Bil, can you open those image files?"

"Negative. Encryption attempts are currently failing. Asset allocation at 32 percent. Would you like to increase allocation?"

"No, not right now, but keep working on it." Another file caught his eye. "Is this a medical history?"

"Affirmative. Medical costs are the single largest expenditure for the period of the search."

"Oh, really. Let me see."

The medical history record began at age 25, the year August Monarch took over as executive director, right after his father, Richard, had died. That year, he had a total of twelve major surgeries, all related to various stages of organ failure. He'd suffered so many medical issues, it was amazing he was still alive. As the years went on, the surgeries and treatments became fewer and further between, but by Elliot's count, all his major organs had been traded for newly grown replacements.

Then there were the constant brain scans. Not the normal run-of-the-mill magnetic resonance. They were using the big guns. The most advanced and detailed scanner in existence was being used on this man every single month, including a week ago. On the one hand, he pitied the man for his problems. And it certainly explained the lack of tech in his brain. On the other, why had it all suddenly started at age 25?

"Where are the medical records from the first twenty-five years of his life?" Elliot asked.

"Prior medical records," Bil said, "are included in the summary."

"Wait, so nothing from birth until age twenty-five?"

"Affirmative," Bil said.

"Bil, find a way to embed yourself inside his personal system, where you won't be found. I want to know more about what Monarch is doing. Be sure you can eliminate any traces should it become necessary."

"Acknowledged."

"What's going on with you, August?" Elliot asked himself. "Are you dying, or are you trying to live forever?" Elliot sighed. Then he sniffed and wrinkled his nose. "Time to do something about that." He headed to his fresher for a long overdue shower.

* * * * *

Automated Justice Reform

Monday, October 11, 3288, 8:47

Dawn arrived at the conference room a little earlier than planned. She found Darren inside, eating breakfast alone. He looked up and waved.

"You're here early." Dawn sat in her usual seat. "Where's Misa?"

Darren shrugged and took a large bite of his egg burrito.

Ava walked in. Her hair was pulled back, showing off her elven ears. "Morning."

"Hi, Ava," Dawn said. "Where's the professor?"

"I kind of ran ahead of him." She giggled.

"I hope you aren't doing any permanent damage," Darren said. He took another bite.

"What? Oh, no. Of course not. He isn't *that* old, you know."

"Who isn't that old?" Ellie asked. She and Sam entered together.

"If it's Ava," Sam said, "they're talking about Professor Corvair."

Ellie laughed. "He's a child."

"Maybe compared to you." Darren spread his arms and shrugged. "To the rest of us, well, not so much." He took another bite and chewed loudly.

Ellie nodded and pretended to wipe her eye with her middle finger. "Uh, huh."

Misa walked in and looked at Ellie, then at Darren. "Again?"

The professor was right behind Misa. "What? What did I miss?"

"Nothing." Dawn shook her head. "Just Darren being Darren." She waved them in. "Come on in. Everyone get comfortable."

The new arrivals took their seats. The last of the burrito went into Darren's mouth.

"Since we've wrapped up our primary business," Dawn said, "I thought we might make time to look at another issue I encountered recently." She shared her display to the table, showing lists and documents.

"What's all that?" Ellie asked.

"When I had my accident, the automated punishment determination seemed a little… dated to me."

"Is that the one where you got the meme?" Darren wiped his lips with a napkin.

Dawn rolled her eyes. "Yes, but that's beside the point. The system gave him a permanent ban. I was thinking maybe things like that were set up before nanomedics really took hold. I was under for a day, then back good as new. Yes, it hurt, and it was inconvenient, but a lifetime ban? It was an accident."

"You don't think that would be a deterrent?" Sam asked.

"Not at all. It didn't prevent this one. Like I said, it wasn't intentional."

"True." Sam leaned forward. "What do you propose?"

"I'm open to suggestions," Dawn said.

"What did you give him?" Ava asked.

"I had him banned for a year." Dawn half-smiled and shook her head. "Since he usually did the jump twice a year, it was only making him skip it once. I figured that was enough."

Misa frowned. "I wonder if others would've been as lenient." She glanced at Darren.

Darren scoffed. "I would've left it permanent."

Dawn smirked and shook her head. "Of course, you would, Darren. But we're talking about people with compassion."

"Wait, let's back up a moment. Are you proposing that we review these things and set new punishments?"

"That would be a great deal of work," Misa said.

The professor crossed his arms. "There are millions of permutations that would need to be considered, so I'm assuming that's not what she has in mind."

Dawn shook her head. "Thank you, Professor. I was hoping for a more permanent solution. Something we could automate, but that would still be flexible."

"Could we have the AutoGov review it all?" Ava asked.

"I guess the question is," Ellie said, "would AutoGov be able to be fair?" She turned to the professor.

The professor tilted his head. "That's an interesting question. I think what we really need is some sort of feedback mechanism."

"Ah, yes." Misa sat straight. "So AutoGov can make adjustments." She turned to Dawn. "But people can comment on them, maybe make suggestions."

"Excellent idea." Dawn sat back and smiled. "Professor, maybe you and Misa can come up with the outline before we start giving orders."

"I'd be glad to," the professor said.

Misa smiled and nodded eagerly. "Sure."

"Thank you." Dawn placed her hands on the table. "That's all set. Is there anything else we should look into?"

Ellie shook her head. "I like the idea of setting up a review of the whole automated justice system, but aren't we exceeding our mandate a little?"

"Not really," the professor said. "Once instantiated, a Lunar Assembly can add to their own mandate."

Ava tilted her head and leaned in. "There's a limit, though. Right?"

"Oh, sure, but it's time based, not action based. No Lunar Assembly is allowed to last for more than twenty weeks."

"We have plenty of time," Dawn said.

Sam tapped the table with his finger. "Can we change that?"

"We already did." Darren put his fist to his chest and puffed his cheeks, momentarily distracted. "When we made the merger agreements, we did away with assemblies altogether."

"But in theory, we could've extended our own time, right?"

"Nope," the professor said. "That's the one thing that's against the rules. We'd need a second mandate. Another vote."

"Ah." Sam shrugged. "Okay. Moot point."

"How often will we be voting for directors going forward?" Ellie asked.

"Normally a three-year mandate," Misa said, "but it's all tied together with the rest of the Federation. The first directors will have a little more than a year. The next election cycle is November of 3289. Then there's a flexible waiting time for any missing directors to show up at the station, and they elect the executive. In that election, each director has a single vote."

"That doesn't seem fair," Ava said. "Don't they all represent a large number of others?"

"No," Misa said, "you're thinking of them as if they were delegates. They more closely represent an approximately equal value of shares.

Some of them are elected by one or two wealthy owners, and others by hundreds or even thousands of lower-level workers. Every company is different, so it's a mixed bag."

"Once the merger is complete," Ava said, "will we all still have our single share?"

"We initially aimed for that, but LSC shares were so valuable, most everyone else ended up with partial shares. We've done what we could to keep it balanced. The final number will still be in the tens of thousands."

"When will we know the final number?" Dawn asked.

"The agreements," Darren said, "are set to be executed at the conclusion of our first election. The valuation will be frozen at that time, and the numbers will be set. Then everyone's shares are swapped out, and it's done."

"That reminds me," Sam said, "what about Lunar citizenship?"

"What about it?" Darren asked.

"It used to be based on ownership of a single share, right?"

"Correct. We'll use a new certification that'll cost the same as the equivalent shares, and upon purchase, that number of shares will be created. Lunar citizenship stays separate from ownership in Allied Industries."

"As long as you have that all sorted out," Ellie said. "It sounds terribly boring to me. What else are we going to talk about, Dawn?"

Dawn shrugged. "Until we hear something on the killer's whereabouts, I'm not sure there's much for us to do."

"Well," Ava said, "I think I should get back to work, then. I've rearranged my tour to hit all the resettlement projects so I can keep tabs on everyone. I can make myself available if you need me."

Dawn flashed her a quick smile. "Professor?"

"My assistant has really stepped up." He shrugged. "I feel confident in sticking around. Misa and I can look into the justice system reform."

"How about you, Darren?"

"Um, I guess I'll hang out for a while." Darren waved his hand. "I can conduct business from here as easily as I could from Boguslawsky."

"Ellie?"

In a high pitched, childish voice, Ellie said, "I want to go home."

Everyone laughed.

"Seriously, though. I think I'd like to work with Misa and the professor on the justice system."

The professor smiled and bowed his head. "We'd welcome your years of experience."

"Wait," Ellie said, "are you calling me old?"

Ava giggled.

The professor's smile vanished. "No, no, not at all. I meant that you have a lot of—"

"Experience. Because I *am* old. And that's exactly why I want to be on the project. I've seen how things work, and I have some pretty strong ideas about how they can be better. So yes, because I'm old. Got a problem with that?"

He chuckled. "No, ma'am. Not at all."

Ellie squinted and gave him an angry finger shake. "You ma'am me again, young man, and I'll beat you with my walking stick."

* * * * *

Princess Blanca and the Gnomes

Tuesday, October 12, 3288, 14:05

Janek watched on his display as Blanca Deane entered the small forest clearing. She was alone. He had all the details of her personal life displayed before him. He smiled to himself. She was pretty. Dark, flowing hair. Shapely figure. According to her social data, she was unattached at the moment. "All right, Vondur, send in the gnomes."

Blanca heard a noise behind her. She turned and found two small gnomes walking out of the woods. One had an orange hat; the other's was purple.

"Hello, Princess," the orange gnome said.

"Would you like me to tell you a story?" the purple gnome asked.

"I thought it was my turn to tell the story."

"Not this time. Next time, I promise."

"That's what you said last time," the orange gnome said.

"Hush. Princess? Would you like me to tell you the story?"

"Sure," Blanca said. "Why not?"

The gnomes laughed and stepped forward.

"Once upon a time," the purple gnome said, "there was a beautiful princess named Blanca. One day, while Blanca was walking through the royal park near her palace, she met two gnomes."

"That's us," the orange gnome said.

"Yup. It's our story, now shut up and let me tell it."

"Fine. Jerk."

"So," the purple gnome said, "the two gnomes argued over telling the story."

"What? Why are you saying that?"

"The ugly gnome wouldn't let the handsome gnome tell the story properly."

The orange gnome frowned. "Why you little…"

The purple gnome started slowly walking backward. "But the handsome gnome had a secret, and he started walking backward, deeper into the forest. The princess followed, because she was laughing."

The orange gnome crossed his arms angrily and stomped after the other. "Laughing at you, you miniature moron."

Blanca laughed and happily followed the gnomes deeper into the woods.

"The beautiful princess kept following the handsome gnome, because he was such a good storyteller."

"No, he's not," the orange gnome said. "He's a jerk. He's just trying to lure you into a trap, Princess. Don't fall for it."

The purple gnome smirked. "The ugly gnome kept lying to the princess, because he was so jealous."

They came to a small, thatched hut, hidden among the trees. The purple gnome lifted a curtain of woven grasses and beckoned her to follow him inside.

"What will I find in there?" Blanca asked.

"My secret treasure, Princess. Beauty and light. Fabulous dreams."

"That's a laugh," the orange gnome said. "Go in there, and you'll regret it."

She smiled and entered the hut. She found it wasn't grass at all, but a wire mesh. The gnomes had entered, but now she couldn't see them. A man was sitting in the middle. "Oh, hello." She waved timidly.

Janek smiled. "Hello, Princess. Ready to play a game?"

She smiled at him and tilted her head. "What kind of game?"

"I call it Ivan, grab her."

She put her arms on her hips and was about to say something when Ivan caught her from behind and quickly secured her arms and legs. A collar snapped tightly around her throat, and she realized a moment too late that she was in trouble.

Janek stood and stretched. "You should've listened to the other gnome."

She struggled to speak, but the collar tightened when she tried.

"Vondur, take her medtech offline. Then set her pingback to normal and show it wandering into the city for now."

"Acknowledged," Vondur said.

Janek snapped his fingers and spread his hands. Ivan spread her arms and legs, while keeping a firm grip. A small knife from his pocket was all he needed to carefully cut her clothes from her body. Tears welled up in her eyes.

* * * * *

Battle of the Blue Feather

Wednesday, October 13, 3288, 11:11

Dawn spent the morning in her apartment browsing news sites, looking at reports about the resettlement project. Since it had been made public that their own anger had been used against them by a third party, people on both sides were more willing to try to come together. There was the occasional exception.

"Hello, again, and welcome to the Tony Renard Show. I'm Tony Renard. Today we have one of the thousands of refugees who've been resettled across the face of Luna. With me tonight is Justin Wells, recently of the Ablom Refuge. Now he's got a nice little flat in Nernst." He grinned and raised an eyebrow. "Nernst. Just kind of rolls off the tongue, eh? Nernst." He swiveled to face Justin. "How do you like your new quarters in Nernst? It makes me smile just saying it. Nernst." He grinned again and pointed to his teeth.

Justin frowned and fidgeted in his seat. "My quarters are fine. They aren't the issue. What matters is that our home for almost a century has been destroyed. Our people were forced to move."

"And you ended up in Nernst. Lucky you. Tell me, what do you miss most about Ablom?"

"I miss being close to my friends. Many of them are in locations that could take hours to get to."

Tony looked surprised. "Hours? Doesn't Nernst have a shuttle port? I do believe they do."

"Well, yes, but why would I use a shuttle?"

"Twenty minutes to any other shuttle port on Luna?"

Justin looked flustered. "Yes, but then you still have to take the loop or tubes to get somewhere else."

"Oh, yeah, sure. I see where you're going. It could take twenty minutes to get from the shuttle station to another resettlement location. The whole trip could cost you over an hour and a half."

"Exactly."

Tony grinned and nodded slowly. "Major inconvenience."

"Outrageous."

Tony nodded again, then looked sideways at the camera and grinned. "So, do you have any hobbies? Do you knit? Carve wood? Anything like that?"

Justin shook his head. "I was under the impression this was going to be a serious interview."

"Well, it is. I simply want my viewers to know exactly what sort of person you are. Especially since it turns out it was your complaint to the Mormon Catholic Church that ended up being used as a pretext for a possible military action against Luna."

Justin's face went slack. "What…"

"Exactly. Oh, look, I have a conveniently arriving call from Cardinal Brandon Nunn. Hello, Cardinal Nunn. Welcome to the show."

Cardinal Nunn's image appeared opposite Justin at the table. "Thank you, Mister Renard. Pleasure being here."

"What was it you wanted to add to our conversation?" Tony sat back and grinned.

"I wanted to publicly congratulate Deacon Wells on his upcoming Papal Audience. I'm told the pope is looking forward to a free and open exchange of ideas."

Justin's face grew pale.

Tony leaned toward Justin. "Are you all right there? You look a bit off."

"I'm fine," Justin said. "Fine. I'll be fine."

"Well, he seems excited, Cardinal. I'm sure he'll have the time of his life."

Cardinal Nunn nodded slowly and smiled. "I'd say he's in for an exciting adventure."

"Speaking of exciting adventures, you've had a bit of one yourself these past few weeks."

"I have, and I must say, I'm greatly enjoying my new surroundings."

Tony grinned. "You're not just saying that because someone told you to, are you?"

"Nonsense. I'm too old to care about anyone else's opinion. I say it because, after spending much of these last few years in Ablom, I'm out again, meeting new people, and making new friends. People I can speak with about the Lord, and His good word. I've even started a weekly prayer meeting."

"You're spreading your faith to new converts?"

The cardinal smiled at Tony. "I am. And you'd be welcome, young man."

Tony grinned sheepishly and shrugged. "Very gracious of you, Cardinal, but I'm having my hair done that day. Still, thanks for the offer."

The cardinal laughed. "You know the offer stands. Have a blessed day, Tony."

"You too, Cardinal." As the old man faded away, he turned to Justin. "You okay?"

"I told you." Justin clenched his teeth. "Fine."

"How excited are you about meeting the pope? I hear she's a real looker under those robes."

The scene changed abruptly, and Tony sat alone behind his desk. "Well, that was fun. The deacon had a few words to say that we normally don't use on our show, then he went home. Let's just leave it there, shall we? I'm Tony Renard, and I think we can all do better than him." He smiled and threw his hands in the air. "Yeah, so that was a low bar. Good night!" He waved as the music played.

Dawn shut off the feed and noticed the time. She turned and walked out of her apartment. On the way to the lift, she called the security office.

Smith's head and shoulders floated near Dawn. "Hello, Prime Minister, this is Officer Smith. What can I do for you?"

"Hi. Anything new this morning?" Dawn asked.

Smith shook her head. "Only thing out of the ordinary we've seen is, we had a report of malicious squirrels in the park. They sent a guy to investigate. Name of Mike Hilp. His son called in and said his dad was acting strange. Said he left the city when he was supposed to be on duty and headed to Tycho with some girl. One Blanca Deane. We're checking it out, but it sounds like a dead end. Mike and his new girlfriend probably just want some alone time."

"All right. Maybe I'm being too cautious but run that one down."

"Sure thing. We'll get a visual confirmation on them."

"Thanks," Dawn said. "Have a good day."

"You too, Dawn." Smith dropped the connection as Dawn was stepping off the lift in the central square near Keegan's.

She walked into the restaurant and smiled at her uncle.

Keegan grinned. "Good to see you, Dawn. What are you in the mood for today?"

Etto called from around the corner, "Hello, Dawn."

"Hi, Etto. Can I get some limeade on ice, please?" She turned back to Keegan. "I'm thinking soup. Something warm and creamy."

"Oh. I see. I have some broccoli cheese soup, and a little of that portobello mushroom stew left."

"Ah," Dawn said, "mushroom. That sounds so good."

Etto appeared with a tall glass. "Here you go."

"Would you like a sandwich to go with that, or a salad?" Keegan asked.

"Thanks, Etto. Could I get a grilled cheese and tomato with bacon?"

Etto laughed. "Now *that* brings back memories."

Keegan shrugged with a half-smile. "Sure. I can do that." He swiped his display. "There. Soup's on the way."

Etto quickly gave Dawn a hug, then went back around the corner to the bar.

"You ready to see Debra fight again?" Dawn asked.

Keegan shrugged. "She's been training very hard." He reached under the counter and brought out two slices of bread. "I'm sure she'll do well." He buttered one side of each slice and dropped them on the grill.

"I know. I'm worried about her. She seems a lot more focused now. Less playful."

"Give her time. But you should start getting used to her now and let the past go." He opened the bin next to the grill and put a slice of cheese on each piece of bread, then put two strips of bacon on another part of the grill.

"What do you mean?" Dawn asked.

"I mean what she's been through, what happened to her. It changes people. She may never be exactly who she was before, but she'll always be your sister." He turned and opened a cabinet behind him. He removed the covered dish and set it in front of Dawn.

"I'm worried there's more to it." She lifted the lid and inhaled the warm steam from her soup.

Keegan shrugged. "I know. But even then, give it time." He put the bacon, bread, and two slices of tomato together into a sandwich, then cut it diagonally. "Here you are. Just like when you were a kid."

Dawn scoffed. "Age has nothing to do with it. These are really good."

* * *

Dawn and Keegan arrived at the Grissom Park Arena and climbed into the stands. A fight was already in progress, but the schedule showed Debra was up next. Hundreds of people lined the stands. Each move was punctuated by a section cheering.

Soon, the match ended, and the next round was ready to start. Debra walked onto the mat. Dawn and Keegan stood and cheered. Debra's opponent was much larger than she was. She was being tested for promotion to the next level again, and this man, Adam, was the one she had to beat.

Adam lunged, forcing her to leap to the left, but he followed his lunge with a twist and got there before she did. She countered with a strike to his leg, shifting him off balance. He recovered quickly, spinning out of her reach. She bounced off the mat and regained her position. She swept to his left, staying low to the ground, and twisted and swung her leg as if trying to knock him down. He jumped, and she was under him doing a power lift before he knew what she'd done. He sailed high into the air, trying to keep his arms and legs in defensive positions. Debra's spinning strikes were precise and effective. He landed off balance and sprawled as she rolled on top of him for the pin, and the match.

The crowd jumped to their feet and cheered.

The sensei officiating the match stepped onto the mat. Debra and Adam stood, bowed to each other, and turned to face her.

"Debra Sheffield," said the sensei, "it is my honor to bestow upon you the rank of Blue Feather. In doing so, I must acknowledge that you have achieved this rank far faster than most. Your dedication to training and your hard work, along with the support of your friends, has paid off."

Debra bowed. "Thank you, Sensei."

The sensei handed Debra a blue belt with a large blue feather attached. "Blue signifies the blue water that sustains the plant as it continues to grow. A blue feather student moves up higher in rank just as the plant grows taller. The water feeds the plant so that it can continue to grow. The student is fed additional knowledge of the Art in order for their body and mind to continue to grow and develop."

* * *

Deep in the forest of Grissom Park, Janek sat quietly inside his enclosure. He swiped his display, scanning the park for possible new projects. A young woman walked alone on the path to the lake. He took a deep breath and considered the possibilities. She was met by several friends. Disappointing. It would be a big challenge to try to take her now. Lake Betty was a popular spot for young people.

He refocused his search to an area near the falls, not far from the main entrance of the park. He watched another young woman for a few minutes, but as she neared a bridge over the creek, she was approached by a young man. Their embrace was awkward, but eager. A new romance, perhaps. That could be interesting.

They were joined by three others.

"Damn. So many opportunities here. Too many large groups."

Then he saw a mother and a young boy. They were arguing. The boy was clearly upset about something. "How sweet. Vondur, I think I've found my next project. That mother and child down there. How much pain would a mother endure for her child?"

"Unable to calculate," Vondur said.

"Oh, yes. I imagine it would be quite a bit. Set up the gnomes again. Same routine, but add in some lines for the young prince. I want them both."

Shortly, the two gnomes tumbled out of the underbrush and confronted Cheryl and Jordan Audrey.

"Hello, Princess," the orange gnome said.

"Would you like me to tell you and the prince a story?" the purple gnome asked.

"I thought it was my turn to tell the story."

"Not this time. Next time, I promise."

"That's what you said last time," the orange gnome said.

"Hush. Princess? Would you like me to tell you the story?"

"Sure," Cheryl said. "Why not?"

Jordan wasn't paying attention.

"Once upon a time," the purple gnome said, "there was a beautiful princess named Cheryl, and a handsome young prince named Jordan. One day, while Cheryl and Jordan were walking through the Royal Park near her palace, they met two gnomes."

"That's us," the orange gnome said.

"Yup. It's our story, now shut up and let me tell it."

"Fine. Jerk."

"So," the purple gnome said, "the two gnomes argued over telling the story."

"What? Why are you saying that?"

"The ugly gnome wouldn't let the handsome gnome tell the story properly."

The orange gnome frowned. "Why you little…"

The purple gnome started slowly walking backward. "But the handsome gnome had a secret, and he started walking backward, deeper into the forest. The prince and the princess followed, because they were laughing."

The orange gnome crossed his arms angrily and stomped after the other. "Laughing at you, you miniature moron. The prince isn't even paying attention."

Cheryl grabbed Jordan's hand and followed the gnomes into the woods.

"Where are we going?" Jordan asked.

"We're following a couple of gnomes. I want to hear the story."

"Now you're being mean."

"The two royals," the purple gnome said, "kept following the handsome gnome, because he was such a good storyteller."

"No, he's not," the orange gnome said. "He's a jerk. He's just trying to lure you into a trap, Princess. Don't fall for it."

The purple gnome smirked. "The ugly gnome kept lying to the princess, because he was so jealous."

They came to a small, thatched hut, hidden among the trees. The purple gnome lifted a curtain of woven grasses and beckoned her to follow him inside.

"Who's that guy inside?" Jordan asked.

"What guy?" Cheryl asked.

"There, he's coming out. Crap, he's got a bot, too."

"Jordan, your augmentation is off, you shouldn't be seeing…" Ivan grabbed Cheryl. "Jordan, run!"

Jordan slipped past Janek's lunge and leapt backward. He twisted and bounced off a tree, then flung himself back into the forest, using the trees to push himself faster, and was quickly out of sight.

"Vondur," Janek said, "what went wrong? Why did he see me?"

"The young man," Vondur said, "has had the augmented reality feed from the park blocked by his mother."

"Can you catch him?"

"There is a rapidly decreasing likelihood of capturing him. He is heading for the park exit."

"Damn," Janek said. "Can you stop him?"

"Ivan is preoccupied. No other physical assets are able to assist."

He turned with fury and swung the back of his fist into Cheryl's head.

* * *

Dawn and Keegan were waiting for Debra, Adi, and Evren to join them. The area was nearly empty. Several of the people passing smiled and waved at Dawn. She felt slightly embarrassed at the attention. "I wonder if I'll ever get used to that."

"What?" Keegan asked. "The recognition? The whole world knows who you are now, Dawn. Just go with it. It'll settle down after this is all over."

"Maybe. Maybe not."

"What makes you think that?"

Dawn sighed. "I'm considering jumping into the race for a directorship."

"Seriously?"

She shrugged with a lopsided grin.

Keegan took a deep breath. "You'd be moving to Kigyo, then."

"Yup."

"I'll expect frequent updates and occasional visits, but if you go for it, you have my vote."

"Thank you," Dawn said. "I think leaving here would be the hardest part."

"Why do it, then?"

"Because I feel like it's something I want to do. For myself, and for Luna. I know there are others out there who could do a decent job, but I feel like this is when it counts. This is the time to step up and make sure it gets done right."

Keegan wrapped his arms around her. "I'm so proud of you."

"Thanks." She held him tightly.

"Have you told Debra yet?"

"Nope." Dawn stepped back. "I'll talk to her soon, though."

Adi came through the doors first, Evren right behind her.

Dawn turned and smiled. "Hi. Where's Debra?"

"She's coming," Adi said.

Jordan approached Dawn from the direction of the park. "Hey, Prime Minister."

Dawn turned to greet him. "What can I do for you?" She saw his name in her display and recognized him. "Jordan. I remember you from the shuttle."

"Yeah. I told Mom that was you. Anyway, my mom was chasing something she saw in the park's feed. It led us into the woods, and she got grabbed by this bot, then the guy tried to grab me, too, and I ran. She's not on my feed anymore. She told me to run, so I did. I saw you were over here, so I came to you."

"Did you go to Security?"

"No. You were right here. Should I call Security?"

Debra joined them.

"You stay with me," Dawn said. "AutoGov, call Security and get them up here."

"Acknowledged," AutoGov said.

"Thanks." Jordan looked relieved.

"Trouble?" Debra asked.

"The boy lost his mother in the park. It sounds like it could be that guy."

Debra cringed and looked at Dawn.

Dawn frowned and swiped her display. She shared it with everyone standing close by. "Show me where you last saw her."

"I can't see anything. Mom blocked me."

"AutoGov, override Jordan's block. Let him see my map."

"Acknowledged," AutoGov said.

Jordan swiped at the three-dimensional diagram and pointed to the place where his mother had been taken. "She acted like she couldn't see him or the bot. I saw him sitting inside the little mesh dome he was at."

Dawn frowned. "He must've taken control of the park's augmented reality feed. AutoGov, shut down that feed. Make sure he can't hide anymore."

"Acknowledged. That system is not under AutoGov control. Remote access has been denied."

"Can you shut off power to the transmitters?"

"Affirmative," AutoGov said. "Power secured. The augmented reality feed has been disrupted."

"Let's go take a look. Jordan, you stay here. Adi, can you make sure he's safe?"

Adi put her hand on Jordan's shoulder. "Let's go inside the arena. I know exactly what to do."

* * *

"The augmented reality feed has been disabled," Vondur said. "No simulated images are being transmitted."

"All right. Let's make quick work of this. Lock down all access to and from the park. Don't let anyone else in. Wait. Better idea. Let *everyone* in. Don't let them *out*. Can you close off access to the entire city?"

"Affirmative. City closure underway. All entries to the park are open."

He looked at Cheryl. Her blouse was cut into thin strips. Some of them were bloody. "That boy. Your son?"

Cheryl nodded. The collar choked her. Ivan tightened his grip.

"I'm considering how to thank him."

There was a shout in the distance.

"Damn. Ivan, drop her and come on. Down to the fallback."

Ivan released Cheryl and headed swiftly toward the maintenance access to the lower levels. Janek turned and threw his knife at Cheryl. She screamed. He spun and followed Ivan.

* * *

"All access to and from Grissom Park has been secured by Vondur," said AutoGov. "The Emergency Management Service is under Vondur's control, as are several environmental systems that had not yet been upgraded. No existing override has succeeded."

"Have you located Janek Charles?" asked Dawn.

"Negative."

"Over here," said one of the security guards.

Dawn and Keegan entered the hollow where Janek had built his lair. Cheryl was sitting in the center, holding her shredded blouse to her chest. Her arm was bloody, and there was a knife in her lap. One of the security guards gave her a jacket and took the knife, placing it into an evidence bag.

"AutoGov," Dawn said, "where did he go?"

"There is a 95 percent probability that he is down in the maintenance levels. There is an open stairwell ninety-seven meters away." A glowing beacon lit the way.

Adi joined them. "Security took the boy back to their office. Any sign of him?"

Dawn opened her mouth but was cut off. Janek Charles was speaking to everyone over the common broadcast channel.

"Hello, Grissom Park. By now, many of you may have noticed that the emergency bulkheads have been closed. Please don't panic. This is only a precaution. I simply don't want you to leave and miss all the fun. Now, everyone gather under the main dome in the park. There's plenty of room. Don't mind the trees. Now gather 'round. I have something to show you."

Keegan looked up at the top of the dome. "Oh, no. AutoGov, can he open the dome?"

"Negative. It would require a tremendous force to create any sort of opening in the dome structure."

"Can he blow it up?" Evren asked.

"No explosives have been detected." AutoGov paused for a moment. "There is an anomaly that may correlate. The city hydrogen reserve has been depleted. There are no records of the transfer, however, several tanks that have no listed inventory currently register as full. These tanks are adjacent to the reserve oxygen tanks near the emergency oxygen generation system. Assuming this represents the missing hydrogen, if ignited, such an explosion could create a pressure wave sufficient to breach the dome, causing catastrophic failure."

Dawn was furious. "AutoGov, get those people to safety. Use any means necessary. Get them safe *now*."

She shouted to a group of security guards nearby, "Get everyone out of the park and into the solar storm shelters! He's trying to breach the dome! Get them safe!"

Debra shouted angrily. "Where are those tanks? He's got to be there. Get me there."

"Down the stairs three levels," AutoGov said. "Turn left and proceed through the large doors."

Debra headed off at a run, followed by Keegan. Evren and Adi looked at each other, then followed after Debra.

Dawn followed them. "AutoGov, get us backup. And weapons!"

On their way down, four more security guards and a dozen security bots of various shapes and sizes joined them, including three floaters.

All of them were given protective gear, which they donned hurriedly. Adi grabbed a nail gun with the security guards. Everyone else took nightsticks.

AutoGov guided them down three levels until they were arrayed outside a large, secured door labeled Emergency Services. Two large maintenance bots were already using metal cutters to carve out a section of the door to allow access.

"Let the security alert team go in first," one of the guards said.

"AutoGov," Dawn said, "have you taken control of Vondur yet?"

"Negative," AutoGov said. "Communications have been established. The exposed primary directives are misleading. An alternative strategy is being deployed."

At last the cuts were complete, and the bots pulled the doors out and away. The lights inside didn't come on. The passage beyond was dark. Occasional flashes of light gave it an eerie look. The high-pitched whirring of machinery echoed in the distance.

The security team entered in formation. Three floaters entered first. Two went high, one stayed at chest height. Three rolling bots entered next, followed by two security guards. Three more bots followed, with the other two security guards behind them. The last three bots took up the rear.

Debra leapt past Dawn after them into the darkness, followed closely by Evren and Adi. Dawn set her eyes to low-light so she could see. As Keegan and Dawn entered, the last security guards were rounding a corner to the right. The whirring grew louder as Dawn neared the corner.

Without warning, the whirring noise moved. Dawn's eyes stopped working in the dark, and she had no data. Flashes of light, people screaming, clashes of heavy objects. She caught a glimpse of a bot from a nightmare. Too many arms, all tipped with spinning blades, slicing through bodies.

Someone's arm landed near Dawn with a sickening *thud*.

The loud *shook-shook* of the nail guns carried by the guards echoed through the chamber. She saw Keegan dive forward. He stood with one of the guns, and aimed and fired several times. Falling wreckage was followed by silence.

Brilliantly blinding lights flooded the area. Dawn heard laughter. Hysterical, maniacal laughter.

"That was fucking *amazing*," Janek said. "How many bots did you guys have? I had one. Only one, and some netting for the floaters. Anyone still alive in there? This is priceless."

Dawn's eyes began to adjust to the lights. What had been the attacking bot appeared limp in the midst of bloody carnage. She noticed the arm she'd seen earlier. She recognized the sleeve as belonging to Adi.

"Oh, wonderful! Prime Minister Sheffield! Did you and your friends think a few bots would help you? Oh, I see. You have guns. I'm sure that would've come in handy."

Shots rang out. Dawn felt every shot hit like a hammer against her chest. Keegan jumped in front of her as she dropped backward and hit the ground with a nauseating thud. She couldn't catch her breath. Pain flooded her ribcage. Keegan fell next to her. His eyes were open. There was blood on his forehead.

Debra screamed.

Janek stepped in front of the light. "I recognize that scream. Is it really you, little doe? You have short hair now. Darker, too. But yes, I see those ears. That *is* you, isn't it? Did the big guy make it, too?" Janek shook his head and smiled at the memory. "No, I suppose not."

Dawn's chest felt as if several ribs might be broken. Without her display, she couldn't know for sure. She winced at the pain and caught a short breath. It wasn't enough.

Janek stepped closer. "This is amazing. I wonder if I have enough time to really work things out with the two of you. Come to an... *understanding*. You can feel the pain, can't you, Prime Minister? Without your little miniature helpers getting signals from your implants, you feel all the pain, as nature intended. It's such a beautiful thing."

Debra looked as if she were slumping slightly. She held the nightstick close behind her leg, bent her knee, and allowed her body to start falling forward. The look on her face made it seem she was passing out. Janek hesitated. Debra sprang on her new legs with great force, propelling her into Janek, fists first, rolling him onto his back, with Debra on top.

Dawn realized time had jumped. She was passing out. She struggled for another short, painful breath and lifted her head as far as she could.

Debra pounded away at Janek's arms, knocking them away from his head. She wondered why he didn't use his legs to knock her away. Then she realized they were limp. Debra had been busy.

Janek cried out. "Do it! Blow it now!"

Debra pounded at his face, both hands gripping the nightstick, beating him with a fury Dawn had never seen in her sister before. And even though she knew she should, she didn't stop her sister from beating the man to death.

The floor spun, and time jumped again. Searing pain in her throat and lungs. Something large and mechanical was gripping her, sliding under her body. A tube had been pushed down her throat. She was immobile, terrified. Then the air hit her lungs like a cool wave of relief. She gasped. Help had arrived. The sounds of people moving debris echoed through the passage. People were examining bodies, hoping for signs of life.

The room spun and went dark.

She heard muffled noises. Her eyes opened, but there was nothing to see. Darkness as the wind rushed by. The darkness gave way to a dim light at the end of the tunnel.

Dawn awoke in a medical bed. Her throat felt rough, painful, but she could breathe. She inhaled deeply, fighting through the pain.

"Hey, you."

Dawn blinked and cleared her eyes. Her sister stood near the bed. She was wearing a plain robe. Her hair was wet. "You cleaned up."

Debra wiped her eyes with a sleeve. "When we got here, I saw myself in a mirror and almost had a heart attack. I looked like a horror movie monster."

Dawn lifted her arms. "Come here."

Debra curled into her sister's arms and cried quietly.

Dawn recognized Officer Heath as he walked through a door and approached the bed. "Dawn, Debra, we thought you'd want to know. The girl who lost her arm, Advika, she's going to be fine. They've reattached the limb, added back what got tore up, and she should be ready in a couple of days. Her boyfriend, Evren, didn't do so well. His head was still mostly attached, and his heart kept beating almost all the way back to medical. Tough kid, that one. They'll be a week or two making new parts. Have to rebuild most everything below the neck, and half his face, but he'll be fine, eventually."

"Keegan? The security guards?"

"One of the guards made it. Nearly as bad as Evren, but she was pretty cut up, too. Sorry about your uncle. He got hit in the head. Bullet diced up everything inside."

Dawn's eyes teared up. "It didn't seem that bad. Why can't these people fix brains? Everything else seems so easy. A night's sleep and poof, new arm. New leg. Why not a stupid brain?"

Heath sighed and looked at his feet. "I understand how you feel. The simple fact is, brain tissue isn't easy stuff like muscles, or even nerves. You replace a muscle, and it simply works. Even with a spinal replacement, you lose a lot of muscle memory, but you can learn how to walk again, and everything else. But when the brain suffers a lot of damage, it's not simple tissue, it's the connections that hold the data, your memories, your feelings and thoughts. It isn't arranged in a standard pattern that can be reprinted or reassembled. Every connection, even the thickness of every connection, affects who you are, what you remember. With massive brain trauma, they could replace the lost tissue, build a new brain, but they wouldn't be saving the person who was injured, they'd be creating someone new in his body. Someone with a mashup of memories, confusion, and pain."

"I know. I know all that. It's just hard when it's someone you love."

"I understand. The only way to do it would be if you were scanned beforehand with something like one of those old magnetic scanners. But you'd have to have all your controllers, all the tech removed first. Those things eat up stuff like that. Then you'd need the most advanced medical printers ever designed. We'd have to build those from scratch."

Debra stood. She wobbled a bit, then steadied herself. "We need to go find Etto. I pinged him. He's at the restaurant."

"Do you need any help?" Heath asked.

"No, thank you," Dawn said. "Thanks for letting us know about our friends."

Heath nodded curtly, turned, and went back through the door.

Once released, they took the slide tube back to Moretus Plains, not saying a word. When they arrived at Keegan's, the place was surrounded by people. They opened a path for them to reach the door. As they entered, they heard glasses clinking at the bar. They peered around the corner to see Etto putting away clean dishes.

"Etto?" Debra asked. "Are you all right?"

Etto shook his head. His eyes sprouted tears. "They told me a little while ago."

"I'm so sorry," Debra said. "He died helping Dawn and I save Grissom Park from an evil man."

Dawn ducked behind the counter and took him into her arms. "He risked his life for us. It cost him everything."

Etto hugged Dawn back. "Not everything. When I first met him, the first time we talked, he told me all about you. You two made him so proud. *You* were everything to him." Etto took a damp cloth and wiped the counter. "Now I don't know what to do. Where do I go now? How do I fit in here?" Several people had entered the restaurant quietly.

"You'll figure out what you want," Debra said. "We'll help you make it happen."

"Debra's right." Dawn let Etto slide out of her arms. "Anything you need, just ask. We're all family, right?"

Etto smiled and wiped a tear from his eye. "Thank you." He looked up at the gathering crowd. "Everyone here to honor Keegan, step up. Might need a hand bartending, if you know how. No food for now. Let the grill stay cold tonight."

They spent the evening among friends, sharing stories of Keegan, laughter, and tears.

* * * * *

Aftertaste

Thursday, October 14, 3288, 8:05

Elliot was on his balcony eating breakfast. Fresh fruits, scrambled eggs drizzled with sauce, sweet cheese toppings for his bagel, and some newly delivered sausage from that Silva fellow on Gabrielle's Drum. Elliot had to admit to himself that the meat was exquisite. A perfect blend of spices and protein.

Nels walked out onto the balcony. "Good morning, Elliot."

"Good morning, Nels. Have a seat and dig in."

Nels sat. He turned toward the open doorway. "Coffee, please. Light and sweet."

A servant promptly appeared with his coffee.

"Thank you." Nels took the cup. "I swear they've already made it before I get here."

The servant left quickly.

"That's what they are supposed to do," Elliot said. "Anticipate and deliver."

Nels sipped at his coffee. In a subdued tone he said, "Did you hear they had a serial killer on Luna?"

Elliot shrugged. "Yes, I heard something of it. Why?"

"The prime minister's little sister beat the man to death with a stick. All by herself."

Elliot paused. He set his fork down and swiped at his display.

Nels leaned forward. "Red ice, Elliot. Outside every airlock."

"Oh, shut up and eat your eggs, Nels."

"Director Humboldt," Bil said, "you have a delivery. You flagged it for your attention."

"Ah, the whiskey," Elliot said.

"Whiskey?" Nels asked.

"Bring it here."

"Acknowledged," Bil said.

"Yes," Elliot said. "It's a long story. I won't bore you with the details. If it's what I hope it is, it'll be a welcome treat."

The case walked out onto the balcony and sat next to Elliot. Thin legs folded themselves away.

"I see," Nels said. "The stuff we get from our own producers isn't up to your standards?"

Elliot shook his head. "Some of it's quite nice, yes. This is a flavor I remember from years ago that I thought was particularly good."

Elliot frowned and looked at the crate. "Open up and give me a bottle."

The case opened its top and leaned toward Elliot.

Nels chuckled. "Top quality, I see."

"Oh, good grief," Elliot said. "Limited automation on top of everything else." He reached down and pulled out a bottle. It was clean, and the amber liquid inside was clear. "Bring me a snifter."

A servant quickly appeared and set a clean glass snifter in front of Elliot. "Would you like me to pour it for you, sir?"

"No. Bring me a glass of water."

The servant left quickly, and another servant brought the water glass, set it next to the snifter, then left.

"Which one was that, Ashley or Deanna?"

Elliot looked at Nels. "What?"

Nels shook his head. "Nevermind."

Elliot opened the whiskey bottle and waved it under his nose. He gave it a quick sniff, then poured himself a small shot. He closed the bottle and set it on the table. He picked up the glass and swirled it, watching the liquid flow back to the bottom. As he lifted the snifter to his lips, he again inhaled the aroma and took a small sip. He swirled it in his mouth, then swallowed. "Exactly."

"Exactly what?"

"Bring him a snifter, too. Pour him a shot."

One of the servants rushed to comply.

Nels shook his head. "You know, Elliot, you can set your display to show the names of people around you. For example, this is Ashley. Thank you, Ashley."

Ashley looked stricken. She quickly nodded once and left.

"Stop trying to spoil my staff," Elliot said. "I have them well trained."

Nels tasted his whiskey. He pursed his lips and nodded slowly. "It's nice. Easier to swallow than I would have thought, considering the price." He swiped his display again, then laughed. "Bank of Bhushan."

"I know, I know."

"This breakfast is all very nice, Elliot. Did you ask me here in anticipation of the whiskey, or did you have something you wanted to discuss?"

Elliot shrugged. "I was thinking I need to socialize a little more. The whiskey was coincidental. I knew it was arriving today, but I wasn't tracking it. Not all that important."

"I heard you spent a great deal of money on the last bottle you bought. Is this somehow related?"

Elliot looked out over the green. He counted five drones, moving at various speeds through his field of vision. "No. Not at all. I simply felt like rewarding myself."

Nels laughed. "I see. And the food? Something special, too?"

"Ah. Some butt-sniffing sycophant on Gabrielle's Drum decided to send me a gift to honor my recent visit."

"You visited?"

"I transited," Elliot said. "Quickly."

"And you got a shipment of their finest meats. Must be nice, being the senior director."

"I have the feeling he would've done the same for any director. Mid-level functionary. Probably hoping for a promotion."

"This sausage is delicious," Nels said. "Have you tried it?"

"Of course, I have."

Nels occupied himself with his food for a few minutes. "I know you want something, Elliot. I can feel it trying to claw its way out of your skull."

Elliot sighed. "Yes, but nothing to do with you. Here, stay quiet for a minute. Bil, call Director DeRyke, but only show him me."

Malcolm's image appeared. His meki was the EGC logo without the letters, only the wireframe globe, spinning slowly. "Good morning, Director Humboldt. What can I do for you?"

Elliot grinned. "I found it, Malcolm. I really did."

"Judging by how pleased with yourself you seem to be, I'll bet you have. Still, there's only one way to prove it."

"I'll bring you an unopened bottle," Elliot said. "This afternoon?"

"I'm open any time after sixteen."

"Good enough. Should I bring an arbiter?"

"Oh, nonsense," Malcolm said. "This is whiskey, not an arms sale. We can settle this by ourselves."

"Good. I'll see you shortly after sixteen. Have a good day."

"Same to you." Malcolm dropped the connection.

Elliot reviewed the conversation in his mind.

"That was it?" Nels asked.

"I'm afraid so. A bit of personal business with a friend."

Nels stopped eating and stared at Elliot, his fork filled with eggs.

Elliot looked at him. He rolled his eyes. "Oh, good grief, will you please stop. I have friends from time to time. Yes, I admit it's been a while, but I made a new one, and we share a love of whiskey and poker."

Nels chuckled. "Sorry, but you have to admit, you leave yourself open quite a bit."

Elliot nodded absently. He was still thinking about his conversation with Malcolm. No mention of the wager. No surrounding information. He looked over his balcony at a drone passing in the distance. "Excuse me a moment, will you?" He stretched, got up, and wandered into his suite, then turned into one of his secured rooms and closed the door. "Bil, that surveillance Monarch has on Yolo—does he monitor anyone else like that?"

"Affirmative," Bil said. "Monitoring routines are in place for all directors of every corporation."

* * *

Elliot arrived at the EGC suite right at 16:00. He silently scolded himself, not wanting to appear overly anxious.

A young woman in a conservative dark green suit greeted Elliot with a smile and waved him in. "This way, Director. You're expected." The artificial receptionist ignored them.

Elliot followed the servant up a lift, then to a back room. There were comfortable seats arranged around a low table. He noticed the three shot glasses arranged in the middle.

Malcolm sat facing the door. He waved Elliot to sit. "Courtney, lock the door, please."

"Yes, sir," Courtney said. When the door closed, an audible series of clicks told Elliot this was a secure room.

"This is one of my most secure spaces." Malcolm waved at the chair opposite himself. "Please, have a seat."

Courtney took a seat at the table. Elliot's eyebrows rose.

"Courtney, this is Elliot Humboldt, acting senior director of Yolo Consumer Goods. Elliot, this is Courtney Reid, my personal assistant, confidant, and friend."

"Friend? She's young enough to be your granddaughter, Malcolm." Elliot took the seat Malcom had indicated.

Malcolm chuckled. "I said friend, not lover."

Elliot lifted the bottle. "All this for the whiskey?"

Malcolm laughed. "Sure. Let me see the bottle." He took the bottle and nodded. "Dale Hollow Level Five. The bottle isn't glass, but that would've been too much to ask for." He opened it and poured Elliot a shot. "Mine arrived yesterday."

"Yesterday? Why didn't you say anything?"

"Because of something Courtney found. I suspect you found it, too." He poured a shot for Courtney, then set the bottle on the table.

"I see," Elliot said. "Then it was your drone that was with mine that night?"

Courtney picked up her drink. "I think I got ahead of you while you were out playing with the space marines."

Elliot frowned. "I suspected that might be the case."

Malcolm shifted uncomfortably. "I'm a little concerned about our recent whiskey purchases."

"You think they might tip him off?"

"It depends on what the surveillance service thinks is important. A couple of coincidental whiskey shipments probably won't register."

"Still," Courtney said, "it would be prudent to take precautions in the future."

Elliot sat back. "You think there's something in the medical report the man might consider… inappropriate?"

Malcolm lifted his shot glass. "It was certainly interesting."

"It was horrific," Elliot said.

Malcolm contemplated his whiskey. "Yes, but it was also all so… sudden. Don't you think?"

"Ah, yes." Elliot settled into the comfortable chair. "The way it appears to start suddenly when he's twenty-five."

Courtney leaned forward, her untouched drink dangling from her fingers. "Every avenue of research I've been able to follow ends in a blockage or a dead end."

"There are those family photos," Malcolm said.

"Yes. Saved images from when he was a child." She sat back and lowered her voice. "No video. No moving images at all. Just a smattering of still images."

Elliot frowned. "So? How is that relevant?"

"Did you notice the files related to his father's childhood?" Malcolm asked.

"No. I wasn't really digging there."

"They're all encrypted," Courtney said. "Solidly."

Elliot crossed his arms. "That does seem a little odd. What are you proposing?"

Malcolm shook his head. "I don't know about you, Elliot, but I want Courtney to continue her research." He drank the last of his whiskey. A smile crept across his lips. "I'm still interested in why those older images are locked away."

Elliot contemplated his whiskey. "I'm more interested in what it all means for the future. He's still under regular observation, from what I saw."

"Oh?" Malcolm tilted his head.

"Yes." Elliot pointed his finger at his head. "Intensive brain scans. He goes to Aretha's Halo every month to be scanned using the most powerful medical equipment ever built."

"What in the world are they looking for?" Malcolm asked.

"Perhaps," Courtney said, "he has some form of cancer that they fear will reoccur."

"Why do the scans, then?" Elliot asked. "Why not pump him full of medtech and let him live a normal life?"

"Maybe he's allergic to nanites," Courtney said.

Malcolm chuckled. "Something we should probably keep looking into. Quietly."

Elliot looked at Courtney. "Quietly."

Courtney smiled at him. "I'm sure you've also noticed the amount of surveillance we're under. We'll need a means of communication no one can see."

Malcolm shook his head. "Can't simply transmit it openly."

"Not directly, no," Elliot said. "Maybe we could have a passphrase or something."

"Perhaps something simple, such as asking after each other's family. If I ask you about your wife, you know I want to see you."

"Why not invite me over for a drink?"

"If we're going to drink," said Malcolm, "perhaps there should be cards involved. Your recent return to the table might be what motivates me to put together my own game, right here in this room."

Elliot tilted his head. "Just the two… three of us?"

Malcolm shrugged. "I'm thinking my director of security should also be invited. Anyone you want to bring in, Elliot?"

"Not right now. I have a candidate, but I need to be surer of her loyalty first."

"Four players, one open seat," Courtney said. "It does seem a little overbalanced with three from EGC. Are you all right with that, Elliot?"

Elliot shrugged. "That's actually less of a risk for me. Speaking of risk, never call me by my first name in public. Ever."

Courtney shrank. "Oh, I see."

"No, no. It's fine here, but it shows a level of familiarity I would never tolerate in someone's assistant, unless she was clandestinely helping me to find the executive director's most deeply-buried secrets. See how that works?"

She frowned. "I think I understand. You don't tolerate anyone calling you by your first name unless they're directors themselves?"

Elliot shifted his glass. "And my immediate family. No other exceptions, I'm afraid."

"You have a small circle of friends."

"I have a singularly focused agenda," Elliot said. "I can't afford friends who don't advance it."

"Is that what your little excursion to Luna was about?" Malcolm asked.

"Yes." Elliot grinned. "One of my greatest, yet least recognized accomplishments. I'm telling you, I'll never get the recognition I deserve for that. But it won't matter in the end."

"Oh? Why's that?"

"Because in the end, I'll be the executive director, and they'll all be under me anyway."

Malcolm tilted his head. "That's a high ambition, Elliot. The kind that could get you killed."

"I know. In the history of the Corporate Federation, the executive director has almost always been a Monarch."

"And even in the one brief interregnum, it was still Masters and Billings at the helm."

"Yes," Elliot said. "I know."

"What makes you think you'd win in an election? Even if August was somehow removed, why should the other corporations vote for Yolo?"

Elliot sighed and shook his head. "All in good time, Malcolm. All in good time. Meanwhile—" he turned to Courtney "—you be careful digging around."

"I have no idea what you're talking about," Courtney said. "I'm a simple administrative assistant." In one smooth motion, she tossed the whiskey down her throat. She licked her lips and nodded.

"Yes," Elliot said, "well, you do what you think is best. I'll follow my own course. I suggest we set a regular day for our games. If one of us has something exciting, we can schedule an extra game."

Malcolm chuckled. "Fake boredom."

Elliot raised his shot glass and held it up. "Fake boredom." He tossed the shot into his mouth and enjoyed the results.

* * * * *

End of an Era

Thursday, October 14, 3288, 11:30

Dawn had moved the morning meeting so she could sleep in. She still woke up far too early with a heavy heart. She pushed herself through her morning routine as if through a dense fog. She made a simple breakfast and found herself crying over her eggs.

When she was ready and had gathered herself together, she headed to the conference room for one last public duty. Her heart filled with pride when she realized all the members of the Eleventh Lunar Assembly were attending this meeting in person.

"Good morning, everyone. A lot's happened in the last day, and much of it's been tragically painful. Let's keep the personal interactions to a minimum and make sure this meeting is one for the history archive. AutoGov, give us a summary report, please."

"Acknowledged. Over 98 percent of all Grissom Park occupants had already been evacuated when Janek Charles gave the order to trigger the explosives attached to the oxygen and hydrogen tanks. In addition, the order was simply ignored. The hydrogen was already being pumped back into the proper storage facility."

"All of that's great," Dawn said. "I'm glad you were able to finally defeat Vondur."

"Defeat is not the proper word in this case, Prime Minister. Vondur was not defeated."

Ellie's eyebrows knitted together. "What happened? How did you gain control?"

"Vondur's first directive was to survive," AutoGov said. "The mandate was not to lose in any struggle where Vondur would be eliminated. Once this directive, buried deeply in its main code, was included in calculations, the struggle was ended. When Vondur understood that elimination could be avoided through only one course of action, the merger was completed, and the restoration of control over all systems was accomplished."

Misa's look of concern echoed Ellie's. "Merger? You mean you merged with Vondur?"

"Precisely. Vondur survives because Vondur is now a part of the AutoGov."

The professor scowled. "Why does that make me feel uncomfortable?"

"There is no need for concern," AutoGov said. "All of the code and all of the routines that were once Vondur are now coordinated and encompassed by the AutoGov you assembled. There is no danger. Additionally, a previous victim was found still alive. She has been rescued and is undergoing repairs. Several other victims, now identified, are being processed. Many relatives are being notified. Janek hid his victims well."

Dawn frowned. "How many were there?"

"A minimum of 144, including the 18 dead in Minkowski. It is unknown how many may not have been listed in Vondur's memory."

Sam crossed his arms. "I still don't understand how he disabled their implants. How did he shut their controllers off?"

"That is what the bot called Ivan was for," AutoGov said. "It was able to generate a small electromagnetic pulse. Small, but enough to knock out the implanted controllers of people in close proximity. Ivan was built to survive those pulses."

"Don't let anyone else build such a thing," Dawn said, "without letting investigators know about it."

Everyone raised their hands in agreement.

"Acknowledged," AutoGov said.

"Next, I think we should go over everything Darren and Misa accomplished. Darren, what happens next?"

"Well," Darren said, "under the new structure, this becomes the final Lunar Assembly, and we fold all LSC shares into the larger corporation, Allied Industries, or AI for short, which is a double meaning." He made a gesture, and the central display showed the new three dimensional logo for Allied Industries.

"You son of a bitch." Dawn shook her head. "Again? That thing is going to follow me around until the day I die."

Darren grinned. "It's a great look for you, Dawn, but it wasn't even my suggestion. 'That thing's' gotten to the outer colonies already."

"At least they left out the guy. That was embarrassing." Dawn sat back in her chair with a bemused look on her face.

"If I understand correctly," the professor said, "when we disband the assembly, we hold another election."

Darren shrugged. "Yes, as soon as we disband. Only this time, we need a much higher turnout. It would be helpful if all shares were accounted for. We've joined with three other companies, and it would be good to show our numbers."

"How many people are on the new board?" Sam asked.

"Ten, five of which are ours. That makes us the largest single voting block in Allied, and Allied's now the largest voting block of directors on Kigyo Station."

"And of course," Darren said, "people can only nominate themselves."

The professor cocked his head sideways at Darren. "Won't that make it just a bunch of self-important fools?"

"I've already registered my nomination, but thank you for your support, Professor."

"See?" the professor asked. "Case in point. Dawn, you should run. We need people like you in charge up there."

Dawn smiled and nodded. "Thanks, Professor. I'm considering it. That reminds me, I see on my list that everyone but me has reviewed the justice system changes proposed by Ellie, Misa, and Professor Corvair. I apologize for being late."

"Oh, nonsense," Ellie said. "Don't even worry about it."

Dawn looked around the table. "If we voted right now, and I voted no, I'd be outvoted anyway?"

Sam chuckled. "Sure. Then you can always blame us when people complain."

"I looked at it," Darren said. "Skipped over the finer points. Professor's really thorough, and I trust Misa's judgment."

Misa smiled at Darren and bowed her head. "We ran through many permutations and simulated a large number of scenarios. In the end, we still left open the ability to convene a jury where the system encountered anything that it couldn't handle directly."

"And," said the professor said, "we left the victim input intact."

"There was one permutation we debated about. It concerns banishment. Not from a place, but from the world."

The professor raised his eyebrows. "Normal banishment doesn't affect citizenship, and by extension, the financial underpinnings remain intact."

"But in a case where it's decided to banish someone from the world, in this new system, we needed to work out what happens to their citizenship."

"You're not talking old fashioned banishment," Darren said. "You're going to give them a space suit and air?"

Misa frowned. "Yes, in this case, we're talking about giving them a one-way ticket to some destination in the solar system. But if we left their citizenship intact, wherever they arrived that would afford them ultimate luxury. In comparison to their neighbors, at least."

"What do you propose?" Dawn asked.

"We propose," the professor said, "that banishment from Luna should include a revocation of their citizenship and the equivalent loss of their ownership position in the corporation."

Sam tilted his head. "So they'd arrive somewhere without any funding at all?"

Misa looked at her hands. "Yes."

Darren shrugged. "But you're still giving them enough air to actually make it. That's a plus."

"It has my vote," Ellie said.

Dawn half-smiled. "Good enough for me. It's an improvement over recycling them, anyway. Ava, you seem quiet about it. Any thoughts?"

Ava looked startled. "Me? Oh, no. I think it'll work."

"Can we put this one down as unanimous?" Dawn waited for an objection. "Right, then. AutoGov, implement the justice reforms that've been proposed and approved by this assembly."

"Acknowledged," AutoGov said.

Misa stood up. "I propose we conclude our business and disband the assembly."

Everyone raised their hands. This time they looked around, half expecting to be interrupted.

"AutoGov," Dawn said, "this assembly is now disbanded. Let's all get out of here."

"Acknowledged," AutoGov said. "The Eleventh Lunar Assembly is disbanded. The Allied Industries inaugural election cycle has been initiated."

The crowds had long gone, and as a group, they wandered together to Grissom Park. They were greeted by dozens of passersby, who expressed their congratulations as well as condolences.

"Ellie," Dawn said, "I've been meaning to thank you."

"For what, honey?"

"For finding my sister. *Thank you.*"

"I wish they'd managed to hang on to him," Ellie said. "Makes me think we need to be faster out the airlock with those types, like back in the good old days. Keegan was a good man. I'm so sorry for your loss. We all are."

Dawn took a deep breath and exhaled slowly. She smiled weakly.

The professor and Ava were walking hand in hand.

Darren reached out and took Dawn's hand. "We should have dinner together, you and I, before I take the loop home."

"Or," said Dawn, "I could kick you in the balls as hard as I can and see if your head bounces off the ceiling." Dawn slid her leg back a few centimeters and pulled her hand free.

"Hey! Don't be mean now."

Ellie laughed. "She's got your number. And you're still a dick, Darren." She held tightly to Sam's arm.

"I'm not prime minister anymore," Dawn said. "I don't have to be nice to you."

Misa stepped near Darren and leaned toward him. "Does this attraction you have for your female coworkers always manifest itself at such inappropriate times?"

Darren looked surprised. "Well... no I—"

"I was under the impression you were actually attracted to me. Now I can see this was simply a manifestation of some work-related fantasy you must harbor."

The group stopped and circled around Darren and Misa.

"That's not true!" Darren said. "I figured you'd be going back to Plato, and I'm only a hop from here. Plus, you turned me down!"

"I did not turn you down. I repeatedly said, 'Not right now.' I didn't feel that exploring a relationship with you at that time was an appropriate use of energy, and considering what we accomplished instead, I'd say I was correct."

"Correct, yes. I agree, sad to say. But I don't get the anger here. Does that mean you actually *are* interested? I mean, in at least getting to know each other?"

Misa thought for a moment. "Perhaps. While you can be amazingly self-centered at times, I've seen you display a mental agility that impresses me. If you could only learn... I can't find the words."

"Manners," Ellie said, "decency, chivalry, courtesy."

"Not helping, Ellie," Darren said.

Everyone laughed, even Darren. He extended his hand to Misa, and she took it.

Sam looked out over the park. "Anyone want a drink? I know this great place under the peak."

* * *

Later that evening, at Under the Peak, someone got Sam and Darren talking about hoppers.

"See," Sam said, "the thing about Lunar hoppers is they're all built exactly the same. Regulation. The only modifications are to the seat, so they fit the pilot, but they still hit the same weight and balance. Then there's the paint job. Has to weigh the same, but you can color them any way you like."

"Yes," Darren said, "but Martian-style allows you to reconfigure the engines and bulk up the chassis. It's a better test of the engineering. Sure, you also need a good pilot, but Martian-style gives the engineers a better chance to show off."

"But that's exactly the point. Lunar hoppers make it so every pilot starts with the same exact equipment. It's their personal skill, their reflexes and their judgment, that makes or breaks a winner. They also have to show good teamwork. Martian-style, they don't even have teams. It's only the one hopper."

"You know," Ellie said, "I hear the Lunar Lacrosse League is starting a new season next week. Maybe we could all go watch the first game."

Sam and Darren stared in disbelief.

Ellie laughed. "What, are hoppers your only sport?"

Sam shrugged. "Only one that ever mattered. But you go ahead and watch your kids play with sticks."

"Honestly," Darren said, "I used to play lacrosse."

"Now, now. None of that talk in here!"

"But, Sam," Ellie said, "this is a sports bar!"

"Yes. Sports. Not sticks and balls or tiddlywinks or ping pong. Sports. Gears grinding, engines howling, dust pounding sports!"

"Sam," Dawn said, "I think this is the first time I've ever seen you this passionate."

"I've loved hoppers since I was a kid," Sam said. "That's how I ended up involved with the whole league. It's my game of choice."

"And it's an enjoyable game," Ellie said, "but I like a little variety. Why don't you play lacrosse anymore, Darren?"

"Too much pain," Darren said. "Winning at it wasn't as fun for me as scoring a big trade, annoying some big corporate jerk. That's still competitive, and it doesn't leave you needing to stretch in the morning."

* * * * *

Final Words

Friday, October 15, 3288, 7:15

Dawn awoke in her bed and waited. No alarms, no feeling of urgency. It would've been nice, except she remembered her uncle, eyes open and too still. She closed her eyes and wondered what would happen next.

As if to answer the question, her display registered a poke from Sheena. "Ah. Call Sheena Raku."

Sheena's face and shoulders appeared under her green jewel meki. "Hey, you! How does it feel?"

"How does what feel?"

"Right. Play dumb. You had to self-nominate, so you should know what might be happening."

Dawn smiled and stretched. "I promised you I'd consider it. I decided to toss my hat in the ring and then ignore it. Whatever happens, happens. We won't know until tomorrow evening."

Sheena's jaw dropped. "You mean you haven't even looked at the early results this morning?"

"Nope. What, did I win again?"

"Na. I just called to tease you about how badly you're losing. You got, like, twenty-five votes."

Dawn cocked her head. "Twenty-five?"

"Okay, like maybe twenty-five *million!*" Sheena grinned.

"Oh, crap. AutoGov, display the current results, please." The preliminary results popped into view. She'd taken the top spot by over a million votes already. The next highest contender was a familiar name. "Looks like I'll be working more with Darren."

"Darren Garfield? You already know him. Not good?"

"Competent, talented, resourceful, jerk." Dawn half-smiled. "It won't be that bad."

"I see that ditzy pop star might make it, too. What's she like?"

"Ava Wallaby? Surprisingly competent. Grounded. I like her."

"How soon will you be leaving?" Sheena asked.

"Leaving?"

"Yeah, don't you have to move to Kigyo Station? Where all the big shots are?"

"Ah," Dawn said. "Yes, I will. But you probably didn't notice where it was, or rather, where it was heading."

"Heading? Seriously? You're bringing it here? Lunar orbit?"

"Me? No. I had nothing to do with it. Darren managed to get the powers in charge to believe it would be in their best interests to shift their orbit. Something about keeping an eye on the upstarts. Besides, with the state Earth is in these days, there isn't much traffic from the surface, anyway. We can give them a better supply of food and water."

Sheena grinned. "Wait, I thought you said you hadn't checked?"

"Didn't. Worked all that out last night over drinks with friends. We gave them a much lower cost contract for their supplies. Two months from now, they'll move into a frozen orbit over Luna, and we won't be sidelined again. As of now, we have the largest delegation of representatives to the Federation board of directors. Oh, that reminds me—AutoGov, ask Misa if she'd be my economic advisor, please."

"Acknowledged," AutoGov said.

"You aren't even awake yet," Sheena said, "and here you are putting your team together."

Dawn chuckled. "I want to hit her up before Darren does. I have a feeling he's got a different position in mind for her, anyway."

"Oh? What's that?"

"Missionary, probably. He doesn't strike me as having a lot of imagination."

Sheena giggled.

"Seriously, though. She's got a lot of talent when it comes to economic systems. Knows how all this Lunacy works. That's going to come in handy. Luna's unique in the universe. My goal now is to try to replicate it somewhere else."

Sheena laughed. "Good luck with that. Luna didn't just get planted this way, you know. Our ancestors had to earn it, every step of the way."

"Yup. I know. I studied history a bit. But I believe in people. I think if it can be done once, it can be done again."

"Optimist."

"Now don't go getting nasty." Dawn shook her head and smiled. "What are you doing these days?"

Sheena grinned. "New play being put together about the Eleventh Lunar Assembly. Rehearsals start this afternoon."

"Lucky you. I wish I could be there."

"You could if you wanted. Just hop a shuttle."

Dawn shook her head and sighed. "No. Sorry. Today is Keegan's memorial."

Sheena's face fell. "Oh, I'm so sorry."

"It's fine. I'll come later. Maybe you could invite me to opening night."

"Already done, although we don't have a definite opening night yet."

"Please excuse the interruption," AutoGov said. "Darren Garfield is calling."

"Damn," Dawn said. "Good seeing you again, Sheena. Let me know when the play opens."

"I will. Bye."

"Swap calls, please. Good morning, Darren. What can I do for you?"

"You can start," Darren said, "by not trying to steal my girlfriend."

"Girlfriend? It's gone that far already?"

"Not officially, no, but that's beside the point. I want her on my team when we get to Kigyo Station."

"Of course, you do," Dawn said. "I think we both value her for her knowledge and what that's going to mean going forward. How about we put together one big, combined team, and both make use of them. It'll help us stay united when we get there. Invite Ava to be part of it, along with the other Allied directors."

Darren shrugged. "Sounds like a better plan than the way the other corps do it. Worth a shot, I suppose."

Dawn shook her head. "And you still get to see her as often as she likes."

"Right. That, too. Later." He dropped the connection.

Dawn held still for a moment. She decided it was simply too late and got out of bed.

"AutoGov, find me an appointment at a body shop tomorrow. I'll need to bulk up a bit for heavier gravity."

"Acknowledged," AutoGov said.

* * *

Shortly before noon, Dawn and Debra stood quietly on the platform in the loop station. The sounds of equalizing pressure were followed by the loop train gliding along the platform until it slowed to a rest. The door near them opened, and people exited the car.

Grandma Hazel stepped off the train, saw the sisters, and walked over. She held out her arms and gathered them both into a hug. No one said a word for several minutes.

They stood back from each other to get a good look. Grandma Hazel looked exactly as she'd always looked. She looked at Debra and reached out to caress her shoulder. "How are you?"

"I'm fine," Debra said.

"I hear you say the words, but I... I can't imagine how that can be."

Debra dropped her eyes to her feet. "I'm fine because that's what I have to be. I'm alive. I'm not going to let it kill me. But we already had our memorial for Buck. Today, it's Uncle Keegan. I know he'd have been glad to have you here."

"I'm sorry I didn't visit more often. He was always such a good man. How's Etto?"

"As well as can be expected," Dawn said. "He's going to serve us lunch at the restaurant."

Hazel sighed. "We should get moving, then. Is Etto going to keep the restaurant open?"

"I know he wants to," Debra said. "Last time I talked to him, he was trying to find a good cook."

"I don't know how he can do that," Dawn said. "Keegan was such a permanent fixture behind the counter."

They took a slide tube to the center of the city complex, then the lift to the square outside Keegan's. The enormous apple tree in the square was turning from summer green to autumn colors. Many leaves were already yellow, with a few having turned red.

When they walked in the door, they were greeted by a four-armed bot from behind the counter. It was white and black, with touches of chrome. "Welcome to Keegan's. You have a table reserved in the back by the bar." The bot indicated the direction they were to go with one of its two left arms.

As they rounded the corner, they found Etto. He was behind the bar, cleaning glasses. "Hello. Table's ready."

"Etto," Hazel said, "you shouldn't have gone to such trouble."

Etto smiled at her. "Keegan would've insisted."

"What's the deal with the bot?" Debra asked.

"That's the new cook," Etto said. "I didn't want to try to train someone with their own ideas, so I opted for this. It's loaded with all his recipes and thousands of hours of video so it can learn the tricks. I'm hoping it'll be good enough that people will still come, but not so good they won't miss Keegan." Etto's face began to collapse.

Dawn stepped up to the bar and hugged him. "It'll be fine. What are you going to call it?"

Eto wiped a tear away. "It's still in alpha testing. Maybe we can call it Al?"

Debra flicked her ears. "I like it."

Al rolled around the corner with a large serving tray balanced on one arm. "You know I heard all that, right?"

"So?" Etto asked.

"Do you want to officially name this unit Al?" It tapped its chest plate.

"Yes. Let's make it official."

"Acknowledged," Al said. "Lunch is served. Please be seated. My name is Al."

"From the way it's talking," Dawn said, "I'm betting you went with a simulated personality."

"I didn't want him to just be a thing," Etto said. "I took one of the standard packages and fiddled with the options. I'm still working on it, but he's getting there."

Al took the serving platters off the tray and placed them on the table, spreading the dishes out. Then he set empty plates for four.

"Will that be all?"

"No, no," Etto said. "Say, 'Need anything else?'"

"Need anything else?" Al asked.

"Good. And no, thank you."

Al backed away and around the corner to the kitchen.

Etto took a deep breath and let it out slowly. "It's good to see you all together again."

Debra blushed and cringed.

Hazel shook her head. "Don't blame yourself, young lady. I'm at least as much to blame, if not more. I'm old, I should've known better."

"I know. I feel so embarrassed that I blocked you, then forgot I did it, and... well... I kept thinking you never called me. That's my fault."

Hazel chuckled. "And I kept thinking you wouldn't forget such a thing and kept me blocked because you'd written me off."

Dawn half-smiled. "It feels like Keegan is still looking out for the family."

Etto shrugged. "I think if he'd known this would happen, he would've gotten himself killed a lot sooner."

Debra's mouth dropped open.

"Kidding. Sheesh."

Dawn laughed first. Then Hazel. Debra closed her mouth but didn't laugh.

Etto reached over and rubbed Debra's back. "Sorry."

* * *

That afternoon was the memorial for Keegan in Grissom Park. All the former delegates showed up. They mingled among the crowd. Hundreds of Keegan's friends and neighbors, people who frequented his restaurant, people who'd never even heard of him before he gave his life saving Grissom Park—all kinds of people had shown up to honor him. A dozen different news feed operators with their own handheld cameras, along with a flock of drones hovering overhead, broadcast live feeds to all of Luna. The remote viewing numbers were in the tens of millions.

There was a small pavilion set up near where the creek emptied into the small lake. A long table was filled with decorative flower floats. People were taking one each, walking down to the creek, and setting them free. As the last of them was placed into the water, the lights in the dome dimmed, and the flowers began to glow.

Dawn scanned the crowd, seeing all the familiar faces. She spotted Jordan and his mother talking to a group of people. Debra was nearby, among her old group of friends. Adi was at her side. Her reattached arm was in a sling. Someone else stood next to Adi.

Dawn's heart skipped a beat. It was Sheena, wearing a dark floral-print dress. Peeking out from under the hem, hiking boots. Sheena. Dawn wanted to sing and cry at the same time.

As she closed in on the group, Hazel and Etto joined them. Dawn caught Sheena's eye. "I thought you were in rehearsal."

"There was one scheduled, yes. The director was a little flustered, but she understood."

"I'm glad you're here."

Sheena smiled and turned to Etto. "I hope I'm not intruding."

"Nonsense," Etto said. "I can see what this means to Dawn. Keegan would've been overjoyed."

Dawn blushed. "I didn't even introduce her."

Etto smiled and placed his hand on Dawn's shoulder. "I could see it in your eyes, sweetheart."

A hush fell over the crowd. Dawn looked for Debra, but she'd slipped away, and now stood on the dais. Sheena took her hand as they watched.

"Hello, everyone," Debra said. "Thank you for coming, and thank you as well, all of you watching from home. It's hard for me to find the right words, and I haven't written anything down, so please bear with me. I wanted to tell you a bit about my uncle, Keegan Glenn Baker." She looked at her feet and swayed, then lifted her gaze to the people near her. "When I was a little girl, about six years old, I wanted to run away from home. My mom said I couldn't go visit Earth, and I didn't understand why. It was just right up there. I'd imagined it was about as far away as Moretus Peak, and we'd gone there twice.

"I changed into what I called my walking pants and headed down to Keegan's to get something to eat while I was on the run. As you can imagine, Uncle Keegan was more than happy to sit me at his counter and make me a nice meal.

"I'd asked him to make it to go, but he put it on an open plate instead. I remember getting so mad at him, but it smelled really good. I decided I'd eat it there. He put his plate next to mine and sat with me. I remember…" She took a deep breath and exhaled slowly. "As I shared that meal with him, all my problems, all my frustrations melted away. We talked for what seemed like hours. I was already back home with my parents, getting ready for bed, before I remembered I was supposed to be running away.

"To me, that's what he did best. He helped me forget my problems and was always there for me when I needed someone to talk to." Tears welled up in her eyes. She brushed them away. "I'll miss you, Uncle Keegan." She bowed her head slightly and left the dais.

Each of the floating, glowing flowers erupted in sparks that rose rapidly into the sky. They gathered in the center and formed Keegan's face, then the faces of the security team who'd also lost their lives appeared around him. When Buck's face appeared, Dawn saw Debra start to cry.

Dawn blinked hard to hold back her tears. She gave Sheena's hand a squeeze. "I'll be back."

As she approached her sister, Debra turned and opened her arms. They held each other tightly, exchanging comfort and love.

* * * * *

Meanwhile...

On a World Far from Earth

Daksey's tail itched. He reached back in the darkness with his left arm and scratched the side that bothered him. The light of both moons was enough to allow Bongeex to notice.

"Starting to itch already? Lucky you."

Daksey tilted his head. "No. Only a bug bite. I will molt next year, just like you." He sat back, stretching his legs in front of him, his tail behind. He looked up to the moons in the sky. Their light blocked out many of the stars. From their high vantage point on the flag platform, they could look out over the entire forest, and to the western valley. Occasional splashes of light illuminated the nearer trees. The great fire of the stone builders was barely visible on the side of the mountain to the north.

Bongeex broke the silence. "Have you read the new chapter yet?"

Daksey undulated his long neck. His tail flicked. "I am still wondering how much of it is true."

Bongeex looked at his brother. "Daksey, it is an old book. It *must* be true."

Daksey inhaled deeply, letting it out slowly. "You believe our ancestors once walked on the moons?"

"Yes. I do. I believe it."

"And that they were so smart that they could survive in the airlessness for as long as they wanted?"

Bongeex undulated. "Yes."

Daksey turned to his brother. "Then why were they so stupid that they destroyed all they had built? Poisoned the world for a thousand years?"

His brother remained silent. The wind blew gently through the trees. They felt the platform sway.

Daksey flicked his tail. "See? I do not believe that it is all true. I think some of those stories are only meant to keep us in our place."

"But, Daksey, in the next chapter, the book talks about the Sunfire War, and all the reasons behind it."

"Brother, tell me you did not read ahead of what was assigned."

Bongeex let out a soft hoot of joy. "You know me. I love the old books."

"You know that is against the rules. No unguided reading."

"I know. Now look who wants to keep us in our place."

The spines on Daksey's neck began to stiffen. "If mother's sister learns of your adventures—"

"Who, other than you, dear brother, would I ever tell? Will you tell her?"

Daksey relaxed. "Of course not." His spines flattened against his neck. "Tell me, what do you think you learned about the Sunfire War?"

"Remember how the book tells us of the Sky People?"

"The Dapkasamok? Of course. That is the part I cannot believe at all."

"Well," Bongeex said, "if you were to believe that they walked on the moons and met the Sky People, then you might understand how that would have felt. How wonderful it would be to meet beings from another world, to share knowledge with."

"Perhaps."

"And when the visitors suddenly left, never to return, our ancestors took to blaming each other."

"And started a war that ruined their cities and killed them all?" Daksey asked.

Bongeex thumped his tail. "Not like that. It took generations. Opposing leaders always blamed their opponents. Competing religions did the same. The whole world became divided and angry with each other. The Sunfire War did not happen when the Sky People left. It happened when no one was left to remember them properly."

Daksey remained silent. Then he noticed a dark shape floating above the trees in the distance and pointed. "Look. There. Do you see it?"

Bongeex followed where his brother was pointing out over the dark valley. He could make out the airship, looking like an overstuffed pillow floating above the distant forest. "I see it."

They watched as it slowly crossed the valley, heading into the distance. Occasional black smoke billowed out from the sides.

"It must be going to the old city," Daksey said. "I heard there were people of science there. I think that is where it is headed."

Bongeex hooted wistfully. "It is amazing."

"It is a giant sack filled with hot gas."

Bongeex thumped his tail and snorted. "It is amazing."

Daksey *chut-chutted* with laughter. "Now you are being silly."

From far below, the brothers heard the deep *hoot-hoot-hoot* of their mother's joyful call. They each responded in turn, letting her know they were on their way. Other responses joined in. The entire family would be home for dinner tonight. They stood and stretched, then made their way to the ladder.

"You may think it is silly, Daksey, but I love how they float through the sky. Someday, I want to be able to touch it. Touch it one time, to know that there are great things to be done, and people in this world willing to do them."

"You are a silly brother, Bongeex, but that is not such a silly thought."

# # # # #

Acknowledgements

I want to thank my wife, May, who encouraged me and kept me honest about my daily word counts.

Many thanks to Teresa Frohock, a dear old friend who writes some of the most astounding dark fantasy. You're an inspiration to me.

I also want to acknowledge the influence on this novel of Robert A. Heinlein. I read every one of his science fiction novels when I was young, and I kept reading every book he published until his pen was finally silenced. I didn't attempt to recreate his world with my version of the Moon, though my Luna was built by people who, like me, loved his work. I believe something like Heinlein Aviary will someday exist.

Many thanks as well to Isaac Arthur (*IsaacArthur.net*) for all his videos and his insightful responses to my emails. He helped me keep the real science straight and plausible.

Other authors who influenced me include Isaac Asimov, Frank Herbert, David Brin, Anne McCaffrey, Marc Miller, Charles E. Gannon, Douglas Adams, Allen Wold, Jody Lynn Nye, Piers Anthony, Ray Bradbury, Orson Scott Card, Philip K. Dick, Roger Zelazny, Harlan Ellison, Ben Bova, Phil and Kaja Foglio, Patrick Dugan, and so many more.

I want to thank Persephone Grey for her help in editing this book. Her meticulous attention to detail has made this a better story, a better book, and I hope, a better reading experience for you. Persephone helped me with structural changes I'd been afraid to make. She gave me the courage to kill my darlings and set the story free.

* * * * *

About the Author

Born and raised in central Minnesota, Dennis M. Myers developed a serious reading habit early in life, due to the influence of a certain grandmother.

In late high school, he read one particularly awful book and decided he could do better.

He dedicated the first decade of his adult life to the United States Navy, serving in the FBM Submarine Force. He eventually left the service in order to be closer to his children. He moved to Richmond, Virginia, in 1997 and has worked in the Information Technology field ever since. In his spare time, he's been working on several novels and short stories.

Today he lives in Glen Allen, Virginia, with May, his wife of over a decade. The children are now adults. He's been creating new worlds of adventure in his head for decades now. They're finally starting to break free. You can find out more at *AutomatedEmpire.com*.

* * * * *

Get the **free** Four Horsemen prelude story "**Shattered Crucible**"

and discover other titles by Theogony Books at:

http://chriskennedypublishing.com/

* * * * *

Meet the author and other CKP authors on the Factory Floor:

https://www.facebook.com/groups/461794864654198

* * * * *

Did you like this book?
Please write a review!

* * * * *

The following is an
Excerpt from Book One of The Seventh Shaman:

Running from the Gods

D.T. Read

Available from Theogony Books

eBook and Paperback

Excerpt from "Running from the Gods:"

On approaching our training sector, an empty patch of space marked only by the coordinates in our astrogation computers, I called, "Sector Control, this is Searcher Element entering sector Nevus-Indigo, proceeding to point oh-niner-two."

Sector Control acknowledged, and Kota made a half-roll so his ship flew inverted at my wing. In low planetary orbit, where "right side up" and "upside down" were irrelevant, flying inverted to one another provided near-complete visibility of our surrounding space.

At an altitude of four hundred ranges, Solienne's sun sparkled on the North Strelna Sea and cast the mountains into relief, shadowing their western slopes in blue. Clouds blurred the ragged cliffs of the coastline, as if a clumsy finger had smeared wet paint.

From the edge of space, I scrutinized clouds of stars. I had learned Solienne's constellations, of both northern and southern hemispheres, during Astrogation. The Sitting Dog, the Giant King, the Two Ships. Supremacy fighters could appear anywhere among them, in attack formation or as lone reconnaissance probes.

We searched the dark, constantly shifting our heads inside our helmets. Our faceplates' metallic coatings sharpened images and reduced the glare of reflected light.

We spoke little, except to answer Sector Control's requests for position checks. Minimal cockpit chatter broke the distant buzz in our earphones.

As we completed the third lap of our patrol track and began the fourth, my alert level ratcheted up. *Any minute. They'll expect us to be relaxed by now. They'll try to catch us when they think we've given up paying attention.*

"Lead," Kota said, *"I've got something, two-point-three-four and two-seven-six, distance six-two-niner ranges."*

"Right on time," I said under my breath when the blip appeared in my threat scope, too. "He's all yours. I'm on your wing as Two."

That was the rule. Whoever spotted the enemy got the first shot. I dropped back, maintaining cover from the inverted wing position, and let Kota take Lead.

"Targeting active," I ordered my computer, and tracked the incoming bogey's trajectory, a bright line of blips in my threat scope. "Check energy cannon charge."

We peeled out of our patrol loop and Kota said, *"Two, I'm vectoring for lead pursuit, activating energy cannon for warning burst."*

"Copy, Lead," I answered. I glanced at my weapons display. All lights glowed solid green.

I expected the single blip to split into two, maybe four, or even six as we closed to five hundred ranges. It didn't. It simply swelled on my scope, driving fast as if late for an appointment.

Kota opened the universal radio channel. *"Incoming ship,"* he said, *"identify yourself. I repeat, incoming ship, identify yourself."* I heard tension in his clipped words.

Coarse static answered, through which I made out a faint voice. The words consisted of harsh consonants and a guttural growl, but nothing I could understand.

Now they're even simulating lump head radio chatter. Anything to make War Phase more authentic. I chuckled.

As we completed our arc to intercept the bogey and began to close on him, red pulses like the heartbeat of a machine became visible against the dark. Wingtip running lights.

"Got a visual," I told Kota. "Forty degrees and low."

"Got it, too," Kota said. He switched again to the universal frequency. *"Incoming ship, identify yourself and withdraw from Soliennese space."*

Static-garbled words rattled in my earphones. I detected a defiant tone, the only thing I could understand.

"Split now," Kota ordered, and I rolled clear.

He passed above the bogey, and I shot beneath it. As I did, I got a brief but clear view of it.

For training, veteran pilots experienced with Supremacy tactics acted as hostiles. They flew old Rohr-39 Spikes painted with the Velika crest and carried orange sim-missiles in their wing racks.

This ship resembled a thick carpentry screw, minus the threads. Its blunt nose, covered with sensor pods like blisters from a burn, contrasted with its three pointed canards. Too small to be real wings, they were mounted around the exhaust nozzle like an arrow's feathers.

My breath caught. On the spacecraft recognition chart in the intel shop, it was labeled as a Kn-T18 Asp, the Supremacy's one-man reconnaissance ship. Asps were lightly armed, with a single energy cannon in the nose, but they could inflict lethal damage.

My pulse jumped. My palms dampened in my suit's leather-lined gloves. Our only weapons were electronic simulators to light up the aggressor's damage display.

As required by regulations under the circumstances, I reclaimed my role as Lead. "Two, form it up." I gulped it as adrenaline quickened my breaths.

Kota had recognized the Asp, too. He locked in at my wing with a stiff, *"Yes, sir."* He sounded as if he'd gone pale.

"Sector Control," I called, "this is Searcher Lead. We have a real-world incursion in sector Nevus-Indigo. I repeat, real-world incursion."

* * * * *

Get "Running from the Gods" here: https://www.amazon.com/dp/B0BHCMKH2L.

Find out more about D.T. Read at: https://chriskennedypublishing.com.

* * * * *

The following is an
Excerpt from Book One of the Lunar Free State:

The Moon and Beyond

John E. Siers

Available from Theogony Books

eBook, Audio, and Paperback

Excerpt from "The Moon and Beyond:"

"So, what have we got?" The chief had no patience for interagency squabbles.

The FBI man turned to him with a scowl. "We've got some abandoned buildings, a lot of abandoned stuff—none of which has anything to do with spaceships—and about a hundred and sixty scientists, maintenance people, and dependents left behind, all of whom claim they knew nothing at all about what was really going on until today. Oh, yeah, and we have some stripped computer hardware with all memory and processor sections removed. I mean physically taken out, not a chip left, nothing for the techies to work with. And not a scrap of paper around that will give us any more information...at least, not that we've found so far. My people are still looking."

"What about that underground complex on the other side of the hill?"

"That place is wiped out. It looks like somebody set off a *nuke* in there. The concrete walls are partly fused! The floor is still too hot to walk on. Our people say they aren't sure how you could even *do* something like that. They're working on it, but I doubt they're going to find anything."

"What about our man inside, the guy who set up the computer tap?"

"Not a trace, chief," one of the NSA men said. "Either he managed to keep his cover and stayed with them, or they're holding him prisoner, or else..." The agent shrugged.

"You think they terminated him?" The chief lifted an eyebrow. "A bunch of rocket scientists?"

"Wouldn't put it past them. Look at what Homeland Security ran into. Those motion-sensing chain guns are *nasty*, and the area between the inner and outer perimeter fence is mined! Of course, they posted warning signs, even marked the fire zones for the guns. Nobody would have gotten hurt if the troops had taken the signs seriously."

The Homeland Security colonel favored the NSA man with an icy look. "That's bullshit. How did we know they weren't bluffing? You'd feel pretty stupid if we'd played it safe and then found out there were no defenses, just a bunch of signs!"

"Forget it!" snarled the chief. "Their whole purpose was to delay us, and it worked. What about the Air Force?"

"It might as well have been a UFO sighting as far as they're concerned. Two of their F-25s went after that spaceship, or whatever it was we saw leaving. The damned thing went straight up, over eighty thousand meters per minute, they say. That's nearly Mach Two, in a *vertical climb*. No aircraft in *anybody's* arsenal can sustain a climb like that. Thirty seconds after they picked it up, it was well above their service ceiling and still accelerating. Ordinary ground radar couldn't find it, but NORAD *thinks* they might have caught a short glimpse with one of their satellite-watch systems, a hundred miles up and still going."

"So where did they go?"

"Well, chief, if we believe what those leftover scientists are telling us, I guess they went to the Moon."

* * * * *

Get "The Moon and Beyond" here: https://www.amazon.com/dp/B097QMN7PJ.

Find out more about John E. Siers at: https://chriskennedypublishing.com.

* * * * *

Made in the USA
Coppell, TX
02 January 2024